Cranberry
HEARTS

Cranberry HEARTS

Trust Opens Doors to Love

LISA HARRIS
LENA NELSON DOOLEY
ELIZABETH GODDARD

BARBOUR
PUBLISHING

Who Am I? © 2007 by Lena Nelson Dooley
A Matter of Trust © 2007 by Lisa Harris
Seasons of Love © 2008 by Elizabeth Goddard

ISBN 978-1-60260-488-9

Scripture quotations are taken from the HOLY BIBLE, NEW INTERNATIONAL VERSION®. NIV®. Copyright © 1973, 1978, 1984 by International Bible Society. Used by permission of Zondervan. All rights reserved.

This book is a work of fiction. Names, characters, places, and incidents are either products of the author's imagination or used fictitiously. Any similarity to actual people, organizations, and/or events is purely coincidental.

Cover model photography: Jim Celuch, Celuch Creative Imaging

Published by Barbour Publishing, Inc., P.O. Box 719, Uhrichsville, Ohio 44683, www.barbourbooks.com

Our mission is to publish and distribute inspirational products offering exceptional value and biblical encouragement to the masses.

ecpa Member of the
Evangelical Christian
Publishers Association

Printed in the United States of America.

WHO AM I?

Lena Nelson Dooley

Dedication

Special thanks to everyone who gave me expert help. You rock! Who knew it would be so much fun to ask a doctor how to poison someone?

This book is dedicated to my good friends and writing partners, Lisa Harris and Beth Goddard. I enjoyed working on this three-book project with you. Also to my two editors, JoAnne Simmons, who contracted this series, and Kathy Ide, whose expert advice makes my books better.

This book is also dedicated to my wonderful husband of forty-five years, James Allen Dooley. You love me, cherish me, encourage me, support me, and make my life richer, fuller, and a lot more fun.

Chapter 1

Leiann Hambrick clutched her upper arms, holding herself together while she stared through the sheer curtains that veiled the picture window. Would she have to leave all this behind? She no longer saw the Hurst athletic complex, which had been built a few years earlier. In her mind's eye she saw the thicket full of wild mustang grapevines that used to grow on that spot. Grapes she had picked so her mother could make her famous jelly. Jelly her father loved on his biscuits in the morning. She longed for that simpler time, when she knew who her father was. When she knew who she was.

Leiann swiped at the tears that streamed down her cheeks, ruining the makeup she had taken such pains to apply a few hours ago as she prepared for the reading of her mother's will. How different her world had been this morning.

The Hambricks had moved to this house on Cimarron Trail in Hurst, Texas, when Leiann was in fourth grade. Leiann had been excited when they moved to this ranch-style house on the quiet street. A lot of undeveloped property surrounded them. Besides the thicket across the road—and it had been a country road then, not a four lane street as it was now a creek ran along the back of the property. Leiann and her friends played there often, wading and hunting bullfrogs on hot summer evenings.

Leiann yearned to go back to that time when she knew what her life was all about. She wanted to hug her mother and have her daddy tell her that everything was all right because they were together. Of course, that was impossible. She didn't think anything would ever be all right again.

Squeezing her eyes shut could not erase the pictures dancing through her mind. The lawyer's office. The reading of the will. . .

"And to my daughter, I leave all my worldly goods." The lawyer's voice had droned on, listing the things that had belonged to her mother, which were now Leiann's. Family heirlooms, bank accounts, furniture and household goods, jewelry. But not the house. Her mother hadn't owned the house.

"Leiann?" From across the living room, the soft voice of her best friend brought Leiann out of her confused thoughts. When Leiann didn't respond, Arlene came to stand beside her. "You really need to eat something."

She turned, but she didn't loosen the grip she held on her upper arms. If she did, she might fly apart. "I'm not really hungry." Forcing the words past the desert that had taken up residence in her throat took a major effort.

Arlene put her arm around Leiann. "I know. But you need sustenance, whether you're hungry or not."

Leiann stared into the familiar azure eyes for a moment. Then the precarious hold on her emotions broke. Arlene pulled Leiann into her arms and patted her back while murmuring soothing words into her ear. Leiann sobbed so hard she couldn't make out the words, but the soft sound was like a balm that began to calm her soul. . .at least a little.

After Leiann had cried for what seemed like an eternity, Arlene convinced her to go to the kitchen. Thankfully, people weren't hovering around the house as they had after the funeral yesterday.

Arlene settled Leiann at the table, then dished up two plates of leftover food from the refrigerator. "I know it's too hot to eat much, but we have a nice assortment of salads."

She placed a plate in front of Leiann, then sat across the table from her with her own plate of food. After taking a bite, she waved her fork as she talked. "This salmon salad Mrs. Howard brought is really good. It has apples, celery, and walnuts in it. Try some."

Leiann took a bite. The food awakened her taste buds and ignited the realization that she really was hungry. How long had it been since she had last eaten? Not breakfast. Not supper last night. It must have been after the funeral, and then only a few nibbles. No wonder she felt ravenous.

"Thanks, Arlene. I needed this."

For a few minutes, the two friends ate in silence, enjoying the mixed green salad and fruit salad, too. When Leiann laid her fork on her plate, she pushed back from the table and started to stack the dishes.

Arlene stopped her with a gentle hand on her arm. "When are you going to tell me what happened at the lawyer's office?"

She went straight to the point. Of course, that was the kind of friend she was. They had gone all through public school together, were college roommates, and now both taught at Thompson Elementary. If Leiann hadn't chosen to stay in the house with her mother when Milton died of a heart attack, the two friends probably would have moved into an apartment or house together.

"He read my mother's will. What makes you think anything else happened?" Leiann looked away, hoping Arlene would let it go at that. She wasn't sure she could verbalize what she felt.

Arlene huffed. "You're much more upset today than you were yesterday." Her eyes bored into Leiann's with an intensity that penetrated the wall Leiann had tried to erect around her heart.

Leiann slumped like a marionette that just had its strings cut. "So I'm upset.

My mother just died. What do you expect?" She hoped her clipped words would be a barrier her friend wouldn't cross.

"Do you think it would help to talk about it?"

Leiann knew Arlene had only her best interests in mind. "I've never kept secrets from you. I guess I shouldn't start now." Her gaze roved around the room. "Where did I put my purse?"

"I think you left it in the front room."

The two young women went to the living room. Leiann sat on the couch, where she'd dropped her bag when she returned home earlier. She opened it and dug through the papers stuck in the side pocket. Arlene settled into the rocker across from her.

"Here it is." Leiann pulled out an envelope. She opened it and extracted a letter.

"That looks like your mother's handwriting." Arlene leaned forward.

"It is." Leiann took a deep breath. She didn't want to start crying again. "She wrote this to me some time ago."

"And she gave it to the lawyer instead of you?" Arlene sounded as surprised as Leiann had been.

"Yes. He was instructed to give it to me after the reading of her will."

Confusion puckered Arlene's brows. "Why would she do that?"

Leiann couldn't read the words aloud. Without comment, she handed the letter to Arlene.

"Are you sure you want me to do this?"

She nodded slowly. Arlene turned her attention to the letter.

Leiann knew the moment Arlene reached the part that was most upsetting. Her eyes widened, and she gasped. After lowering the paper, she stared at Leiann for a long moment then picked up the missive again and continued to read. Tears slipped down her cheeks as they had down Leiann's the first time she went through the confusing document.

"Well, that's"—Arlene folded the paper precisely the way it had been in the envelope and handed it back—"really a shock."

A shock that had caused Leiann's world to spin out of control. Milton Hambrick, the man she'd always thought was her dad, wasn't her biological father. Apparently her natural father was no longer alive. But she had a grandfather she'd never been told about—and he owned the house they lived in. If she wanted to continue living there, she had to go to his home in Massachusetts and meet the man. Unbelievable.

"What are you going to do?"

Leiann didn't have an answer. What could she do? If she didn't comply with the instructions in the letter, she wouldn't have a home.

"I'll tell you what *I'd* do." Arlene sounded as if she were on a crusade. "I'd go to Massachusetts and tell that Mr. Johnson what I thought of him."

Once more clutching her arms across her chest, Leiann stood and crossed to the window. After gazing out for a moment, she turned halfway around. "The problem is, I don't know what I think of him. I can't process this information overload." She whirled back to stare out the window.

What was she thinking about when she stood here earlier? Anything to take her mind off the stark message. Oh yes, the grapes. When her mother made green grape pie the first time, she told Leiann that magic made the juice in the pie pink when the unripe fruit was green. For years, she'd believed her mother. Somehow, being lost in thoughts of the past didn't keep the present from breaking through. Arlene joined Leiann. "You could go see the guy and deck him. I'll help you."

Leiann chuckled. "That *guy* is my grandfather." There, she'd said it.

All these years she'd thought her grandparents were dead. Her dad's parents had been killed in a car crash when she was a baby. Mother's parents had died when she was in high school; she never would have been able to go to college if she hadn't received scholarships. And she wouldn't have met Daddy if she hadn't gone to college.

"This is complicated, isn't it?" Arlene sank into the chair again.

"I may never know the whole story unless I go talk to this man."

Arlene smiled. "According to the letter, all you have to do is meet him and the house becomes yours."

Leiann looked around the room her mother had lovingly decorated. All the furniture, knickknacks, doilies, pictures, and even the rug belonged to Leiann. But not the house. It belonged to a man who was supposedly her grandfather but had rejected her mother. And rejected Leiann, as well. And now he wanted to meet her. If only Mother's letter hadn't been so sketchy. Why couldn't she have told Leiann more details? Then she'd be better able to make a decision about how to proceed.

Did she really want to meet this stranger? If she did, could any good come of it?

Chapter 2

As his eyes scanned the document he'd just received over the secure line, Gerome fisted his hand against the low-slung waist of his pajama bottoms. He couldn't let this continue. He hoped he hadn't waited too long to take care of it. No one should be allowed to take advantage of the Old Man like this.

After slamming the paper on the table beside the fax machine, Gerome extracted his cell phone from its holster on the belt dangling across the chair and punched a speed-dial number. "Mays here," he said when his boss picked up. "When can I come in to see you?"

Fifteen minutes later, Gerome emerged from the elevator of his apartment building onto the middle level of the parking garage below the Houston highrise. He scanned the area, making sure no one else was around, a long-ingrained habit. As the door swished shut, the final *snap* echoed in the concrete cavern. He clicked the remote to unlock his Corvette, his one real extravagance.

When he arrived at the office building, which always reminded him of a fortress with narrow windows, Gerome took the express elevator to the top floor. "He's expecting me." He threw the words over his right shoulder at the receptionist, never slowing his pace.

She leaned her arms on the desk and smiled up at him. "What? No greeting for me today?"

He stopped in his tracks and turned back. He couldn't antagonize one of his greatest allies in the company. Forcing a smile, he gave a husky whisper. "Morning, Sheree. You look ravishing as always."

The bleached blond leaned back in her leather chair, which squeaked as she gently rocked it. "It's too late for your honeyed words. Go on. He told me to send you right in. Must be important."

You don't know how important. Gerome pushed open the massive door, quickly closing it behind him. He strode across the plush carpet.

The older man behind the desk looked up, the overhead light glinting off the threads of silver in his dark hair. "Have a seat, Mays. What can I do for you today?"

Gerome dropped into one of the two chairs in front of the desk. "I want to take a leave of absence."

His boss steepled his fingers, tapping the tips together in an irregular rhythm, and stared at Gerome. "How long are we talking about?"

"I'm not sure. Some questionable things are going on in my family." Gerome didn't flinch away from the man's sharp perusal. He'd learned long ago to hide his feelings and hold his own in any situation.

After a few clicks on the keys of his laptop, his boss studied the page he pulled up. "According to the files, it's been quite awhile since you took a vacation." He swiveled back toward Gerome. "You know that's not good. I've told you before that you should take all your allotted time off."

Gerome gave a quick laugh. "Yeah, it's not easy to take off when you're in the middle of a desert or jungle."

The man joined in the laughter. "I know how hard it is for you to shut down, but you're always sharper after time away from the job." He turned back toward the computer. "How about if I make your leave open-ended?"

"Sounds good to me."

A few more clicks, and the man faced him once again. "When do you want to start?"

Gerome stuck his long legs out in front of him, trying to look nonchalant. He didn't want his employer to know what was going on, at least not yet. "Is right now too soon?"

☙

Back at his apartment, Gerome grabbed a beat-up duffel bag. He dug through his closet and drawers to find his oldest and rattiest jeans and T-shirts. Just in case, he threw in a couple of oxford cloth shirts, too. He chose one pair of running shoes to pack and another one to wear. Although they'd been worn a lot, they would still support his feet in case he had to chase anyone.

He wished he could take his leather jacket, but he threw in a worn camo jacket instead. His toiletries would have to be pared down, too. By the time he traveled halfway across the country, he needed to look disreputable. He was already several weeks overdue for a good haircut. That should add to his bad-boy appearance.

He collected a few disposable razors, a can of cheap shaving foam, nondescript deodorant, and soap, then thrust them into a denim drawstring sack.

Gerome returned to the parking garage, descending to the lowest level. He approached a dented, rusty pickup off in the corner. Its appearance belied its abilities. Gerome kept this vehicle in tip-top shape. He never knew when he'd need its power in a crunch. He unlocked the door and threw the duffel onto the floorboard on the passenger side.

Before he started the engine, he leaned his forehead against the steering wheel to clear his mind. Focus was essential to the success of this venture.

Gerome drove almost straight through from Houston to Boston, taking only a few short naps in rest areas along the way. After crossing the Massachusetts state line, he enjoyed the lush countryside and abundant trees, with the fresh green leaves of late spring. A few patches of wild lupines, his mother's favorite flower, gave the landscape a blue haze. Every time he came back to this part of the country, he felt like he was coming home. At least, the only true home he'd ever known.

He didn't want to take the time to go through the city, even though he was drawn to its historical significance. When he reached 128, he looped west, then took 117. But every mile he drew closer to the Old Man's private domain, he tensed. Knowing how important his mission was, he was afraid to lose his edge to nostalgia.

Gerome turned onto the private road that led to the mansion. He began to mentally assume the personality he would need for the time he was there. How long had it been since he was that young man drifting in the quagmire of the world before Herman Johnson became his stepfather? Too many years and too many miles to think about.

When Gerome reached the front gates, they stood open, inviting anyone to enter. He frowned. That didn't bode well. Herman had always been very careful, knowing people would take advantage of his wealth if they had half a chance.

Gerome drove up the long drive leading through a corridor of trees whose branches formed a canopy, then around the cobblestone circle to the front door.

As he killed the engine, he flicked the hidden switch that made his pickup backfire. That should convince anyone who might be watching that the vehicle was on its last legs—or wheels, in this case.

Before Gerome reached the front door, the heavy carved slab of cherry wood, with stained-glass fan windows in the top section, opened. An austere stranger in a black suit lowered his brows and frowned at him. *Who's he? A new butler?* Interesting. Gerome would have to check into this, too.

"How may I help you?" The man's frozen expression was probably meant to discourage him from entering.

"I'm here to see Mr. Johnson." Gerome hooked his thumbs in the empty belt loops on the front of his jeans.

"Is he expecting you?" The icy tone didn't soften.

"No, but I think he'll see me. Just tell him Jerry's here."

When the door closed in his face, Gerome slouched against one of the pillars that lined the front of the imposing house. Crossing one ankle over the other, he waited in alert repose.

Unobtrusively, he scanned the perimeter. All around him were shrubbery and flower beds that needed attention. The fountain, which usually shot sparkling water high in intricate patterns, wasn't on. He wondered what other changes he'd find once he got inside.

The man returned and opened the door wider, but his expression was no more inviting than before. "Mr. Johnson will see you now."

After Gerome entered the circular two-story foyer, the butler closed the door behind him then led him down the hallway toward Herman's office. Their footsteps on the marble floor echoed in the tomblike quietness. Everything looked the same inside the house. But he felt as if hidden eyes were watching. It made the hairs on the back of his neck stand up.

Something isn't right.

❦

"Come in, Jerry, my boy."

Gerome complied with Herman Johnson's directive, standing still while his stepfather gave him a shrewd once-over.

"What a surprise. I wish you'd let me know you were coming." Herman's eyes widened slightly then hardened before a mask dropped over his features. "What can I do for you?"

Gerome knew he'd achieved the impression he wanted. He hunched his shoulders and shoved his hands into his front pockets, waiting until the new servant was out of earshot behind the closed door. This room was almost soundproof—nothing could be heard through that thick door unless someone had his ear pressed against the keyhole. Gerome had done that often enough in times past.

"I was wondering if you need another handyman around the place." He tried to keep a lazy expression on his face as he took in his stepfather's appearance. He'd aged considerably in the years since Gerome had been home. Somehow, he looked shriveled, sitting behind his massive desk in a pin-striped suit, but his intelligent eyes held the same spark they always had.

"If you need money, I'd be glad to write you a check." With a resigned sigh, Herman reached toward one of the desk drawers.

"No. I really want to work for what I get. You taught me that lesson." Gerome knew he had said the right thing when a faint smile flitted across Herman's face.

"What if I don't need anyone else working here?" His stepfather studied him through squinted eyes.

This was a test. "Then I'll just look elsewhere."

The older man's smile returned. "Well said. Actually, most of my help have gone on to other positions, so some things aren't getting done. I'd like to have you work for me." He gave Gerome another piercing gaze that softened at the end. "It'll be good to have you home again, Jerry."

14

Gerome dropped into one of the leather chairs across the desk from Herman. "I'd rather no one knows about our relationship. They might feel uncomfortable around me when I'm working."

Herman slowly swiped his hand across his mouth and chin, a habit he'd always had when thinking. "Maybe you're right. Most of the people who are in the house now weren't here when you and your mother lived with me. But won't they wonder when I have the housekeeper get your old room ready for you?"

"How about I stay in the servants' quarters out back?"

After a pause, Herman asked, "Are you all right, Jerry?"

"Yeah. I just need a place for some downtime and to make a little money."

Herman's gaze traveled over his worn clothing, shaggy hair, and unshaven face. "Okay. I'll have Prudence put you on the payroll."

Chapter 3

When Arlene drove her Honda into the driveway, Leiann was already packed and ready to go. After making one last walk through the house, she set three pieces of luggage beside the front door.

She took a deep breath and let it out slowly. *Am I doing the right thing?* The arrangements for the trip had taken only a week. Was she ready for this?

Before her friend could ring the bell, Leiann opened the door. "Thank you for driving me to the airport." She started pulling the two larger bags toward the car, leaving the carry-on for Arlene.

"You know I'm glad to do it." Arlene popped the lid of her trunk and helped Leiann lift in one of the large suitcases. "This is heavy. What do you have in it?"

Leiann brushed at a strand of hair tickling her forehead. "Since I'm not sure how long I'll stay, I put in a few books. Maybe I can catch up on my reading."

With the luggage stowed in the trunk, Arlene slammed it closed. She crossed her arms and turned toward Leiann, a serious expression on her face. "I'd be glad to go with you."

"I know, but this is something I have to do on my own. Besides, I need you to make sure everything is okay here at the house while I'm gone." Leiann rubbed the muscle above her eye that had started jumping. Usually the movement was barely discernible, but she always felt like it was a huge, ugly tic. "Just be sure to keep your cell phone close by."

Once they were in the car, Arlene backed out and headed east. "So, how did your meeting with Mr. Malone go?"

"He understood my need to go on this trip." Leiann almost cried remembering the concern in her principal's eyes. "He knows how hard things were during Mother's battle with breast cancer before she. . ." She blinked away her tears. "I can't believe it took her so quickly."

"Me either. But at least now she's not in pain."

Even coming from her best friend, the words sounded trite, and they didn't bring any comfort. "Mr. Malone said that since it's only a month until the end of school, he'd get a sub to finish the year for me. I'm really relieved. I was dreading all the sympathetic glances from students. Maybe I'll be better able to cope when the fall semester starts."

As they drove along Mid-Cities Boulevard, Arlene kept up a stream of casual conversation. Even though Leiann wasn't really into what her best friend talked about, she enjoyed having her familiar voice as a background to her own turbulent thoughts.

When they arrived at the terminal at Dallas Fort Worth International Airport, both women worked to extract the bags from the back of the sedan.

"How are you set for money?" Concern wrinkled Arlene's forehead.

"I'm fine. After Mr. Connor, Mother's lawyer, read the will and handed me her letter, he gave me an envelope of cash from my...grandfather." Leiann knew the word sounded bitter; it tasted that way, too. "I decided that if Mr. Johnson wanted me to come see him, I'd let him pay for it. Mr. Connor booked the flight, and he got me a seat in first class. That'll be a new experience."

Leiann hugged her friend good-bye then checked in. It didn't take as long as she'd anticipated. After going through security, she had a lot of time to kill. Feeling too nervous to sit still, she walked up and down the terminal, dragging her carry-on. She'd probably be glad she'd exercised when she sat during the three-and-a-half-hour flight.

She stopped at Starbucks and bought a decaf frozen mocha latté. As hyper as she felt right now, Leiann knew she didn't need any caffeine, but she wanted the comfort of her favorite treat. On the way back to her gate, she noticed a cute T-shirt in one of the shops. Might as well spend the extra time shopping. She could afford a few indulgences.

With her purchases scrunched into an outside pocket of the carry-on, she sat down near her gate and waited for the departure announcement.

On the flight, even though she was in first class, Leiann couldn't enjoy all the pampering by the flight attendant. Between the servings of food and soft drinks, her mind kept revisiting her plight. Every minute of her life had been a lie. All those hours spent with her father—stepfather—Milton, a lie. She'd loved her dad. Enjoyed spending time with him, being his special daughter. How could he not tell her that he wasn't her biological father? Why didn't he tell her the truth after his heart attack? Why did he have to lie to her all his life?

The mother she had loved and trusted had lived the lie, too. After Milton died, why didn't she tell Leiann the truth? When she had breast cancer, she knew her daughter would find out after she was gone. She could have prepared her for the truth. But she went to her grave still clinging to the lie.

And God had let it happen, too. All the subterfuge. People who should have loved her had played games with her life. How could the God she'd grown up loving let her live a life built on a lie?

When the pilot announced that they were approaching Logan Airport, Leiann moved into the empty seat beside her so she could look out the window. The countryside was greener, the buildings closer together than back home.

After crossing what had to be downtown, the airplane circled out over water.

She had pictured the airport somewhere outside Boston in open country, much like DFW. Instead, the runway ended at the edge of an island. Her heart jumped into her throat. She could almost feel the plane hitting the water. Leiann held her breath and took a death grip on the leather armrest. She didn't release either until they were safely on solid ground.

God, I feel abandoned and alone. And I don't even know who I really am. Why have You taken everything I know and love away from me?

She listened, but no voice answered either question. Just as well. She didn't know if she could still trust the God she'd grown up with. All of her life had been a lie. What part did He have in that?

When her feet hit the industrial-grade carpet of the terminal, she turned on her cell phone and called Arlene. "I've landed."

"Are you doing okay?" Her friend's sensitive words reached that hurting place deep inside.

"So many thoughts are jumbled in my head."

"Try to push them aside." Arlene's voice took on a tender tone. "I can come if you need me."

"And leave Mr. Malone to find another substitute? I don't think so." Leiann tried to sound cheerful. "I'll be all right, at least until school is out."

"Call me if you need to."

After assuring Arlene that she would, Leiann snapped her cell phone shut.

Mr. Connor had told her someone would meet her where she picked up her bags, so she made her way through the airport to baggage claim. There she found a man in a dark navy uniform and cap holding a sign with her name on it. He noticed her staring at him and moved toward her.

"Are you Miss Hambrick?" His voice sounded pleasant enough.

She nodded.

"Mr. Johnson sent me. After we retrieve your bags, I'll have you home in a jiffy."

Home? The man was treating her like she was one of the family.

Then it hit her. Mr. Johnson must be wealthier than she had imagined if he had his own driver.

"Are you his chauffeur?"

The man smiled and nodded. "I've been with Mr. Johnson for over twenty years. My father worked for him, too."

Leiann turned toward the baggage carousel, scanning each piece as it appeared so she could grab hers when they first came out. The chauffeur took both her checked bags out the door. She followed, lugging the carry-on.

He stopped beside a black limousine. She'd never been in one, not even for the funeral. This vehicle was a far cry from her five-year-old Kia. At least it wasn't one of those long stretch limos.

Feeling much like Dorothy when the tornado took her from the Kansas farm, Leiann stopped for a moment to let her mind settle. One of the reasons she'd agreed to this trip was to make some connection to her real heritage—or at least find out what it was. Everything was happening way too fast.

The driver put her bags in the trunk then opened the back door for her. Leiann didn't want to sit back there alone, but he probably wouldn't understand if she asked to ride up front with him. She climbed in.

The car slipped into a tunnel that took traffic from Logan into Boston. Even with the lights along the sides of the interior, she felt closed in.

Realizing how tired she was, she leaned her head against the back of the plush leather seat and closed her eyes for just a moment. For years, she'd thought of visiting the East Coast and some of the important historical sites in the Boston area. Maybe she'd be here long enough to do that.

"Miss Hambrick."

The words woke her from her nap. She glanced toward the open car door.

"We've arrived." The chauffeur held out his hand.

She took it and slid from the comfortable leather seat. She'd missed the drive through Boston. They were somewhere in the country now. "I never did ask your name."

"No, ma'am."

"What is it?"

"Greene, Miss. Forrest Greene." A chuckle followed his pronouncement.

She laughed, too. "That's some name."

"I don't mind, though it was sometimes a problem when I was a lad."

She glanced at the tall trees gracing the lawn as she moved toward the back of the car. Mr. Johnson must have a whole team of groundskeepers. "May I get my bags now?"

He pulled on the bill of his hat. "Someone will take them up to your room for you."

Of course Mr. Johnson would have servants to do things like that if he had a chauffeur. Leiann took a deep breath and turned toward the house. Tall marble columns reached to the roof of the porch above the second-story balcony. The opulence almost overwhelmed her.

The front door of the mansion opened, and a woman came out. She was dressed in a crimson suit expertly tailored to her willowy form, making Leiann feel dowdy and dull.

"Miss Hambrick, I'm Prudence Smith, Mr. Johnson's administrative assistant."

What an old-fashioned name for such a modern-looking woman.

"He wants to see you right away." The woman whirled back toward the house so fast her sleek chin-length hair riffled in the wind. Leiann had to walk fast to keep up. She wondered how she moved so quickly in those heels. They had to be more than three inches high.

They hurried through a large foyer and down a long hall, stopping outside a closed door. Leiann didn't get a chance to take in much of the surroundings, but the feeling of great wealth seeped into her consciousness.

Prudence opened the door to allow Leiann's entry then closed it behind her.

A man on the other side of a large carved desk stood. "Leiann! We finally meet." The kindness in his voice pulled her toward him a few steps.

She didn't know what to say. So she just stood and studied the man. Snow-white hair framed a face lined with deep grooves, and his bright blue eyes held a sparkling vitality. His stooped posture spoke of long years. He had to be older than she had thought he would be, maybe even in his eighties. Leiann didn't know what she expected to feel when she met him—maybe some kind of unspoken connection. But nothing came.

"You look a lot like your mother, but you have your father's eyes."

The quiet words went straight to her heart. Finally, a distinct connection. She'd often wondered why her eyes weren't like either her mother's or her father's.

"I wouldn't know." She bit off the last word. Leiann didn't want to antagonize the man right from the start, but she was having a hard time understanding everything that swirled inside her. "I'm sorry. The trip was long, and I'm tired."

He walked around the desk and approached her. "I'm sure you are, so I won't keep you. I just wanted to see you. We can talk later." His words continued to hold kindness. "I'll have Pru take you up to your room. I've given you one on the second floor that overlooks the back gardens. I hope the view will bring you some peace."

Leiann didn't want him to touch her, and he must have instinctively understood that. But his eyes probed every part of her, making her feel even more vulnerable. How did he know she needed peace?

He leaned across the desk and depressed a lever. "Please come in here, Miss Smith."

His assistant entered with a smile. "Yes, Mr. Johnson?"

"I want you to take my granddaughter to her room."

She glanced at Leiann then turned back to the man. "I'll be right back in case you need anything else." She stood beside the open door, waiting for Leiann to exit.

This time, as they walked down the hallway, Leiann went slower so she could study her surroundings. This house had the feel of old money. The knickknacks on several pieces of polished wood furniture appeared to be priceless treasures. Most looked like museum pieces. Her shoes sank so deep in the thick carpet that the ends of her toes disappeared into the fibers.

When she arrived in the bedroom suite, she found a maid unpacking her bags. The door to a private bath stood open, and the young servant arranged Leiann's toiletries on mirrored trays on a marble counter.

"I can do that."

Prudence frowned. "She's only doing her job."

Leiann nodded, and Prudence left. Leiann smiled at the young woman, who was now hanging up her clothes. "What's your name?"

"I'm Charity Gilcrest, ma'am. Mr. Johnson said I would be your personal maid while you're here." She curtseyed as if Leiann were royalty.

"You don't have to do that."

Leiann took off her light jacket and laid it on the bed. Charity picked it up and hung it in the walk-in closet. Leiann's bedroom back home was smaller than that closet.

"Would you like me to turn back your covers so you can rest?"

The thought of having a maid to turn down her bed unnerved Leiann. But she certainly did feel the need for some rest.

❦

Leiann awoke in the late afternoon to find a tea tray on the bedside table. Someone had been in her room while she slept. Surely Charity had brought the food in. She bristled at the idea of anyone prowling around her while she slept.

When she removed the cozy from the teapot, she breathed in the pungent aroma of orange and spices. After savoring a couple of the sugar cookies along with the tea, Leiann felt refreshed.

She glanced around the room, wondering what changes the next few days would bring to her life. She wished she'd let Arlene come with her. Her best friend would enjoy spending time in this mansion, and having her around would keep Leiann from feeling so alone. She wondered why Mr. Johnson had gone to so much trouble to make sure she came here. What could he have to say to her that was so important?

Leiann put on clean clothes, walked to the large window, and pulled open the drapes. The peaceful view stole her breath. She opened the French doors and stepped out onto the balcony. Fresh air carried the mingled fragrances of flowers.

She leaned against the ornate railing and gazed into the distance. A forest surrounded the estate on this side. The dense trees and underbrush gave a sense of being cut off from the world. But more than just trees stood between her and the person she had always been.

Although she saw no houses nearby, Leiann felt as if someone was watching her. Her gaze slowly traced the carefully laid-out gardens, stopping on a tall man who leaned against a large elm tree with spreading branches that stood a short distance from the house. He appeared to be a gardener or handyman, dressed in jeans and a red T-shirt that stretched over his broad shoulders. Of course, Mr. Johnson would need many workers to keep the property in shape.

When her eyes met those of the man, her breath hitched. Handsome didn't even begin to describe him. Hard muscles glistened below his rolled-up shirt sleeves. His wavy hair was too long to be fashionable, and the style needed to be tamed. He exuded a strong masculinity with a touch of wildness.

His dark, brooding eyes glinted in the sinking sunlight. Why was he studying her so intently? When that question entered her mind, she realized that she was staring at him, too. She quickly averted her gaze.

🍂

Gerome was cutting dead limbs out of the overgrown elm trees in the back garden when the French doors in one of the guest suites opened. A woman stepped out onto the balcony.

Who is this, and where does she fit into the equation? Something about the way her light brown curls tumbled around her head gave her a fluffy halo in the late-afternoon sun. None of Herman's other employees had said anything to him about someone coming to visit. Maybe he could discover something about her while he ate with the servants this evening.

After he cleaned up from work, he walked to the big house and went in through the back door to the kitchen.

Gerome found the cook alone, mashing potatoes in a large pot. Since she was the only other person who knew he was Herman's stepson, he could relax around her. When he arrived a week ago, she had assured him she wouldn't tell anyone about the relationship.

He sniffed the delicious aromas. "Smells like we're having a feast tonight."

"Of course." Mrs. Martha Shields stirred something in a pan on the gleaming industrial-sized range. "Your stepfather's granddaughter is here."

Gerome felt as if he'd been poleaxed. "His granddaughter? I didn't know he had a granddaughter."

"I didn't either." She turned and put one hand on an ample hip. "Mr. Johnson's son died in a motorcycle accident years ago, soon after I came to work here. Evidently, young Lee married a woman his father didn't approve of. According to the rumors, they had a child several months after his death. Mr. Johnson and his granddaughter haven't been in contact before." Martha shook her head and tsked. "Such goings-on."

"Do you know her name?" Gerome walked to the large sink and filled a glass with water.

"Leiann Hambrick. Such a pretty name." Martha went back to stirring the pot on the stove. "My granddaughter, Charity, is serving as her maid. She saw it engraved on a leather portfolio. She couldn't get over the strange spelling. L-E-I-A-N-N."

"That is unusual."

When Gerome returned to his room that night, he took out his secure satellite cell phone and punched in the number of his best friend and coworker. "I need some information, Greg. Find out everything you can about a Leiann Hambrick." He spelled her first name the way Martha had told him. "She's from somewhere in Texas." Gerome raked one hand through his unruly curls. "I need the information ASAP."

"I'll get right on it."

Gerome snapped the phone shut and stared out into the darkening twilight. Why did this woman show up now? Was she part of what he came to check out?

She could even be a gold digger out to get what she could from the Old Man. *If she came here to get her hands on his millions, she'll have to go through a brick wall—me.*

Chapter 4

As she prepared for dinner, Leiann put on her favorite outfit. Whenever she wore the chocolate brown pantsuit and tailored blouse in muted greens and blues, she felt very professional. That's the impression she wanted to make on Mr. Johnson. During the mealtime together, maybe she would be able to find out a little more about her family background.

Charity led her down the stairs and into the large dining room. Leiann glanced around the room. Huge chandeliers hung above both ends of the table, which could seat more than twenty people. Four places were set at one end. *So much for a quiet dinner.* She wondered who else would be joining them.

"I see you got here before we did."

Leiann turned at the sound of Prudence's voice. She was accompanied by a man Leiann hadn't seen before.

Prudence stopped in front of her. "This is my brother, Eric."

After brief introductions, Prudence sat closest to the head of the table. She waved toward the chair at the head of the table. "Herman usually sits there."

Leiann slipped into the chair on the other side of the table from Prudence.

Charity entered with a tray that she set on the sideboard. She picked up a soup bowl and set it before Leiann. "I hope you like cream of asparagus."

Leiann welcomed her friendly smile. "Yes, thank you."

While Charity served the other two people, Leiann asked, "Isn't my grandfather going to join us?"

"No. He isn't feeling well this evening." Prudence sipped a spoonful of the soup. "Charity, tell Martha this soup is delicious."

"Yes, ma'am." Charity backed out through the door.

Disappointment robbed Leiann of her appetite. She had really hoped this mealtime would be productive, an opportunity for her to talk to Mr. Johnson alone. Leiann wondered about Prudence. Was she more than just Mr. Johnson's assistant? She sure was acting like it.

Prudence turned her attention to her brother. "So, what did you do today?"

"Nothing important." He kept his attention on Leiann. "I'd like to get to know Herman's granddaughter better."

Evidently, Eric was used to taking his meals here. *Wonder what he does. Maybe he works for Grandfather, too.*

Eric was a handsome man, but Leiann wasn't interested. As quickly as she could, she ate a few bites of each course then excused herself after dessert.

🍂

Sleep eluded Leiann that night. *That's what I get for taking a nap in the car and another one after I arrived here.* After midnight, she rose from tossing and turning in the bed and decided to read awhile. Maybe that would help her relax and get to sleep.

A walnut bookcase sat against one wall in the sitting area of her suite, and the books she'd brought with her lined one shelf. Her fingers trailed along the spines. She didn't want one of the suspense novels. Enough drama filled her life already. Finally, she extracted a women's fiction that everyone had been raving about and took it to the comfortable chair near the window. She pulled her legs up beside her and tucked her gown around them.

No matter how hard she tried to stay focused, her thoughts roamed far from the story. After an hour, she stood and stretched. Her rumbling stomach reminded her how little she'd eaten that day.

Maybe she could go to the kitchen and get a snack. Her grandfather had told her to make herself at home, hadn't he?

Leiann walked into the closet and found her robe. She removed the terry cloth garment from the hanger and put it on, cinching the belt tight.

She opened the bedroom door and listened. Probably no one else was up. As she tiptoed down the hall, the thick carpeting swallowed the sound of her footsteps.

She stood in the foyer and looked around. *Now, if I were a kitchen, where would I be?*

After making a few wrong turns, Leiann finally found the right doorway. Most of her house would fit into the cavernous space. She found the light switch and flipped it on, then went to the large stainless-steel refrigerators that lined one wall and opened one. The bottom drawer spread across the whole width, filled with fruit. She took an orange and a paper towel to the table and perched on a high stool, taking her time peeling it while studying the rest of the room.

Her mother would have loved all the copper-bottomed pans hanging above the island. What other wonders did the cabinets hold?

After she savored the last juicy slice, she went to the large double sink and wet the paper towel, planning to wipe off the table.

"What are you doing in here?"

Leiann jumped at the strident voice that echoed in the room. She spun around and gasped. Prudence Smith stood in the doorway, clad in a long silk robe that did little to mask her fabulous figure.

"I. . .uh, I. . .was hungry." Leiann felt like a stammering schoolchild as she clutched the soggy paper towel.

The other woman walked across the room toward her.

"I showed you the bellpull that would summon a servant." Prudence took a glass from the cabinet and filled it with water. "Why didn't you use it? Someone would have brought you whatever you wanted."

Leiann wondered why the woman cared what Leiann did. Her grandfather had invited her here, and he didn't tell her she had to obey his assistant. "I didn't see any reason to disturb anyone else's sleep."

"That's what servants are paid for." Disdain dripped from every word. Prudence swept through the door, her robe swishing behind her.

Trembling, Leiann took another paper towel from the roll and returned to the table. While she mopped up the few drops of juice from her orange, her thoughts followed the other woman down the hall and up the stairs. Prudence acted more like the mistress of the house than an employee. Dressed as she was, she had to be staying in the main house, not one of the cottages behind, where Leiann assumed the employees lived. Why did Miss Smith live here?

❧

Charity brought Leiann's breakfast to her room. Leiann asked her to set the tray on the table beside the window. That way she could enjoy the view while she ate.

"Have you worked here long?" Leiann liked having the cheerful young woman around.

The maid looked up from smoothing the covers over the mattress. "Just since I finished junior college a year ago. I'm saving money so I can transfer to a four-year school."

Leiann took a sip of orange juice. "What are you majoring in?"

"I really want to be a lawyer, but I'll probably end up a paralegal. Law school takes a long time and a lot of money." She picked up Leiann's robe from the chair beside the bed and headed toward the closet.

After taking a bite of the delicious waffles, Leiann studied Charity. "If you don't mind my asking, why did you choose to work here?"

"Martha, the cook, is my grandmother. I spent a lot of time here during the summers." Charity came out of the closet and went back to the bed. "I've always liked Mr. Johnson. He's been good to my family."

Charity finished tucking the comforter under the pillows and smoothed it. Leiann wanted to ask the girl more about what was going on in the house, but she didn't want to make her feel uncomfortable. Maybe she could find out later.

❧

The butler brought Leiann a summons to Mr. Johnson's office soon after she finished breakfast. She brushed her teeth, splashed on cologne, and defined her lips with a subtle shade of lipstick. She'd never worn much makeup except when she had a special event to attend, which hadn't been often. Leiann fluffed her curls and took a deep breath before heading down the stairs.

When she knocked on the door, her grandfather opened it. "Come in, Leiann."

She smiled, not knowing what to say as he led her toward a sofa and a couple of chairs that sat on one side of the office. He eased into one of the chairs, so she decided to sit on the sofa. After sinking into the deeply cushioned seat, she picked up one of the decorative pillows and held it in front of her, fingering the fringe. At least this was less intimidating than sitting across the large desk from him.

A moment of uncomfortable silence lengthened. Finally, she looked at the elderly man. His intense gaze rested on her.

"Why did you want me to come here?"

He took awhile before saying anything. A myriad of expressions crossed his face. "The most important reason was to ask your forgiveness."

"I have no idea what I need to forgive you for." Leiann's heart raced under his scrutiny. She looked away, her gaze roaming from the glossy paneled walls to the thick draperies that framed the floor-to-ceiling windows. Everything seemed dark. Definitely a man's domain.

"This is hard for me." He rubbed the bridge of his nose. "No man wants to admit his failings, and I've had lots of them."

Leiann didn't comment.

Herman Johnson steepled his fingers and rested his chin against the tips. "I am not proud of what I did to your mother. But she was finally able to forgive me."

Leiann couldn't hold back any longer. "Why didn't she ever tell me about my father and you?"

"I asked her not to until you were grown. She and Milton were good parents, and I didn't think I deserved to upset your life. She chose to keep you in the dark longer." He sighed and swiped a hand across his eyes. "I thought she would eventually tell you."

Leiann rose and paced across the Persian carpet before turning back toward the man. "Do you have any idea how all this has affected me?"

"Dear Leiann, I hope you can give me the time it will take to get to know me. During your visit, I'll answer all your questions." Weariness painted his features, and his shoulders stooped. "Can we do this a little at a time?"

The thought panicked Leiann. She had only thought she'd be here for a short visit. "How long?"

His eyes drifted closed. Without opening them, he said, "I know your school year is almost over." He opened his eyes and fastened his gaze on her. "Could you stay at least until the middle of summer?"

She gasped. She'd only planned on a few days at the most.

Before she could answer, he held up a hand. "I know that's a lot to ask, but I have much to atone for, and I don't think I can go into it all at once." His eyes took on a pleading expression that looked foreign on his strong but wizened face.

Leiann lowered her gaze to the carpet. She did want to know about her father. And did she really have to hurry back to the house that reminded her so much of her lost past? The principal had told her the substitute could finish out the year. And she needed time to grieve for her mother. Could she do that in this foreign setting?

"Will you at least think about it?"

She gave a slow nod.

"Good." A faint smile stretched his thin lips. "Now, if you'll excuse me, I need to lie down. I've been ill, and it's taking me awhile to regain my strength."

Leiann followed him out the door into the hallway. He turned the opposite direction from the foyer, which contained the staircase.

As she walked to her room, she realized she hadn't learned one single fact about her life. Except that her mother evidently had forgiven her grandfather for whatever he did to her.

Tonight she would call Arlene and tell her about Mr. Johnson's request.

❦

Even in this large house, Leiann felt as if the walls were closing in on her. Deciding she needed a walk in the sunshine, she took off her skirt and flats and put on khaki slacks and sneakers.

"Charity," Leiann called to the girl cleaning the bathroom in her suite. The maid came into the bedroom. "I want to get outside for a while. I'd like to visit the gardens. Is there anything I need to know before I go out there?"

Charity raised her eyebrows. "Like what?"

"I just don't want to do anything that would cause a problem." As soon as the words left her lips, Leiann knew they sounded silly.

"You're family. You can do anything you want." Charity wiped her hands on a towel.

Of course the servants would think that. Leiann opened the door to the hallway. "If Mr. Johnson wants to talk to me, can you tell him where I've gone?"

"Yes, ma'am."

She considered going out the front door and walking around to the back of the house but instead decided to make her way through the mansion. She wished someone had given her a tour of the house.

First she found the library, which was lined with floor-to-ceiling shelves, except for a section across the back where French doors opened to the garden. She definitely wanted to go out there, but first she had to explore this room. Like something out of a Victorian novel, the library sported hanging ladders that slid along the top shelves. She moved a couple of them and climbed in several places around the room. The selection of books was phenomenal—leather-bound classics, some first editions, reference books, a large selection of fiction from different eras. She even found a collection of current Christian fiction. She wouldn't have needed to bring her own after all. Maybe she'd read a few of these and save hers for when she went home. She wondered who in this house enjoyed them.

Leiann stepped through the French doors into the late-morning sunlight that bathed the multilevel flagstone terrace. The sun brought warmth, but not the heat she was used to in Texas at this time of year.

The terrace held several glass-topped, wrought-iron tables with comfortable-looking chairs. Maybe she could ask to have her breakfast here sometimes. If she decided to stay.

At the end of the terrace, stone steps led down into the garden. Paths meandered in different directions through well-manicured lawns and flower beds. She chose one and strolled through a long arbor that gave shade from the sun and sheltered a wide variety of flowering bushes and shrubs, many of them roses. Their perfume infused the air, reminding Leiann of her mother. Every year, Mom had toiled over her rose beds, but never had they bloomed as profusely as those surrounding this path.

Leiann took a deep breath to keep from crying at the thought of her mother then strode down the stone path. When she found a white wrought-iron bench, she sat and gazed at the verdant hillside in the distance, trying to lose herself in its beauty to keep from concentrating on her recent loss.

Footsteps brought her from her musings, and she looked up in time to see Eric Smith come around the corner.

"Ah, there you are. May I join you?"

Since she didn't know any reason why not, she nodded.

He dropped onto the short bench. "Has anyone given you the grand tour?"

Leiann shook her head and unobtrusively slid as close to her end of the bench as she could. The man was much too close to her.

Eric's eyes brightened. "May I do the honors?" He gave her a moment to answer before continuing. "Or not." His engaging smile drew her. Besides, if she was going to stay here awhile, she needed to get to know the layout of the place.

"Sure." She stood and brushed the back of her slacks in case there was dust on the bench.

He joined her and offered her his arm. She took it and let him lead her farther down the path.

They laughed and talked as he showed her through the grounds and the house. By the time Leiann returned to her room, she didn't feel so much like a stranger in this strange place. At least she had one tenuous friendship, and she knew her way around. Eric had even offered to take her sightseeing.

♡

Gerome kept working in the flower beds while he watched Smith take Leiann on a tour of the gardens before going into the house with her. He had a bad feeling about that man. Something about him didn't sit right. In his line of work, Gerome had learned to recognize certain personality traits almost in an instant, and this guy was as phony as a three-dollar bill. Why couldn't the Old Man's granddaughter, if that was really who she was, see through him?

Maybe Leiann already knew Eric Smith before she came here. Maybe she knew Prudence, too. He hoped to hear back on his inquiry into her background by tonight. Until then, he'd try to keep an eye on all three. *Talk about a difficult situation!*

For a moment, Gerome wished he'd come sooner so he could protect his stepfather. Then again, he could be wrong about someone trying to swindle him.

He'd always thought the Old Man—the pet name he'd given Herman as a rebellious teenager but which stuck through adulthood—was astute enough not to let anything like that happen to him. Evidently, he had been wrong in his assessment.

♡

When Leiann arrived at her grandfather's office the next morning, he looked better than he had the day before. His eyes twinkled and his skin had a healthier color.

"Let's sit over here again." He led the way to the sofa.

After he was seated, she took her place on the other end, turning to lean against the cushiony arm so she could face him.

"Can I tell you about your father?" He sounded almost eager.

Leiann nodded.

"Lee was born when I was old enough to be a grandfather." He chuckled. "Talk about a generation gap. It was as wide as the Grand Canyon."

She understood how that could happen. She'd seen it more than once as a teacher. Older parents with a teen they couldn't connect with.

"Unfortunately, my first wife never recovered from the toll of having a baby in her forties. By the time Lee was a toddler, we'd lost her." Her grandfather's voice broke on the last word. A tear slipped down his cheek.

For a moment, Leiann wanted to wipe it away. "So who raised. . .my father?"

Mr. Johnson took out a white handkerchief and wiped his nose. "A succession

30

of nannies." He shook his head. "I was so devastated at losing Miriam that I kept myself very busy. That's when I added to the family's wealth. I fought my grief by working hard."

Leiann noticed that the longer her grandfather talked, the more tired he looked. "Everyone has to deal with their grief some way."

"But mine was wrong for Lee. Although I saw him sometime every day, I didn't spend the amount of quality time with him that he needed. I'm sure that added to the gap between us."

A knock sounded on the door. "Who is it?"

"Prudence."

"Come in." Mr. Johnson stood and started toward his desk.

When his assistant came, she glanced at Leiann on her way toward her employer. "You have an important call from Hanson in Hong Kong."

Her grandfather turned toward Leiann. "I need to take this call, and it could last a long time. Will you excuse me?"

"Of course."

"We'll get together tomorrow morning again, if that's okay with you, Leiann."

"I'd like that."

Chapter 5

A week later, Leiann sat at the table on the terrace, eating breakfast as she watched dawn break over the wooded hills. Mrs. Shields had insisted on feeding Leiann when she came outside to enjoy the early-morning beauty. The cook said she always got up early anyway, so it was no trouble. Feeling pampered by the grandmotherly woman, Leiann agreed.

Mrs. Shields's culinary prowess amazed her. Today she'd had a light omelet with sliced kiwi ringing the plate. A separate plate held toast made from hearty whole-grain bread. Yesterday she'd had fluffy French toast with circles of Canadian bacon, accompanied by slices of some kind of melon. At home Leiann usually had bagels, cereal bars, or occasionally scrambled eggs and toast. She never got up this early, but she'd begun to enjoy the solitude.

Her grandfather had met with her in the late morning every day. For the most part, they'd been getting acquainted with each other rather than delving into the past. He expressed genuine interest in her. Whenever she shared something about herself with him, he seemed happy. As if he cared about everything in her life. She was glad of that, but it wasn't getting her any closer to finding out about her past and why he owned the house. Every time she felt like pressuring him for more of that kind of information, his frailty stopped her.

These early-morning times of respite always refreshed her before she went to his office. But today, for some reason, she felt as if someone was watching her again. As she ate slowly, she surreptitiously glanced around the area. Nothing looked out of place. Finally, she spied movement among the trees off to the right. The handyman she'd seen that first day here was standing beside a tree, pulling himself up to a horizontal limb and raising his chin over it, then slowly dropping to the ground. He wore jogging clothes, and his hair had been cut. The man looked more appealing than ever.

Leiann averted her gaze and stared at her nearly empty plate, heat filling her cheeks. She should concentrate on her breakfast and ignore the enigmatic man.

"Enjoying your breakfast?" The question came from behind her.

She turned around to find Eric framed in the doorway of the large den, which also faced the terrace. Why hadn't she heard him open the door? Surely she'd closed it when she came outside.

"I'm almost finished." Leiann ignored his question. She quickly stood and started gathering the utensils.

"Leave everything. The servants will clean up." Eric came toward her. "How about going sightseeing with me today?" He stopped a little too close for her comfort. Eric amused her when they were together, but he didn't seem to understand about personal space.

"I'm meeting with my grandfather soon. I'll let you know after that."

Charity stuck her head out the doorway. "Miss Leiann, Mr. Johnson had to go back to bed. He apologizes, but he must cancel your time together."

Leiann glanced at Eric.

He gave her a dazzling smile. "Great. Now you can come with me."

"Actually, today wouldn't be a good time for me." She hurried inside the house and made her way up to her room. She did want to do some sightseeing, but by herself, not with Eric Smith. He was charming and polite, but she was beginning to worry about her grandfather. Some days he seemed vigorous; others, he was fragile and weak.

~

Gerome worked his way through the garden, checking on the plants and getting rid of a few weeds, trying to get close enough to hear what Eric was saying to Leiann. He slid behind the shelter of the shrubs beside the house.

He wondered at the motives of both of them. Eric seemed to be a ne'er-do-well who hung on his sister's coattails. As far as Gerome could tell, he didn't have a job.

Gerome wished he could ask Leiann Hambrick what she was really doing here. But he didn't want to tip his hand before he knew more about the relationships between all these people.

~

After lunch, Gerome moved to the front of the house to hoe the flower beds and mow the grass. A Mercedes, driven by Eric Smith, pulled through the gates and started up the long drive. Gerome squatted to clean the grass off the riding mower while monitoring the vehicle's approach out of the corner of his eye.

So, the freeloader was driving the Old Man's vehicle. This man was up to no good.

The reports Gerome had received from Greg had convinced him that someone was defrauding his stepfather. The question was, who else was working with him?

Greg's latest report indicated the Hambrick woman was who she said she was: a schoolteacher from Texas. His colleague at Ozbourne Global Security hadn't found any proof that she was kin to Herman, but no one had found any criminal record for her, either—not even a traffic ticket.

❦

Leiann planned to have a light supper in her room or on the terrace, but Charity brought a message that her grandfather would like to dine with her.

When she arrived in the large dining room, the long table was set at just one end, as it had been when she dined with Prudence and Eric. Grandfather looked regal in the heavy chair at the head. The seat to his right was empty, but across from it, Prudence Smith leaned toward her boss, talking rapidly. Eric lounged beside his sister, but when he noticed Leiann enter the room, he straightened and smiled at her. Evidently her rebuff this morning hadn't affected him.

As she approached, her grandfather gestured for her to take the empty seat beside him. Prudence leaned back in her chair and lifted her water glass for a sip.

As soon as Leiann was seated, the first course appeared, served by a maid Leiann hadn't seen before. The creamy soup smelled enticing. It was followed by a large salad full of her favorite vegetables. Hot, steaming rolls melted the butter she spread on them.

By the time the main course arrived, Leiann felt stuffed. But the conversation had proved pleasant.

During a lull, her grandfather laid a lumpy envelope on the table between them, giving it a little shove in her direction. "This is for you." His eyes twinkled while she opened it.

A set of car keys slid onto the table with a clatter. The keychain had a Mercedes logo on it. "What are these for?"

"They fit the dark blue sedan in the garage. I want you to use it while you're here."

Prudence gasped then set her lips in a grim line.

"I don't drive anymore, so the only time it's used is when Forrest takes it out to have it serviced." He picked up a fluffy roll and slathered butter on it. "I thought you might want to do a little exploring."

She smiled at her grandfather. "Thank you for your thoughtfulness."

During the rest of the meal, her grandfather asked a lot of questions that kept her talking about herself. She learned that he shared the same interest in history that she had. As soon as he was finished eating, her grandfather excused himself.

When Leiann left the dining room, she went out on the terrace to watch twilight fall over the garden. Soon stars popped into the indigo canopy overhead. This time of day was just as pleasing as the early morning had been.

One of the doors behind her opened, and she glanced back to see Eric sauntering across the flagstones toward her.

"You like looking at the property, don't you?"

"It's beautiful country." She watched the rising moon paint a silver rim on the trees.

"Almost everything you can see from here belongs to Mr. Johnson." Eric jingled something metallic in his front pocket. "Would you like me to take you to the mountain that overlooks the property?"

What would it hurt? "I'd like that."

"We'll go tomorrow." He dropped into the chair across the table from Leiann. "What time?"

"After I meet with my grandfather."

☙

Eric picked her up in a Jeep Wrangler.

"Is this yours?" She reached to buckle the seat belt.

"No, it belongs to the estate."

To the estate? Why didn't he just say it belonged to her grandfather? "So, do you work for my grandfather?"

The muscles in his face tightened. "I'm not actually on the payroll. Sometimes I do what would be considered contract work, running errands for my sister or for Mr. Johnson. Prudence wanted me to come stay here after we lost our parents. It helps her to have me near. I'm all the family she has now."

Leiann could understand how Prudence might feel this way. If she had a sibling, she'd want to keep him close to her, too. "And my grandfather lets you use his vehicles?"

He gave her a jaunty grin. "I couldn't run errands otherwise."

"How many vehicles are in his garage?"

Eric drove around the house and down a track that went past the outbuildings. "Quite a few. When we get back, I'll take you to see them."

As they started through the forest, the dirt road became rougher, so Leiann held on to the seat. The path was overgrown with tall grass, but she could see the indentations of the tracks.

"Are we still on Grandfather's property?"

Eric didn't take his eyes off the path that wound between the trees. "He owns the whole mountain."

When they arrived at a clearing near the top of the hill, a view spread before them like a landscape painting. It was definitely worth all the bumping along the journey.

She climbed out of the Jeep and walked to the front of it. Crossing her arms, she leaned against the vehicle.

He came up and leaned beside her. "If you want a really good view of the property, there's an observation tower closer to the top of the mountain. We'd have to climb a little to get to it."

Leiann's adventurous spirit came to the forefront. "Lead the way."

By the time they reached the wooden tower, Leiann was glad to take the opportunity to sit on a large rock near the base. "I'm not used to climbing mountains."

Eric reached the ladder and tapped it with his foot. "When you've caught your breath, you should go on up there. The view is amazing."

The tower looked well maintained. Its ladder went straight up the side. But with the metal handrails, it shouldn't be hard to climb. After a few moments of rest, she tested the first step. It felt solid.

She took a few tentative steps then became bolder. She glanced over her shoulder and saw Eric standing near the edge of the cliff, his hands clasped behind him. Maybe he'd been up here so many times, he didn't want to join her. Or he could want her to savor the view without distractions. She focused on the climb and continued up the long ladder. The closer to the top she came, the bolder she felt. Wait until she called Arlene and told her how she'd climbed this tall thing. It had to be more than fifty feet high.

With a loud *crack*, the step Leiann stood on broke. She clung to the railings, trying to decide whether to try to go back down or to step up. What if the next one broke, too?

She went back down one level without letting go of the railing. After she stood on it for a moment, that step also gave way. Her feet dangled in thin air. Panic filled her, and her palms began to sweat. How long could she hold on?

"Eric!" Her scream echoed.

He looked up, and his eyes widened. "I'll go get help."

"Nooo! Don't leave me here!"

Ignoring her plea, he ran back toward the Jeep.

Her hands slowly slid down the metal rails until they reached a support. Afraid to place her weight on yet another step, she left her feet dangling. Her arms ached. Her weight pressed against the sides of her hands, making them ache, too. But she was afraid to let go with either hand to move it past the support. She knew she wouldn't be able to hold on until Eric reached the Jeep, much less brought back help.

She squeezed her eyes shut, her breath coming in gasps. Tears trickled down her cheeks.

The ladder shook, and her eyes flew open. What was happening? She ventured a glance down. Below her on the ladder, the handyman climbed toward her like a monkey.

"Let go," he called to her from a dozen steps below. "I'll catch you."

She clung tighter. "I don't want to knock you down."

"You won't. I'm wedged in here." He stared up at her with concern crinkling his eyes. "I promise I'll catch you."

There was nothing else to do. Her hands were getting weaker every second.

She closed her eyes and released her hold, wondering if this was her time to die.

She thudded against the man, but he caught her weight and held her steady. He enclosed her with his strong arms and pulled her against his chest. "You're all right now," he crooned over and over as she sobbed against him.

She clung to him while she breathed in great gulps of air. With her ear pressed so close to his chest, his heartbeat sounded as accelerated as hers felt. Leiann didn't know why the man had been out on the mountain at this moment, but she was glad he was.

Chapter 6

Leiann stood in the shower, letting the hot water pour over her sore shoulders and arms, thankful that her grandfather hadn't found out what happened on the tower. She'd begun to care about the curious gentleman and didn't want him worried. He seemed old enough to be her great-grandfather. Sometimes when they were talking, weariness deepened the lines on his face and his hands shook. Other times he was full of energy.

She'd always heard that your life flashed before your eyes when you thought you were going to die. Hers hadn't. She'd been too busy concentrating on holding on to the railings to think about anything else. And when she was finally safe in the arms of the mysterious handyman, his hard muscles cushioning her, she felt safe. For the first time in quite a while.

Her unusual hero hadn't put her down right away when he reached the ground. He held her as if she didn't weigh anything and rushed through the trees to a beat-up pickup, which ran surprisingly well. He'd taken her to the house and carried her through the kitchen and up the back staircase to her room. She'd never seen the stairs the servants used, but he seemed to know where he was going. She felt so shaken, she'd just clung to the front of his shirt.

Charity had been sitting on a high stool next to the kitchen sink when they rushed by. Her eyes wide, she'd jumped down and hurried after them.

While the water in the shower rushed down her back, Leiann could hear her maid and her rescuer talking in her bedroom. The bathroom door opened. Leiann wrapped the ornate shower curtain around her wet body.

"Miss Hambrick, I've put a robe on the vanity for you." Charity's comment was followed by the bathroom door opening and closing again.

Leiann turned off the water and leaned her head against the shower wall, letting the marble tiles cool her. *What is going on?* The whole incident on the mountain felt bizarre. She towel-dried her hair then wrapped another one around her head before drying off and donning the plush terrycloth robe. Leiann hadn't heard any voices since her maid brought the robe. Perhaps her rescuer had left.

Charity sat in the chair beside the balcony door, waiting for her to emerge from the bathroom. "Would you like something to eat. . .or maybe a pot of tea?"

"Tea would be nice." Leiann walked into the closet to choose something to put on.

When Charity returned from downstairs, Leiann stood in the bathroom blow-drying her hair.

"Would you like me to stay with you?" Her maid's words made Leiann realize she didn't want to be alone right now.

"Did you bring an extra cup?"

The girl giggled. "I did."

Leiann unplugged the dryer and stepped into her bedroom. Charity had set places on the table by the window.

"I brought some finger sandwiches, too." She glanced at Leiann. "Grandma said you'd need something to eat."

While Leiann slipped into one of the chairs, Charity settled into the other and poured two cups of tea. She added a few heaping spoonfuls of sugar into one and stirred it before handing it to Leiann. "Grandma told me to load it up with sugar to stave off shock."

"We don't drink much hot tea in Texas." Leiann breathed in the fragrant steam wafting from her cup then took a sip. "It feels funny to be drinking it near Boston. Makes me think about the Boston Tea Party from history class." She knew she was babbling, but she didn't want to start crying. This felt like a safe topic.

Charity passed her the plate of sandwiches.

Leiann looked over the variety. "What kind are they?"

"The ones on the white bread are cream cheese and cucumber. Grandma likes those best. Egg salad is on the wheat bread, and chicken salad in the croissants."

Leiann shook her head. "This is way too much food for me."

"Don't worry about it. Someone else will eat whatever we don't."

After taking a sample of each kind, Leiann had another thought. "Charity, why were you so formal when you brought the robe to me in the bathroom? You haven't called me Miss Hambrick since we became friends."

A sheepish grin covered the girl's face. "Mr. Mays was just leaving, and I didn't want him to think I'd forgotten my place."

"So his name is Mays." Leiann sank her teeth into the cucumber sandwich.

"Yes. Gerome Mays. He's only been here a couple of weeks."

Now her hero had a name.

🌿

Gerome drove so fast up the track toward the observation tower that he bumped all over the truck seat and had a hard time keeping his foot on the accelerator. He wanted to pick up all the evidence he could before anyone else took it.

He stopped the truck at the end of the track and, leaving the door open, scrambled the rest of the way up to the structure. The strenuous exercise reminded him that he hadn't kept to his regimen as well as he should have since arriving here. He leaned his hands on his knees and breathed through his mouth, trying to calm his racing pulse.

Scanning the area, he knew something was wrong. Things had changed since he left here with the girl.

Who was he kidding? She was a woman. Catching her and holding her may have been part of the reason his pulse rate had shifted to double time. Leiann Hambrick had curves in all the right places, and the floral fragrance from her hair tingled in his nostrils even now. In different circumstances, he might have wanted to get to know her better. But at this juncture, he had to remain vigilant.

Gerome stood tall and raked the tower with his intense gaze. His rambling thoughts came to a screeching halt when he finally found what had changed. The wood from the two broken steps no longer hung between the railings. He circled the structure, searching the ground for even a sliver of the lumber. Someone had come up here and removed all of it. He gripped his hands into fists and pounded one of the wooden supports with his right hand. Not a smart move. As he rushed back down to his truck, he rubbed his sore knuckles.

❧

When Eric called Leiann's room, asking if she would go for a drive with him, she told him no. He'd left her on the tower, hanging on for dear life.

"Where did you go?" Her voice sounded strident, but she didn't care.

"I went for help. Evidently I needn't have bothered."

Leiann took a deep breath. "How did you know I was back at the house?"

"I saw Mays bring you in." He paused. "Leiann, I have to talk to you." His voice held an urgency that startled her. "There are things you need to know."

"Like what?"

"I don't want to risk anyone overhearing. You don't understand the danger."

Because he sounded so upset, she agreed to meet him on the terrace at four. That would give her a little while to get dressed and fix her hair.

She wasn't comfortable with the way he had disappeared while she dangled from the tower. She could have been killed. To her, that spelled danger with capital letters. How was he going to explain that? As if any explanation would be acceptable.

When she got to the terrace, he wasn't there. Leiann sat in one of the chairs and let her gaze travel over the back gardens. She hoped to catch a glimpse of Gerome Mays. She wanted to thank him for rescuing her. She'd been so rattled before, she didn't even think to do it. But he was nowhere in sight.

"Why so glum, Leiann?"

Eric had come up on her without making a sound. She wondered if he did that on purpose or if she was so lost in her own thoughts that she didn't hear him.

Leiann stood and faced Eric with her hands on her hips. "What a stupid question. This has been a horrible day."

He held up both hands as if to ward off her anger. "Wait a minute. I went for help."

"You left me dangling who knows how many feet up in the air. If I'd fallen to the ground, I could've been killed."

His gaze made a lazy trip up and down her body. "You don't look hurt to me."

Leiann fisted her hands to keep from slapping his face. "My arms, hands, and shoulders hurt plenty."

Eric's expression softened. "I'm sorry. But I have acrophobia. You know, a fear of heights. So I couldn't climb up there after you. I hoped to get help before it was too late."

Leiann crossed her arms and looked out over the rose garden, allowing the rich perfume to calm her nerves while she let this new information sink in. When she looked back at Eric, his eyes were focused on her.

"It's a good thing Mr. Mays was there. He saved me and brought me home." When she realized what she said, she gasped. Why had she called this *home*?

"Yeah, good thing." Eric sounded skeptical. "Didn't you wonder what the moody gardener was doing up there at that time of day?"

"Why should I? I'm just thankful he came to my rescue."

Eric stuck one hand in the front pocket of his slacks and jingled the contents. "The reason I want you to go for a ride with me is so I can show you what I found when I got back up there."

"What did you find?" Leiann was losing her patience.

"The boards had been cut almost all the way through. Someone tried to kill you. It could have been anyone. It could even have been Mays. Maybe he was hiding so he could watch you fall."

"Then why did he rescue me?"

"Probably because he didn't want to leave a witness, and I'd seen it happen."

Leiann couldn't imagine a reason anyone would want to kill her. She rubbed her forehead. All this gave her a headache. Suddenly, another thought popped into her head. "How did you get the wood down from the steps if you have acrophobia?" She glared at Eric.

The jingling stopped. "It fell when you did. I found it on the ground at the base of the tower."

That makes sense, doesn't it? Leiann wondered who she could trust. The only person who'd told her about the sabotage was Eric. And he'd always been a gentleman with her. Maybe she could trust him. "What do we do now? Should we call the police?"

"That would upset your grandfather. I think it would be better to wait until we know for sure what happened. That way we don't worry him without reason. He had a bout with his heart before you came, and even though the doctor says he's okay, I wouldn't want to cause more trouble."

Concern wrinkled Eric's brow. "How about if I do a little more checking on my own? I've done private investigation before. I'll call the law in after I see what I can dig up myself."

Perhaps he was right. Leiann didn't want to disturb her grandfather until it was necessary. She just hoped that Eric would quickly be able to dig up the information.

℘

Leiann spent part of every day with her grandfather, and the more she got to know him, the better she liked him. She'd seen how quickly he tired, so she didn't want him upset needlessly, but Eric's investigation was taking longer than she'd hoped.

Three days after the accident, Leiann's grandfather sent word that he wanted to have a long talk with her after breakfast. When she finished eating, she walked the familiar hallways to his office.

"Come in, my dear." Her grandfather waited for her in the conversation area of the office. "Close the door behind you."

She did then sat on the couch across from his easy chair. "What do you want to talk about today?"

He clasped his hands loosely in his lap. "I need to tell you the rest of the story about what happened to your mother. I hope that since you've come to know me, you can forgive an old man for the many mistakes he has made in his life."

The time she had anticipated and dreaded was finally here. Leiann felt expectant and apprehensive at the same time. "I'll try."

Herman Johnson began to fidget with his clasped hands. He kept his eyes trained toward the floor instead of looking at her. "I was a very hard man when I was younger. I came from a poor family, but I vowed that I wouldn't stay that way. I fought and clawed my way to success, eventually owning many businesses. I was ruthless in the takeovers, never caring who was hurt in the process."

He leaned forward. "When my wife died, I became even harder. . .and bitter. As my son grew older, I wanted to control him. When Lee told me he was going to marry your mother, I forbade the marriage. I thought Geneva was a nobody, not worthy of my son's attention."

The words felt like bullets to Leiann's heart, but she tried not to show how much they hurt.

"Lee was strong and stubborn, just like me. He married her anyway." His tight smile indicated his pride in her father. "I'm most ashamed of the way I tried to buy off your mother by offering her a lot of money to never see my son again.

But Geneva told me she loved him and rejected my offer—and me. I thought all my money would buy me anything I wanted." He wilted against the back of the chair. "I was furious at her, but I couldn't blame her."

Something inside Leiann wanted to comfort him, but she held back. She needed to hear more.

"Within three months of their elopement, your father was killed in a motorcycle accident. I hadn't wanted Lee to have that bike, and he knew it. Riding it was another form of rebellion from my controlling ways. I'll always blame myself for pushing him away when all I wanted was to hold him in my arms and love him. Too bad I hadn't built the connection with him when he was younger."

Tears filled Leiann's eyes. She blinked to clear them.

"When he died, I didn't know that your mother was carrying you. That probably was a good thing. I would have tried to control her life, too. When she quickly married Milton Hambrick, I thought that proved she hadn't really loved Lee."

When his voice broke, Leiann took a deep breath. This wasn't easy to hear.

"Leiann." Her grandfather's tone grew softer. "Do you know why your mother gave you the name you have?"

She shook her head. "I asked her more than once, but she never told me."

"It's a combination of Lee and her middle name, Ann. That was her tribute to my son." His smile took on a faraway quality. "How I misjudged that fine woman." He took out a pristine linen handkerchief and wiped his eyes. "When I went to her in contrition, she forgave me."

Leiann wanted to get him back to the story. "Where did she meet Milton?"

"He was a fellow student in college. She was working toward a nursing degree, and Milton was a ministerial student."

"But Mother was never a nurse." Leiann felt bewildered, something like Alice when she fell down the rabbit hole.

"No. She dropped out of school after they married. Milton knew she was carrying Lee's child, but he wanted to help raise you. Because of an illness when he was young, Milton could never father a child of his own. They both loved you very much."

Grief welled up inside her. Leiann pulled a tissue from the box on the table beside the couch.

Her grandfather leaned toward her and patted her hand. "I didn't want to make you cry. But I knew I couldn't tell you the whole story without doing that."

She hiccuped a sob. "Please go ahead. I need to know it all."

"When I realized what a selfish man I'd been, I asked Milton to come see me. I asked him why he would marry a woman he knew was pregnant with another man's child and raise that child as his own. He shared Jesus with me."

That sounds like Milton.

"When I became a Christian, my outlook on life changed. All the money meant nothing to me."

Leiann had often heard that many wealthy people weren't happy or fulfilled. Her grandfather exemplified that.

"I wanted to become a part of your life, but Milton asked me to allow him to continue raising you as if he were your natural father. How could I do anything else? He rescued Geneva and you when you both needed it."

Tears blurred Leiann's vision, but she didn't wipe them away.

"I did keep up with what was going on with you. I knew when you broke your arm, when you had your first violin recital. . ."

"I never did learn to play very well." Leiann gave a self-deprecating laugh.

"I know. I heard all about it."

Leiann wondered who told him. Her mother and Milton had always said she played well. She wondered if her grandfather had someone shadowing her. The thought made her feel a little creepy.

"Milton and Geneva corresponded with me over the years. They also sent me pictures of you. I have an album in my bedroom that I look at whenever I have trouble falling asleep."

Leiann had twisted the wet tissue until it disintegrated. She stood and threw it in the wastebasket beside the desk before sitting in the chair beside her grandfather's.

"Milton had his heart attack when he was still a young man. Your mother almost lost the house. Even if she took a job, she knew she couldn't afford to keep it. So I talked her into letting me help. I bought the house and convinced Geneva that the monthly checks I sent would have been your father's anyway, so she should use it for you. That way she could continue to stay home and raise you."

"I assumed Daddy had taken out a really good insurance policy since Mom was able to do that." So much began to make sense now.

"I thought Geneva would tell you the whole story when you grew up, but she never did. I didn't think I had a right to push for it, but I've wanted to get to know you for years. I probably should have signed the house over to her, but I guess enough of my old nature remained for me to want to keep it in case I needed it for leverage to see you." The elderly man's voice shook.

Leiann patted his hand, wondering what would happen next. Although the story she'd just heard answered many questions, it brought to mind several others. But she'd wait until she had a chance to mull all this over before deciding what to ask.

Chapter 7

After her grandfather said he needed to rest, Leiann told Mrs. Shields she would like to have her lunch out on the terrace. While she waited for the meal to arrive, she strolled along the many paths through the arbors and between flower beds. In Texas this time of the year, midday would be scorching. She enjoyed the more temperate climate in Massachusetts.

As she rounded one corner, she came face-to-face with the man she'd been hoping to see for three days. Gerome Mays looked as startled as she felt.

"I've been looking for you, but you haven't been around." She reached up to brush from her eyes the strands of hair a capricious breeze had been playing with. "I wanted to thank you for saving me."

☙

Gerome stared into intriguing eyes that changed color every time he saw them. Today, against the backdrop of lush leaves and flowers, they took on a greenish hue.

"I'm glad I was there to help." He couldn't tear his gaze from hers.

The woman was beautiful. No wonder Eric Smith was always trying to spend time with her.

Gerome wondered how he ever could have thought she could be a part of the swindle. Innocence surrounded her like a cloak.

He cleared his throat, and she glanced at his Adam's apple, then his mouth.

He steeled his senses against the emotional assault that battered him every time he was around her.

"I have to get back to work." He pulled a dead leaf off the climbing rose that almost completely covered the arbor.

Leiann swallowed, and he watched the pulse beating in the hollow of her throat. She felt the same connection he did. He jerked around and strode back through the garden toward his cottage.

☙

As Leiann watched Gerome walk away, she felt bereft. What was there about the man that tugged at her senses? Sure, he was handsome, but so was Eric, and she didn't have to fight an attraction to him.

She didn't need any kind of emotional attachments right now, at least until she sorted out all the ramifications of the story from her grandfather. He'd asked her to stay at least until the middle of summer, and she'd decided to grant his request. She still had a lot of questions buzzing around in her head.

Before she left, Leiann wanted to find out all she could about her natural father. What he liked when he was growing up. What activities he participated in. What he looked like. Surely her grandfather had photos she could look at.

Hearing someone come out onto the terrace, she retraced her steps. Leiann felt ravenous, and she was confident that Mrs. Shields had created some culinary delight to tease her taste buds.

Leiann enjoyed a cup of cool cantaloupe soup and a chicken salad croissant, accompanied by a tall glass of ice-cold, fresh-squeezed lemonade. As she finished the last bite, Charity brought a serving of pound cake topped with fresh strawberries and a sprig of mint.

"Can you join me for dessert?" Leiann looked up hopefully.

"Not today." Charity held the empty tray under one arm. "I need to go to town for Grandma."

Even though she was disappointed to have to eat alone, Leiann savored every juice-soaked morsel of the dessert. She leaned back in the chair and gazed across the gardens toward the mountain where she'd had the accident. That's what it had to have been. An accident. She hadn't seen any proof the step had been cut. Eric probably didn't like Gerome, so he'd planted the seeds of doubt in her mind.

This time, she heard the door open before Eric spoke to her. "I'm glad you're here. I just found out something very interesting." He probably thought dragging out the last two words would make her want to know more.

She watched him over her shoulder as he approached. "And what is that?"

"A reason Gerome Mays might want you out of the way."

Leiann sat up straight. "What are you talking about?"

Eric dropped into the chair across the table from her. "Prudence said he's Herman's stepson. I'm sure he hopes to inherit the fortune, which is purportedly worth millions, maybe billions. He wouldn't want some long-lost granddaughter to get in his way."

Chills gripped her spine. Her life was getting weirder by the minute. Gerome Mays was her grandfather's stepson? Neither one of them had mentioned anything like that to her. Why not? If it were true, that would make the man her. . .

"He's your uncle, sort of, isn't he?" Eric grinned.

Who could she trust? She'd felt safe around Gerome and her grandfather. But apparently they'd both lied to her, or at least hidden a vital truth.

🍃

Sleep that night proved elusive. Leiann paced across the vast room from the closet, past her king-sized bed, to the French doors, then back. Snatches of conversations from the day flitted through her mind. Finally, one of the things Eric said stuck. *Millions or billions*. Could her grandfather really be that wealthy? If so, would that make her a target for Gerome?

Unsettled, she went downstairs, careful not to make a sound. She didn't want to awaken anyone.

She was more comfortable raiding the kitchen now that Mrs. Shields had given her permission. After noticing the pound cake under a crystal dome, she searched through the refrigerators, hoping to find more strawberries. When she did, Leiann cut a piece of the cake and topped it with the fruit. She sat on a stool beside the worktable with the dessert and a glass of milk.

Leiann almost felt as if she were the only person in the house. She wished she'd brought a book downstairs so she could read while she enjoyed her midnight snack.

Leaving the food sitting on the table, Leiann went to the library to get one of the Christian novels. When she opened the door, a lamp across the room cast a soft glow, dispelling part of the darkness. Gerome Mays, dressed in sweats, stood near the shadows, holding an open paperback book.

"What are you doing in here?" If he were a gardener or handyman, he shouldn't be in the main house at this time of night. However, if he really was Herman's stepson...

He closed the book but held his finger between the pages. "I could ask you the same thing. Isn't it a little late for you to be roaming around?"

"I came down for a snack. I forgot to bring a book with me, so I decided to choose one of these."

Gerome stepped away from the shelves. "Be my guest. I've decided to borrow this one. Mr. Johnson gives all the employees access to his library."

Leiann walked past him and pulled *Midnight Zone* from the shelf. She turned back to face him.

He studied her so intently she felt uncomfortable.

"I'll just be on my way." Without looking back, she exited the room.

After closing the door, she leaned against it and took a deep breath. That man was much too virile for her peace of mind. In the muted light, the hard planes of his face stood out in sharp relief from the shadowed hollows in his cheeks. The dusting of dark hair along his strong jawline shouted masculinity, and his brooding eyes made her think of Mr. Rochester in *Jane Eyre*. Finally, she understood why Jane felt so drawn to the man.

She took a deep breath and went to the kitchen. Leiann tried to read the book while she ate her snack, but vivid images kept jumping in front of the words. Gerome Mays, standing in the library. Eric telling her about her grandfather's fortune. She didn't want to believe that anyone would want her out of the way, especially not her rescuer. Wishing she knew the extent of the possible danger, she decided to see if she could find anything that would indicate how much her grandfather was worth.

❦

Gerome hadn't expected to meet anyone in the library after midnight. When Leiann came through the door, dressed in a robe, he almost lost the ability to talk. The woman was ravishing with her tumbled, light brown curls. The intimacy of being in the darkened room with her made his pulse race.

Gerome heard a light thump outside the door and knew she'd slumped against it. Somehow, he instinctively knew when she moved on. He was attuned to her every move. He'd never experienced anything like this with the women he had known over the years.

He quietly opened the door and peeked into the corridor in time to see her heading into the kitchen. She left the door open, and he peered through the crack, watching her eat some of Mrs. Shields's wonderful pound cake. For a moment, Gerome thought about joining her, until he noticed how unsettled she appeared to be. Something was bothering Herman's lovely granddaughter. He hoped it wasn't a guilty conscience. He still wasn't completely certain she wasn't involved in the swindle.

Leiann took her plate and glass to the sink and drank the last of the milk before she rinsed the dishes. Gerome moved out of sight down the hall.

Instead of going up to her room, she went to Herman's office. What was she doing there? She tried to turn the doorknob, but it didn't budge.

She leaned against the door frame and rubbed her eyes. When she stood up straight, one arm hit the door with a thump, and it swung open. A startled look covered her face. Evidently, the locked door hadn't been closed properly. Leiann went in without shutting the door completely behind her.

Gerome crept down the hall until he could press his eye against the slim opening between the door and its facing. He watched her go to the desk and try to open each of the drawers. She found them all locked. She wandered over to the bookshelves and searched every shelf. What was she looking for?

She picked up a box from the corner of the bottom shelf and set it on the desk, turning on the lamp before she opened it. The first book she pulled out looked like a ledger. Why didn't Herman keep that locked up? Probably he thought it was safe with the office door locked.

Taking her time, Leiann studied several pages of the book then turned to the front. He'd seen those kinds of ledgers before when he and his mother lived here. The front pages gave the dates covered by each ledger.

Leiann looked into all the books stored in the box. Gerome wished he knew which years these covered. He knew Herman kept the current ledger locked in his desk. At least, he used to. Although the Old Man kept all his files on a computer, he'd told Gerome he liked to have a hard copy he could hold in his hands, the way he did when he was younger. Surely the ones in the box were from years ago and wouldn't be useful to anyone, especially the young woman who pored over them.

After she returned the box to its space, she headed toward the door. Gerome crept to the end of the hall and watched from around the corner as she went to her room.

What was Leiann trying to find in Herman's office? Was she working with Eric Smith and his sister? Maybe she came here on her own, looking for what she could get from the Old Man.

When he returned to his cottage, Gerome had a hard time going to sleep.

෯

After her foray into her grandfather's office, Leiann felt restless and distressed. Although the ledgers she perused were not current, they painted the picture of a true billionaire. Her grandfather's wealth might have fluctuated since then, but probably not a great deal.

If he wanted to make her his heir, or at least one of them, and if someone else wanted to be the sole heir, she could be in danger. Maybe Eric was right about the steps on the tower being tampered with. Her intuition told her that Gerome was a hero. What if the opposite were true?

A week went by without her being able to make any headway in her thoughts. It was hard to hide her distress from her grandfather. Wanting to get away from all the turmoil, she decided to go to Boston to do some sightseeing on her own. This metropolitan area had as strong a tie to the past as it did to the present. She might as well see all she could while she was here. It could be her only chance.

Her grandfather had started taking his breakfast with her. Over the fluffiest omelet she had ever eaten, she enjoyed visiting with him and talking about Massachusetts. "I'd like to take you up on your offer to let me borrow the car today."

"I'm glad. I want you to enjoy your time here. Maybe you'll want to come visit me often." When he set his coffee cup onto its saucer, the china clattered.

She didn't like the way his hands trembled. Now that she knew him, she wanted him to stay around for a long time. He was the only real family she had left.

"So, where are you going today?"

She leaned toward him. "I'd like to check out several things. Boston Common, *Old Ironsides*, Boston Harbor. I want to walk on the cobblestone streets, and I love poking around in museums."

"I'd enjoy going with you, but that's a lot of walking for an old man."

"Maybe we could go somewhere together on another day. A place that wouldn't be too much for you." Leiann took another bite of the omelet.

"We must go to my house on the Cape while you're here. Maybe we can do that next week." The statement brought a sparkle to his smile.

"The Cape? Where's that?"

His hearty laugh belied his frailty. "That's what the locals call Cape Cod. It's that funny-shaped loop of land that juts out from the southeast corner of the state."

"I'd like that."

❦

When Leiann reached the garage, she found the doors open, revealing several vehicles. She noticed her grandfather's chauffeur polishing the windows of the limousine. "Mr. Greene, I'd like to use the Mercedes today."

He turned toward her. "Mr. Johnson sent word to be sure she was gassed up. I didn't have to do anything, though, because no one has driven her since I filled her up last time."

Leiann hoped it wouldn't be too much different from driving her compact. She hoped she wouldn't have any trouble backing it out. "Is there anything I need to know before I take it out?"

"No, she drives like a dream. I've put some maps in the front seat for you. They'll help you get wherever you want to go." He laid the rag and bottle of glass cleaner on a shelf. "Let me pull her out for you."

After he stopped the car facing the drive, Mr. Greene got out and held the door for her. Leiann slid into the butter-soft leather seat. He closed her door and she pushed the button that slid down the front window. She took a deep breath and exhaled.

"You'll do fine, Miss Hambrick. Have a nice day." He waved her off.

After adjusting the seat and mirrors, Leiann sat in the car and studied the maps for a few minutes. She marked the places she wanted to go today. She'd always been good at directions, so she didn't think she'd have any problem finding them.

Leiann eased the car around the circle drive in front of the house, trying to get a feel for driving it. She stopped and tried all the controls to make sure she knew what they did. When she turned on the radio, the dial was set on an easy-listening station. She decided to leave it there. Her nerves needed to be soothed.

She pulled out of the gate and accelerated on the winding downhill drive. The mountain behind the house wasn't the only steep incline on the property.

After taking several of the curves, Leiann began to feel comfortable with the automobile, so she drove a little faster on a longer section of straight road.

When a sharp hairpin curve appeared up ahead, she applied the brakes.

50

Nothing happened. Adrenaline coursed through her. She pumped the brakes. Again, nothing.

Leiann's breathing accelerated right along with her pulse that pounded through her veins. She frantically pumped several times, her hands fused with the steering wheel. Still the car didn't slow. *God, help me!*

Would He want to? She had been avoiding Him since she'd found out about her grandfather. Could He help her in time?

She jerked the wheel to take the turn, but the vehicle kept going much too fast. The tires screeched.

The road rose a little, slowing the car's momentum slightly. But when she topped the rise, the next section went straight down at an alarming angle. She felt as helpless as she had hanging on the side of the tower.

The car barreled down the mountain, gaining momentum. This time her life did flash before her eyes. She fully expected to join her mother, father, and Milton any minute.

Chapter 8

After going to town to buy fertilizer, Gerome was making his way through the mountainous drive to the house when he noticed a car racing toward a deadly curve. It looked like Herman's Mercedes. Who was the crazy driver? And why was he going so fast? Didn't he know how dangerous this road was?

He went around a curve that hid the oncoming car from his line of sight. Was the driver in danger? Should he pull off on the upcoming bypass in case he could help?

After slowing the pickup, he drove onto the widened shoulder. He stepped out of the truck and listened to the approaching vehicle's engine, still coming at full speed. If that car didn't slow down, it wouldn't make the next curve. He jogged along the edge of the pavement until he could see the hidden section of the drive.

As he topped the rise, he caught a glimpse of Leiann's frightened face through the windshield of the hurtling car. Drained of color with her wide eyes dark against their too-white background, her features contorted in fear. What did she think she was doing?

While he watched, horrified, the car missed the curve. It sailed into the deep ditch on the mountain side of the drive. Small trees and bushes impeded its forward motion enough to slow it down before it hit the trunk of a giant elm. The impact shook the tree, and green leaves showered down.

Gerome sprinted back to his truck and jumped in, gunning it as he backed onto the road. He topped the hill faster than he should have. After pulling his cell phone from his belt, he punched 9-1-1 with one hand.

"There's been an accident." He rattled out all the information he had then flipped the phone closed, despite the operator's asking him to stay on the line.

He came to a screeching halt far enough off the road so he wouldn't be hit if someone else came by. Gerome shuddered to think what would've happened if her car had gone off the other side of the road. By the time the vehicle hit the bottom of the deep gorge, it probably would've burst into flames. Leiann wouldn't have survived that wreck. Hopefully, she did this one.

Making his way down to the car, he slid on topsoil and rocks the Mercedes had loosened on its descent. He fell but quickly picked himself up, dug in his heels, and continued. Two bushes he tried to use as support came out of the ground, roots and all.

When he arrived beside the car, he saw steam rising from the radiator, which had probably cracked on impact. But he didn't smell gasoline, so hopefully the tank was intact.

He tried to open the driver's door, but it was either jammed or locked. The deflated air bag draped across the bottom of the steering wheel. Leiann slumped in the seat belt, not moving. At least he couldn't see any blood.

Gerome scrambled around the car, trying each of the doors. None of them budged. He went back to Leiann.

He knocked on the glass, hoping to rouse her. "Leiann! Can you hear me?"

She moaned and rolled her head then opened her eyes. They looked glazed.

❦

Leiann blinked several times. What was that loud thumping? She glanced out the window straight into Gerome's worried face. She closed her eyes. The sunlight hurt them. Where was she?

The last thing she remembered was leaving the house. . .driving the Mercedes. . .losing control. . .tapping the brakes. . . missing the curve. Frantic, she opened her eyes and looked around.

She looked down and noticed the deflated air bag between her chest and the steering wheel. The seat belt held her tight. She felt closed in, restricted. She unbuckled the belt and reached for the door handle. The door screeched and only opened a few inches.

Gerome knelt beside the opening. "Leiann, are you hurt?"

"I don't know." She ran her hands down both sides, then her legs. "I don't feel any pain."

"Then maybe it'll be okay to move you." He took hold of the edge of the door and gave it a pull, scraping it across the rocky ground, widening the space enough that she might be able to slip through.

Leiann started to swing toward the door, but there wasn't room to get her legs and feet out.

"Look at me, Leiann." Gerome's voice sounded gentler than she'd ever heard it.

She turned her gaze toward him.

He stared at her for a moment. "Your pupils are dilating, so you may be going into shock. Let me get my arms around your back. I'm going to extract you through this space." He lowered his head closer to hers. "You need to trust me. Okay?"

Leiann closed her eyes against the bright sunlight and nodded.

"Lean forward a little."

When she did, his arm slid between her and the seat. He gripped her under the arms and pulled. With one shoulder, Gerome pushed harder on the door, moving it a little. Leiann relaxed, allowing him to maneuver her. As he lifted her into his muscular arms, she heard sirens.

When the paramedics arrived, they checked Leiann thoroughly. They didn't find anything seriously wrong with her, but they said they wanted to take her to the hospital just in case.

"No," she blurted out. "I don't want to go there. Just take me home."

Gerome leaned close. "I think you should let them take you."

She stared into his chocolate brown eyes. "I had enough of hospitals before my mother died."

He agreed. After pulling her against his side, he walked her to his pickup. All the way, he kept asking her if she was all right. She got tired of telling him that she was okay.

When she arrived in her room, she took a warm shower, trying to forget the frightening feelings that still gripped her. She'd always thought a Mercedes was a safe automobile. How could the brakes fail? Didn't Grandfather say that Mr. Greene checked the cars often? Then again, the driver had said the Mercedes hadn't been driven in a while.

Leiann stepped out into the steamy bathroom and wrapped a fluffy bath towel around her. Though she still felt a little shaky, she was glad she hadn't gone to the hospital. She sat on the stool and leaned her elbows on the dressing table. One more thing going wrong in her topsy-turvy world.

She remembered crying out to God when she thought she was going to die. She wondered why she'd done that. She was pretty sure He didn't care what happened to her. If He did, why had He let all these things occur?

☙

Gerome knew Greene kept all the vehicles in tip-top shape. When Leiann told him the brakes hadn't worked, he decided to have the car checked. The brakes shouldn't have failed. Unless they'd been sabotaged.

Gerome knocked on the door to Herman's office.

"Come in, Prudence," the Old Man's voice called faintly.

After opening the door a little, Gerome stuck his head around the edge. "It's me. I'd like to talk to you."

Herman rose behind his desk and leaned both hands on the top. "Come in, my boy. How can I help you?"

"Leiann had a wreck on her way to town."

The Old Man frowned. "Was she hurt?"

"I don't think so. The paramedics checked her over and said she'd only have a few bruises."

"Good." Herman's eyes glistened. "That girl is important to me."

"But your car's another story." Gerome slid into one of the chairs in front of the desk. "It's been banged up pretty badly. If it's okay with you, I'd like to check it out personally."

"Whatever you think is best." Herman slumped into his chair. "Gerome, I wish you'd move into your old room here in the house."

"I don't think that's a good idea." Gerome stood, glad he'd been able to downplay the wreck enough so Herman wasn't really worried. "Not yet anyway." He still didn't need anyone else to know the connection between him and his stepfather.

Just before he got out the door, Herman called him back. "Why don't we all go to the house on the Cape for a while? I'll need to take Prudence along—we're working on a special merger right now. But we won't work all the time. Salty has been telling me he needs some help with repairs around the place. Maybe you and Eric can assist with those. Charity could come along to help take care of Leiann. What do you think?"

Gerome took a moment to mull over the idea. "I'm sure your granddaughter would enjoy the change of scenery. When do you want to go?"

"Day after tomorrow." Herman stared into his eyes. "That'll give you a day to get everything ready."

"Sounds good to me. I'll have time to check out the Mercedes, too." Gerome opened the door and started to step into the hallway.

"Could you please send Prudence in? I need her to do some letters for me."

"Sure." Gerome left Herman's door open and knocked on the one next door. When Prudence answered, he stuck his head in to tell her what Herman had said then headed out of the house.

Gerome had to get the Ozbourne Global team started on the Mercedes before the group left for the Cape. He hurried toward his cottage so he could talk to Greg about it.

❦

Two days later, a caravan of cars eased away from the mansion. Leiann rode in the limousine with her grandfather, Prudence, and Charity. Eric drove the Jeep, and Gerome trailed in his old pickup.

Leiann was encouraged because her grandfather seemed in high spirits. His color was better, and he even helped load the last few things into the back of the pickup. As soon as they were under way, he started a lively conversation that captured her interest. She had dreaded going by the place where she had the wreck, but they were past it before she noticed.

After they maneuvered the mountainous drive to Highway 117, Mr. Greene turned the limo the opposite direction from Boston.

Leiann glanced toward her grandfather. "Don't we have to go through Boston to get to Cape Cod?"

He shook his head. "There are several ways we could go, but I like to miss all the traffic of the metropolitan area. We'll be on I-495. It's farther, but it takes less time."

"I guess I'll get to see more of Massachusetts this way." She leaned back and turned her attention out the windows.

When they crossed the bridge over the canal at Cape Cod, Leiann didn't see any difference between that area and much of the rest of the scenery they'd come through. "I thought I'd be able to see the beach."

"There's a lot of waterfront, but the Cape consists of much more than that." Prudence sounded like a teacher correcting a student.

"When you look at it on the map, it looks small."

"I guess it would to someone from Texas." Prudence pursed her lips into a tight, disapproving pucker.

They traveled through several small towns before going through the gated entrance into a community of elegant homes nestled among trees. They stopped in a driveway wide enough to hold several vehicles. This house couldn't compare to the mansion on the estate, but it was still much more than Leiann was used to. Of course, considering what she'd found out about her grandfather's finances, maintaining two grand homes wouldn't be a problem.

When the vehicles stopped in a car park behind the house, a man and woman came out the back door. "Who are they?" Leiann asked.

"Salty and Sharon Styles are my full-time caretakers at this house." Her grandfather got out of the car and reached back for her hand. "Come on, I'll introduce you."

Herman seemed like a new man today—stronger somehow. Maybe the change was good for him.

After introductions, Sharon said she had a cold lunch ready.

"We'll eat after we unload the vehicles." Herman started back toward the limo, but Gerome insisted he accompany the women into the house.

Grandfather took Leiann to a room on the second floor, where she had a view of the ocean from her windows. Charity had the room next to her. Prudence had voiced her disapproval, saying the girl should be in the servants' quarters over the garage. Herman overruled her objection. The rooms connected with a large bathroom between. Leiann welcomed sharing the space with Charity.

She and her maid went down to the kitchen together.

After the meal, Eric came up behind Leiann. "Would you like to go with me in the dune buggy? We could have a lot of fun, and you'll see more of the Cape. Salty said it's all gassed up and ready to go."

At first, Leiann refused. Memories of the wreck still haunted her. But Herman encouraged her to go, insisting that she would enjoy the beach. Evidently, Gerome didn't agree, because he watched her with a frown creasing his forehead.

Leiann waited in the driveway while Eric went to the garage. He returned driving a bright yellow vehicle that looked like a cross between a VW Beetle and a Jeep, with two bucket seats, monster tires, and a roll bar. When Leiann saw the heavy-duty seat belts, she felt safer.

They drove over dunes covered with tall, scraggly grass as well as bare, sandy hills, careful to skirt around boggy areas. Eric proved to be a good companion, keeping a constant flow of pleasant conversation going, and Leiann enjoyed the ride. She hadn't been anywhere like this in Texas.

Finally, he turned back toward the house. "It's probably time to head home. We've been out here several hours."

"You're kidding." Leiann glanced at her watch, and he was right. "Do you come from here? You know your way around so well."

Eric laughed. "No, but Pru and I have been down here a few times."

After he stopped the buggy in the driveway, she turned toward him. "I had a really good time today."

He smiled. "I did, too. Maybe we can do some more things together while we're at the Cape."

That sounded good to Leiann.

☙

Every time Gerome saw Leiann over the next two days, she had plans with Eric. Prudence had actually started smiling at them. Something fishy was going on. Though he hadn't received the full report he expected from Greg, Eric and his sister were still his prime suspects for the scheme to defraud Herman. Without solid proof, he couldn't do anything about what was happening here at the Cape.

Gerome didn't see Prudence Smith much. Evidently, she had a lot of work that kept her busy.

When he wasn't helping Salty with the house or grounds, he spent time with Herman. They reconnected the way they had years ago when he had been a rebellious teen and his mother married Herman. They even took a walk on the beach one afternoon. As they strolled through the sand, Herman talked about the mistakes he'd made with his son and why he was just now getting to know his granddaughter. Gerome admired the strength of character his stepfather exhibited.

Without the influence of this godly man, no telling where Gerome would be today. Probably in prison, where his biological father went shortly after he divorced Mother. Gerome had forgiven him before he died behind bars, but not until Herman helped him understand about people making mistakes and having to pay for them.

The best thing Gerome's mother ever did for him was marry Herman Johnson. Too bad she didn't live long enough to know how much good it had done for her son. Ovarian cancer took her quickly. His stepfather kept him from blaming God for that, too.

While Leiann and Eric traipsed all over the Cape and Prudence holed up in the office working, Gerome and Herman spent a lot of time studying the Bible together. This seemed to lift the Old Man's spirits. Gerome welcomed the change in him. Too bad his granddaughter wasn't around to see it.

🍃

Eric asked Leiann to ride with him in the Jeep for the trip back to the mansion. She'd had so much fun with him the past two days that she agreed without hesitation. Her grandfather told her that if she changed her mind and wanted to spend part of the trip in the limo, she could call him on the cell phone.

She tied her hair back with a scarf, hoping to keep it from blowing in her face, but it didn't help. With the force of the wind created at the speeds they traveled, conversation was almost impossible.

Partway home, the limo pulled off the interstate for a rest stop. After Leiann took her turn in the bathroom, she returned to the Jeep.

While she waited for everyone else to get back to the vehicles, Eric took her hand. "Leiann, we've had a lot of fun this week, and I've come to care a great deal for you."

Although Eric's declaration surprised her, she realized that the idea pleased her. She gave him her sweetest smile. "I like you a lot, too."

"I was hoping you'd say that." He leaned closer. "This will probably sound awfully sudden, but, well, what can I say? I'm a spontaneous kind of guy." He dropped a quick kiss on her cheek. "Leiann, I'd like very much to marry you."

Her eyes widened. Had he really said that? She'd begun to think of him as a good friend, but the idea of a romance with him hadn't occurred to her. And quite frankly, it didn't particularly interest her.

She tugged her hand back into her lap. "We've only known each other for a few days."

He cupped her cheek with one hand, but she pulled back.

"Too much is going on in my life for me to consider anything romantic right now."

"Would you at least think about it?" The earnest expression in his eyes pleaded with her.

Leiann turned her gaze from his, noticing that the others were returning to their vehicles. She opened the door of the Jeep. "I think I'll join Grandfather in the limo." She didn't look back to see how he took her rejection.

🍃

The next evening, Gerome stepped out of his cottage to go for a walk. Charity approached with a message from Herman. When she left, he opened the envelope.

After quickly reading the note, he hurried toward the house. Herman hadn't asked him to come to his private suite since he'd returned to Massachusetts. Gerome went to the Old Man as quickly as he could.

He'd just received notification from the guys at Ozbourne Global Security's garage that someone had tampered with the brakes on the Mercedes. He'd asked Greg to get a complete report as soon as possible. Surely no one would try to hurt the Old Man physically, but Gerome couldn't be sure.

After a quick knock, he opened the door to the bedroom suite. Herman sat in one of the easy chairs beside the couch. Gerome took the other chair. "What can I do for you?"

Herman smiled. "You're a good boy, Jerry. Oh, I know, you don't like to be called that, but you'll always be Jerry to me."

"I don't mind it so much coming from you." He grinned.

"Jerry, I want you to drive me to church tomorrow. Forrest's daughter is having a baby in Boston, so I told him to take his wife and go be with her. I knew he wanted to."

"You're such an old softie."

"Don't tell anyone. Can't have information like that getting around, ruining my reputation." He chuckled. "So, how about it?"

"Of course I'll drive you. I've been having a worship time in my cottage on Sundays, but it'll be good to fellowship with other believers again. What time do we need to leave?"

Herman thought for a moment. "If we start by ten, we'll get there in plenty of time for the eleven o'clock service."

"Ten it is." Gerome stood and started toward the door then turned back. "Will Leiann be going with us?"

A frown covered the Old Man's face. "She hasn't gone to church since she's been here. I always give her the option of accompanying me. She's turned me down every time. I haven't wanted to push with everything that's happened to her. But I've been praying for her. I'll invite her again this week. Maybe this time she'll say yes."

"We can hope so," Gerome agreed before he left Herman.

While Gerome walked to his cottage, he pondered this new information. The reports he'd received from Greg said that Leiann's stepfather had been a preacher and she'd been active in her church in Texas. He'd always tried to go to church wherever he was. He wondered why she didn't.

Another thing kept bothering him. Why were she and Eric so chummy?

Chapter 9

Just before Gerome arrived at his cottage, his cell phone vibrated. He pulled it from his pocket. "Mays here."

"You were right." Greg sounded serious.

"About what?" Gerome stepped inside and closed the door behind him.

"The car." He heard Greg shuffling papers then clicking a few computer keys. "Sorry we couldn't check it right away. Most of the team was called away for an emergency."

"So get to the point." Gerome hurried across the carpeted floor and dropped into the chair beside the desk. He knew he sounded impatient, but he didn't care. Enough of this chitchat.

"Whoever did this was clever. The way the line was rigged, it wouldn't leak until quite a bit of pressure was placed on the brakes, more than what would happen in regular driving. That kept any brake fluid from leaking onto the garage floor."

Gerome rubbed the back of his neck. The long, hilly drive from the house to the highway would require a driver to use the brakes a lot. "Is there any way to tell who did it? Were there any prints?"

"Not a one."

"Thanks." Gerome flipped his phone shut and laid it on the table.

He shucked off his clothes and stepped into his favorite ratty jeans, then stretched a snug red T-shirt over his torso. He could hardly wait to get to his favorite place to spend time with God under the stars.

He struck out toward a copse of trees several yards behind his cottage. Soon after he arrived at the estate, he'd used his free time to throw together a bench between two large elms.

He sat on one end of the seat and leaned back against the tree trunk. After meditating on the Bible verses he'd read that morning, his mind roamed over the events of the last few days.

"Lord, I need Your discernment in this situation. Help me protect Herman from whoever is working against him. Thank You for the renewed relationship we have."

As his words died away, his thoughts wandered toward the woman who took up far too much of his thoughts. He shouldn't be interested in her, especially if she was estranged from God. Then again, perhaps it was his Christian duty to help her find her way back to the fold. Of course, he didn't know what kept her from attending church. Maybe whatever it was wouldn't be a problem tomorrow. He hoped she'd be accompanying them to the service.

The more he thought about it, the more sure Gerome felt that Prudence Smith and her brother, Eric, were behind the intel he'd received about his stepfather's finances. Would they do him actual harm? Were the tampered brakes meant for him? But he didn't drive anymore.

He suspected the steps on the tower had also been tampered with. But that couldn't have been meant to damage Herman. He'd never climb the tower.

Were both of those things meant for Leiann? His heart thumped at the idea.

He wished he'd thought to retrieve the wood before someone else did.

What was he supposed to do now?

"Watch over Leiann."

"Is that You, Lord?" Or had his own interest in her brought that thought to mind?

"Watch over Leiann."

When the words came again, Gerome was sure they were from the God he trusted above all else. "But what if she's involved with whoever is defrauding Herman?"

"Watch over Leiann."

"Okay, Lord."

Sometimes she seemed so vulnerable. Then she'd do something that made her look like a gold digger or somehow in cahoots with Eric and his sister. Why did she spend so much time with the man? Every time she'd left the house on Cape Cod with Eric, something inside Gerome felt unsettled. He'd been glad she hadn't ridden all the way home with Eric. For Herman's sake, he hoped Leiann was innocent.

Gerome slid off the bench then turned around and knelt with his head in his hands on the seat. "Lord, draw her close to You and to fellowship with other Christians. Let her know You're looking out for her and that You have people around her to help her."

Before he finished praying, a realization crept into Gerome's heart. He cared more for her than he wanted to. He didn't have time develop a relationship with any woman. "God, please change my heart, too, so I won't feel so torn about her."

He had to keep his sharp edge to stay on top of things. He didn't want to miss something that would keep him from protecting Herman—or Leiann.

When Leiann awoke on Sunday, she dressed and went down to the kitchen to make herself some breakfast. All the hired help had Sundays off, so soon after she arrived, Leiann started rising early and eating something before sitting on the balcony outside her room and reading.

When she opened the kitchen door, she heard, "Good morning, Leiann." Her grandfather's greeting startled her.

Her hand flew to her chest. "I'm surprised to see you here."

A smile lit his face. "I can tell."

She took a deep breath and went to the refrigerator to get out eggs for an omelet. "You don't usually come to the kitchen on Sunday mornings."

"But you do." He folded the newspaper he'd been reading and placed it on the table. "I wanted to see you before I left." He stood from his stool. "Would you like to go to church with Gerome and me?"

"Gerome's going?" Leiann reached for a crockery bowl in the cabinet beside the fridge. "I didn't know he went to church with you."

"I asked him to drive me today because I gave Forrest some time off." He came to stand beside her. "I'd really like your company."

Leiann smiled, hoping to take the sting of rejection out of her words. "I'd rather stay at the house if you don't mind."

Disappointment clouded her grandfather's expression. "Of course not. I want you to be happy here." He turned and left the kitchen.

She slumped against the cabinet, disappointed that the only thing Grandfather wanted to talk about today was going to church. She didn't want to go, feeling the way she did about God—knowing He'd let her whole life be a lie. Leiann still believed in God, but she wasn't sure she could trust Him with her life anymore. If she went to church, it would be hypocritical.

Ever since Eric told her Gerome was her grandfather's stepson, she'd been waiting for one of them to reveal the truth to her. She didn't want to ask them about it, because if it wasn't true, she'd feel foolish. Besides, she didn't want to explain why it was important to her. Unfortunately, because neither one had said anything, she wasn't sure she could completely trust either of them.

Gerome drove the limo around to the front of the mansion. He got out and started toward the door, but Herman emerged before he reached it. "I don't see Leiann. Did you ask her to come?"

The older man nodded. "She declined my invitation." He stopped beside the car door. "I'm going to sit up front with you so we can talk."

"If the Mercedes hadn't been wrecked, we could take it." While Gerome walked around the vehicle, he wondered if he should share his concerns about the embezzlement with Herman. He didn't want to upset his stepfather without concrete proof, so he decided now wasn't the time.

When they arrived at church, Herman was surrounded by friends before he was halfway to the door. Gerome leaned against the car and watched, glad to see the Old Man so happy. After that group went inside, he followed them. Instead of sitting by Herman, Gerome dropped onto one of the back pews. He didn't want to intrude on the group of friends.

He enjoyed the worship, which contained a mix of contemporary music and traditional hymns. So often when he was on an assignment, he didn't have the chance to attend church. He'd enjoy attending here as long as he could.

On the way home after the service, Herman turned toward Gerome with a worried expression. "I'm concerned about my granddaughter. The sheriff's report said the brakes failed. But Forrest checks everything at least once a week. He took the car in to the dealership for a routine brake inspection a couple of months ago. Everything was working fine."

How much information could Gerome tell him without worrying him? "That concerned me, too, so I had a mechanic friend tow the car to his garage. He found a hole in the brake line."

Herman glared at him. "If the brake line was leaking, fluid would have dripped onto the floor of the garage."

"Someone cut the line in such a way that the fluid didn't leak until Leiann was going down the drive. When was the last time someone used that car?"

"I had Forrest drive me in it when we went to town a couple of weeks ago. But the brakes were fine." Herman wrinkled his forehead and gazed out the windshield.

Gerome huffed out a breath. "Who knew Leiann was going to use the Mercedes?"

Herman turned his attention toward Gerome. "Most of the people at the house. I gave her a set of keys at dinner one evening. Prudence and Eric were there. One of the maids. And of course, Forrest knew because I asked him to get the keys made for her."

That didn't narrow the field much. Gerome kept his eyes on the road as they went up the winding drive.

His stepfather remained silent a few minutes. "Jerry, I want to ask you a big favor."

"Sure. What is it?"

"I'm just getting acquainted with Leiann, and she's all I have left of Lee. I made so many mistakes with that boy. I wish I could go back and change things. Then I'd have known her while she was growing up. I don't want to lose the chance to get to know her now." Herman's voice took on a husky tone.

"Watch over Leiann for me."

His words echoed the ones God had spoken into Gerome's heart, confirming them.

🍂

By the time her grandfather and Gerome arrived home from church, Leiann had lunch ready for them. When she heard the men coming down the hallway, she began putting the hot dishes on the kitchen table.

Gerome opened the door and held it for her grandfather. "What's this I smell?" A grin split his face.

Leiann held up the platter of fried chicken. "I fixed dinner. A real Southern meal."

Grandfather smiled, too. "Smells good, and I'm really hungry."

She wiped her hands on Mrs. Shields's apron, which she'd worn to protect her clothes. "I set the table in the breakfast area. It's more informal than the dining room." She untied the strings and pulled off the apron.

The meal proved to be a big success. Both men took heaping helpings of the mashed potatoes and creamy gravy, as well as the buttered English peas and pearl onions. Pleasant conversation flowed smoothly throughout the meal. It did Leiann's heart good to see her grandfather really eat. Since she'd been here, he'd picked at his food, taking only a few bites at each meal she'd shared with him.

He pushed back from the table and patted his stomach. "I haven't enjoyed eating this much in a long time. But now I want a nap."

After his stepfather left, Gerome pitched in and helped wash the dishes. He looked funny with soapsuds up to his elbows.

"I don't understand why we didn't put the dishes in the dishwasher." He swiped down his arms, trying to dislodge some of the foam.

Leiann glanced at the machine that was so big it looked like it belonged in a restaurant. It didn't even fit under the cabinet. "I've never used a dishwasher like that one. It's easier to wash and dry them myself. But you insisted on helping me, remember? And I know which cabinet I took each dish from."

When his laughter pealed across the kitchen, something in her heart turned over. This man was too attractive for his own good. Or hers.

🍂

Herman asked Gerome to come to his office first thing Monday morning. When he stuck his head through the open doorway, he saw Leiann sitting in the chair next to her grandfather's desk.

His stepfather glanced up and beckoned him. "Come in, Jerry."

Leiann mouthed the last word with a questioning look on her face.

"Sometimes Herman calls me Jerry." He liked the twinkle of laughter that lit her eyes. "But no one else does."

She turned toward her grandfather. "If you need to talk to Gerome, I can come back later."

Herman clasped his hands together on the top of the desk. "Actually, I wanted to see both of you."

Gerome took the chair beside Leiann's. He caught a whiff of the light floral fragrance he'd smelled in her hair when he carried her down from the tower.

"I've been in touch with my insurance agent, and he tells me there isn't much hope for the Mercedes."

Leiann crossed one leg over the other knee and swung her foot in tight circles. "I'm really sorry about the car."

The Old Man leaned toward his granddaughter. "It wasn't your fault. Don't worry about it. I'm just glad you weren't hurt."

"Will you be replacing the Mercedes then?" Gerome concentrated on the man across the desk from them.

"I want to. But I don't feel up to shopping for a car right now. I was hoping the two of you could do it for me."

Leiann's foot dropped to the floor. "Go shopping for a car? Just like that?" She rubbed her thumb and fingers together, but they didn't snap.

"What's wrong, my dear? Don't you want to help me?" Concern laced Herman's words.

"You caught me by surprise, that's all." She started tapping one foot on the floor.

Why did that bother her? Gerome thought she'd jump at the chance to do this for her grandfather.

Herman rose from his chair and leaned his hands on the desk. "You don't have to do anything you don't want to, Leiann. Gerome can do it for me. I just thought you should help him pick it out since you'll be driving it while you're here."

Her foot stilled, and she tucked an errant strand of hair behind one ear. "What kind of car did you want us to buy?"

"If you don't like a Mercedes, you can get something else." The older man sank back into his chair. "What would you like?" He tented his fingers and studied her.

She glanced at Gerome. Her look told him she wanted him to take over the conversation, but he wanted to hear how it would play out.

"The only car I've ever purchased was a used car from a good friend. I've never been inside a new-car dealership." She rubbed a spot on her forehead between her eyes.

"Then it's time we remedied that." Herman laughed. "Don't you think so, Jerry?"

It could prove interesting. Gerome nodded and smiled at Leiann.

❦

Less than an hour later, Leiann rode beside Gerome in his pickup truck as they headed down the long drive toward the highway. "Are we going all the way into Boston?"

"I thought we'd try the suburbs first. Might get a better deal out there."

Leiann kept her eyes trained on the road as they drove down the mountainous drive, dreading the moment when they would pass the place where she'd missed the curve.

"Are you all right?" Gerome's concern felt like a tangible thing, reaching out to her.

"Yeah, I'm fine."

"Then why are your knuckles white?" His voice held a hint of humor.

She flexed her hands and rubbed them to get the circulation back.

He covered her hands with one of his. His strong fingers wrapped around all of hers, giving her a feeling of security yet unsettling her at the same time. "You're safe with me, Leiann."

How she wanted to believe that. But if what Eric said was true and this man was her grandfather's stepson, Gerome was keeping a gigantic secret from her. A secret that could affect her life. She couldn't let her emotions lead her down the wrong path with this handsome man.

❦

When Gerome stopped in front of the luxury-car dealership, he almost laughed out loud at the expression on the face of one of the salesmen when he saw the beat-up pickup. Without a word to either of them, the man walked right back into his tiny but luxurious office. Wouldn't he be surprised when they paid cash for a new car?

A different salesman came out and let Leiann sit in each model in the showroom, fiddling with all the gadgets while he stood by and watched her every move.

When she got out of the last one, Gerome pulled her aside and leaned close to her ear. "So, which model should we buy?"

Her hazel eyes gleamed with a golden light. "Are we really going to get one today?"

She rested her hand on his forearm. The feathery weight of it burned through his skin, making him aware of her in an even deeper way. *Lord, I asked You to guard my heart.* He exhaled a deep breath.

"Yes, Herman expects us to come home with a new car." He didn't move a muscle, hoping she'd not step away from him.

She leaned closer but glanced toward a model on the other side of the showroom. "I like that one the best, but I don't care for the color."

When she stood back from him, Gerome turned to the salesman and gestured toward the vehicle. "Do you have that model in any other colors?"

"Yes, sir. Please follow me." The man led them out a side door to an area covered with varying heights of canopies. "These are the colors we have now. Do you see anything you like?"

Leiann made her way through the vehicles until she reached one in a red metallic paint. "I like this." Then she pointed to another car in blue metallic. "But that one's pretty, too."

How like a woman not to be able to make up her mind. But Gerome was glad she'd chosen vibrant colors instead of silver or black. They fit her personality more.

He turned toward the salesman, who was watching a more prosperous-looking couple approach another sales associate. The man probably thought he was wasting his time, but he didn't desert them.

"We'd like to take one of these out for a test drive."

Though the man sighed, he went inside to retrieve the keys.

Leiann gazed up at Gerome. "Which one do you like best?"

He crossed his arms over his chest. "Oh, no, you don't. Herman said for you to choose the car, so I'm not going to try to influence you." He studied first one car then the other. "They're both good-looking vehicles."

The salesman returned and gave Gerome the keys. He handed them to Leiann. "I'll ride shotgun." The salesman sat behind her.

After driving around for about half an hour, Leiann stopped the car. "I want you to drive it, too." They changed places.

The sedan performed like a dream—as smooth as his Corvette. He drove only a few minutes before returning to the dealership. When they got out of the vehicle, the salesman held out his hand for the keys.

Gerome clutched the key chain. "We'll take this one." He turned to Leiann. "Unless you want the blue one."

"I think I like the red one better."

"Okay." Gerome had to bite his lip to keep from laughing at the incredulous look on the man's face.

"If you and your wife will follow me." He swiveled and marched into the showroom.

"Oh, we're not. . ." Leiann's voice trailed off because the man was too far away to hear. She frowned at Gerome. "Aren't you going to tell him the truth?"

"It doesn't matter." Gerome followed her into the glass-walled cubicle. He urged Leiann toward a comfortable chair before extracting his billfold.

After looking at the bank card and Gerome's ID, the salesman called the bank. When the president assured him that Gerome was indeed on the account, the man wrote up the sale. Since it took him three times before he got the papers filled out right, this was probably his first cash transaction. After thanking them profusely and shaking their hands, he watched them walk to the car.

They headed back toward the estate, with Leiann driving the new car and Gerome following her in his pickup. She drove the speed limit until she pulled onto the long drive. She crept along it, especially the curve she'd missed before.

When Leiann entered her grandfather's office the next morning, she found Gerome there with him.

Her grandfather stood. "Jerry, why don't you take Leiann to town today to see some of the sights she's been wanting to visit? You can take the new Mercedes."

Gerome turned toward her. "What do you think?"

"I'd enjoy that."

While Gerome drove around Boston, Leiann watched the scenery rush past the windows, forming a kaleidoscope of spring colors. All during the journey he kept her amused with tour-guide chatter.

"Have you ever worked for a tour company?"

"No." He looked at her for a moment before returning his attention to the heavy traffic. "I've just shown the sights to several friends and family members."

"Do you have a large family?" Leiann wanted to know more about this man who had been her hero.

"I have cousins who live on a cranberry farm not far from Plymouth. Maybe we'll go there sometime. They're on my father's side of the family, and I haven't had any contact with them since my parents divorced." A wry grin twisted his mouth. "I haven't thought much about them in a long time."

Leiann mulled over that information. If she had extended family, she'd have had plenty of contact with them.

Gerome interrupted her thoughts. "Very soon, you'll catch sight of Plymouth Bay." He pointed ahead toward the left.

The historical commentary continued. Leiann found herself immersed in the surroundings and the information. She hadn't realized Gerome was as interested in history as she was.

When they reached the parking lot near Plymouth Rock, Leiann felt a little disappointed. She'd wanted to stand on the rock and look out to sea, trying to feel what the Pilgrims must have experienced when they first landed. But the huge stone was canopied by a columned granite portico and surrounded by a security fence to keep people from touching it. She realized the rock needed to be protected or it wouldn't have lasted this long. Tourists probably would try to take souvenir chips home so they could own a piece of history.

Her image of a straggly group of weary travelers landing in an unknown land was lost in the grandeur of the portico and the white columned mansion that sat high on a green hill behind the monument. At some time in the past, someone had engraved "1620" into the top of the rock. She pulled out her digital camera and took several shots from different angles.

"It's too bad the simplicity of the rock is overshadowed by all the trappings." Gerome's words echoed her thoughts.

Leiann studied his face. Intelligence shone from his eyes as he stared out over the moving water.

He turned toward her with a spark in his eyes. He reached for the camera. "Let me take a couple of pictures with you in them."

He posed her against the portico, then with the mansion in the background. She took back the camera and clicked a shot of him leaning against a column.

One of the other tourists approached Gerome. "Would you like me to take a picture of you and your wife together?"

"Sure." Gerome reached for the camera and handed it to him. Then he put his arm around Leiann.

She held herself stiff, waiting for him to correct the man. Just as he did at the dealership, Gerome didn't say a word. Why couldn't he just be honest?

Not wanting to cause a scene in front of the other tourists, she held her tongue as she walked closer to the rocks that lined the short beach and stared out over the water.

"You seem intent." Gerome stood so close behind her that his breath fluttered her hair, sending a skitter up her spine. Though she was upset that he hadn't corrected the man, she wasn't immune to his charm.

She turned and looked up at him, taking a step back so she could breathe easier. "I guess I expected to be able to see everything the way the Pilgrims did." She shrugged. "Silly, wasn't it?"

"Not at all." Gerome shoved his hands into the front pockets of his Dockers. "If you want to get closer to the experience of the settlers, we can go to Plimoth Plantation."

When she agreed, he took her hand and led her away from the portico toward the entrance to the restored settlement. The calluses on his palm spread warmth up her arm.

Walking through the reconstructed village and watching reenactments of the everyday life of the first settlers proved interesting. Leiann felt a connection to the early history of her country. She marveled at the ingenious ways the Pilgrims were able to make their own place in a strange land—not unlike how she felt being in Massachusetts, which was so different from Texas.

Leiann enjoyed watching Gerome talk to the costumed role-players. He asked intelligent questions that helped her understand how hard life had been for the Pilgrims. They watched artisans create authentic-looking period furniture and clothing. At the Nye Barn, Gerome talked at length to the personnel about the rare historical breeds of cattle cultivated there.

"I didn't know you were interested in livestock." Leiann glanced up at him as they walked toward the Wampanoag Homesite to find out more about the history and culture of the original Americans.

"At one time, I planned to buy a farm when I was ready to settle down." He smiled at her. "Sounds funny, right?"

She shook her head. "We all have our dreams."

"And what are your dreams, Leiann?" He stopped walking and studied her intently.

"I'm not sure right now." She started down the path, and he fell into step with her. She couldn't even think about her dreams when so much of her life was still unsettled.

As they left Plimoth Plantation, Gerome held her elbow so they could stay together in the busload of tourists massed around the entrance. The parking lot was a lot more crowded than it had been when they arrived. Leiann liked the feel of his touch.

"Are you hungry?" Gerome asked as he started the car.

"It has been awhile since breakfast."

His rich laughter filled the car. "Especially since you ate at the crack of dawn."

Leiann laughed with him. "I enjoy getting up to watch the sunrise."

He took her to a little café near a wharf up the coast. She felt sure this place wasn't in any tourist brochure. Weathered boards covered the outside, and well-used fishnets hung at odd angles over them. FRESH SEAFOOD was hand painted in bright red near the roofline.

"This doesn't look like much, but the food is awesome." Gerome took her elbow as they wound their way between tables that were crowded too close together.

Most of the seats were taken, but he found two at the end of one table.

"We're not going to sit with strangers, are we?" Leiann held back.

"If we want to eat here, we'll have to." He pulled out one of the chairs for her. "It's this busy all the time."

After they were seated, Leiann looked around. The mixture of customers appeared to be a cross-section of the citizens of the area. A few men in suits were scattered among those dressed casually. The noise level, though not deafening, was a few decibels higher than normal conversation, and the clipped speech sounded far different from the Texas drawl.

When the waitress finally reached them, she asked, "What'll ya have?"

70

"What's the special today?" Gerome didn't even pick up the typewritten menu the woman placed in front of him.

She poised a pen over the pad in her hand. "Shrimp Boil. It's real fresh. Wouldja like that?" She spoke so fast Leiann had a hard time understanding her.

Gerome glanced at Leiann, who was still trying to figure out the rapid-fire words. When she finally nodded, he ordered for both of them.

The waitress punctuated her confirmation of the order with a loud pop of her gum.

The meal was just as delicious as he'd promised. While they ate, they discussed all they'd seen that morning. Leiann enjoyed his company more than ever. He was even more fun to be around than Eric. But he hadn't said anything about his connection with Grandfather. And it still bothered her that he'd let the salesman and the tourist think they were married. Was that a further sign of his deceptive nature?

For the next two days, Leiann's grandfather sent her on several errands, always accompanied by Gerome. The more time she spent with the man, the more she felt drawn to him. If only she could trust him completely.

The third day, they went to a place that had flowering plants so she could choose some to add to the gardens. She enjoyed picturing the colorful blossoms in various flower beds.

On the drive back to the estate, Gerome brought up another subject. "Since you've been here, you've spent a lot of time with Prudence's brother."

Leiann stared at him. "What's wrong with that?"

He kept his eyes on the winding road. "I'm not saying anything is wrong with that. I just wanted to caution you to be careful."

"About what?" She crossed her arms.

"Nothing in particular." He turned into the circle drive in front of the house. "Just be careful."

If she didn't know better, she'd think Gerome was jealous of her time with Eric, but there was no reason to be. She was just friends with both men.

If Gerome really was Herman's stepson, Leiann wondered why her grandfather hadn't told her there was a connection between them.

She was tired of waiting for him to offer the information. Tomorrow she would ask her grandfather and get it all out in the open.

Chapter 10

Once again, Gerome sat under the elm trees in the dark of night. The day had been wonderful—and terrible. Leiann was fun, open, vulnerable. And far too beautiful.

Was she using her looks to get what she wanted? Did Eric truly find her attractive—or was he using her?

Gerome had to find out for sure what Smith and his sister were up to. All the information he'd received from Greg pointed only to them, but he needed irrefutable proof. Maybe it was time to break into the office files and do a search.

But not tonight. He was too keyed up after the day he'd spent with Leiann. Actually, he'd spent four wonderful days with her, compliments of his stepfather. The Old Man must trust him to keep throwing them together.

Seeing her reaction to driving by the site of the wreck brought out all kinds of protective feelings in Gerome. Watching her at the car dealership intensified them. Then following her around, carrying packages for her while she shopped in a mall made him feel almost domesticated. When they spent the day picking out flowers for him to plant in the gardens, he began to wonder if Herman had some ulterior motive.

Lord, I'm watching out for her as both You and Herman asked me to, but I need to put aside these personal feelings I'm having. I need to concentrate on what brought me here. Help me, Lord. I need You more than I did when I came. Show me what I need to know. Give me discernment into what's going on to harm my stepfather. Thank You, Lord.

The restlessness that had kept him from falling asleep fell away. He yawned and stretched. Time to get some shut-eye before the sun came up.

❦

Leiann had a hard time going to sleep. The last few days had been full of excitement. Buying a new luxury car was over the top. But right up there was her awareness of Gerome. Strong. Good-looking. Tender.

Imagining running her fingers through the thick waves of his hair sent heat coursing through her. Add to that the way his muscles rippled and stretched his T-shirts. His brooding brown eyes added a mysterious look that called to something inside her.

She'd never felt like this with any man. When they were away from her grandfather's estate, Gerome seemed almost carefree. They'd had a lot of fun, even though he fussed about carrying all those packages at the mall. Their conversations had been interesting. He shared her love of history. They even liked the same kinds of food.

But while he gently probed about her past, he didn't reveal anything about his. That fact bothered her. Why couldn't he be open with her? What did he have to hide? Was he Grandfather's stepson or not? If so, why was he living out behind the big house? Tomorrow would reveal the secret—if it existed.

After her third trip into the bathroom to get a drink of water, she finally fell into a fitful sleep. Dreams flitted through her mind. Snatches of reality morphed into crazy and weird situations.

Something woke her before the sun rose. She lay still and listened, gripping her hands into fists. After a moment, she heard the soft sound of breathing. It moved closer. Someone was in her room.

Her scream pierced the air a moment before a pillow covered her face, cutting off the sound. She fought, bucking and rolling, trying to scratch her assailant. She finally jerked free and lunged toward the lamp on the other side of the bed. When the light came on, she saw a man slip through the partially opened French doors to the balcony.

The door to the hallway burst open, and Prudence hurried into the room. "What's the matter?"

Leiann pointed toward the balcony. Her grandfather's assistant rushed to the parted draperies. After closing the door and locking it, she turned back. "What happened?"

"Someone was in my room." Leiann clutched her arms across her chest. She couldn't stop shaking. "He tried to smother me."

Prudence sat on the edge of her bed. For the first time, the woman softened toward her. "Did you see who it was?"

"No." Leiann closed her eyes and replayed what had happened in her mind. "He wore a ski mask. I didn't see his eyes. It was too dark."

"Are you sure it was a man?"

"I think so. . .yes. . .I'm sure it was." She opened her eyes and stared at the woman. A sudden realization dawned on her.

Prudence scooted closer. "Do you remember anything else?"

Should she trust this woman? She hadn't felt comfortable with her until tonight. But she had to tell someone.

"He wore old jeans and a red T-shirt."

"Like that Mays man had on today?" Surprise colored Prudence's tone.

Something inside Leiann quaked. "Yes. Just like Gerome's."

Prudence patted Leiann's arm. "Don't worry. I'll get the lock changed on your bedroom door and the French doors and give you the only key."

Tears streamed down Leiann's face.

The other woman stood. "We needn't tell Herman about this. He's worried enough. We don't want to cause him any more distress. His heart, you know."

Leiann stared at her. "What's wrong with his heart?"

Prudence looked genuinely worried. "He had a couple of cardiac episodes before you came here. But he's been better with you around. We want to keep it that way, don't we?"

"Of course." Leiann clasped her hands in a tight grip.

Prudence stared at the draperies then turned back to Leiann. "I'll have Eric take you to the Cape Cod house right away. You'll be out of danger there."

"Shouldn't we call the police?"

She crossed the room. "I'll call the sheriff's department first thing in the morning. They can take your statement there."

Leiann rubbed her forehead, unable to think about anything but the feeling of helplessness with the pillow over her face.

"You probably won't have to stay there long. The sheriff should be able to apprehend Mays quickly."

Leiann nodded slowly.

"I'll go get Eric." Prudence exited, quietly closing the door.

Leiann picked up her cell phone and speed-dialed Arlene. With the time difference, maybe her friend was still awake.

"Hello." Arlene sounded sleepy.

"I wish you were here." Leiann tried to keep the panic from her voice.

"What's wrong?" Now Arlene was more alert.

"Someone tried to smother me." Her voice broke.

"Who would want to smother you?" Arlene's hysterical voice screamed through the phone. "Do you want me to come up there?"

"No." Leiann held the phone to her ear with one hand while she gathered things and stuffed them into a tote bag with the other. "I'm going to the Cape Cod house. The Styleses should be able to protect me."

"How are you going to get there?"

"Eric will drive me."

Arlene paused. "What about Gerome? I thought you were spending a lot of time with him."

Leiann took a deep breath. "He may be the person who tried to smother me."

When a quiet knock sounded on the door, Leiann told Arlene good-bye. She accompanied Prudence downstairs and out the front door. Eric waited in the Jeep. They drove into the dark night.

Chapter 11

The Jeep was a lot more crowded than the sedan. Leiann felt cramped and too close to Eric. Even though he had her best interests in mind, she didn't want to be near any man right now. He turned on a radio station with music that grated on her nerves. He drove carefully, but faster on the winding drive than she would have. When they neared the site of her wreck, she clenched her fists and closed her eyes.

"Are you all right?" His voice sounded as if he cared.

Leiann glanced at him, but his eyes were on the road. "I'm fine."

At the end of the drive, he headed the vehicle toward Boston.

"This isn't the way we went last time."

He smiled. "Herman likes to take the long way. I don't."

When they reached I-95, Eric went under the highway and hooked a left. Leiann had always had a good sense of direction, and she knew they were going in the opposite direction from Cape Cod.

After they merged onto the freeway, she studied Eric.

"Do you like what you see?" He grinned at her then looked back toward the road.

"I'm just wondering why we're not going the right direction."

He laughed. "You're smarter than I thought." He shot a quick glance at her. "The Cape Cod story was a cover to keep Mays from knowing where we're going. I'm just trying to protect you."

Leiann didn't like the fact that Eric had lied to her. She wondered if he had told Prudence where he was really taking her.

An uncomfortable feeling overwhelmed her. She gritted her teeth. "So, where are we going?"

"To the Johnson hunting lodge."

She stared through the windshield. Everything felt surreal. Like something in a movie or TV show, happening to someone else, not her. Why was her life such a mess? Maybe she should have stayed in Texas and found an apartment.

"Where is this lodge?" Leiann tried not to sound as panicked as she felt.

"It's in Maine, near the Canadian border." Eric readjusted the mirror.

She didn't want to go that far. The only reason she'd agreed to go to Cape

Cod was because the Styleses would be there. She didn't want to go anywhere alone with Eric.

She wanted to shriek, but she tried to keep her voice even. "If Gerome is Grandfather's stepson, won't he know about the lodge?"

He shook his head. "He's been gone from here for a long time. Herman purchased this place maybe ten years ago. I don't think they stayed in touch."

Leiann couldn't imagine the man she had spent the last several days with harming her. But what did she really know about him?

She longed to call Arlene and tell her what was going on. But she was worried that might upset Eric. The first time they stopped, she would call her friend on the cell phone, even if she had to do it from the bathroom. Maybe the two of them could come up with another plan.

❦

Gerome spent most of the day planting the flowers Leiann had chosen for the gardens. When he picked up each pot, he remembered her face when she saw that particular plant. Her laughing eyes. The way she didn't mind getting dirt on her hands. Her smile. How interesting she was to talk to.

Shaking his head, he stood and picked up the empty wooden flat. The woman was getting under his skin, and he had a feeling that was what Herman wanted.

After he finished planting he went to his cottage to clean up. While he was there, Greg called.

"There's no question that money is being siphoned off," his friend said. "And the only person close enough to do it is Prudence Smith."

"Are you sure?"

"I found several dummy companies, but the amounts that have been deposited into them were small enough not to arouse suspicion."

Gerome had always teased Greg for being such a computer whiz. Now he was glad the man was on his side.

"I'll fax you the names of the dummy companies, along with pictures of several documents and files pertaining to those companies. You might see if you can find a computer trail from that end."

After thanking Greg for his thorough work, Gerome walked through the gardens toward the kitchen. No enticing smell met him at the door. Maybe everyone had already eaten. He'd just look in on them in the dining room. However, when he entered the hallway, he saw the room was dark.

He went into the kitchen, where Mrs. Shields was hanging up a damp dish towel. "Where is everyone?"

She shook her head. "I don't know. Mr. Johnson had an early dinner, and Miss Smith said her brother and Miss Hambrick wouldn't be eating here tonight."

Something about this didn't feel right. He needed to talk to Herman.

When he headed toward his stepfather's office, the man's assistant came out. "Is Herman in there?" Gerome asked her.

"No. I was just finishing up some work he left for me." Prudence held a few file folders in one arm. "He wasn't feeling well, so he went to bed after dinner."

Talking to his stepfather would have to wait until tomorrow, but tonight might be the time to check out the office. Thanks to Greg's latest intel, Gerome knew exactly what kind of files to look for.

Was Prudence the only person involved, or did her brother also play a part? With Eric hanging around here all the time, Gerome had a gut feeling he was in it up to his eyeballs. They had to be the people who'd made the two attempts on Leiann's life. But he needed solid proof.

When he went back to the kitchen, Mrs. Shields gave him a plate with a roast beef sandwich on thick-sliced homemade bread. He thanked her before wolfing it down, accompanied by a large glass of milk.

He took up his post at the back of the house, hidden in the dark shadows under the elm trees. He prayed and repeated memorized scripture verses while he watched the light in the window of Prudence's office. After it was extinguished, he trained his eyes on the suite of rooms she occupied.

Gerome didn't know what the woman did that took so long, but finally, all those lights went out. He made several reconnaissance runs around the mansion, looking for anything that might be out of the ordinary.

He went back to his cottage and changed into black clothing, even masking his face with black makeup. He rummaged through his duffel bag and took out the tools he'd use to help him quickly access the files. Before returning to the house, he whispered another prayer for protection.

Gerome moved from hiding place to hiding place as he once again checked out the grounds. He couldn't go in through the back door, where anyone could see him. He carefully disconnected the security system and quickly picked the lock on the French doors to Herman's office.

He checked all the files. Nothing seemed amiss. He went next door to Prudence's office. At her computer, he plugged in his flash drive, which contained a software program for breaking passwords. Hers took longer than he expected, but the effort was well worth it. After downloading onto the flash drive all the files with the information he needed, he made sure everything in the room was back the way he found it.

While he reconnected the alarm, he thanked God for his special training.

✆

When Leiann told Eric she needed to make a pit stop, he frowned at her. But he left the interstate and pulled into a drive-in grocery with a small dining room.

"Might as well get dinner while we're here. What do you want?"

Leiann glanced at the lighted menu board. "I'll have a grilled chicken sandwich on whole wheat." She grabbed her purse from the counter and headed toward the door at the back of the dining room.

When she reached the hall, she found three women in line outside the door. That might be good. An excuse to take longer. She moved a little ways from the other women and reached into her purse for her cell phone. It wasn't in the corner where she usually stowed it.

She hurried back under the light and pulled the purse open as wide as she could. After digging through everything in the bag, she still hadn't found the flip phone. She looked again, even checking to see if it was in her wallet. The phone was missing.

One of the women in front of her went into the bathroom, so the line shifted. Leiann followed. She closed her eyes and tried to remember the last time she'd seen her phone. She'd used it to call Arlene back in her bedroom at the mansion. But what did she do with it after that? She thought she'd put it in her purse, but she couldn't be sure.

Leiann didn't want to panic. Maybe it had dropped out when they were leaving the house, or maybe she'd left it on her bed.

Another woman came out of the bathroom, and the two in front of her went in together. Leiann leaned against the rough, wooden-paneled wall.

Leiann didn't want to upset Eric. But she desperately wanted to talk to Arlene. She didn't feel like she was thinking straight right now. Frustration gripped her like a vise.

Chapter 12

Leiann didn't think Eric would ever stop for the night, but finally he pulled into the parking lot of a run-down motel in the middle of nowhere. She didn't want to stay there, but maybe she'd get a chance to use the room phone. To keep Eric from knowing she wasn't happy about going so far with him, she could reverse the charges. First she'd call Arlene, then maybe Prudence, or even the sheriff.

"You stay here. I'll go get us a room." The long time without sleep made him look haggard and older.

"I'm not sharing a room with you."

He huffed out a breath. "Of course not. I was planning on separate rooms."

She crossed her arms and glared at him. "Good."

He slammed the door and loped into the office.

Leiann watched his every move through the grimy picture window of the office. The man behind the counter glanced toward the vehicle. When the clerk looked at her, a knowing smirk slid over his face. She felt like going in and slapping it off.

Eric opened the door and jumped into the driver's seat. He drove down the length of the one-story building until he came to an empty parking space near the far end. He held up two brass keys. "Adjoining rooms."

He jumped out and ran around to her side of the Jeep. When he opened her door, he gave her a little bow. Leiann couldn't appreciate his attempt at gallantry after the way he'd lied to her and dragged her across another state. She grabbed her overnight bag from behind her seat before he could get it for her.

The peeling paint on the exterior walls was so faded, Leiann wasn't sure whether it was green or blue. At least the narrow sidewalk was free of debris. She hoped the rooms would be clean.

Eric gave her a key and waited while she opened the door.

Leiann closed the door in his face. She locked the doorknob and pulled the security chain across. Both looked flimsy. A good kick to the door from the outside would open it.

She stood with her back against the door and her hands gripping her upper arms. How had her life spiraled this far out of control in so short a time? All she'd wanted was to know who she really was.

If she could believe Eric and Prudence, Gerome had tried to kill her two times: once at the tower and last night with the pillow in her face. But could she really believe them?

She took stock of the room. Fading paint on these walls, too. The mattress was lumpy, but when she pulled the comforter back, the sheets looked and smelled clean. The tile floor had been swept and mopped. Maybe it wouldn't be too bad. After all, it was only for one night.

She spied a black rotary phone on the nightstand between the bed and the tiny bathroom. After hurrying over, she picked up the receiver. No dial tone. A sign on the wall above the telephone said that occupants had to pay a fee to have the phone turned on. Obviously, Eric hadn't paid extra for her phone.

Leiann dug out her billfold, intending to slip out and go to the office and pay for it herself. She didn't carry cash, but most places accepted debit cards. She opened her wallet. The card wasn't where she usually kept it. After going through every pocket, she sat on the bed, frustrated.

This was almost more than she could take. She felt as if she were at the bottom of a very dark pit.

❦

When Gerome got up the next day, he went for his usual run in the predawn twilight. While his feet pounded a steady rhythm, his heart lifted in praise to the Lord. Then he moved to prayer for Leiann, for Herman, and for wisdom that he would know how to proceed with the information he'd retrieved from Prudence's computer.

He showered and shaved before going to the house for breakfast. He didn't want to wait any longer to see Leiann. On the walk to the house, he wondered where she had been yesterday.

Prudence Smith was the only person in the dining room when he arrived. Gerome greeted her coolly, then loaded up a plate. Moments after he sat down and started to eat, Charity walked by the open door. He scooted his chair back and hurried after her.

Gerome caught her just before she started up the stairs. "Charity, is Leiann coming down to breakfast?"

"She's not here."

Her words hit him like heavy rocks. "What do you mean?" His voice came out harsh.

Charity backed up a step. "Mr. Smith took her to the Cape yesterday."

That didn't make sense. "Are you sure?"

"That's what Prudence told me."

"Thank you." He walked to the front door and looked out one of the sidelight windows. Every instinct went on high alert. When he turned back, Charity was at the top of the stairs. "Does Mr. Johnson know about this?"

"I don't know. I suppose so."

Gerome wanted to make sure Leiann was all right. Someone had made two attempts on her life, and he suspected the Smiths. He hurried back to the dining room. Prudence wasn't there. He quickly polished off his food. He wasn't sure when he'd be able to eat again, and he needed to keep up his strength.

He returned to his cottage and threw a few essentials into his duffel bag. His cell was fully charged, but he tossed in the car charger anyway. He didn't know what he would find when he got to the Cape.

Within five minutes, he was on the way, and he didn't drive slowly on the winding road. Prayers for Leiann's safety, and his own, filled the cab.

He pulled into the drive at the house on Cape Cod in record time. God must have been watching out for him, because no one stopped him for speeding. Urgency ate at his gut. He had to find Leiann and make sure she was all right.

Salty came out of the garage at the other side of the car park. "Mays, what are you doing here? I didn't know you were coming."

Gerome met him halfway. "I came to see Leiann and Eric. Are they around?" He didn't want to upset the man.

"No. Haven't seen them." Concern puckered around the older man's eyes. "Are they missing?"

"Don't worry." Gerome clapped him on the shoulder. "I'll find them."

He ran the few steps to the pickup, jumped in, and shot back out into the street. *Let's see if I can get to the house as quickly as I got here.*

He briefly considered calling the house. But Prudence usually answered the phone, and she was undoubtedly in on whatever was going on.

Once more, prayers filled his heart. He might need backup, but he wouldn't call until he was sure of what was going on.

The first place he went when he got to the mansion was Prudence Smith's office. When he burst through the door, she looked up from her computer, startled.

"What do you want?" Her hands rested on the keyboard.

"Where are your brother and Leiann?"

Her gaze darted toward the wall behind him. "They went to Cape Cod."

Gerome stomped across the office and leaned his fists on her desk, his face close to hers. "I just came from there." He glared at her, his muscles twitching.

Prudence thrust her hands into her lap and trained her eyes on them. "That's what I heard."

He wanted to yank her out of her chair and make her tell him what was going on, but he didn't want her to know what he really suspected. Maybe she would just think he was jealous. Perhaps he was.

After going back out front, he drove his truck to his cottage, parking it at the rear.

Where would Smith have taken her?

As he went in his front door, Gerome reached for his satellite cell and punched Greg's speed-dial number. "Hey, buddy, I need a huge favor." As succinctly as possible, he laid out what he knew and what he suspected.

"Sounds ominous. What do you need from me?"

"For now, this can't be official, but I need to find out where Eric has taken her. If she went willingly, I can't interfere, but if she's in danger, I'll need help. Off the record, can you run their credit cards and see if they've been used in the last forty-eight hours?"

"Will do."

"I need it yesterday. I'll wait for your call."

While Gerome paced his cottage, he poured out his heart to God. After a few minutes, a peace he didn't understand settled over him. He hoped it meant he wouldn't be too late to help Leiann.

His cell rang. "Mays here."

"You're on to something." Greg's eager voice sparked a hint of optimism. "I found one debit card for her—no activity on it. But Eric Smith has several cards. One was used to buy gas near the Massachusetts-New Hampshire border. Then at a small rural grocery near the New Hampshire border, and finally at a motel on the other side of New Hampshire. One last time for gas in Maine."

Gerome hit his forehead with the palm of his hand. "That's it. Herman owns a hunting lodge near the Canadian border. He's offered to let me use it several times, but I've never been there. Do you think you can find it?"

"Shouldn't take long." The staccato sound of clicking computer keys filled the silence.

Gerome walked to the kitchen and snatched a half bottle of water from the fridge. He opened the sports top with one hand and took a swig while he waited with the phone clutched against his ear.

"Got it!"

The shout over the phone almost burst Gerome's eardrum.

"This place is really out in the woods. Past Moosehead Lake. I'll fax you a map right now."

Gerome set the water down and swiped his hand across the back of his neck. "Why would he take her there?" The sight of Leiann hanging on to the handrails on the tower flashed into his mind. Then her frightened face as the Mercedes approached the hairpin curve. "Do you suppose he intends to kill her?"

Silence hung between the phones.

"I've got to get there right away. If she didn't go willingly, it's kidnapping."

The chilling sound of those words hung between them.

Greg broke the silence. "Your instincts have saved us from a lot of tight places."

Gerome let out the breath he was holding. "I'm not sure I can trust my instincts about this one."

"Because you have feelings for the girl?"

Gerome laughed. He never had been able to hide anything from Greg. Not since they were in grade school. "Yeah. So, am I too close to this?"

His friend snorted. "No woman could destroy your instincts. What does your gut tell you?"

"That she didn't know they were going up there. Telling Prudence and Charity they're going to the Cape, then not going. And the way Prudence acted when I questioned her. The whole scenario feels wrong."

"You want backup?"

"Yes. I'd rather take the heat for this being a wild goose chase than take a chance of letting him kill the woman I love."

The woman I love. Those words danced in the air around Gerome like a melody from heaven.

"Okay." Greg's voice broke into the silence. "I'll get a chopper and pick you up. With a good tailwind, we could get to the cabin by the time Eric and Leiann do."

Gerome's fax machine started printing, and he walked over to grab the map. He studied it for a moment. "Contact the FBI. We've cooperated on cases with them before. Since he's taken her across state lines, they'll have jurisdiction. Tell them it's a kidnapping. If we wait until we know for sure whether she went willingly, it may be too late to save her. Have local agents take a four-wheel drive vehicle to Hunter's Glen. That's probably the closest place to Moosehead Lake to set the helo down."

Chapter 13

On the way through New Hampshire, Eric drove like a madman. Sometimes he'd take a road, then double back and go another way.

"Do you even know where you're going?"

He turned a fierce scowl toward her. "Of course I do."

They passed a sign that said WELCOME TO MAINE. She didn't see a city, just a little hamlet with a few stores and several houses. Her stomach let out a loud grumble.

"You hungry?"

"Yes. But I don't see a restaurant."

Eric pulled up in front of a corner store. A sign in the front window proclaimed ITALIAN SANDWICHES.

"We'll go in here. You can use the restroom while I buy us something to eat. What do you want?"

"A cola and an Italian sandwich. And could you get a few bottles of water to take with us?"

She assumed his grunt meant yes.

An older man stood behind the counter near an ancient cash register. "What can I do for you and the missus?"

Leiann cringed, but Eric didn't seem to notice. She hadn't liked it when the car salesman and the tourist assumed she and Gerome were married, but somehow this bothered her more. The man turned away before she could say anything.

After threading around the haphazard displays of all kinds of canned foods and snacks, she found the restroom in a back corner. The lock on the door was an old hook-and-eye kind. When she turned around after locking it, she wasn't sure she wanted to touch anything. She couldn't tell what was stained and what was soiled.

When Leiann emerged, she found Eric standing outside the door. "This is the last stop before we reach Hunter's Glen, which isn't far from the lodge."

She wandered through the store, gazing at the products while trying to find a phone. If the store had one, it must be in an office or under the counter. If only Arlene or Grandfather knew where she was. Her stomach muscles clenched at the thought.

Eric picked up a brown paper sack from a smiling woman behind the sandwich counter. "Thank you, ma'am."

While he paid the man by the register, Leiann went outside. No phone booth in sight. If she tried to get help from anyone, what would she say? It wasn't against the law to lie. So far, Eric hadn't done anything overt to cause her not to trust him. But the farther they went, the harder uneasiness gripped her.

After they were back on the road, Eric asked her to open his sandwich for him. Leiann pulled back the paper on one of them and handed it to him, then opened her own.

She picked off the onions and wadded them in a napkin. She was hungry, but the thought of eating made her stomach clench more.

"There are some chips in there, too. Open a package for me." He laid the sandwich on one leg and reached over to take the potato chips.

After she ate as much as she could get past the lump in her throat, Leiann felt drowsy. She stretched her neck and rolled her shoulders. She made sure the door was locked and leaned against it. Soon she fell asleep.

"We're here." Eric gave her shoulder a shake. "Hunter's Glen."

Leiann sat up straight and rubbed her eyes. He'd stopped the Jeep at a store with a couple of gas pumps out front. A few other buildings were scattered up and down two roads that crossed beside the store.

An open phone booth stood not far from where they parked. She followed Eric into the store, going immediately to the restroom. When she came out, he was picking up groceries from the shelves and piling them in his arms. She went around the other side of the display from him and slipped out the door.

While she approached the telephone, she dug through her purse, looking for enough coins to get through to Arlene. Leiann set her purse on the hood of the Jeep so she could reach every corner.

"What are you doing?" Eric stood behind her with a sack in his arms.

"I want to call my grandfather. He'll be worried about me."

He frowned. "I talked to my sister last night from the motel. She said Herman had another spell with his heart. She thought it best not to tell him about us leaving."

"Your sister knows where we are?"

"Of course. I had to get the key to the lodge from her." He opened the car door and shoved the sack into the backseat. "She'll make sure everything is all right on that end."

"Did she call the sheriff? Are they investigating? Have they found anything?" Questions tumbled from Leiann's lips.

"Don't worry about all that. Pru is taking care of everything."

Leiann huffed out a deep breath. "She told me the sheriff would need to get a statement from me, so we need to go back."

"We will when it's safe." Eric's placating tone grated on her nerves.

"I still want to call my grandfather and let him know I'm all right." Stress ate at Leiann's insides. "But I don't have enough change."

"I'm afraid you'd be in more danger if you made that call. Just get in so we can be on our way." Eric took his place behind the steering wheel.

Leiann climbed into her seat. She wondered how long he planned for them to stay at the lodge. She didn't like the idea of them being there alone.

The rest of the drive to the hunting lodge was over rough roads through heavily wooded areas. They crossed several streams with bridges. The roads were narrow. Leiann was glad they hadn't met any other traffic.

When they finally pulled into a clearing around a log house, Leiann welcomed the chance to leave the vehicle and really stretch her legs. The building fit the surroundings. Power lines ran from an outbuilding to the house.

"Do they have electricity out here?" She rubbed the small of her back to get the kinks out.

"That building holds the generator. I'll get it turned on."

The lodge was surprisingly large, with enough windows letting in light that she had no trouble exploring. The furniture was sturdy wood and leather, and rugs were scattered on the hardwood floors.

She inspected each upstairs bedroom until she found one with a lock on the inside of the door.

By the time she came back downstairs, Eric had returned, and the lights worked. He unloaded several items out of the sack of things he'd bought at Hunter's Glen and put them into the small refrigerator.

"Where does the water come from?" She turned toward Eric.

"There's a well. With the generator on, the pump works. I just lit the water heater. I'm going to check out the surrounding area." Eric headed out the door but turned back toward her. "Don't leave the cabin until I get back. Dangers lurk in the woods."

❧

Gerome's anxiety for Leiann had him pacing the floor of his cottage as he waited for Greg's call. When his cell finally vibrated, he grabbed it off his belt. "Mays here."

"Hey, man." Greg's welcome voice came through loud and clear. "Everything's in place. Where do we set the bird down?"

Gerome rubbed the back of his neck. Tension had tied it in knots. "Not close enough for Prudence to suspect anything. I'm going to drive to a meadow on the far end of the estate, near the highway. The people at the house won't be able to see or hear the helo from there. Go ahead and head this direction. I'll give you the coordinates from my GPS after I get there."

He clicked off the cell and hurried to his pickup. Thankful that the estate was so large, Gerome headed across country toward the open field. While he bounced on the seat, gripping the steering wheel so tight his knuckles whitened, he prayed he'd achieve success.

Soon after he gave Greg the coordinates, the helicopter settled in the long grass. Gerome grabbed the duffel bag he always kept in his pickup, ran under the whirling blades, and jumped aboard, nodding to the pilot as well as his best friend. The chopper lifted off and headed northeast.

Greg pressed a finger on his earpiece, his brows knit in concentration. "A couple of FBI agents were on a hunting trip near Hunter's Glen. They found the lodge. They're hidden in the woods, awaiting our arrival. Local agents are in a four-wheel-drive SUV parked in an open field behind the only store in town. They sent the pilot the coordinates."

Gerome blew out a relieved breath. For the first time since he discovered Leiann was gone, hope sparked in his heart. He'd trusted his life to these men more than once, and they always came through.

The helicopter skimmed through the air just above the treetops. All the colors ran together in a shifting collage, like an impressionist painting. Gerome never did understand why anyone wanted art that was blurry. He liked things in sharp focus. That way he could see everything around him and quickly assess any danger. But he'd almost dropped the ball when it came to Leiann.

He hoped he was wrong about Smith, but something in his gut wouldn't let go of the feeling that Leiann was in mortal danger.

Lord, don't let us be too late.

Gerome hadn't been able to figure out why Prudence and Eric would want to get rid of Leiann. Even if they killed her, Gerome was still an heir to the Johnson fortune, unless Herman had cut him out of his will back when he'd been a rebellious youth. Gerome didn't believe the Old Man had done that. Herman had always accepted him, caring for him more than his own father did.

Were Prudence and Eric afraid that he or Leiann might find out they'd been embezzling from the estate? The Smiths didn't know the kind of work he did, so they wouldn't know that he could keep close tabs on anyone around the Old Man. Gerome had been in enough sticky situations to know that people preyed on the wealthy, and he wanted to make sure Herman was well protected. So he regularly checked on what was going on. That's how he'd detected the discrepancies. And he wanted them to pay for what they'd done to Herman.

As soon as the chopper set down, Gerome and Greg jumped out and joined the local agents. Gerome suggested that all of them dress like hunters who'd become lost and were seeking help. They purchased everything they needed from the store and were quickly on their way.

❦

Leiann went upstairs to the room she'd chosen. She sat on the bed and tried not to cry. When had her life started getting out of control?

"*When you turned your back on Me, Leiann.*"

She recognized the voice in her spirit. She'd grown up with it. When the foundations of her life were shaken in that lawyer's office, she couldn't understand how God had let it happen. The man who'd raised her as his own was a strong man of God. Or so she'd thought. How could he keep the truth from her? How could her mother?

Didn't God demand honesty and integrity? Why hadn't He protected her?

"*I created you in your mother's womb. I knit you together, and I made sure you were protected and loved.*"

"But why was the truth withheld from me?" She spoke the question into the heavy air.

"*I don't overrule the free will I gave your mother and father.*"

Tears streamed down Leiann's face.

"*Just as I didn't overrule your free will when you hardened your heart against Me.*"

The wall around Leiann's heart cracked. "I need Your help, Lord. Someone is trying to kill me. But I don't know who."

"Talking to yourself, Leiann?" Eric's voice startled her. She hadn't heard him open the door. "Let's go for a walk. That should clear your head."

"I'd rather stay here." She turned her back on him.

"Big mistake." He grabbed her arm and jerked her around. Light gleamed off the barrel of a pistol in his other hand. It was pointed at her.

"What are you doing?"

"Just do what I say." Eric dragged her through the doorway and shoved her toward the top of the stairs. "I won't hesitate to use this."

Numb, she staggered down the steps, using the banister to steady herself. "Where are you taking me?"

He motioned with the gun toward the open back door. A path beyond it led through the thick woods.

Seeing no choice, she started down it. The humid air intensified the earthy fragrance of soil, brush, and trees. "Why are you doing this?"

"You messed up everything." His words held a sinister ring as they echoed through the tall trees.

Her eyes darted all around, looking for something she could use as a weapon. Finally, she noticed a sturdy limb lying beside the path. She glanced out the corners of her eyes, without moving her head, to see if there was someplace to hide if she picked it up and whacked him with it.

"Don't even think about it. Kick the branch out of the way." He prodded her with the barrel of the gun, so she complied.

The cold touch of the weapon against her back made Leiann tremble, but she tried to hide her fear from Eric. "What did I mess up?"

"Prudence has worked this gig for a long time. The old coot's worth a ton of money, but she barely made enough to live on. For the past fifteen years, she's managed to skim a little bit off the top here and there without his noticing. But we wanted more. So she planned to convince him to marry her."

Leiann turned toward him. "Are you crazy? I saw no indication that he cared for her like that."

Eric forced her back around with the barrel of the gun. "Pru's real smart. She'd been gradually weakening him. Soon he'd need her to take care of him, and she felt sure she could convince him to marry her so she could do a better job of it. It wouldn't be a love match, of course. We just wanted his money—all of it."

"How much money is there?" Although Leiann had some idea about the amount, she hoped all the questions would help her catch Eric off guard.

"Not as much as there was when she first came to work for him." He barked out a hard laugh. "But your coming messed up everything. I tried to get you to marry me. That would've been another way to get access to the money. But you weren't interested."

God, if I've ever needed You, I need You now. "So what are you going to do?"

"You're about to have an unfortunate accident."

Leiann didn't like the sound of that.

"If by some chance your *boyfriend*"—he spat out the word—"figures out where we are, he'll come after us. By the time he drives up here, you'll already be dead. When the authorities start snooping around, I'll tell them I tried to stop him from killing you, but I had to shoot him in self-defense. That way we get rid of both heirs at the same time." His maniacal laugh resounded in the remote forest.

This man is insane! "How am I supposed to die?"

"There's a high cliff up ahead. You're going to fall off it."

Not if I can help it. Show me what to do, Lord.

Chapter 14

Gerome, Greg, and the two FBI agents made good time up the road toward the lodge. Gerome studied the heavy forest bisected by the one-lane drive. No wonder Herman had bought this property. A far cry from his everyday world of high finance, it could take him back to simplicity and nature. When Gerome was younger, the old man had often told him the importance of not losing touch with the simple life.

Majestic trees soared above them, sentinels of God's magnificent creation. The density of the underbrush probably held a myriad of wildlife. Gerome wasn't sure Herman ever hunted when he was at the lodge. He probably spent the time communing with God.

Now Gerome wished he had taken Herman up on one of his offers to use the property. Herman thought Gerome needed it for a refuge since he thought his stepson was shiftless. When this was over, Herman would finally know the truth about what Gerome had done with his life.

One of the agents who'd been watching the lodge met them on the road before they reached the clearing barely visible up the hill a ways. Gerome jumped out of the vehicle. "What's happening, Hilton?"

"We're not sure." The man kept his hand on his holster. "They arrived awhile ago and went into the lodge."

Maybe she wasn't here against her will after all. Gerome frowned. Hopefully, his gut finally had made a mistake. "Did she look all right?"

The man nodded. "She seemed to be. Although she didn't look happy. Shortly after they went inside, the man came out and scouted the area. Then he went down a path behind the house. One of our agents followed him but kept out of sight."

"Where does the path lead?" Gerome visualized what happened as the agent described it.

"It ends at a large slab of rock above a steep cliff."

Gerome rubbed the sides of his forehead with the thumb and middle finger of one hand. "Did Smith go that far?"

"He stood on the rock for a few minutes. Studied everything around him."

"Did he go all the way to the edge?" A frightening scenario formed in Gerome's mind.

"Yes. He stood there for a few moments, looking down." The agent pressed a hand against his earpiece. "The man is almost back at the house."

"What happens now?"

"Myers and I will go around to the back of the house." Hilton, the senior agent, turned toward his partner. "You take the north side, and I'll take the south."

Gerome had seen these men handle a case before. He knew they were good. "Would it be all right if Greg and I go, too?"

"If you stay back in the cover of the woods."

Greg followed Myers, and Gerome went after Hilton, being careful to stay in the underbrush.

When they were almost even with the front of the lodge, Hilton whispered, "Targets sighted exiting the rear of the structure. Male is armed and holding female hostage."

Gerome's heart double-timed as he zigzagged through the dense forestation, trying to get close enough to see what was going on.

"Keep them in sight. Do not engage unless absolutely necessary." Hilton continued toward the back of the lodge.

Gerome strained to hear what Eric was saying to Leiann. From what he could make out, it was obvious the man and his sister had been swindling Herman for a long time. Gerome almost laughed out loud when Eric said Prudence was going to try to convince Herman to marry her. The two must not realize just how astute his stepfather really was. He wouldn't be fooled by any wiles that woman tried to exert on him.

When Eric jabbed the gun into Leiann's back, Gerome wanted to tackle him and give him the beating he deserved. He whispered a prayer for patience. The man sounded insane, and crazy people were unpredictable.

Gerome studied Leiann. She seemed to be taking in her surroundings, as if looking for a way of escape. That could work to their advantage.

Hilton walked around the lodge toward the pathway, stopping a few feet behind Eric and Leiann. "Is anybody here? I need some help." His words resounded through the trees as he walked toward the couple. "I think I'm lost."

Eric whirled around. With his attention diverted, Leiann ducked behind the wide trunk of a nearby tree.

Myers launched himself toward Eric, grabbing him from behind. Eric twisted and turned, trying to point the gun at the agent. But Myers managed to keep Eric's hand turned away from him.

The woods exploded with other agents, all leveling their weapons at Eric. The man's eyes widened, and he let his guard down for an instant. Hilton grabbed the hand with the gun and forced Eric to drop the weapon before pulling both arms behind his back.

"Don't move," Hilton hissed.

Agent Myers pulled out handcuffs while the other agents kept their weapons trained on the prisoner.

Once Eric was subdued, Leiann stepped out from behind the tree. She crossed her arms over her chest and gripped her biceps with white knuckles, shaking from head to toe.

Gerome hurried toward her and gathered her against him. He pressed his face against her hair and whispered soothing words into her ear. Grabbing his shirt with both fists, she leaned against him and burst into tears. He pulled her even closer. His love for her swelled in his chest. She felt so right in his arms.

※

Is this Your answer to my cry for help, Lord?

Leiann clung to the front of Gerome's shirt and reveled in the feeling of his arms cradling her to his chest. How could she have been so wrong?

Because I'm stubborn, of course. She had turned her back on the Lord when she felt He had let her down, and she no longer had His discernment active in her thoughts.

She thanked God for intervening in the dangerous situation. How could she ever have thought Eric was a friend? And Gerome had never given her any reason not to trust him. Eric's lies had planted those doubts.

She raised her head and gazed up at the handsome face above hers. His eyes were trained on her even though chaos reigned around them.

"Are you all right?" His gentle tone arrowed straight to her heart.

"I am. Thanks to you."

Gerome's gaze caressed her features. For a moment, she thought he was going to kiss her, but he loosened his hold. "Did he hurt you?"

Leiann shook her head. "No. But he would have if everyone hadn't shown up when they did."

He leaned closer when her words became a whisper. This wonderful man was her hero in more ways than one.

※

Gerome stepped back from Leiann and glanced around. Eric was lashing out with loud, vile language. He strode over to the prisoner. "If you don't want them to gag you, you'll watch what you say around the lady."

Eric held his head high. Curses belched from his mouth, blistering the air.

Gerome reached for the man's throat, gripping it hard, but not enough to do any real damage. "I'd like nothing better than to beat you to a pulp. But I think the FBI has other plans for you."

Eric spat on the closest agent.

Leiann gasped, and Gerome pushed her behind him, shielding her from Eric.

"How did you know about this place, Mays? Herman bought it after you left home to become a bum." The sneer on Eric's face scorched Gerome.

If the man knew the truth, he wouldn't be so condescending. "Contrary to what you might believe, my stepfather and I have always had a good relationship, even though he thought I was wasting my life without a good job." Gerome glanced at the large log house. "More than once, he offered to let me stay here if I needed to."

Two FBI agents hauled Eric toward their vehicle. He continued to fight, trying to get out of their grasp.

Gerome turned toward Leiann and nodded at his friend, who stood nearby. "This is Greg. We work for a global security firm. He helped me track you down."

Leiann's eyes widened as she held out her hand. "Thank you very much." Her voice had a catch in it.

Greg grinned while he shook her hand. "Glad to help, Miss Hambrick."

The three of them stopped outside the back door of the lodge. Agent Myers stood just inside.

Gerome looked down at Leiann. "This a crime scene. We don't want to contaminate it." He glanced at the FBI agent. "When do you think you'll be finished?"

"Can't say." Myers shrugged. "We'll let you know when we're through."

Gerome nodded.

Leiann leaned toward him. "My purse is in one of the bedrooms upstairs."

"You'll get it back after the agents finish with the crime scene." Gerome put his arm around her shoulders. "In the meantime, you, Greg, and I are going to fly back to Massachusetts. We want to be there when the FBI arrests Prudence."

Hilton came into the kitchen and saw them beside the door. "Mays, as usual you were right about this one. I radioed headquarters. They're sending a team to the mansion."

"Could you wait to close in until we have Leiann back home? Herman has had some trouble with his heart. And he'll be worried about his granddaughter if she's not there when the agents close in."

"Okay. We'll have them on the premises, but they won't make the arrest until after you're there."

"Thanks." Gerome headed around the lodge with Leiann.

Greg and Myers stood beside the SUV, waiting for them. Gerome helped Leiann into the backseat then sat beside her, pulling her close to his side. He didn't want to let her out of his sight.

❦

Leiann welcomed the comfort of the SUV, and the trip to Hunter's Glen from the lodge didn't seem to take as long as the journey up with Eric had. Greg and

Gerome must have been longtime friends, because their banter filled the vehicle with laughter, helping her relax.

She watched these men interact and realized that even though she had fallen in love with Gerome, she didn't really know him. She'd had fun with him before, when she thought of him as just a handyman. What had happened here today revealed his true character. From his conversation with Eric when he was in custody, she knew he was her grandfather's stepson, but this man would never try to get her out of the way so he could be the only heir.

So Gerome worked for a global security firm. And he had tracked her down and saved her life. This was a lot of information to process at once. She wondered if they could have a future together.

When the SUV arrived in the tiny town near the lake, the driver stopped in a field behind the store where Leiann had tried to use the outside phone. A large helicopter, with OZBOURNE GLOBAL SECURITY painted in gold letters along the tail, waited for them. Gerome introduced her to the pilot when they got into the craft, and within a short time they were airborne.

Leiann had never flown in a helicopter. Being so close to the tops of the trees unsettled her. Even though she knew the pilot wouldn't hit anything, everything felt very close.

Wrinkles puckered Gerome's forehead. "Herman's doctor should be waiting for us when we arrive, just in case."

"So what Prudence and Eric said about my grandfather having heart trouble wasn't a lie?"

"No, but it's a recent development." Gerome smiled at her. "He has always been very healthy."

While she and Eric had made the cross-country jaunt, she'd hoped Prudence had called the sheriff so they would investigate the attempts on her life. And all the time, Prudence and Eric had been the ones trying to kill her. "Eric probably doesn't have acrophobia, either."

Gerome frowned. "What?"

"He told me he couldn't come up the tower to rescue me because he has a fear of heights." She tucked her hair behind her ears.

Gerome snorted. "Yeah, I'm sure he doesn't."

"I'm glad you don't, either."

🍂

When the helicopter touched down in the same field they had picked him up from earlier, Gerome unbuckled his seat belt and helped Leiann to the ground. They ran across the field toward his pickup, followed closely by Greg.

Gerome liked the way they fit so closely together on the bench seat. As they drove toward the mansion, Leiann's shoulder brushed against his arm whenever they hit a bump.

Halfway across the estate, they came upon an FBI command post. Three SUVs and one paneled van clustered together, and agents in full gear filled the seats. Two others stood in front of the van, watching the pickup approach. Gerome stopped the truck and rolled down the window so he could talk to the agent coming toward them.

"You heading to the mansion, Mays?" The man crossed his arms, his eyes shielded by reflective sunglasses.

Gerome nodded. "I want Leiann to be with her grandfather while the arrest is going down."

"We asked Mr. Johnson's doctor to be present, too," Greg added.

"Good idea." The agent stepped back.

After Gerome started driving again, Leiann touched his forearm. "Do you think Grandfather will be all right?"

"I've talked to his doctor. He doesn't think the heart problems are life-threatening, but we don't want to take any chances."

Leiann stared through the windshield toward the mansion, which was barely visible over the next hill. "I hope he lives a long time. We have a lot of lost years to make up for."

When Gerome stopped at the side of the house, the doctor's car pulled up in front. Gerome and Greg took Leiann around to greet him.

"What are you going to tell Herman about why you're here?" Gerome asked the doctor.

"That I wasn't satisfied with his blood pressure the last time I took it." A grin split the man's wrinkled face. "I've always wanted to put one over on Herman. He's a hard man to fool. This'll be fun." He offered his arm to Leiann, and they entered the house, leaving Gerome and Greg outside.

An FBI agent came from around the building. "If you can get the Smith woman out of her office, we'll secure her computers without giving her time to erase any of her files."

Gerome liked the way this man worked. "Her office has doors that open onto the back terrace. I'll point out which ones they are. Greg and I will go in the front and get her to come out into the hall. Your agents can enter her office through the back doors."

After all the details were worked out, Gerome and Greg went inside, talking loud and joking. As expected, Prudence came out of her office before they were very far down the long hallway.

She stalked toward them, meeting them close to the foyer. "What are you doing in here, Mr. Mays? Aren't you supposed to be working in the gardens? And who is this with you?"

Just wait until you see who's here. Gerome shoved his hands into the front pockets of his jeans.

☙

Leiann knocked on the French door of her grandfather's office then opened the door. "Can I come in?"

He raised his gaze from the open laptop on his desk to look at her. "Leiann, I thought you and Eric went to the Cape."

"I came back." Smiling, she approached, trying to decide how much to tell him.

"Herman." The doctor followed her in and went around to the front of the desk. "I've come to check your blood pressure."

Her grandfather stood and held out his hand. "You old saw-bones. Don't you have anyone else who needs to be poked or prodded?" He winked at Leiann. "I think you just wanted an excuse for some of Mrs. Shields's good cooking."

"I can't hide anything from you, can I?" After the handshake, the doctor set his bag on the desk and had Herman sit down. "Your blood pressure hasn't remained as stable as I'd like it to be, so I wanted to do a spot check. Roll up your sleeve."

Grandfather leaned forward, took off his suit jacket, and slung it across the desk. Then he turned up his shirtsleeve. The doctor took a blood pressure cuff out of his bag and fitted it around his upper arm.

Herman turned his attention toward Leiann. "Did you enjoy your time at the Cape?"

While the doctor pumped up the cuff, he chided his long-time friend. "You're going to have to sit perfectly still so I can get an accurate reading. You can talk to your granddaughter when I'm finished."

Out of the corners of her eyes, Leiann glanced out the window. She saw several agents taking up positions outside the office next door. She was glad the doorway to the hall was closed and the doctor had him facing that way. No need to upset him before they had to.

Chapter 15

"This is my friend Greg." Gerome gave his most potent smile to the woman. Beside her closed office door, Prudence remained stony faced, except for one eyebrow that arched like a cat ready to spit. "He stopped by, and I wanted to give him a tour of the place."

Her other eyebrow rose. "You did, did you? Do you think that's appropriate?"

While maintaining his relaxed pose, Gerome kept one ear attuned to the faint sounds in the background. The slight *whoosh* coming from the air conditioner vents. A tiny tinkle of the crystals on the chandelier in the entry as they swayed in the gentle breeze caused by the cooling unit. Voices coming from Herman's office. Nothing to indicate that FBI agents were gathering outside. These men were good.

He hooked his thumbs in the front belt loops on his jeans. "I didn't think it would hurt anything."

Prudence puckered her lips in an unbecoming way. "Really, Mr. Mays, you shouldn't make such assumptions."

"I'm sorry." Gerome put all the sincerity he could into his tone. "I'll go ask Mr. Johnson. I'm sure he won't mind."

She crossed her arms and tapped her toe, reminding him of an old-maidish schoolteacher from his junior high days. "I don't think you should bother him about anything so trivial. He's a busy man."

"Well, now, this is a dilemma." Gerome shifted his weight from one foot to the other. "We're already inside the house. What are we supposed to do now?"

"Maybe we should leave," Greg chimed in.

"No." Gerome stood straighter. "I want to continue what we started."

As if trying to match his height, Prudence stiffened and tilted her chin. "I said it isn't a good idea for you to take him through the house, Mr. Mays." She spat out his name as if it tasted bitter on her tongue.

A slight *thump* sounded from inside her office. She whirled and hurried toward her door then pushed it open. A look of horror covered her features. "What's going on here?" She pivoted toward the two men in the hall. "Did you have anything to do with these intruders getting into my office?" Gerome was sure her screeching could be heard in the next county.

One of the FBI agents stepped into the hall. "We have a search warrant for these premises."

Prudence's face paled to a papery white before red suffused it. "But. . .but. . ." Her eyes took on a steely glint as her gaze shot daggers toward Gerome. "I know you're involved with this." Her words zinged through the air like bullets. "Did you come back to try to lay claim to Herman's fortune?"

For a moment, Gerome felt sorry for the woman. She'd wasted fifteen years trying to pull this off. She gave a whole new meaning to the term *long con*. "I don't need to lay claim to his money. I have plenty of my own."

Prudence huffed then glanced into her office. "What are they doing with my computer?" Her voice reached a high pitch.

Another agent came out into the hallway and stood beside her. "It's evidence. Ms. Smith, you're under arrest for fraud, embezzlement, and conspiracy to kidnap. You have the right to remain silent. . ."

While the agent recited her Miranda rights, Prudence seemed to shrink before Gerome's eyes.

Why couldn't people realize that crime had a high cost? Sometime, somewhere, somehow, they always had to pay. If not in this lifetime, then in eternity.

❦

The doctor hadn't finished taking Grandfather's blood pressure when Leiann heard a screech from Prudence. The clever medical man had dawdled over the process.

"What's going on?" Grandfather started to rise.

"I'm not finished." The doctor kept listening through the stethoscope. "Your blood pressure is increasing right now."

Leiann dropped to her knees beside his chair. "Everything's okay. You don't have to be upset."

Grandfather relaxed against the back of the chair and took a couple of deep breaths. "Just get this over with, Doc. I have to find out what's wrong with Prudence."

Just as the doctor removed the cuff from Herman's upper arm, another shrill scream resounded. Grandfather jumped up and started toward the door. Leiann wanted to stop him, but she didn't know if she should or even could. At the doorway he clutched his hand against his chest and started to slump. The doctor reached him in time to keep him from hitting the floor.

"Leiann," the doctor said over his shoulder, "would you wait outside while I take care of Herman?"

She stepped into the hallway, shutting the door behind her. *Please, Lord, don't let him die.*

Her attention was snagged by the agent reading Prudence her rights. This whole thing felt surreal. Like something out of one of those police or FBI shows on TV. Leiann had always enjoyed watching them, but she doubted she would after this. At least not for a while."

Gerome came to stand beside her. "It's almost over." His arm slipped around her waist.

She leaned against him. "I'm glad."

"How's Herman?" He whispered the words into her ear, his breath warm on her cheek.

"Not so good."

Gerome knocked on the office door. The doctor's voice invited them in. When they entered, the doctor was leaning over her grandfather, who was lying on the couch.

He looked up. "Can you help me? We need to get him to his bedroom."

Gerome pulled the leather office chair close to the couch. "Why don't we put him in this and push it down the hall to his room? It'd be easier than trying to carry him and probably cause him less stress."

"Sounds like a good idea." The doctor lifted Grandfather and put him in the chair while Gerome held it steady. The doctor led the way, Gerome pushed the chair, and Leiann followed.

When they got out into the hallway, Prudence and the agents were no longer there. Leiann heard voices coming from behind the closed door of Prudence's office.

She waited outside the bedroom door while Gerome and the doctor got her grandfather settled in his bed. Gerome soon came outside.

Once again, he pulled her into his arms and rested his chin on the top of her head. She relaxed against his chest. "Is Grandfather going to be okay?"

"He has a good doctor." Gerome's words comforted her. "He knows all about Herman, and he told me not to worry."

Gerome leaned back from her, and she peered up at him. His tender smile reached her heart.

The doctor opened the door. "He's awake and he wants to talk to both of you. He won't rest until you tell him what's happening. I'll stay until I'm sure he doesn't need me anymore."

Leiann and Gerome walked toward the bed while the doctor sat in one of the rockers across the room. Grandfather rested against fluffy pillows on a king-sized bed. A smile lit his face. She didn't know what the doctor had done, but her grandfather looked better than he did when she last saw him. Color had returned to his cheeks, and a light sparked in his piercing eyes.

Grandfather took her hand with a healthy grip. "So, when are you two going to tell me what's going on?"

Gerome pulled a chair close to the bed for Leiann.

She sat in it, never letting go of Grandfather's hand. "Eric and I didn't go to

Cape Cod." Her grandfather raised a questioning brow. She glanced at the doctor. "Is he okay to hear all this?"

When the man nodded, she continued. "He took me to your hunting lodge in Maine."

Her grandfather frowned. "Why would he do that?"

"It's a long story." She fisted the hand lying in her lap.

"Maybe I should tell it from the beginning." Gerome stood behind her with his strong hands resting on her shoulders. "Herman, I came here because I had information that led me to believe someone was embezzling money from you, maybe a lot of money over a long period of time."

Her grandfather tried to rise.

"Just relax and let them talk," the doctor advised.

Leiann was glad Grandfather listened to him.

❦

Gerome shoved his hands into the front pockets of his jeans. "I work for a global security firm. That's how I came across the information."

Herman took Gerome's hand. "I'm sorry I misjudged you so long. I'm proud of you, Jerry."

A lump formed in Gerome's throat. "Thank you, sir." He told Herman what he'd found and why he came to the estate.

Herman chuckled. "So you didn't need the charitable job I gave you."

"Sure I did, but not for the money." Gerome was glad to see some animation return to his stepfather. "Then the attempts on Leiann's life started."

"Attempts? I only knew about the car. What else happened?" With every word, strength seemed to pour into him.

"She fell from the lookout tower after the steps were tampered with."

Herman stared into Gerome's eyes. "Anything else?"

"Not that I know of."

"Yes."

Gerome's and Leiann's differing answers came at the same time.

"What do you mean?" Gerome's heartbeat accelerated, and not just because she was near.

"Someone came into my room from the balcony night before last and tried to smother me with a pillow." Leiann looked from one man to the other. "That's why Eric was able to talk me into going to Cape Cod. The person wore the same kind of jeans and T-shirt Gerome had on that day. Eric convinced me Gerome had sabotaged the tower, too." She turned to look up at Gerome. "I don't know how I could have believed that about you."

He didn't want to add to her stress, so he nodded at her. Then he explained to Herman everything that went on after he arrived at the estate a few weeks ago.

Gerome knew the Old Man wouldn't rest easy until he knew all the details, and he wasn't wrong about that. Herman asked penetrating questions.

🍂

Gerome, Grandfather, and the doctor sent Leiann upstairs to get some rest. She shed her clothes and stepped into the shower. Steamy water poured over her skin until she felt more than the dirt float down the drain. Could this be a new beginning for her? She hoped so.

After the shower, Leiann slipped into her robe. Charity soon arrived with a teapot and finger sandwiches. She set the tray on the table and poured some tea for Leiann.

"Thank you." She took the cup from her maid and friend. She inhaled the spicy steam curling from the dark liquid.

As usual, Charity brought an extra cup and sat with her. Curiosity danced in her eyes, but she didn't voice any questions. Leiann was glad. She wasn't ready to talk about what had happened. Of course, the whole household would find out eventually, but not today. Not from her.

Leiann asked Charity what she did on her last day off. The girl chattered on about her afternoon at the beach. Leiann relaxed, enjoying the light tale.

After her maid left to take the dishes back to the kitchen, Leiann lay down. Though her body felt weighted from all that had transpired, her thoughts took wing, flitting through the events of the last few days.

Restless, she got up and stood at the window, looking toward the mountainous terrain across the gardens. Even in the twilight, the variegated shades of green interspersed with colorful flowers proved to be a balm to her spirit. Finally, she slipped into bed and enjoyed dreamless sleep.

After dressing the next morning, Leiann once again stood looking out over the gardens. July was almost here, and by the middle of the month, she'd be returning to Texas. Part of her wanted to go back home, but another part didn't want to leave Massachusetts—or her grandfather.

Did a tall man with muscular shoulders and arms play into that feeling? But wouldn't he be going back to his high-powered job?

Her cell phone's ringing snagged Leiann's attention. But where was the sound coming from? Over near the bed. She rushed toward it then homed in on the nightstand. After pulling the drawer open, she grabbed her phone before it could go to voice mail. She glanced at the screen as she flicked it open.

"Arlene, I've been wanting to talk to you." Leiann pushed a strand of hair behind her other ear and sat on the side of the bed.

"I tried to call you all day yesterday. Where were you?" Leiann could imagine the worry wrinkles in her friend's forehead.

"A lot has happened."

"It has here, too."

Leiann wondered what Arlene meant.

"Our contracts for next school year came in the mail. Mr. Malone told me you could wait until you return home to sign yours."

"That's good. I don't need another thing to think about right now."

The phone was silent for a moment before Arlene asked, "So, what happened yesterday?"

"You won't believe it when I tell you. It was like something out of a movie." Leiann chuckled and glanced into the open drawer. Her debit card had been under her phone. She guessed that Prudence must have slipped them out of her purse while Leiann was packing her bag. She picked it up and put it in her purse while she continued talking.

Leiann explained the previous day's adventure in great detail, and Arlene interrupted often with squeals and questions.

After the two friends finished their call, Leiann walked out onto the balcony. She leaned her arms on the railing and let peace settle in her spirit. How could she leave so soon after realizing how much she loved her grandfather and wanted to get to know him better? In spite of their ulterior motives, Prudence and Eric had been company for Grandfather, and Prudence had helped him run his business. Now that they were in custody, and once Gerome went back to his company, Grandfather would be alone in this huge mansion—except for the servants who lived in the cottages behind the house.

Leiann could always come back and visit him, maybe every summer. But was that enough? What if he collapsed at night? With no one living here, he might die before someone discovered him. How could she leave him alone?

A soft knock sounded on the door. Leiann crossed the room to open it. Charity stood on the other side. "Your grandfather wants to talk to you. If you aren't up to it, I can tell him you're resting."

"I'll be right down." Leiann went into the bathroom to comb her hair, spritz on her favorite light fragrance, and put on some lip gloss before heading downstairs.

Gerome waited at the bottom of the steps. "He sent for me, too."

Instead of the usual jeans and T-shirt, he wore a tan oxford shirt and brown dress slacks. The clothes set off his wavy black hair and brought out the chocolate brown of his eyes. He looked like a different man from the one she'd come to know. Somehow even more mysterious and enticing.

Something of what she was feeling must have shown in her expression, because he leaned toward her and whispered, "It's still me, Leiann. The clothes don't make the man. He defines the clothes."

Oh, he did that all right. She took a deep breath, trying to still her racing pulse. All the things she had liked about him intensified.

Gerome and Leiann started down the hall toward Herman's bedroom. The floral scent that engulfed Leiann wound its tendrils around his head. And his heart. How could he consider walking away from this woman?

As they started past the open doorway to Herman's office, his voice stopped them. "I'm in here."

Gerome placed his hand on the small of her back and followed her inside. His stepfather, sitting in his chair behind the imposing desk, looked fully recovered. *Good.*

Herman gestured toward the chairs in front of the desk, and Leiann took one of them. Gerome dropped into the other.

The Old Man leaned his elbows on the desk and steepled his fingers. "I've been thinking about some things. With Prudence gone, I need an administrative assistant." His gaze turned toward Leiann. "Would you consider coming to work for me?"

Her eyes widened, but she didn't say anything.

"I know you're a successful teacher in Texas, and I'll understand if you turn me down. But I'd love to have you close by so we can get to know each other better."

She nodded. "I'd like that. But I don't know anything about your business."

Herman gazed at Leiann. "Evidently, Jerry knows a lot about my business. I've been in contact with his boss, checking him out." He glanced at Gerome. "I hope you don't mind, but you did keep tabs on me and my business, and I'm glad."

Gerome squirmed in the chair. He wasn't sure where this conversation was going.

"Your boss gave you a glowing endorsement, Jerry." Herman clasped his hands loosely on the large blotter on his desk. "I'd like you to come to work for me, too. Together the three of us could straighten out this mess Prudence made."

A comfortable silence settled over the room. Leiann stood and walked to the French doors, where she stared out across the terrace.

Gerome stood and smiled at his stepfather. "I'd like a little time to think about this."

This could be the answer he had been seeking. A way to help Herman and pursue a relationship with Leiann.

Chapter 16

Gerome stood in the main room of the cottage, considering Herman's offer. The Old Man had told him and Leiann that they could take some time before giving him their answers. Of course, he'd have to hire someone else pretty quickly if they didn't accept.

Greg had headed back home by helicopter shortly after the confrontation at the mansion. Gerome wished his best friend were here to brainstorm with. Of course he could link up with him over the secure satellite phone, but face-to-face worked better.

When he thought about how good he was at his job, he felt pulled toward Ozbourne Global Security. But what was his heart telling him? And could he trust that?

Gerome loved Herman Johnson. And with minimal encouragement from Leiann, he could see himself married to her. He'd already fallen in love with her, and when she was in mortal danger, that love had intensified, consuming him. Of course, there was still the question of her not going to church. He'd pray that would work out, too.

He rubbed the knotted muscles in the back of his neck. A massage would feel good right now. Where was his trainer when he needed him? *Not in Massachusetts, that's for sure.*

His cell phone vibrated against his waist. He flipped it open. *Greg.* He held the phone up to his ear. "What do you want, buddy?"

"How are things there?"

"Prudence's screech brought on a spell with Herman's heart."

"Is he all right?"

"Yeah." Gerome went to the window and gazed toward the big house.

"How are you and Leiann?"

Trust his best friend to zero in on that subject. "She's fine." Gerome's comment met with a pause.

"So, what gives with the two of you? Anyone within a hundred yards could feel the sizzle."

Gerome snorted. "Your imagination is running away with you."

"I don't think so." Greg laughed. "Look, I've got to go. Lots to do, as usual. When do you think you'll be coming back?"

"I don't know. I've got some. . .loose ends to tie up."

"Okay, but I hope you make a decision soon. I could use your help."

Gerome flipped the phone closed and holstered it.

Greg had made an interesting observation. The only thing Gerome could do was pray.

❦

Leiann stood in the walk-in closet of her bedroom. She'd paced the floor for more than an hour, mulling over her grandfather's offer. Acceptance would mean a complete change in her life. These few weeks had been a pleasant interlude, but would she like living here permanently?

The chance to really get to know her grandfather—and more about her father—enticed her. But she was a good teacher, and she loved her students. And if she moved, she'd miss her friends, especially Arlene. Of course, cell phones made it affordable to talk often, and they could get together. She could fly to Texas, and maybe Arlene could fly to Massachusetts at least once a year.

Lord, I need Your direction now more than ever. She spent most of the day sequestered in her room, seeking God's answer.

Leiann needed to give Grandfather an answer tonight.

He'd asked Gerome and her to dress for dinner. Leiann looked through the clothes she'd bought the day she and Gerome spent at the mall. She held a lime green bolero against her chest. He had told her it brought out the green in her eyes. And it complemented the brown silk sundress with tiny white flowers and leaves the same shade as the matching short-sleeved jacket.

As she started down the staircase, her stomach fluttered. Her decision was made. *Lord, I need Your strength to go through with this.*

❦

Gerome reached the dining room before Leiann. He took the chair across from where she would sit. The table was set in readiness for a feast, and enticing smells came from the kitchen. When she stood in the doorway, his breath caught in his throat. She wore that dress they'd found at the mall. He remembered the fun they'd had there, even if he did complain about carrying all those packages. Looking at her now made it all worthwhile.

She'd swept her hair up and fastened it with a sparkly clip, but curly tendrils rested against the slender column of her neck. For a moment, Gerome had a vision of pushing them aside and replacing them with his lips. The palms of his hands turned clammy, and he rubbed them down the legs of his chinos before rising. He hurried around the table to pull out her chair.

Leiann floated across the carpet and sank against the tapestry seat. She looked up at him. "Thank you."

Gerome nodded and returned to his chair. "You look lovely."

A blush stole across her cheeks, intensifying her beauty. "You look pretty good yourself." A nervous laugh punctuated her sentence.

Gerome straightened his tie then bracketed the plate with his elbows, something his mother would have abhorred, and leaned toward Leiann. "We're the same people who bought a new car together, went to the mall, shopped for garden plants, and went through an FBI raid together. Just remember that."

With a sigh, she relaxed. "You're right."

Herman came into the room, and the atmosphere lifted. "Here are my two favorite people." He strode across the floor as if nothing had happened to him.

The moment he took his seat, Charity entered, followed by Mary, another maid. The two young women placed steaming bowls of creamy soup in front of each of the diners. Gerome loved Mrs. Shields's lobster bisque. This was beginning to feel like a party.

"Gerome." Herman held out a hand to each of them. "Would you bless the meal for us?"

After expressing his thanks to God, Gerome raised his head and caught Leiann looking at him. She quickly turned her attention to her grandfather, who released their hands.

"I don't want to pressure you two." Herman wiped one hand across his eyes. "But I'm anxious to know if you've come to a decision." He picked up his spoon and sampled the soup.

How like Herman to get right to the point.

❦

Leiann let her hands drop to her lap. She took a deep breath and glanced from one of the men to the other. "I've thought of nothing else." She slumped against the back of her chair. "It was a hard decision, because I'd be leaving a lot behind in Texas." *Lord, I hope I heard You right.* Her chin dropped against her chest for a moment before she raised it and sat up straight. "But I believe God wants me to accept your offer. . . if you think I can do what you need."

A bright smile spread across her grandfather's face. "You've made me very happy."

She glanced at Gerome. His magnificent smile shone like the Texas sun.

"I contacted my superior and told him he would receive my resignation tomorrow." Gerome's words lifted her spirits even more.

"Okay." Her grandfather clapped his hands. "Let's enjoy this wonderful meal Mrs. Shields prepared for us. We can discuss the particulars tomorrow."

Leiann took a sip of her iced tea and wondered what tomorrow would bring.

❦

The FBI hadn't released the office Prudence had used, so Gerome helped Leiann set up a space in a study close to Herman's. Since the computers Prudence had used were evidence, Leiann needed a new one. His training and experience with Ozbourne helped him remain on task, which was difficult in close proximity to Leiann.

For the next two days, he helped her familiarize herself with the computer. Then they started looking at the overall structure of the companies Herman owned. Each of the organizations had competent people running them, but Herman oversaw much of the ongoing work.

"I had no idea Grandfather's companies were so diversified." Leiann scanned down the document. "He has interests in computers and electronics, power companies, construction, banking, even retail. No wonder he's so wealthy."

Gerome chuckled. "We haven't even started on the financial part yet."

Later, he'd get a forensic accountant to help them follow the trail of the money Prudence had embezzled. Hopefully, since he had all of Prudence's personal files on his flash drive, they might be able to retrieve some of the funds. Getting all of it back was highly improbable. But he'd leave no stone unturned to recover all he could.

"Tomorrow's Sunday." Gerome glanced quickly at Leiann, who was studying the computer screen over his shoulder. "Would you like to go to church with me in the morning?"

"I'd like that." Leiann's words were soft.

Startled, he turned to look at her fully and noticed a light in her eyes. "I thought you'd turn me down."

"I know I haven't gone since I came to Massachusetts, but I had things I needed to deal with." She cleared her throat. "Do you think Grandfather will go with us?"

"I'm sure he'll want to if he feels up to it." Gerome closed the file. "He has been better the last few days."

Gerome had been thinking about sitting down with Herman's doctor and discussing his health. He knew the man was bound by privacy regulations, but maybe they could skirt the issues without being too specific.

Chapter 17

When Leiann walked into the sanctuary of the picturesque church with its hand-carved wooden columns and beams, a feeling of peace settled on her like a familiar cloak. She basked in the multicolored light streaming through stained-glass windows. The music lifted her heart toward heaven, reminding her of what she'd missed by staying away from fellowship with other believers. *Father, I'm sorry I turned my back on You.*

After the congregation sat down, the middle-aged pastor in a long black robe and white stole stepped up to the pulpit. "Please turn to Jeremiah 29. We'll start with verse 11."

Leiann had always carried her Bible to church. But she hadn't put it in her luggage when she came to visit Grandfather. When she went back to Texas to get the rest of her things, she'd make sure to pack it.

Gerome opened his Bible and offered to share it with her. She glanced down at the words. While the preacher read them, tears filled her eyes, blurring the letters.

" ' "I know the plans I have for you," declares the Lord, "plans to prosper you and not to harm you, plans to give you hope and a future. Then you will call upon me and come and pray to me, and I will listen to you. You will seek me and find me when you seek me with all your heart. I will be found by you," declares the Lord.' "

The preacher paused. "I'm going to stop reading right there, even though it's not the end of verse 14."

"Plans to prosper you and not to harm you." The words played over and over in her heart. God had plans for her from the very beginning. Why hadn't she turned to Him in her hurt instead of turning away? She knew better.

The pastor's words penetrated her thoughts. "Many times things go on in our lives that we don't understand. Things that at first seem to hurt us. But God. . . Remember those words: *But God.* He is always there, through every hurt, every mistake, every wrong turn. He'll work all things out for our good if we let Him."

Leiann felt as if the preacher were speaking straight to her. She knew God had laid this message on the man's heart because He knew she would be here to listen.

Thank You, Lord, for loving me so much.

On Monday afternoon, Gerome joined Leiann on the terrace for a midafternoon break. They sat in the shade, enjoying colas and a snack mix with nuts, dried fruit, and cereal squares.

"Leiann, I've been wondering about something."

She turned an expectant expression toward him.

"You haven't gone to church since you came to the estate. Why did you go yesterday?"

She took a sip of her drink then clasped her hands on the table.

By the distress in her eyes, he could tell this was hard for her. "You don't have to tell me any more than you want to."

She stared into his eyes. "Oh, but I want to. Maybe after it's all out in the open, I'll feel better about it."

He leaned back and relaxed, hoping it would help her do the same.

She told him the whole story about how her life had been turned upside down.

Gerome pulled one foot across the other knee. Things were beginning to fall into place.

She turned her gaze toward Gerome, and he saw anguish in her soul. "I blamed God for my life being out of control. For a while, I turned my back on Him."

Gerome placed his foot back on the floor and took her hands in his. "What changed that?"

Her grip tightened. "When I was at the lodge, I cried out to Him. God sent you, your friends, and the FBI to rescue me."

Warmth spread from his heart. *She thinks I'm a hero sent by God.* Maybe she was right. God had led him every step of the way. "I'm glad you've found your way back to the Lord."

The next morning, Gerome walked into the doctor's office. He'd spent a great deal of time there when he was younger. Not much about the office had changed.

"Have a seat, young man." Gerome guessed the older man would always call him that no matter how old he was. "My receptionist said you want to talk to me. What can I do for you?" The doctor leaned back in his wooden swivel chair, and it squeaked like it used to.

"I want to ask some questions about Herman." Gerome rested his forearms against his thighs. "I know you can't tell me everything, but I have serious concerns."

The man steepled his fingers. "Such as?"

"When did Herman's health start this decline?" Gerome sat up straight. "He's always been robust and sharp."

The doctor studied Gerome for a minute before answering. "I've had concerns, too, even before you came home. He started having spells of weakness a few months ago. He'd be better for a while, but the weakness would return. This happened several times before he really got frail. If I didn't know better, I'd think he was being poisoned."

Gerome stood and held out his hand to the doctor. "I've been suspecting that, too. Thank you for the information."

As he drove his car back toward the estate, Gerome pulled out his cell phone and speed-dialed Greg.

"Computer lab." Greg sounded distracted. *He must be busy.*

"I won't take much of your time, but I need a favor."

Greg laughed. "I can do you a favor as a friend, but not as part of the company. You don't work here anymore, remember?"

Gerome didn't have time for friendly banter. "Then, as a friend, find out if the FBI found any kind of poison in Prudence Smith's possessions."

"Poison?" Now he had Greg's attention.

"Yeah. I'm wondering if she was slowly poisoning Herman Johnson."

"I'll see what I can find out."

As Gerome hung up the phone, he realized there was one good side to this theory. If what he suspected was true, Herman should make a complete recovery.

❦

When he arrived in the dining room for the evening meal, Gerome heard Leiann tell Herman, "My flight leaves in three days."

Not what Gerome wanted to hear right now. He wasn't ready for her to be gone for even a short time.

Herman's brows furrowed. "So soon, my dear?"

"There are several things I need to take care of. And I have to pack up the things I want to have shipped here. I haven't even gone through Mother's belongings yet. Everything happened so fast after she died."

Herman nodded. "I understand. I've been making arrangements to have several rooms turned into a private apartment for you." Leiann's eyes widened. "I'd like your input on the decorating. Maybe we could go over the details before you leave. That way, you'll have a better idea about what to ship."

That should take several hours. Gerome planned to be with her as much as possible during the next three days.

❦

Her grandfather's words stunned Leiann. Remodel part of the mansion for her? She'd never even considered such a thing.

Grandfather glanced toward Gerome. "I also plan to expand your quarters into something larger."

110

Surprise painted Gerome's expression as he pulled out his chair and sat opposite her.

Leiann said, "I need to let the principal know I'm not coming back, and I want to do that face-to-face, not over the phone." She picked up the linen napkin beside her plate and placed it in her lap. "I already have my ticket."

"Don't worry about that, Leiann. I own a private jet." Grandfather held out his hands. "Now, let's bless the food and let Charity and Mary start serving it."

All the time she ate and carried on a three-way conversation, thoughts tumbled through Leiann's head. It would take awhile to get used to this way of life.

After he wiped his mouth on his napkin and placed it beside his plate, Grandfather patted her hand. "You've been distracted all through dinner. Anything I can help you with?"

"Not right now."

Gerome stood. "I've been thinking. I'd like to accompany Leiann to Texas."

Her grandfather's eyes lit up. "Good idea, Jerry." He turned back toward her. "So, when did you want to go?"

Leiann glanced toward Gerome then back at Herman. "Would next Monday be too soon?"

"Your wish is my command." Gerome gave her an elegant bow.

Grandfather laughed. "That boy always had a flair about him, even when he was getting into mischief."

Leiann could just imagine what kind of mischief Gerome had gotten into. She looked forward to hearing many stories of his childhood. But right now, she was glad he'd offered to accompany her home. The thought of being away from him had bothered her.

❦

Their luggage stowed in the belly of the jet, Leiann buckled her seat belt. She glanced around. Tables with leather seats around them were scattered across the cabin. "This looks more like a conference room than an airplane."

Gerome sat across a round table from her. "Herman used to travel all around the United States for business."

She leaned as far toward him as the seat belt would allow and whispered, "There's even a flight attendant in the galley."

"Probably for your benefit. He's pulling out all the stops."

After the plane leveled off in the air, the uniformed young woman came and asked them what they wanted, offering several kinds of beverages, fresh fruit, and cheeses. They told her what they'd like, and she quickly returned with their orders. "You may unbuckle your seat belts. The pilot will let you know if you need them during the flight."

Chapter 18

After landing at DFW Airport's terminal B, Leiann saw a uniformed man holding a sign with Gerome's and her names on it. Gerome grabbed her hand, and they made their way toward the man.

"Here we are." Gerome's warm baritone voice sounded like music to her ears.

Grandfather had rented a limo to take them to her house. That should draw attention in her suburban neighborhood.

They were soon ensconced in the backseat of a white Town Car headed toward her childhood home.

Leiann gazed up at Gerome. In the close confines of the car, she could see the shadow of dusky hairs barely visible under the skin of his sculpted chin. Probably because of the inky blackness of his hair. For the first time she fully realized the impact of a five o'clock shadow.

❦

"Tell me about your hometown." Gerome tried to make his tone light.

Leiann chuckled. "There's not much to tell. It's just a typical small Texas town. High school football, church activities, shopping at the mall or WalMart."

He looked out the window. "How soon do we leave this busy freeway behind?"

"We don't. Hurst is in the middle of the metroplex." The melody of her laughter filled the car.

He could get used to hearing that laugh.

"Actually, we're not far from my house." Her gaze roamed over the passing scenery as if she were memorizing it.

He guessed she would need to return to her roots fairly often. He'd make sure it happened for her.

Gerome put his arm around her. "Will it be hard to return to an empty house?"

Her startled gaze met his. "Oh, the house won't be empty. My best friend will be waiting for us."

Gerome looked forward to meeting Leiann's friend.

When the car stopped against the curb, the door of the house flew open and a young woman sprinted down the sidewalk. She was taller and more athletic than Leiann, with a riot of red corkscrew curls. Gerome opened the door, stepped out, and reached back for Leiann's hand.

She grabbed hold and scrambled out. The two women shrieked and hugged, dancing around and talking at the same time. Gerome stood to the side, smiling.

When they broke apart, the taller woman quickly assessed him. "So you're Leiann's hero." She gave him a quick hug. "Thank you for saving her."

Gerome had never experienced such a welcome. So Leiann had called him a hero to her best friend. Interesting.

🙟

Leiann felt a blush climb her cheeks. Why did Arlene have to blurt out those words? What in the world would Gerome think? "I want you to meet Arlene Jamison, my best friend since first grade. Arlene, this is Gerome Mays."

The handshake that followed seemed funny to her, since Arlene had already given him a hug.

Gerome smiled at Arlene. "It's nice to meet one of Leiann's friends."

Arlene returned his smile. "I've been wanting to meet you, too."

Leiann gave Arlene a pointed glance. "Let's go into the house." She started up the walk then turned back to the driver. "Thank you."

He tipped his hat. "My pleasure, ma'am."

Gerome helped the man get the bags out of the trunk of the car, gave him a tip, and then waved him off. Leiann watched, fascinated by the way Gerome always seemed to be in command of any situation.

Arlene linked their arms and leaned close as they walked to the door. "You didn't tell me how handsome he is."

Leiann hoped he couldn't hear the loud whisper. "Yes, he is good-looking."

"So, how long will y'all be here?" Arlene pulled open the storm door, and they entered the house.

"Only long enough to do what we have to." Leiann stepped into the foyer. Memories of the day the will was read assailed her. But now she knew who she really was. The person God created her to be, no matter what circumstances had occurred in her life.

When they moved into the den, Gerome came through the front door. "So, where can I get a room close by?"

"There are a couple of hotels a few blocks away." Leiann sat on the edge of the hearth.

"Don't waste your money," Arlene said. "I'll be staying here, so you can, too."

His eyes sought out Leiann's, and she nodded.

"All right. Where do I put these bags?"

Leiann glanced down the hallway. "My room is on this side of the house. Why don't you take the master bedroom? It's that way."

"Thanks." Gerome headed across the den, pulling his bag behind him.

After they unpacked, Leiann changed into cutoffs and a T-shirt. Might as well be comfortable while they went through things.

🍂

Gerome liked the homey atmosphere of the bedroom, with windows spread across the rear wall of the house. He opened the drapes, letting in the light. Large trees shaded the backyard and kept the Texas sun from baking the room. After shrugging into jeans and a polo shirt, he started back toward the large room where he'd last seen the women.

Arlene stood by the sink in the kitchen, arranging things on a tray. "I thought y'all might like a little something to eat. I made a pitcher of iced tea, too." She glanced up at him. "Do you like iced tea?" Her Southern drawl sounded more pronounced than Leiann's.

He nodded. "I always drink a lot of it in the summer when I'm in Texas."

She led the way to the den. After placing the tray on a low table in front of a comfortably worn, overstuffed couch, she handed him a tall, frosty glass.

Leiann came in from the hall. "Arlene, that looks wonderful."

So do you. The words came unbidden to his mind. He'd never seen her dressed this casually.

"My throat feels like a west Texas desert." When Leiann took a long drink, his eyes were drawn to her long, slender neck.

With her hair pulled up on top of her head and fastened with one of those squiggly things, she looked like a teenager.

Leiann turned to him. "I want to get right to work."

He nodded. "Okay. What do you want me to do?"

"I could use some help packing up all my stuff and Mother's things. I want to get them out of Arlene's way. I told her she can live here rent free at least for the next school year."

Although she didn't have to explain anything to him, he was glad she kept him in the loop.

🍂

After a few hours of packing, Leiann stood and stretched her shoulders. She hadn't done this much manual labor in a long time, but it felt good to have so much of the work behind her. "Is anyone getting hungry?"

Gerome glanced at his watch. "Is it dinnertime already?"

Arlene laughed. "You're in Texas now, so you'll have to use the lingo. We have dinner at noon and supper at night."

He smiled. "Got it."

"Where do we want to go for supper?" Leiann stopped to think. "How about Abuelo's? I've been missing their enchiladas."

"Sorry, no can do." Arlene shook her head. "I've got a committee meeting in an hour. I'll just grab something on the way."

Leiann turned to Gerome. "How about you?"

"Sure. I like Mexican food."

Something else she didn't know about him. Leiann wished she knew more about his likes and dislikes. Everything about him interested her—too much. She wasn't sure he felt the same way about her.

After they changed clothes, Leiann drove her Kia the few short blocks to the restaurant. Several people clustered near the entrance. She knew how popular this place was, but it was Monday. She hadn't expected a long wait.

Gerome approached the hostess stand. "Mays, a party of two." He held up two fingers.

The petite blond smiled up at him, curly hair falling onto her shoulders. "You're in luck, sir. All these other parties are waiting for large tables. We have a table for two beside the fountain if that's all right."

He nodded. While the woman led the way, Gerome's hand rested on the small of Leiann's back. Every woman in the room seemed to give him an appreciative glance. The man had a commanding presence.

"What do you recommend?" Gerome peered at her over the top of the large leather-bound menu.

"I haven't eaten anything here that wasn't good. One of my favorites is the avocado enchilada. I'm having that. You might try one of the combo platters. That way you can taste a variety of things."

As they enjoyed their meal, they learned more about each other and their growing-up years. Gerome even answered a few questions about his job with the security company without revealing anything confidential.

Gerome insisted that the waiter give him the check. To Leiann, that made this feel like a date.

They stepped out into the warm Texas evening. Blossoms in the courtyard and flower beds outside the walls gave a heady fragrance to the still air.

"May I drive back to the house?" Gerome's soft words caressed her.

This makes it feel even more like a date. She dug in her tiny purse and pulled out the keys, then dropped them into his outstretched palm. They stepped into the shadowy darkness on the side of the building where she'd parked.

Her heel caught in a crack of the sidewalk, and she pitched forward. Gerome's arms slid around her, and he pulled her close to his chest. Breathless, she glanced up at the shaded planes of his sculptured cheeks. His eyes burned bright. Mesmerized, she watched his face descend toward hers.

His lips settled gently on hers, almost like the touch of a butterfly's wings. Then they lifted and hovered, waiting for her response. When she didn't pull away, they settled more firmly. Leiann had only been kissed a couple of times in high school. Those kisses were nothing like this. So gentle, giving, and all-consuming.

She returned the caress, pouring all her longings into it. Everything else faded away. This moment in time was a fusing of two hearts. She wanted it to go on forever.

෯

Gerome finally ended the kiss and urged her closer to his chest. He loved this woman. *Lord, thank You for showing me.* Their hearts beat in rhythm. He rested his chin on the top of her head, breathing in the scent that would always be Leiann. His world had made a paradigm shift. For the first time in his life, he wanted to settle down. Be a husband to this woman. Have children with her.

Leiann raised her head from his chest, but she kept her arms around his waist. "We're standing out here in public right next to Hurst City Hall."

He laughed. "We're in the shadows, and I don't think anyone is looking anyway." Holding her felt so good, he didn't want to release her.

"Maybe we should go home." Her whisper mingled with the gentle breeze that rustled the leaves of the shrubbery beside the restaurant.

Home. Anywhere with this woman would be home to him. "Okay."

While they walked the few feet to the car, he kept one arm around her. One of hers remained along his waist. In the vehicle, they talked about everything and nothing, but they didn't discuss the kiss and what it would mean to them.

When they drove into the driveway, Gerome was glad to see that Arlene hadn't returned from her meeting. He wanted to talk with Leiann face-to-face.

After they went into the house, Leiann stood in the middle of the den, staring up at him. "Would you like a soda or some coffee or something?"

Gerome was glad they were a few feet apart. With her too close, he couldn't think straight. "No, thanks. Leiann, I have something to talk to you about."

Her eyes widened slightly, and she nodded.

"I have to tell you what I'm feeling."

She clasped her hands and waited, her sense of expectancy a tangible thing.

He ran a hand across the back of his neck. "I've never done this before."

A smile crept over her lips.

"Leiann, I've prayed about this, and I believe God brought us together."

Her smile widened.

"What I'm trying to say is that I love you and want to marry you. . .if you'll have me."

She walked toward him then raised her arms and slid them around his neck, pulling his head down. "Yes." She whispered the word before she wove her fingers through his curls and kissed him. That powerful kiss spoke her love to his heart.

Epilogue

The day after Thanksgiving

Leiann looked out the French doors of her apartment in the mansion. Today was her wedding day.

So much had happened since that day in Texas when Gerome proposed. They had worked together, worshipped together, spent time with her grandfather, explored most of the historical sites she wanted to see in her new home state, spent time at the Cape—even harvested the crop with Gerome's cousins on the Sanderford cranberry farm off Cranberry Highway.

The FBI had found an old bottle of insect poison containing arsenic hidden in the closet of Prudence's room. Gerome told Leiann he was convinced the woman was giving minute amounts of it to her grandfather to weaken him. His health had improved tremendously since Prudence had been arrested. He was like a different man now. Strong, robust, astute.

Arlene had helped her plan her wedding. She'd spent the first week in August at the estate. Grandfather had flown Arlene to Massachusetts several weekends after that.

Leiann's heart overflowed with love for her husband-to-be, but even more for her Father God. *Lord, I'm so glad You took care of me when I didn't even know You were doing it. Thank You for working things out so I could meet Gerome. . .and Grandfather.*

"It's time to go." Arlene poked her head through the bedroom doorway.

Today her exuberant curls were controlled in a figure-eight chignon. Only a few tendrils escaped. Maybe one of Gerome's buddies from Ozbourne Global Security would recognize what a prize Arlene would be. Leiann had noticed a couple of them watching her covertly during the elaborate rehearsal dinner last night.

"Okay." She picked up her train and held it over one arm so she could turn around in the creamy silk gown covered with lace and pearls.

Arlene inspected Leiann and adjusted the flower-bedecked tiara that held her waist-length veil. Then she led the way to the top of the double staircase in the two-story foyer. Tulle and orchids draped the banister on both sides.

"Is everyone here?" she whispered.

"Yes, they're all seated." Arlene giggled. "Who would ever have guessed the room could hold so many chairs?"

The small orchestral ensemble playing in the sitting room off the foyer moved from prewedding music to the wedding march. Leiann gulped a deep breath. Arlene removed the train from Leiann's arm and arranged it behind her on the carpet and handed her the large orchid bouquet. Then Arlene started slowly descending the staircase. Finally, it was time for Leiann to move forward.

When she came into view, people turned to watch her progress. *Lord, please keep me from stumbling.* She took her first step down. Then she raised her eyes toward the group standing by the front door. Their pastor, Grandfather, Arlene... Gerome. When her gaze connected with his, her heart leaped. The smile that lit his face looked like sunshine drawing her toward its warmth.

Thank You, Lord, for making me who I am. And who I'm soon going to be: Mrs. Gerome Mays.

LENA NELSON DOOLEY

Lena is an author, editor, and speaker. *Cranberry Hearts* is her 21st book release. A full-time writer, she is the president of DFW Ready Writers, the local Dallas-Fort Worth chapter of American Christian Fiction Writers. She has also hosted a critique group in her home for over 20 years. Several of the writers she's mentored have become published authors, too.

Lena lives with the love of her life in North Texas. They enjoy traveling and spending time with family and friends. They're active members of their church, where Lena serves in the bookstore, on the Altar Ministry team, and as a volunteer for the Care ministry and Global Ministries.

The Dooley family includes two daughters, their spouses, two granddaughters, two grandsons, and a great-grandson.

You can find Lena at several places on the Internet: lenanelsondooley.com, lenanelsondooley.blogspot.com, and her monthly newsletter is at lenanelsondooleynewsletter.blogspot.com. You can also visit her on Shoutlife, Facebook, and Twitter.

A MATTER OF TRUST

Lisa Harris

Dedication

To DiAnn Mills, for taking me under her wing as a newbie writer.

To my husband who graciously reads every one of my manuscripts and encourages me to persevere in this ministry.

And for Beth and Lena for coming along on this adventure with me.

Chapter 1

Ty Lawrence was running out of time. He drummed his fingers against the top of his polished mahogany desk that sat near the window of his office and tried to calm his staggered breathing.

One more minute, Lord. That's all I need.

The computer whirred as it copied the files onto his flash drive. He might not have evidence to hand over to the police for an actual conviction, but he did have enough confidential files at his apartment to keep a government official busy for weeks if Abbott Financial Services was ever indicted. These last files, thanks to an unanticipated inside tip and his password, were the best corroboration he'd found so far in linking the CEO, Richard Abbott, to fraud.

And thirty years behind bars if Ty had his way.

Forty-five seconds left.

Ty stuck a dirty coffee mug and a half-eaten bag of peanuts from his desk drawer into the cardboard box he'd brought from home. The corner office with windows overlooking the city, the company Jag, and a yearly bonus that could pay off the debt of a small, third world country hadn't been enough enticement to stay in the game. Not since the morning he'd awakened with a hangover and the front page of the *Boston Times* in his lap with pictures of five executives from Orlando arrested for fraud and conspiracy charges.

It was a sobering thought, requiring little imagination to realize that was where he was headed if he didn't get out before it was too late. The unexpected letter from an old friend offering him a job in Farrington, Massachusetts, had cinched the deal. Never mind the fact that he'd make a third of what he made now, drive his old car, and work from an office smaller than his bedroom closet. He'd have a clean conscience, which was worth more than Richard Abbott could ever give him.

Ty glanced at the computer screen. Twenty seconds. His head throbbed. Once Abbott received the resignation letter with his morning correspondence, security would be sent up to escort Ty off the property.

Voices buzzed in the hallway, growing louder as they neared his office. Five seconds...

His office door slammed against the back wall as his boss crossed the threshold. Ty looked up from the potted plant he was setting in the cardboard box.

"Good morning, Mr. Abbott."

"What is this, Lawrence?" Abbott's face reddened as he held up the resignation letter Ty had composed the night before on company letterhead.

An expensive, pinstriped suit hung across the older man's broad shoulders and thick waist, but with his late-night drinking, high cholesterol, and added stress that came with trying to defraud a company out of millions, the man would be lucky to live past sixty-five.

"I'm guessing you found my resignation letter?" Ty worked to keep his voice calm and prayed for wisdom.

"I want an explanation." Abbott slammed his fist against the desk and let the letter sail across the top. "I've spent three years grooming you for a place on our management team, and you have the gall to walk out of here with nothing more than a paragraph of explanation?"

"I'm moving to Farrington." Ty spoke his well-rehearsed lines out loud. It was all the truth. He had just decided to leave out the part that he preferred not to be involved in the company's alleged illegal activities or the fact he was probably avoiding an inevitable arrest by not sticking around and becoming the chief financial officer. "A friend of mine just offered me a job with Farrington Cranberry Company, and I realized it was time to make a change. I'm not cut out for this anymore."

The veins in Abbott's neck began to bulge. "It was because of your father I gave you this job."

Ty dipped his head. "If he were here right now, I'm sure he'd voice his appreciation for all you've done for me."

"You're telling me you plan to up and leave all of this for some underpaid job in some. . .run-of-the-mill cranberry co-op?"

"Granted, the money's not as good, but the stress will be minimal, and I'll have a friend's boat to use on the weekends."

"You've got accounts to deal with. Clients to placate. You can't leave, Lawrence."

Ty slid a framed picture of the seaside off the wall and set it on the desk beside the box, each move calculated and precise. To Richard Abbott, Ty must appear to be another burnt-out employee needing a slower pace of life before a heart attack took his last ounce of breath.

"I've already gone over everything with Reed." The diploma from Stanford came off the wall next. "The Caldwell account closed last Friday, and that's the main account I've been working on for six months. I skipped the two weeks' notice, figuring once I turned in my resignation you'd throw me out anyway. I'm just making it easier for you."

"Easier? I. . ." Abbott gritted his teeth.

He'd never seen his boss speechless before.

Ty forced a relaxed smile. "I'm tired, sir. Tired of the rat race, the competition, and the sleepless nights. I guess I'm just not cut out for this."

"You ungrateful—"

"No, Mr. Abbott." Ty held up a hand. "Trust me when I say I'm grateful for everything you taught me."

When it came to legal issues and taxes, Abbott knew every nuance of the law. The fact that the man was a criminal didn't obliterate his brilliant mentoring skills.

Abbott spun around on his Italian loafers, knocking over a chair with his hand in the process. "Maurice, search him before he leaves. If you find as much as a thumbtack in his possession that belongs to me, have him arrested."

Maurice appeared from behind his boss, 250 pounds of solid muscle in a coat and tie that were a size too small. Ty never had been sure what the forty-something-year-old did at the company, but at the moment it didn't matter. The bald man's lip twitched as he strode across the carpeted room and began digging through the cardboard box, dumping out the peanuts and spilling dirt from the plant across the desk. Next he turned to face Ty with a grin on his face that made Ty's stomach clench. Even four times a week at the company gym upstairs couldn't prepare him for what this man could do if provoked.

What was I thinking?

"Spread your legs and raise your arms."

Maurice patted down Ty's arms and chest. The flash drive burned a hole in his left sock where he'd stashed it.

It's time for a miracle, Lord.

Maurice frisked his right leg. Ty knew Abbott's threat of arrest was far from empty. On hiring, employees were required to sign all but their lives away. And Abbott knew every trick in the book to cover his backside when it came to hiring and firing whom he pleased.

Maurice started on his left leg. Ty's heart pounded in his chest. What had he been thinking when he planned to take the files out of the building with him?

"Mr. Lawrence?" Penny, his secretary for the past three years, knocked on the door.

Maurice looked up. Ty took advantage of the distraction and quickly moved behind his desk to pick up his box and framed pictures. "What is it, Penny?"

"I was trying to transfer a call through to you, but your phone's not working."

No doubt his password had already been deactivated as well.

"Reed will be taking my calls from now on, Penny. I've just resigned."

"Resigned?"

He wasn't surprised at the confused look she flashed him as he slid past her, but neither was he about to wait until Maurice realized he hadn't finished his job. With all that remained of his life at Abbott Financial Services in his hands, Ty hurried down the stairwell, expecting any moment to hear someone shout out his name. The lobby loomed before him with its tiled floor and expensive artwork hanging on the wall. Another dozen steps and he'd be out the front door.

A vision of silky auburn hair and milk-chocolate brown eyes filled his mind as he slipped through the glass doors of the building into the morning sunlight. He might be leaving behind a six-figure salary, but there was one benefit of moving to Farrington. . .Kayla Marceilo. Kayla was not only his ex-fiancée, but also the only woman he'd ever loved. The only woman he still loved. Losing her had been the most foolish thing he'd let happen, and getting her back was likely going to prove to be more complicated than indicting Richard Abbott in a court of law. Somehow he would have to win her trust and prove to her that turning his life around hadn't been just another one of his acts.

Ty glanced behind his shoulder. He saw no sign of Maurice or Abbott chasing after him. In twenty-four hours he planned to be sipping iced tea and listening to the hum of farmers mowing the banks of the cranberry bogs. And he had no intention of ever looking back.

♡

Kayla Marceilo threw off her shoes and sank into the taupe-colored couch she'd bought at an estate auction last month. Soft strains of Vivaldi filled her two-bedroom apartment as she closed her eyes, relaxing for the first time all day. Moments like these made her grateful she'd moved away from Boston's bustling suburbs to the quiet of Farrington. She loved the winding roads of the countryside filled with apple orchards, quiet woodlands, and the bright red cranberry bogs. Working in her mother's catering business had given her a fresh start, allowing her to leave behind certain ghosts from the past.

The phone rang beside her. Kayla opened her eyes and sighed, wishing she'd remembered to turn off the ringer. She'd spent the past ten hours on her feet, baking seafood cream puffs and petite crab cakes, along with an assortment of other dishes for Sarah Jamison's full buffet wedding reception. Now she wanted nothing more than to sleep for the next week. The answering machine could pick it up. She closed her eyes again then remembered the answering machine had stopped working three days ago and she hadn't had time to replace it.

She answered on the fifth ring. "Hello?"

"Kayla. It's. . .Ty."

The sound of his familiar voice sent a ripple of goose bumps across her skin. She sat up straight. "Ty, it's been a long time." *Twelve months to be exact.*

"Yes, it has. How are you?"

"I'm good." *Extremely good with you out of my life.*

"How is the catering business?"

Kayla hesitated. Most people assumed she had moved back to her home-town a year ago to work in her mother's catering company. The truth was she left Boston to forget about the man she loved. Had loved, she corrected herself.

She cleared her throat and tried to corral her runaway heartbeat. "We manage to stay pretty busy."

"I remember what a great cook you were. I sure could go for a big helping of some of your cream carmel."

"Crème Caramel." Kayla corrected his French, laughing for an instant at his horrible accent before stopping herself. She had to be careful. Ty Lawrence had a way of charming his way into the stickiest of situations. "Where are you?"

"I'm here in Farrington. That's what I called to talk to you about."

"You're in town?" Kayla's pulse raced at the thought of him so near. While she never regretted her decision to call off their wedding, the truth remained that no one had ever affected her the way Ty had. From his charming smile, striking looks, and stirring kisses—at one time he had been her knight in shining armor. Until she'd found out who he really was: a black knight in disguise.

"I know this is a bit awkward." Ty's voice sounded strained. "But I really need to talk to you. . .in person."

"I don't know." The sound of his voice made her lose all sense of reality. She'd left Boston to start a new life without him, something she'd done quite well for the past twelve months. The last thing she wanted was him stirring up buried emotions that were better left to rest. "I don't think that would be wise."

"Please, Kayla. I promise I won't put any pressure on our getting back together. That's not why I want to see you."

"Really?" She didn't believe him.

"I won't deny I still have feelings for you, but I just want to talk. That's it. I have some things I need to tell you."

Kayla bit her lip, knowing she should hang up the phone. She had no reason to trust him. From the beginning of their relationship she'd been naive not to see him, with his Italian suits and expensive gifts, as nothing more than a liar and a manipulator. What made today any different? Her mother had always told her people never really changed, and she believed it.

"Please, Kayla. I promise I won't put any pressure on you."

"All right." She squeezed her eyes shut and prayed she wasn't making a mistake. *Just this one time.* Then she would never see him again.

"I know it's short notice, but what about tomorrow night?"

Thursday. Kayla mentally checked her calendar. She didn't have to be at tomorrow night's catering event, a surprise fiftieth birthday party for Raymond Bridges. Besides, the sooner she saw him, the sooner she could put him out of her mind. "Tomorrow night will be fine."

"Then how about we eat at the country club?"

She hesitated. Another fancy restaurant. Ty knew enough about Farrington to know the Blue Moon was a well-established restaurant that catered to the wealthy in the area. No, Ty had not changed at all. He would only choose the best. This time, though, she knew the real Ty, and she would be ready.

"Come on," he said. "I know how much you love looking over the city lights at night. The view can't be beat, not to mention the food."

"I'll meet you there at seven."

She hung up the phone, shaking inside. If just the sound of his voice could do that, what would she do sitting across the table from him?

Kayla walked to the front closet, opened the door, and rummaged through a box in the back corner until she found the crystal frame that held their engagement picture. She had no idea why she'd even kept the photo. Perhaps a reminder never to make the same mistake again. She ran a finger across Ty's face and wondered how she could have been so wrong about someone. At least she had found out before the wedding and not after.

She would have to be strong tomorrow night. The last thing she needed was to lose her resolve toward this handsome man who had once swept her off her feet before shattering her heart into a million pieces.

☙

Ty set down the phone in his newly rented apartment and took a deep breath. For one usually in control, his legs felt as if they were about to melt into the tan carpet beneath him. He hadn't expected the mere sound of her voice to have that effect on him, but on the other hand, no woman had ever affected him like Kayla. From the first day they met there had been something irresistible about her. Her laugh, her sense of humor, those dark dreamy eyes, and especially her wide smile that never failed to take his breath away.

Ty glanced around the living room cluttered with boxes, his favorite brown leather recliner, a matching sofa, and a few framed prints that lay against the stark white wall. For a moment he missed his apartment in Boston overlooking the bay. This apartment boasted a view of the parking lot and an all-night diner.

Walking to the fireplace, he picked up the framed engagement picture that sat alone on the mantel. For the photo session Kayla had insisted he wear jeans, a far cry from his usual office attire. She'd been right. They seemed totally relaxed in the picture.

And in love.

"Ty Lawrence, you look stunning." Kayla had fumbled with the collar of his forest-green shirt before the photographer snapped the picture in the park a block from his Boston office.

He'd grabbed her hands and wrapped them around his waist. A strand of her reddish-brown hair, shimmering in the late afternoon sunlight, tickled his nose. "You're the one who's beautiful. I don't deserve you."

He hadn't then. But now things had changed. He'd changed. Maybe he still didn't deserve her, but there was one thing he did know. Life without Kayla wasn't the way he wanted to spend it. She was the missing piece in his heart.

He put the framed photo back on the mantel, longing for the warmth of her touch and the feel of her hand in his. He'd have to be careful tomorrow night. It would never do for him to come across too strong and scare her off. But the truth remained. He still loved her and wanted to marry her. There would never be anyone else for him. If only he could convince Kayla of that.

๛

Richard Abbott leaned back in his leather office chair and struggled to loosen his designer tie. How had it come to this? Thirty-five years ago he'd been one of hundreds of ambitious Yale graduates with an empty bank account and a suitcase of dreams. Today he was the CEO of a Fortune 500 company. The *Wall Street Journal, Boston Globe,* and even the *New York Times* had declared him one of America's leading businessmen.

Now he faced the threat of indictment, while questions were being whispered throughout office cubicles. He might have $175 million hidden in off-shore accounts, but if something didn't happen quickly, his name was about to be trampled across Wall Street as the latest executive to have let the lure of money ruin him. He might deserve prison time, but it wasn't going to happen if he could help it. Ty Lawrence flashed in his mind. If he went down, he wasn't going down by himself.

Chapter 2

This was a mistake." Kayla twirled around in front of the full-length mirror and studied the sixth outfit she'd tried on in the past thirty minutes. Normally she loved the semiformal, black-and-white dress, but today it looked too...too inviting. An impression she certainly couldn't leave. How could she ever have agreed to see him again?

She turned to her best friend, Jenny, who sat cross-legged on Kayla's quilt-covered bed for moral support. "So what do you think?"

Jenny flipped one of her bobbed, dark-brown tresses behind her ear and cocked her head. "About the dress or your date with Ty?"

Kayla shot a pointed look, then frowned. This wasn't a date; it was simply a casual get-together. "Both, I suppose."

"The dress looks beautiful. It's the other part of the equation that's incorrect in my opinion."

Kayla fell back on the bed and blew out a sharp breath of air. "You sound like a mathematician."

"I am a mathematician."

Kayla laughed. "Then you sound like my mother."

Her mother's reaction to Ty's dinner invitation had been received about as well as a case of the measles. This was the one disadvantage of living five minutes from her mother's house in a small town where everyone assumed everyone else's business was their own. In Boston, where Sam Peterson ate lunch Sunday after church or who was visiting the Bakers for the Memorial Day weekend wasn't printed in the *Boston Globe*. No doubt tomorrow's leading story of the *Farrington Chronicle* would be a play-by-play recap of her date with Ty. She could see the headlines now: OLD FLAME STIRS UP TROUBLE FOR EX-FIANCÉE. Or if nothing else, stirs up unwanted emotions that were better left buried and forgotten.

No doubt about it. Ty Lawrence spelled trouble. All seventy-four inches of his muscular frame... Kayla groaned. If just the thought of his pale blue eyes and square jawline made her pulse race, how was she going to handle him sitting across from her at an intimate table for two?

"Kayla?"

Kayla jerked her head up and caught her friend's gaze. "Sorry. I was just..."

Just what? Daydreaming about the one man she'd vowed to forget?

Jenny frowned. "You need to focus, Kayla, or he's going to have you wrapped around his little finger by the end of the evening."

"Never."

Jenny began pacing the beige carpet of Kayla's bedroom, her finger tapping the bottom of her chin. "Think of it this way. You're a top military officer—make that a Navy Seal—and you're going in to face the enemy. You have something he wants—"

"Something he wants?" Kayla's eyes widened.

Jenny stopped in front of the window and quirked her left eyebrow. "He wants you back, doesn't he?"

"I don't know that. He told me he just wanted to talk—"

"And you believed him?" Jenny shook her head. "Please, honey. Guys don't call up their ex-girlfriends just because they want to gossip like a group of old ladies sitting around a pile of quilting squares. Either he's getting married, or he's got a plan to win you back."

"Married?" She hadn't thought of that scenario.

"Forget the married picture for now. What are you going to do if he makes a move?"

"Don't you think you're taking things a bit too far?" Kayla fiddled with the top button of the dress. Any anxiety that had been swirling in her stomach had just escalated a notch or two due to Jenny's incessant suspicions. Which she had to admit had merit. Dealing with Ty required the precision of a surgeon paired with the intuitive skills of an undercover agent.

Jenny obviously didn't agree with her assessment of taking things too far. "You didn't answer my question."

"It's just dinner. What could happen?"

"This is serious."

Kayla blew out a sharp breath. "So what do I wear?"

"The purple dress. It's pretty while extra conservative. It will make him think about how much he lost without giving him the impression you're ready to restart your relationship with him."

Kayla jumped off the bed and pulled the dress from the pile. "Are you sure?"

Jenny let out a short breath. "What's up with you? I might be the mathematician, but you're normally the decisive one."

Decisive until Ty had somehow managed to step back into her life. He'd always left her emotions fluctuating wider than a barometer in a storm. "I'm just nervous."

"And I suppose I'm not helping." A sympathetic grin flashed across Jenny's face. "Listen—you're right. It's just dinner. All you need to remember is that when you're finished you have to tell him you don't ever want to see him again. Now get moving. You have to leave, or you're going to be late. Put on that purple dress."

Kayla held the dress in front of her and cocked her head. "First, remind me again why I broke things off with the most gorgeous guy I've ever known. Handsome, considerate, funny—"

"A workaholic, a manipulator, and a liar." Jenny jumped off the bed and rested her hands on Kayla's shoulders. "Listen, honey. You did what you knew was right, and nothing has changed since you gave him back your ring."

Kayla quickly put on the other dress, her heart still heavy with the reminder of what might have been between them if things had been different. "Why couldn't he have been a Christian? Why did he have to lie to me about that?"

"It will all be over before you know it." Jenny handed Kayla a lavender beaded necklace from her dresser to go with the outfit. "Let him say whatever it is he has to say; then you can close that chapter of your life forever. One day you'll find someone ten times better than Ty. Trust me."

Kayla slipped on the earrings and sighed. "How come your life is so simple and mine's so complicated?"

Jenny lowered her glance. "My life is simple?"

"You know what I mean." Kayla turned around and caught her gaze. "You met Greg and fell in love, and before you know it he'll be asking you to marry him."

Kayla stood once more in front of the mirror. Jenny had been right. The outfit was perfect. The simple, sleeveless dress almost reached her ankles, but most important it was extremely modest. No need to give him any ideas and make him think she was reconsidering their relationship.

Besides, she didn't believe in happily ever after anymore. Let Romeo have his Juliet, and Anthony, his Cleopatra. She ran a successful catering business with her mom, had great friends and a wonderful church home—there simply wasn't room for Ty in her life again.

Then why did the thought of seeing him make her knees weak and her palms sweat?

♡

Kayla prayed the entire drive through the small town, down the narrow country road toward the club and up its long, meandering drive. When she found a parking spot outside that overlooked the town below, she said another prayer for added strength. *Keep this line open, Lord. I'm going to need You tonight.*

Acres of velvety green lawns and towering pines surrounded the renovated nineteenth-century farmhouse that loomed before her. She walked past rows of flowers toward the front porch where violin music drifted outside, lending an aura of romance to the evening.

A subject that should have been the last thing on her mind tonight.

She brushed the back of her head with her fingers and tried to calm the nervous flutter in her stomach. Jenny had helped her put up her shoulder-length hair, leaving a few loose wisps around her face to soften the look. Of course it really didn't matter what she looked like. She'd listen to what he had to say, and that would be the end of it.

Kayla started up the wide steps then turned around slowly when she heard a familiar voice call her name. Dressed in khaki slacks and a matching button-down shirt, Ty walked toward her. She drew in a sharp breath.

"If I couldn't drive you here, the least I can do is escort you up to the restaurant, Kayla." He said her name like a familiar caress. Her stomach clenched. "You look beautiful. I always loved that dress. You wore it when you met my mom and dad for the first time."

"I. . .thank you." Kayla looked down at the dress. How could she have forgotten something important like that? She should have worn her new navy pantsuit. It had no history of the two of them together.

"You're not wearing a tie." In the past Ty had rarely shed his coat and tie, because there were few times when he hadn't been working.

"I told you a few things had changed." He stuck his hands in his pockets—a nervous habit she remembered from their two years together. Apparently this evening was going to be as nerve-wracking for him as it was for her.

"Shall we go inside?"

Kayla nodded, taking a second peek at his profile. He looked stunning. Dark hair framed a perfectly proportioned face; from the cleft in his chin to the small scar above his left brow to his blue eyes. They were all so. . .familiar. For a slight second, when he caught her glance, she wanted him to take her in his arms and kiss her.

But that was something she could never do.

"Are you all right?" Ty touched her elbow for a brief second, sending a tremor up her arm.

"Yes." She stammered, disturbed by the lack of control she had over her emotions. "I'm fine."

Ty stopped at the top of the stairs. "Not having second thoughts about seeing me, are you?"

Kayla caught the strain in his voice. "Of course not."

She breathed in deeply and caught a whiff of his cologne. The same cologne she bought him for his thirtieth birthday. Once she had told him it made him irresistible. But not anymore.

Inside the formal entry Kayla glanced toward the Blue Moon's candlelit tables and guests in their starched attire. Ty had always taken her to the finest restaurants, a detail she'd never felt entirely comfortable with. Her family had always preferred a trip to the beach and a plate of soft-shelled crabs.

"Wait." Ty reached for her arm but pulled back before touching her. "I thought we might try the smaller, more informal dining area."

Kayla looked at him with wide eyes.

"You don't mind, do you?" Ty said quickly. "From what I hear, the view is just as stunning, and I thought you might like the casual atmosphere better."

"That's fine," Kayla managed to get out. The Ty she knew would have taken her to the finer restaurant to impress her. On the other hand, he had always been good at portraying the image he wanted, and maybe this was just an act. She couldn't—wouldn't—let herself forget who he really was.

❧

Ty guided Kayla toward the smaller restaurant, afraid that her nearness was enough to make him lose his resolve to keep his distance. From the moment he first saw her, it had taken every ounce of determination he could muster to stop himself from pulling her into his arms and kissing her.

After a year he hadn't forgotten the subtle beauty of her face. But that was not why he had asked to see her tonight. He worked to control his emotions. He could only pray she would accept the one request he had for her tonight. They followed the hostess to an empty table next to the glass walls that overlooked the countryside and, in the distance, the town of Farrington.

"Well, here we are." Ty sat down across from her and pulled his chair toward the table, before clearing his throat. "I hope you don't mind hamburgers and fries."

"Not at all. You were right. The view is fabulous." Kayla bit the edge of her lip. He hated seeing her so uncomfortable, especially knowing he was the reason behind her uneasiness tonight.

"I want to hear all about your business." He'd decided to start off by keeping the conversation light. "And whatever else is going on in your life."

He caught her glance, and she quickly held up the menu to study it, while tapping her fingers on the table. The waiter interrupted, giving them a moment of reprieve, and took their orders of hamburger and fries.

"Business is good," Kayla said after they were alone again. "We do some birthdays, retirement parties, weddings, and anniversary dinners, but our main thrust is business dinners for local clients."

"Sounds like you've done well." He wasn't surprised at all. Kayla had always excelled in whatever she did, but as a culinary expert, she was one of the best. He'd enjoyed more than one home-cooked meal by her while they were together, most of the time while she experimented with different recipes.

Desserts were her specialty. Cheesecake, tortes, sponge cakes, and pies—it was amazing he'd managed to stay in shape while dating her. She'd always had something new for him to try.

"Mom's the one who has really built up the business." She pushed a loose strand of ginger-colored hair behind her ear.

"What's your role?"

Kayla laughed, and his heart melted at her smile. "You name it—I do it. I'm in charge of planning the menus with the clients, but I also do a lot of the cooking and serving."

"Do you miss teaching?" Ty took a sip of his iced tea, keeping his eyes focused on her.

"Part of me does. I know I made a difference in the lives of the students, but I love what I'm doing now, so I can't complain."

"You'd be good at whatever you set your mind to."

Her fingers tapped against the edge of the table. "What about your parents? How are they doing?"

He noted how she avoided his gaze and how she'd changed the subject away from her. "They're fine. Still living in Florida and enjoying every minute of being retired. The only drawback for me is that I rarely get to see them."

After ten more minutes of awkward small talk, the waiter placed two hot plates of food in front of them.

"Shall we pray?" he asked.

Kayla glanced at him, a sadness filling her eyes, and a wave of guilt washed over him. While they were dating he had always prayed before they ate. Then she found out the truth that his prayers were nothing more than empty rituals to win her over. How could he convince her that now he prayed to Someone he knew and had an intimate relationship with?

They bowed their heads, and Ty began his prayer. "Lord, I want to thank You for this time Kayla and I have to spend together. I pray that Your name will be glorified in everything we do and say to one another. Thank You also for the food that is set before us. We know that many people around our world don't have enough to eat. Help us to be grateful for all You have given us. In Jesus' name, amen."

Kayla took a bite of her burger as he fiddled with a fry and tried to eat. Conversation came in spurts, a far cry from the easy dialogue they used to share. Halfway through he lost his appetite. What he had to tell her tonight wasn't going to be easy. "I guess there's no use putting off what I have to say." Ty put down his fork. "Please let me try to get through this before you respond."

Kayla folded her hands in front of her and waited for him to continue.

"So much has happened in the past year I don't even know where to begin." He clutched his napkin between his fingers. "Maybe someday I will get around to telling you the long version, but for now I'll just tell you what's important.

"Eleven months ago Jack committed suicide."

"Oh, Ty. I'm sorry." She leaned forward, her eyes wide with dismay. "I didn't know. I'd heard there had been an accident—but suicide?"

"You had just broken off our engagement, and I have to tell you it was the lowest point I've ever been at in my life."

He watched her expression soften at the declaration. Friends since the fifth grade, Jack was supposed to have been the best man at their wedding. His death had been the second life-changing event in his life. One, like Kayla, he'd probably never get over.

"I really am sorry, Ty."

He combed his fingers through his hair. "I started thinking and searching for answers. Things you told me kept going through my head. I never listened to you back then when you talked about God and religion. It was just an act to win you over."

"You did it very well." The bitterness was evident in her voice.

"I know." He couldn't change the past, but he could at least try to make things right now. "I started spending Saturday afternoons with my grandfather. He's the only Christian in my family, and I sat with him for hours trying to prove that this belief you have for a man who died for our sins wasn't true.

"After about two months, I quit fighting. I realized I was a sinner. Not only for the way I had treated you, but because I had separated myself from God. From the One who created me."

Ty paused and looked intently into Kayla's eyes. "Six months ago I gave my life to Christ, totally and completely."

The fork she'd been twisting between her fingers clamored against the table. He knew it would take a miracle for her to believe him. He'd played games to get what he wanted and had used religion to win her over. She had no reason to believe him this time.

She tilted her head slightly, and her eyes narrowed. With disbelief? He hoped not. "I. . .that's wonderful."

He held up his hand. "Before you say anything else, I want you to know I understand if you don't believe me. In the past I've lied to you and tricked you. If nothing else, I need to ask you to forgive me. If that is as far as tonight goes, then that's okay."

"But you'd like it to go farther?" Kayla asked cautiously.

He closed his eyes and drank in a deep breath, before looking at her again, dreading the response he knew he deserved. "Kayla, I'm still in love with you, and I think I will be until the day I die. There will never be another woman who understands me the way you do."

Kayla stared out the window across the darkening summer skyline but didn't say anything.

"I also realize you have no reason to believe me, and if I'm ever to have a chance with you, then I will have to show you, prove to you, that I'm a different man today from a year ago. I want to win you back, Kayla."

She put her elbows on the table and rubbed her forehead with her fingers. After a moment she leaned her head back and held up her hands, questioning. "I don't know what to say, Ty. You hurt me deeply when I found out the truth. Our entire relationship was based on nothing but lies—your indifferent attitude toward marriage, the excessive social drinking, and, most important, your claims that you were a Christian. I realized I didn't know you at all."

The truth burned through him, but she was right. He was guilty of every one of her accusations. "You have every right to feel that way."

"You ask me to forgive you?" Kayla took a deep breath and steepled her fingers in front of her. "As a Christian I have to forgive you, but as a human it's going to be hard. To trust you again, well, I honestly don't think I'll ever be able to do that."

He'd expected her to say those words, but hearing them hit harder than he'd imagined. "It's up to you, Kayla. I promise, as hard as it would be if you tell me to walk out of your life, I'll respect your wishes and go. But that's not what I want. If you need time, then I'll wait, as long as it takes."

She shook her head slowly. "I don't know, Ty."

"Take as long as you need, but. . ." He had more news for her and wasn't sure at all how she might respond to his next announcement. "You need to know one more thing. I left my job in Boston and just started working for Farrington Cranberry Company here in town."

"What?" She leaned forward, the surprise obvious in her eyes.

"I might not make the same salary I did in Boston, but it's still a great company to work for. They're expanding rapidly by seeking new partnerships with local farms, like Sanderford Cranberry Farm, for example, just down the road."

"You're telling me you're working at an agricultural co-op instead of your high-paying Fortune 500 job?" Kayla held up her hands. "I don't get it."

Ty drew in a deep breath and reminded himself it was going to take her time to come to terms with his moving to Farrington. That it was going to take time for her to trust him again. "Believe me, I hadn't planned to quit, but some unscrupulous things were going on in Boston, and I felt I needed to get out. I'm still not sure what's going to happen, but coming here seemed like the right thing to do."

"You're going to have to give me awhile to think about all of this, Ty. Right now. . .I just don't know."

He caught her gaze and saw the conflict in her eyes. He was certain she still had feelings for him but knew she was trying to hide them. He had changed. If only she could believe him.

Chapter 3

The next morning Ty dialed Kayla's number from his office phone then quickly hung up. He couldn't do it. Hadn't he promised to give her space? Time to think about what he'd told her? If he really wanted to gain her trust, calling her now would undoubtedly lessen any chances he had of winning her back. Something he couldn't afford to do.

On the other hand, in this situation, not calling her could prove to be just as damaging. He had to call her.

Stalling, he drummed his fingers against his desk and stared out the small window that overlooked Benny's Crab Shack. Too bad life wasn't as simple as choosing between the Wednesday special and the steak and potato dinner. Instead, life was full of complex choices, each with its own consequences. And one thing he'd learned, choosing the right thing didn't automatically guarantee everything would turn out like some happily-ever-after fairy tale.

He'd realized that last night. Running his fingers through his hair, he wondered if there really was a chance at all for her ever to trust him again, or if he was simply fooling himself with his wishful thinking. At least last night had gone better than he'd expected. He'd been afraid she'd leave in the middle of his confession, but instead she'd listened to him, forgiven him and, in his mind anyway, hadn't completely dismissed the idea of their getting back together.

He picked up the phone and started dialing. Of course she hadn't encouraged him either, but he could live with that. He was willing to do whatever it took to prove to her he wasn't the same man she'd known a year ago.

She answered on the first ring. "Hello?"

He recognized her sleepy voice and smiled. She always had taken every chance she could to sleep in. Realizing how well he knew her only made him miss her that much more. "I'm sorry. I didn't mean to wake you up."

"I wasn't sleeping. I'm just not fully awake yet." Kayla's voice turned cool and professional. "I didn't expect to hear from you so soon."

"I know." He cleared his throat as his well-rehearsed lines evaporated into the morning breeze. "This...this call isn't about us. I promised to give you as long as you needed, and as hard as it might be, I aim to keep my promise. The reason I'm calling is that something happened at work, and I was afraid it might prove to be a bit awkward."

"What do you mean?"

He shut his eyes for a moment and pictured her snuggled under the favorite quilt her mother bought her for her twenty-eighth birthday. Losing her for a second time would hurt worse than before, but he had to be honest with her. "The company I'm working for now is looking for someone to cater a number of upcoming events."

"And you recommended me?"

"I didn't have to. Your name came up, and they're giving you a call this morning."

"Wow. That's great." For an instant she seemed to forget who she was talking to, because the guarded tone in her voice disappeared. "My mom's been trying to get new accounts with several of the local businesses."

"I felt like I needed to let you know this wasn't some scheme of mine to see you." If he was going to get her back, he would have to be totally honest with her, no matter what the cost.

"I appreciate your telling me."

"Listen—I've got to get back to work."

"Ty. . ." There was a pause on the line.

"Yes?"

"I know you haven't been here long, and, well, I wondered if you had found somewhere to go to church on Sunday."

He froze at her invitation. "Actually no. A guy I work with invited me to his church, but I haven't made any commitments."

"Why don't you pick me up at nine?" She quickly gave him directions.

"Are you sure?"

"Yes."

"I'll see you Sunday then."

Ty hung up the phone wondering if he'd heard her correctly. Had she actually invited him to pick her up for church? He took a deep breath and tried to slow his racing pulse. He hadn't let himself hope she'd give him a second chance. Hadn't let himself dream of the possibility that he could win her back.

Give me wisdom, Lord. You know how much I love Kayla, and yet I know I have to love her enough to let her go if that's Your will.

All he could do now was pray that was something he wouldn't have to do.

❧

Kayla stood in the large kitchen they used for their catering business in town, chopping fresh mint for a couscous salad and replaying in her mind the conversation she'd had this morning with Ty. She had no idea what had gotten into her. Instead of standing firm in her resolve to stay away from him, she'd just complicated matters. He could have gone to church anywhere, yet she'd rushed blindly ahead without thinking and invited him to go with her. Ty was the man who had broken her heart. Why did she keep forgetting that?

Her mother bustled into the kitchen out of breath with a box of fresh peaches in her hands. "How long until the salad's ready? I need to finish up the shortcake, then hurry across town to the Lamberts' and make sure their tables will seat thirty for tonight's reception."

"Relax, Mom." Kayla leaned against the counter. "The tables will work fine. I checked it out yesterday."

"You did, didn't you? I'd forgotten." Her mom set the box on the counter and rubbed her temples with her fingers. "I don't know what's wrong with me today."

A glance at the calendar that morning had reminded Kayla to be prepared for her mother's moodiness. She'd been seven when her father had been killed in a car accident, and while she didn't remember much about him, her mother had never forgotten the pile of bills he'd left behind, or the fact that they'd found alcohol in his blood and an empty six-pack of beer in the backseat. She'd also never forgiven him for the embarrassment of being the last one to find out that her husband's drinking had spiraled out of control.

Maybe some good news would lift her mom's spirits.

"We have a new client." Kayla checked her mom's expression and was thankful to see the smile that played on her lips.

"Really? Who?" Her mom pushed up her gold-rimmed bifocals and raised her penciled brows in interest.

"Someone from Farrington Cranberry Company called this morning to set up a couple of events." She hesitated. "Ty works for them now."

The moment the words left her mouth, Kayla knew she shouldn't have spoken them. Her cautionary attitude toward Ty was only surpassed by her mother who had never forgiven him for breaking her only daughter's heart.

"What?" Her mom didn't bother to mask the look of surprise on her face and placed her hands on her hips. "What happened to your resolution to close the door on Ty Lawrence for good?"

"It's okay, Mom. Nothing has changed. I'm over Ty, 100 percent, and this is just business. Ty had nothing to do with it." She knew she sounded as if she was trying to convince her mother. Truth was, she was still trying to convince herself.

"And you believed him?" Her mom wrinkled her brow and shook her head. "Kayla, I'm worried. First dinner and now this?"

"You know we can't afford to turn away clients, and besides, we'll be catering for his company, not for him personally." Kayla picked up a ripe tomato and resolutely began chopping. "I probably won't even see him."

Her mother shook her head and started cutting up some peaches. "All that man has ever done is lie to you."

"That's not true, Mom."

"Have you so quickly forgotten?" Her mom tossed a pit into the trash can. "Kayla, take a look at the situation. Ty knows exactly how to get to you. He heaps on the charm and claims he's something he's not. Now you tell me. How's that any different from the last time?"

"I don't know, Mom." Kayla picked up the pile of mint and tomatoes and dumped them into a fluted glass bowl. "What am I supposed to do? He's put no pressure on me and even promised me that if I tell him to leave, he'll walk out of my life forever."

Her mother shook her head, her short auburn curls bouncing with emphasis. "I thought you wanted him out of your life."

"I do."

She couldn't tell her mom she'd invited him to church. Not that her mom would be attending Sunday's worship service. Rosa Marceilo had buried her faith in God the same day she buried her husband. And unless someone decided it was their business to inform her mother of Kayla's moment of weakness, then she didn't even have to know. Besides, it was just a onetime thing. It wasn't as if it would become a habit where he picked her up each week. No. Nothing had really changed. Ty Lawrence was out of her life for good.

Kayla sliced a lemon in half and squeezed the tart juice into the salad. The only problem was, if he was out of her life, then how come she couldn't get him out of her heart?

❦

Kayla woke up Sunday morning with a knot in the pit of her stomach. In a little over an hour Ty would be by to pick her up. She rolled out of bed and made her way to the bathroom to brush her teeth. Her mother had once compared Ty to her father who had at one point claimed to be a Christian. After he died, she began telling story after story of Christians whose actions failed to follow their high and mighty words of love and forgiveness. Jenny's family, though, had shown Kayla another side of Christianity. She'd seen the way they acted out their faith, and because of their example, she'd committed her life to Christ when she was fourteen.

Her mother's resentment hadn't stopped Kayla from praying her mother would someday realize Christians were by no means perfect. They were only forgiven. Saved by Christ's blood, thus making them perfect in God's eyes.

Kayla's thoughts switched back to Ty. If Christ had forgiven all of her sins, then surely she could forgive Ty, whether or not he was telling the truth. That was the hard part. She wanted desperately to believe him, and yet how could she?

142

Lord, I need You to help me find a way to forgive him the way You have forgiven me.

An hour later Kayla picked up her Bible from the bed and walked out of her room, not even bothering to glance at the full-length mirror. It didn't matter what she looked like. Forgiveness didn't mean she had to put her heart on the line a second time. A fact she intended to make perfectly clear to Ty today.

The doorbell rang, and Kayla hurried to answer it, praying she wouldn't drop her guard once she saw him. He stood at her door, Bible in hand, with a smile that would have melted the hearts of most women.

Not mine, she reminded herself.

"You look beautiful this morning," he said, as she locked the door behind her and followed him to the car.

Kayla glanced down at her raspberry skirt and matching blouse. "Thanks."

She could have said the same to him but didn't. Still, he did look gorgeous in a gray suit and sky-blue shirt with matching tie. He always knew how to dress.

Ty hurried around to open the passenger side of his two-door car, allowing Kayla to slide into her seat before he shut the door. Her heart hammered in her chest as she leaned back and tried to relax. The car, like Ty, was so familiar. They had dated in this car, and he'd kissed her here for the first time. Kayla slammed the door on the memory.

"You'll have to tell me how to get there," he said, pulling out of the parking lot.

Kayla proceeded to give him directions to the church she had been attending since moving back home.

"Your boss's secretary called our office Friday morning," Kayla began, wanting to ensure that the conversation stayed away from anything personal. "I appreciate your letting me know about the job."

"No problem. I hoped you'd be pleased."

"I was. We already have several functions scheduled for them. Next Friday we'll be providing an Italian dinner for the board and their spouses."

"I'm sure it'll be a hit."

"Then in two weeks we'll be serving a southern-style barbecue for the staff."

"That will be no small dinner."

"Eighty-five people," Kayla said, after telling him to turn left at the light.

"I'll be there for that one. What's on the menu?"

"The powers that be wanted something different, so we decided to try some Southern fare. Barbecue, beans, corn on the cob, corn bread, and cherry cobbler for dessert."

"I can't wait."

The best thing to do was not work that night. Jenny, her mom, and the extra servers they would hire could handle things without her. "Jenny took a year off from teaching and is working for us part-time."

"She planned to be your maid of honor."

"Yes." Kayla wished he hadn't brought up their wedding. There was too much history between them.

"It'll be good to see her."

She grimaced. Without a doubt she needed to make her decision clear and the sooner the better.

Thirty minutes later Kayla sat next to Ty on the pew, barely hearing the words of the sermon. How many times had they gone to church together as she unknowingly succumbed to his deception of being a believer? It had all been an act. What was she doing here with him again?

" 'You see, at just the right time, when we were still powerless, Christ died for the ungodly.' "

Kayla's ears perked up as Pastor Jenkins read from the fifth chapter of Romans. " 'Very rarely will anyone die for a righteous man, though for a good man someone might possibly dare to die. But God demonstrates his own love for us in this: While we were still sinners, Christ died for us.' "

Kayla looked at Ty. For the past year she had seen him as a sinner. One who took advantage of her and in turn broke her heart. Never once had she found the courage to ask God for Ty to find forgiveness in Jesus Christ, a redemption that came so freely.

Now that Ty said he claimed that forgiveness, she refused to believe him because one thing still haunted her. What if he was still lying?

"Now look back at chapter 4 and verses 7 and 8," the minister continued, and Kayla forced herself to listen. " 'Blessed are they whose transgressions are forgiven, whose sins are covered. Blessed is the man whose sin the Lord will never count against him.' "

Kayla swallowed hard and glanced at Ty's lean form. His gaze rested intently on the minister as if he were soaking in the message. Was it just a coincidence that today's lesson spoke on forgiveness, or was God trying to tell her something?

꩜

Ty sat across from Kayla at a corner table in one of the local restaurants. He'd enjoyed the church service, in spite of the fact that he'd been afraid she regretted the moment she'd invited him. If she had, he saw no sign of it in her friendly smile as she introduced him to some of her friends. Afterward she'd told him they needed to talk, and he'd suggested lunch.

"So what did you think about the sermon?" Kayla asked after the waitress had brought them their lunch.

Ty took a bite of his steak sandwich before answering. "It reminded me of just how amazing it is that Christ died for me and how unworthy I am. And I'm thankful I finally figured out I need Him." Ty paused. "I know this is hard for you, Kayla. If our places were reversed, then I would have a difficult time believing you. I only hope I can show you by the way I act that I'm not the same man you broke it off with a year ago."

She nodded. "I am having a hard time trusting you. I want to believe you. I want to believe you've changed, and yet how can you really expect me to do that?"

Ty put down his sandwich and looked at her intently, shaking his head. "I don't know, Kayla. I realize it won't happen overnight."

She still had the same effect on him. He couldn't think straight around her. He reached across the table and took her hand. Kayla pulled hers back as if he had touched her with a burning coal, and immediately he regretted his actions. "I'm sorry, Kayla. I shouldn't have done that. I just. . ."

"Forget it."

What had he been thinking? Ty forced himself to take another bite. Surely she still felt something for him. To have her so near and yet not be able even to touch her was excruciating. He tried to think of something nonpersonal and nonthreatening to say. He had to take it slow so they could get to know each other again.

"I'm enjoying my new job." Surely work was a safe topic. "The company I'm working for is great."

"Really?" Kayla took a bite of her salad, looking as if she were making herself eat. "What do you do?"

"I'm sort of a financial adviser."

The waitress came to refill their drinks, and Kayla pushed her plate aside. "Sounds like fun." Kayla's tone was dry.

Ty sighed. He'd honestly thought that when she invited him to church it had been an unspoken truce, but apparently he was wrong. He watched Kayla check her watch for the tenth time and wondered what he should do.

"Ty. . ." She paused and reached for her purse. "This just isn't going to work. I never should have agreed to see you in the first place. I'm sorry, but we won't be seeing each other again." Without another word Kayla got up from the table and walked out the door.

Just as she had a year ago.

Ty's heart sank as he watched Kayla leave the restaurant, shocked at her abruptness. She must have been sitting there the entire lunch trying to figure out how to tell him there wasn't a chance for them. He had known it wouldn't be easy to win her back, but somehow he'd convinced himself it would work out.

He knew he had changed, but how could he convince Kayla? He possessed a deeper love for her than he had a year ago. If only she could find it in her heart to give him another chance. Ty paid the bill for the uneaten food and left the restaurant.

❦

Kayla felt nauseous as she walked the six blocks home. Things had not gone the way she had intended. She'd planned to be a bit gentler and explain her reasons, but instead it had all come out at once.

What else could she have done but leave? If she hadn't left the moment she did, she knew she would have given in to him. When he took her hand, her entire body had melted at his touch. She couldn't trust him, and she couldn't see him again. There was simply no other way around it.

Chapter 4

Kayla glanced across the lofty barn that had been converted into a meeting hall and wished she could slip off her shoes. The front half of the structure was filled with a dozen round tables covered with red-checkered cloths. She'd spent the afternoon making centerpieces from cowboy hats, balloons, and bandannas. Most of the employees of Farrington Cranberry Company had already filled their plates with the Southern spread and were enjoying the warm July evening, thanks to the bigwigs who were picking up the tab.

The corporate headquarters had made the decision five years ago to settle in the small valley outside Farrington. Landing a catering contract with the company that sold everything from cranberry juice to dried cranberries to cranberry muffins nationwide was a huge blessing for Marceilo Catering. And tonight was key to future catering jobs. Already Kayla had received several compliments on the food as people migrated back to the buffet line for seconds. Her mother had grown up in Memphis and could make barbeque like a pro. They'd added cranberry chutney and cranberry apple crisp to the menu to impress the VIPs, a decision that hadn't gone unnoticed.

"Looks like you've outdone yourself once again."

Kayla glanced up to see Ty filling his plate with a mound of potato salad. A lump swelled in her chest. "Ty. . .I didn't think you were here tonight."

"I got snagged into a conversation outside and somehow missed the first lineup."

She gnawed on the edge of her lip. Great. Now he was going to think she'd been looking for him. Except she hadn't. Not really. Nothing more than a few lingering gazes across the crowded room as she made sure the servers were doing their job and the food warmers stayed full. Of course, that wasn't to say that in the past two weeks she hadn't thought about picking up the phone and calling him to apologize for her abrupt departure at the restaurant. But every time she started to call, she managed to convince herself Ty Lawrence wasn't worth a phone call. The truth was, she didn't owe him anything.

He moved to the beans, and she pretended to stay busy by filling a warming pan with more barbeque beef. Over half the employees had taken the evening's theme seriously and dressed in Western shirts and boots. A number of the men even sported cowboy hats. Ty was no exception. Red plaid shirt, fitted blue jeans, and a black Stetson were enough to woo the heart of any cowgirl. Even she had to admit the rugged look fit him. But Ty always had put appearances first, and she'd learned the hard way that appearances could be very deceiving.

Kayla handed off the empty pan to one of the servers. She was going to have to get rid of any guilt that lingered, because tonight was proof this was a small town and their running into each other was inevitable. If only he didn't manage to tie her emotions into a double knot. At the moment her knees felt like jelly and her heart like the bass drum in a high school marching band. Definitely not a good sign that she'd forgotten the six-foot-two cowboy standing in front of her.

But why does he have to look so amazingly gorgeous?

Ty added a piece of jalapeño corn bread to his plate. "You've got quite a spread here. I don't remember the last time I had barbeque, but it smells absolutely heavenly."

"Once you've got your food, drinks are at the table over there." She cringed at her harsh tone. He'd asked her to forgive him, and she'd practically thrown it back in his face. So much for setting a Christian example. "Love your neighbor as yourself" and "Forgive as the Lord forgave you" were commands she was struggling to follow. Which made it look from the surface as if Ty was more of a Christian than she was. If he really was a Christian at all. Could she help it if her history with the man dictated she guard her heart tighter than the First Bank of Farrington?

"I don't believe I have ever seen you quite so. . ." Kayla searched for the right word.

"So casual?" He chuckled.

"It was always an effort to get you to relax long enough to change out of a tie and jacket and into a pair of blue jeans."

Ty's blue eyes widened. "So you approve?"

"I. . .yes," Kayla stammered.

This definitely wasn't fair. She should have taken her mother's advice and skipped tonight. Except she couldn't keep running. Had she already forgotten she was over him—100 percent? There was no need to run. And the look was perfect for him. All he needed now was a lasso and a mechanical bull.

"Now this looks delicious." He put a spoonful of maple-roasted sweet potatoes on his plate, gave her a slight nod, then walked over to the drink table.

Kayla's jaw dropped. He acted more interested in the food than in her. She grabbed the empty pan and headed for the kitchen. Of course, that was exactly the way it should be. She'd told him the relationship was over, and he'd finally accepted it. Wasn't that what she wanted?

As much as she tried not to notice, Kayla spent the next hour watching Ty mingle with his coworkers. He'd sat down at a table near the buffet, giving her the opportunity to observe him—if she wanted to.

Which of course she didn't.

While the servers normally refilled the drinks, she walked by his table with a pitcher of tea and caught the beginning of a dirty joke by a redheaded man wearing an orange bandanna around his neck. With his typical charm, Ty managed to smoothly change the course of the conversation. She was impressed. Not that she didn't expect him to be sociable and charming; but as she strategically moved throughout the room and caught pieces of his conversation, she was surprised the conversation didn't center on work. A year ago work was the only word in his vocabulary.

But he knows I'm in the room.

Out of the corner of her eye, she watched a woman wearing jeans a size too small and a low-cut white blouse approach Ty and stand behind his chair. Ripples of laughter erupted from the beautiful colleague's mouth.

"Miss Marceilo?"

Kayla jumped. "Yes?"

A tall, willowy woman wearing a denim skirt and a fringed jacket reached out and shook her hand. "I'm one of the vice presidents, and I wanted to let you know I'm quite impressed with all your catering company has to offer tonight."

A roar of laughter came from Ty's table, but Kayla ignored the urge to turn away.

The executive shot her a knowing smile. "He's quite a ladies' man."

"Excuse me?" This time Kayla followed the other woman's gaze.

"Ty Lawrence. He's one of our newest employees, and he seems to have won the hearts of the women."

Kayla swallowed hard. So the truth was about to come out. As far as she knew, he'd never cheated on her while they were together, but on the other hand, she wouldn't have put it past him.

The woman turned back to her. "Funny thing is, rumor has it he isn't interested in any of them."

Kayla cocked her head. "What do you mean?"

"From what I hear there's only one woman in Ty's life."

"There is. . .I mean. . .who?" Kayla worked to steady her breathing. *He had told people he was still in love with her. . . .*

"That I don't know. I was told there was some girl who captured his heart, and he moved here to win her back. Knowing him, he'll get what he wants. Anyway, I just wanted to let you know you'll be hearing from us again for other events."

"Thank you." Kayla swallowed hard. *I'm over him. I'm over him. . . .*

The rest of the evening flew by as she worked with her mother and the staff to ensure the service continued to be exceptional. Once the speaker had finished, they got everything cleaned up and packed in their van.

"I think that's the last of it." Her mom slammed the door shut then rested her hands against her hips. "I noticed Ty appeared to keep his distance."

Kayla frowned. "I told you he would."

"His word is worth about as much as an outlaw's straight out of the Old West. He's just biding his time. You wait and see."

It certainly wouldn't be the last time her mother reminded her she was unhappy with Ty's move to town, but Kayla refused to be dragged into another argument. Glancing into the front seat of the van, she tried to remember where she left her purse. Nothing. She opened the door again and began rummaging through the boxes they'd stacked.

Her mom stood beside her with the van keys dangling in one hand. "What are you looking for?"

"My purse."

"Didn't you put it in one of those cabinets behind the buffet table?"

Kayla slammed the door shut. "You're right. I'll be back in a sec."

ॐ

Ty grabbed his hat from the table and turned to leave with a few of the guys who had lingered behind visiting. He'd enjoyed the chance to meet some more of his coworkers, but it had been impossible for him not to be aware of Kayla's presence the entire evening. He'd wanted to tell her how beautiful she looked in her smart black skirt and red blouse as she bustled around the room ensuring everyone was taken care of—but he hadn't dared.

One of his coworkers came up beside him and slapped him on the back. "Why don't you join us down at Willy's Bar, Ty? Nothing like getting a little drunk on a Friday night."

Ty's hesitation lasted only a moment. A year ago he would have jumped at the invitation. Tonight, getting drunk with a bunch of buddies held none of the appeal it used to. "You know, guys, I think I'll just head on home."

"What's the matter?" A second guy unbuttoned his collar. "You're not one of those Christians who can't stand to have a little bit of harmless fun, are you?"

Ty shook his head. "Actually, I love to have fun just like the next guy, but drinking and waking up with a hangover the next morning doesn't strike me as entertaining anymore. And yes," he added, smiling, "I am a Christian."

He stood there as the men stalked off without him. He might lose a few friends in the process, but the peace he had from his new commitment was worth it.

"Hey."

Ty spun around and felt his heart take a nosedive. "Kayla? I thought you'd left."

"I did, but I forgot something." She held up her purse and shot him a lop-sided grin.

His heart raced as he gazed at the one woman he'd given his heart to.

Her gaze swept the floor. "I've been watching you tonight."

"What do you mean?"

"Never a bad word about anyone. Never a dirty joke thrown in for laughs. Still, you knew I was in the room, and I never could be sure it wasn't just an act."

His stomach clenched as he waited for her to continue.

"It's not an act, is it." She said it as a statement rather than a question.

He fiddled with the brim of the Stetson and tried to keep his hands from shaking. "I told you it wasn't."

"I heard you tell those men you're a Christian, and I'm sure they won't let you down easy. This time you had no idea I was in the room."

"No, I didn't." Ty's voice held steady as he looked at her. He should feel ecstatic that she believed him, but part of him wanted simply to walk out of the room. He refused to spend the rest of his life proving to her who he'd become. "Is this what you were looking for, something to substantiate that I am who I say I am?"

"Yes, no, I. . .I don't know." She took a half dozen steps toward him then stopped.

The room was empty now, and all he could hear was a hum coming from the kitchen and his pulse pounding in his ears. "I won't play games, Kayla. You told me things were off, and I gave you my word I would accept your decision."

She slung the strap of her purse over her shoulder. "It's funny, but as hard as I tried to put you out of my mind this past year, your coming has made me realize I'm not over you. Maybe I'll never be over you."

He was sure he hadn't heard her correctly. Or maybe he was only dreaming. Because Kayla was out of his life. Unless. . . "What are you saying?"

Kayla continued to bridge the gap between them until only a few inches remained. "You've changed, and I. . ."

She stopped, close enough for him to catch a drift of her sweet perfume and see the tears that pooled in the corners of her eyes. How many times in the past few months had he prayed God would let Kayla see him for who he had become? That somehow he could erase the doubts that stopped her from trusting him?

He wiped away the tear that slid down her cheek. "What is it, Kayla?"

"It's you. . .and me. I—I don't know what I'm trying to say."

He'd promised himself he would give her the space she wanted, but with her lips hovering just below his face, he did what any other man would have done in his situation. He leaned down and kissed her, ignoring the Stetson that dropped to the ground as he wrapped his arms around her waist.

A flood of memories washed over him. The scent of honey and roses engulfed him. It was as if the past year never existed between them. . .except it had. And even he couldn't expect them to simply continue where they left off. There was too much hurt folded into their relationship. Too much mistrust.

Pulling away, he cupped her face in his hands and stared into her eyes. "I've missed you so much, but I never expected this."

Kayla took a deep breath and stepped back, but her hands still rested against his chest. "Ty, I—"

"I'm sorry. I promised I wouldn't push you."

"No. This is just as much my fault." She looked down, and he felt a wave of regret wash over him.

He tried to read the expression in her eyes, but her dark lashes swept against her cheeks as she stared at the floor. Surely she didn't regret their kiss. To lose her again—like this—was more than he could handle. He might as well move back to Boston and let Mr. Abbott feed him to the lions.

He tried to swallow the lump that swelled in his throat. "So what happens next?"

"I don't know."

"If you regret—"

"No. I don't regret anything. This has just completely taken me by surprise." She looked up at him, and her lips curled into a smile. "We've both changed in the past year. I need to get to know you again."

"Fair enough." He leaned forward and brushed his lips against her forehead, still not believing she wasn't kicking him out the door.

"Ty." She looked up at him and laughed. "I'm serious."

"So am I." He kissed her one more time before pulling away. "I told you I'd always love you. I just never imagined there was actually hope for the two of us."

❦

Kayla felt her head spin, still uncertain of what had taken place in the past five minutes. His eyes were brighter than she remembered. Blue like the Atlantic Ocean on a warm summer's day. And they seemed to reach all the way into her soul. One thing was clear. Ty had kissed her—and she'd been all too willing to kiss him back. She looked up at his jawline that was sprinkled with a touch of stubble, making him look even more like the rugged, handsome cowboy he'd dressed as tonight.

Needing a distraction from his nearness, she picked up his Stetson and set it on his head. "My mom's waiting for me outside."

He shot her a smile. "Can I take you out for coffee?"

"Are you trying to avoid my mother?"

"You bet."

Kayla laughed. She certainly didn't blame him. The last thing she wanted to do right now was tell her mother she'd just kissed Ty Lawrence. She had no idea what the future held, but for the moment she much preferred staying lost in his gaze. The details of what had transpired could be worked out later. "You didn't think I was going to leave you now, did you?"

"I hope not."

"You wait here, and I'll go tell her."

"No, I'll come with you."

She hurried outside with Ty at her side and headed toward the driver's side of the van, trying to calm the turmoil raging inside. Her mom wasn't going to respond well to this.

"Where have you been?" Her mom stuck her head out of the driver's window then frowned. "Ty? What are you doing here?"

"Mom." Kayla leaned her arm against the door and forced a smile. "Ty and I are going out for a cup of coffee. He'll drop me off later at my apartment."

"Kayla." Her mom grabbed Kayla's arm. "I need to talk to you. Alone."

Kayla glanced at Ty who looked as if he wished he were anywhere else but here. "Do you mind?"

He shook his head. "I'll go get my car."

Once he'd walked away, Kayla caught her mom's fiery gaze. "What is going on?"

Kayla kept her voice steady. "It's only coffee, Mom."

She wasn't ready to supply any further details. And besides, how could she when she didn't know exactly what had happened? One kiss might have left her head spinning, but the future still held no guarantees.

"Kayla, I thought you called things off with that man."

"He's not the same man he was a year ago."

"Apparently you're the same person." Her mother's frown deepened. "You haven't learned a thing."

Kayla stared at the side of the van and tried to control her temper. "Mom—"

"No. I want you to listen to me. Maybe you've forgotten, but the day you came back from Boston you were devastated. Ty Lawrence is a liar, and you know from the past that he will do anything to get what he wants. He's after you, Kayla, and if you don't turn and walk away right now, it's going to be too late."

Kayla clenched her hands until her fingernails bit into her palms. She forced herself to push away any lingering doubts of who Ty really was.

"A lot of things happened during this past year, Mom. Things that forced him to reevaluate his life. I'm not saying we're getting back together, and I know you don't understand, but I believe him."

Her mom slammed her hands against the steering wheel. "Of course I don't understand. That is why I'm trying to stop you from making the biggest mistake of your life. You found out before it was too late last time, but this time. . ."

"Mom—"

"You're old enough to make your own decision, but don't ever come back to me and say I didn't warn you."

Kayla watched as her mom jerked the van into reverse and spun out of the parking lot. A moment later Ty pulled up beside her and reached over to open the passenger door. "Is everything all right?" he asked as she climbed in beside him.

Kayla shook her head. "I knew she'd be upset, but she had so much hurt in her eyes. As if I let her down."

"Do you blame her?" Ty pulled out of the parking lot and headed for an all-night coffee shop around the corner. "She has no reason to believe me."

"You're not doing a very good job of convincing." Kayla laughed, but reality stung. While she might be old enough to make her own decisions, she still respected her mother's experienced opinion.

He reached out and squeezed her hand. "I was hoping I wouldn't have to convince you anymore."

"You don't. But she loves me and doesn't want me to get hurt."

Ty drove into a parking place and shut off the engine before turning to her. He pulled her hand toward his chest and caught her gaze. "I was a fool to lose you the last time, though I know I deserved it. I was never good enough for you."

Kayla struggled to take another breath. "That's not true—"

"Shhh." He pressed his finger against her lips. "Let me finish. I want to do things right this time, with everything out in the open. I am not perfect—you know that—but I promise you I will never intentionally hurt you again. Never."

She squeezed her arms around her waist and blinked back the tears. He was right about one thing. Ty *had* hurt her. He had deceived her. . .and yet she believed he was a changed man.

Oh God, please let me be right.

Chapter 5

Yellow rays of afternoon sunlight filtered through the sheer living room curtains of Chloe Parker's house as Kayla emptied a box of crackers onto a glass plate. Smells of marinated steaks drifted in from the grill on the patio outside, mixing with the German potato salad and tangy coleslaw sitting on the antique mahogany table inside. As good as the spread looked, Kayla wasn't sure she'd be able to eat a single bite. Agreeing to bring Ty to dinner with her two best friends had been a step she'd undoubtedly jumped into sooner than she should have. How could she explain their relationship to her friends when she wasn't even ready to venture her own guess as to where they were headed? No matter what her heart wanted to believe, trust wasn't something that could be repaired overnight.

Chloe nudged Kayla with her elbow before shoving a strand of her long black hair out of her face. "I've yet to hear all the details behind how you and Ty got back together. Spill."

Kayla hesitated as she glanced around Chloe's cozy dining room that opened to the kitchen and living room. Black-and-white photos of her two small boys lined the fireplace mantel. A wooden box of toys sat in the corner of the room beside a rocking chair that was the perfect size for two year old Brandon. Kayla pulled out some crab dip from the picnic basket she'd brought and set it on the table. A home and family were things she'd once planned to have with Ty. Losing that dream had shattered all her childhood illusions of living happily ever after. Having him back in her life had yet to erase the fears that her newfound hopes for the two of them might vanish a second time.

She drew in a breath and tried to calm the butterflies that flitted in her stomach. "There's honestly not much to tell at this point."

Chloe folded her arms across her chest. "Somehow I don't believe that."

"Me either." Jenny shook her head as she added a stack of paper plates from the kitchen bar to the buffet table. "You've been too hush-hush about everything. It's time you gave us a little insider information. We are your best friends, girl."

She couldn't help but laugh as she looked up at Chloe and Jenny who stood side by side like a pair of interrogation officers. She'd given them very few details during the past month, but that hadn't stopped them from arranging an afternoon barbeque where they could check out Ty for themselves.

Kayla tried to shrug off the ridiculous case of nerves that had consumed her all day. These were her friends. Best friends since the seventh grade when the three of them had stood up against Angie Edwards and the Farrington Junior High cheerleaders whose antics had put them at odds outside the classroom more than once.

Kayla gripped the edge of the table with her fingertips. "I promise I'm not trying to keep things from the two of you, but Ty and I still have a lot of things we need to work out. We're completely starting over."

"Right." Jenny's blue eyes widened. "And how long is that going to last?"

"Jenny." Kayla felt a blush cross her cheeks.

Ty's one kiss after the company-catered dinner and observing him when he didn't know she was there had managed to change her entire world and push aside the resolutions she'd put into place over the past year. But until all her doubts were gone she was determined they would take things slowly. Which was exactly what had happened so far.

He'd kept his word, and they'd started seeing each other again as if they were dating for the first time. They'd gone out for dinner, movies at the Rialto Theater, ice cream at Barry's Café, and even a couple of Saturday afternoons on his friend Charlie's boat. In between they'd talked. She'd begun to trust him again—enough to let him into her life—but was still determined to move ahead with their relationship one slow step at a time. Which was exactly why she'd shared little with her mom—or with Jenny and Chloe—about their relationship.

"We're your friends." Jenny flung her arm around Kayla's shoulder. "All we want is what's best for you."

"Or perhaps a chance to check him out up close." Kayla shot her friend a grin as she picked up a serving spoon from the table and stuck it in the coleslaw.

"You bet that's what I mean." Jenny laughed, but her smile melted into a frown. "It's also our job to make sure you don't get your heart broken again."

The innocent comment pierced through the layer of protection Kayla had wrapped around her heart. She knew she had no guarantees Ty wouldn't walk off with the shattered pieces of her heart again. Kayla glanced out the kitchen window that overlooked the backyard and tried to ignore the implications. Ty stood beside the grill with the other two guys, looking as if he were having a good time. His white T-shirt showed off his tan skin, and when he laughed a dimple appeared on his left cheek. He'd always been irresistible. That's why she'd left Boston. Was she only fooling herself into believing things could be different this time around?

No. Things were different this time. Completely different. She was convinced of it.

"Jenny's exactly right, you know." Chloe interrupted Kayla's thoughts. "It's our job to watch out for each other."

"So what do you think about the new Ty?" Kayla dunked a cracker into the crab dip. Maybe food would settle her stomach after all.

Chloe picked up an empty sippy cup from the table then headed into the adjoining kitchen to rinse it out in the sink. "Honestly, while I'm happy for you, it's hard to be objective at this point. I mean, this is the guy who broke your heart, Kayla. I can't forget how many times you cried on my shoulder after you moved back."

"She is right, Kayla." Jenny popped open a jar of salsa and set it next to the chips. "I was supposed to be your maid of honor, and instead you came home with a broken heart."

Kayla frowned. The broken heart was one fact that no one, especially her mother, was willing to forget. And as many times as she'd tried to rationalize it, if she was honest with herself, it was an issue that was hard for her to leave in the past as well. "Things are different now."

"I hope so." Jenny followed Kayla's gaze out the window. "Though there never was any question as to how handsome the guy is."

"Don't let Greg hear you say that." Chloe laughed.

"What about your mom?" Jenny asked, ignoring Chloe's grin. "What does she think about him coming back into your life?"

"We don't talk about it." Kayla grabbed another cracker. "She'd like to pretend none of this is happening. She doesn't trust Ty at all."

"The steaks are done!" Chloe's husband, Nick, burst through the door, interrupting any further conversation.

Chloe took the platter of meat from her husband to set on the table. "Are the kids behaving, honey?"

"Come look for yourself. Jeremy just roped Ty into a game of catch."

Chloe followed Nick outside with a clean plate for the grilled potatoes.

Kayla looked outside at the spacious backyard. It appeared that the game of catch had been postponed. At that moment four-year-old Jeremy was tackling Ty who was on his hands and knees. Two-year-old Brandon had hold of Ty's leg and was pulling with a determined look on his face.

A wave of peace flooded the corners of Kayla's heart as she watched the playful struggle until Ty collapsed to the ground, pretending to admit defeat.

"He's really good with kids," Jenny said, standing beside her.

"Funny thing is, I never knew it." Kayla watched Ty roll over and toss Brandon a foot into the air above him. "A year ago he wouldn't have been out there on the grass wrestling with two little boys. He'd have been too worried about messing up his designer suit."

"Can someone really change that much in such a short time?" Jenny laid her hand on Kayla's arm. "I'm sorry. I had no right—"

"It's okay." Hadn't she asked herself the very same question dozens of times over the past few weeks?

Jenny gave Kayla a hug. "I just don't want you to get hurt again."

Chloe set the potatoes on the table then rang the cast iron dinner bell to bring everyone to the table.

Thirty minutes later Ty leaned back and patted his firm stomach. "Boy, am I full. This was delicious, ladies."

"Absolutely wonderful." Nick reached out and squeezed his wife's hand.

"I think it's time for two little boys to take a nap." Chloe looked at her kids whose eyes were beginning to droop.

Jeremy started to protest, but one look from his mother stopped him.

"Take a good nap for your mom, and I'll turn on the sprinkler later." Their father's offer brought smiles to their faces as they slid off their chairs and into his arms.

The scene brought a smile to Kayla's lips as well. She turned to Chloe. "You're lucky Nick's as good a father as he is a lawyer."

Five minutes later Nick returned from the boys' bedroom and came up behind Chloe to nuzzle his chin in her hair. "Are you into motorcycles, Ty?"

"I've ridden a few times." Ty set his fork down on the plate that had held the second piece of coconut pie Kayla had made. "My father had one when I was in high school—until he broke both legs and my mother made him sell it."

"Don't get any ideas." Nick covered Chloe's ears with his hands, a playful expression on his face. She squirmed out of his grasp before reaching up and planting a firm kiss on his lips.

"Good luck." Jenny reached out and grabbed Greg's hand. "I told Greg I'd never ride a motorcycle. Now he's got me outfitted with everything from a battery-heated vest to a pair of leather boots."

"We all know you're dying to check out Greg's new toy, so go have fun."

Chloe had barely finished her sentence when the men jumped up from the table. Nick kissed his wife again then headed for the garage door.

Kayla laughed, but a part of her still ached in confusion. A year ago holding hands or letting Ty kiss her had seemed a natural part of their relationship. Figuring out where they stood today was a whole other issue.

❦

Kayla let Ty take her hand and lead her down the tree-lined street in front of her apartment building. Walking through the quiet neighborhood was the perfect way to end the day.

"I like your friends." Ty kicked an acorn with the tip of his boot then watched it bounce across the pavement.

"I'm glad." While she knew Chloe and Jenny still held a handful of reservations, the awkwardness of the day had melted into peacefulness as Kayla's friends had worked to make them both feel comfortable with a boisterous game of charades. "You sure seemed to enjoy Nick and Chloe's boys."

"They're sweet kids. It's been a long time since I had so much fun rolling on the grass."

"I don't think I've ever seen you roll on the grass." Kayla laughed. "I liked it."

"I guess you're right. A year ago I would have worried about what the next person might be thinking about me."

"And today?"

Ty stopped and turned so he could look at her.

"Only one person's opinion matters to me now." His blue eyes gazed at her.

"And whose is that?"

Ty tipped her chin and brought his face inches from Kayla's. "Yours."

Kayla could feel his warm breath on her face, but he made no move to lean down farther and kiss her. As much as she wanted his lips on hers, she took a step back. If she let him kiss her, she wouldn't be able to think clearly.

They started walking again in silence, each occupied with their own thoughts.

"Tell me what happened to Jack." It was the one subject they'd put off discussing. And one she needed to understand.

The muscles in his hand flinched, and she knew she'd broached a painful topic. Still, she had to know exactly what led Ty to change his life so drastically.

"I know this is a painful subject for you."

"And one you have every right to know." Ty led Kayla to a bench just off the road, under two large oak trees whose branches spanned the wide street. "Jack's death was a major factor in my finding Christ. It's sad, but in his death I found life."

"God's way of bringing good in the worst of circumstances?"

"Maybe." Ty was silent for a moment. "I'm not sure when Jack started having marital problems. He and his wife had been fighting for months, but shortly after you left Boston, he found out Karen was having an affair with a man at her office."

"I'm sorry to hear that. Jack was a good guy."

"Within a week Karen filed the divorce papers and was gone. I never saw her again. Jack didn't take it well. I think deep down he honestly believed things would work out between them. When she didn't come back, it devastated him. Two weeks later I went by his apartment to pick him up for a basketball game. I found him lying dead on the kitchen floor. He'd shot himself."

Kayla shuddered and squeezed Ty's hand. "I'm so sorry."

"I'm sorry because Jack never knew God. He never knew Christ was the one place where he could have found relief and peace."

"What about you? How did his death change you?"

"My grandfather had a heart attack a month later. I was furious over losing you and then Jack. In a matter of a few weeks I'd lost everything that meant anything to me. It made me start thinking about what was important."

"What happened to your grandfather?"

"When he got out of the hospital, he went into a retirement center. It wasn't what I wanted, but he insisted he didn't want to be a burden on anyone. I tried to visit him at least twice a week, sometimes more if my schedule allowed it. Soon I began to realize the things I had held important in my life weren't that important at all."

Kayla was silent as he continued.

"My grandfather never preached at me, but every time I came he asked me to read to him from the Bible. After a few weeks we had read through the Gospels, and I started asking questions. While the stories of Jesus and His life were not new to me, I had missed the message of the tremendous love behind them: the love of a Savior willing to come to this earth and die for me of all people. I found it hard to believe."

"So what changed your mind?"

"I started thinking about Jack who believed he had nothing to live for, and I wondered very seriously what I had to live for. My job was unfulfilling, and the more hours I put into work, the more resentful I became. What was the point in working twelve to fourteen hours a day, seven days a week? Life seemed meaningless."

"Didn't Solomon write that everything is meaningless?" Kayla fumbled with the shiny red stones on her charm bracelet and pondered her own question.

Ty nodded. " 'To the man who pleases him, God gives wisdom, knowledge and happiness, but to the sinner he gives the task of gathering and storing up wealth to hand it over to the one who pleases God. This too is meaningless, a chasing after the wind.'

"I found that verse at one point, and it struck me so that I memorized it. That's what my life had become. One meaningless day after another, I was chasing after the wind and finding nothing. It took me sinking into the depths to realize I was a sinner who needed a Savior."

Kayla looked up at him, her eyes swelling with tears of joy. "I'm glad, Ty. I'm so glad."

"For the first time I saw a light at the end of the tunnel. I went to the minister of a friend I knew, and he studied with me. It still took awhile to get through my hard head, but finally I saw the truth. I realized the only way I could live was if I died to my sinful nature. I accepted Christ and was baptized one glorious

Sunday afternoon. My grandfather died last January. I think he'd been waiting for me to get my life turned around."

"I wish you would have called me."

He looked at her and caught her gaze. "Before you left I promised you I would stay out of your life. I wasn't ready to see you until I had worked through some things. I actually never planned to come here, but I also know it's not a coincidence I'm here."

For the first time in a long while Kayla smiled at the future.

❦

Richard Abbott threw the rest of his corned beef sandwich into the trash and ran his fingers through his thinning hair. He hadn't left his office in three days, and he was running out of time. Rumors of indictments were getting closer and felt like a noose closing in around his neck. He picked up a file filled with Ty Lawrence's signatures. There was, according to his lawyer, a way out. Now it was only a matter of time before putting things into motion. The way Lawrence walked out on him was something he'd never forgive. He once trusted him, priming him to become his right-hand man. And for what? It didn't really matter anymore. Because Ty Lawrence, former protégé, was going to take the fall for him.

Chapter 6

Ty tapped his finger against the steering wheel and glanced at the rearview mirror. A black sedan swung into the turning lane and stopped three cars behind him. He stared at the red light. He'd noticed the same car in the parking lot at work. And at the gas station where he'd just filled up his car.

His jaw muscles tightened. He'd caught today's headlines from the newsstand five minutes ago. The investigation of Abbott Financial Services made for a riveting front-page story. Not unexpected, but disturbing nevertheless. He might believe Abbott deserved to spend the rest of his life behind bars, but his downfall would affect hundreds of employees if the company ended up filing for bankruptcy.

He punched the speed-dial number for his former secretary into his speakerphone, hoping to catch her at home. She answered on the third ring.

"Penny here."

"Penny, it's Ty." The light turned green, and he pushed on the accelerator to make the left turn.

"Ty?" The line was silent for a moment. "What a nice surprise."

"Did you get the flowers I sent you?"

"They were beautiful, though you didn't have to."

"After all you did for me the past five years, a bunch of flowers seems to pale in comparison."

"You're right about that."

Penny chuckled, and Ty remembered why he liked her. She'd always been efficient and dependable with an added sense of humor.

"Still finding time to sail?"

Ty paused at her question as he checked the rearview mirror again. If only he were out sailing right now instead of being tossed into the middle of some criminal investigation. The black sedan had fallen back into the light five o'clock traffic but was still there. He shot into the left-hand lane before turning onto a residential street to test his theory.

"Sailing? Yeah. A couple of times on my friend's boat, the *Angelina*." He swallowed hard as the other car turned, still on his trail. "How are things at work?"

"Not much has changed. Mr. Abbott's been staying out of sight. The government officially opened up their investigation into the company yesterday."

"I saw the headlines."

"You'll be on the short list of people they want to question."

Ty frowned. "Thanks for the encouragement."

"On the bright side, everyone misses you."

"I don't think that piece of information will impress the government." Ty took another sharp left through a stop sign. The sedan shot straight ahead. He felt himself relax. Either they knew he was on to them or his imagination was working overtime. Of course, there had been other incidents he'd tried to dismiss as coincidence. Misplaced files at the office. The sense that someone had gone through his desk at home. He shook his head. Surely it was nothing. He'd never been someone to overreact in a challenging situation, and he wasn't sure what had him keyed up tonight. The whole idea that someone was after him seemed ridiculous.

He took another sharp left and headed back to the main street. "What's the news from the inside?"

"So far no one's been arrested, so we're all holding our breath and hoping it'll all disappear."

Ty shook his head. That was exactly what Abbott wanted to happen. Cover his tracks well enough, and he'd get the money and the company. Unless he and his dirty lawyers managed to pin the indictment on someone else. "You should leave. I could look into getting you a job here."

"Thanks, but I've decided to stick it out. If the company goes down, which I'm hoping it won't, I won't have lost anything. And it's not that bad. I'd never make this much money in Farrington."

"Trust me, Penny. Money's not always worth the price."

"So you've always tried to tell me. Hey. Before you hang up, how are your parents? Are they back in Massachusetts for the summer?"

"They actually decided to stay in Florida this year. Apparently they're loving every minute of retirement."

"I would have enjoyed seeing them again."

"Me, too." Ty chuckled. "They haven't been up here for months."

"Be sure to tell them hello for me when you see them."

"I will. And, Penny, be careful. I don't trust Abbott. He'll sacrifice the company and all its employees in a second to save his own hide."

"Don't forget I'm a big girl, Ty. I can take care of myself."

"I hope so."

After saying good-bye, Ty hung up, wishing he could simply erase the past five years of his life. He might have left without any illegal involvement, but the truth could easily be twisted and misconstrued. Something at which Abbott was far too proficient.

Not only did this leave his new position vulnerable, but his future with Kayla was at stake. Giving her a reason not to trust him was something he couldn't let happen, and an indictment would come with rumors of corruption and fraud. Ty gripped the steering wheel as he pulled into the parking lot of his apartment building. Richard Abbott had nothing on him. Which meant that all he could do now was pray things stayed that way.

❦

Kayla grabbed the schedule from the color printer in her mom's office and handed a copy to the older woman. "It's going to be a busy week. Three business dinners, a birthday lunch for fifty, and a retirement party."

"Guess we can handle that." Her mom studied the details before sliding it into a clear binder. "Where are you off to in such a hurry?"

Kayla wished she could have avoided the question but knew it was pointless. "Ty and I are taking Chloe's boys to the zoo in Plymouth for the day."

A shadow crossed her mother's face. "So you're still going out with Ty."

Somehow she'd managed to avoid the topic, which in turn had guaranteed any arguments had been dodged as well. But as her relationship with Ty grew, she couldn't avoid the reality that if things continued the way they were, she'd be planning a wedding in the coming months. "I know you don't like him, but—"

"You're right. I don't like him"—her mom flicked the binder onto the desk before setting her fists on her hips—"or trust him or want him in your life."

Kayla grabbed her notebook and purse then started to leave. She'd never win a round head-on with her mom in this arena. The woman was simply too stubborn. "Mom, I don't want to get into this."

Her mom grasped Kayla's forearm, stopping her in the doorway. "Honey, I'm your mother and I love you, but you're setting yourself up again. You can't believe him."

Kayla worked to control her rising frustration. "But I do believe him, and as much as you don't want me to, nothing is going to change that."

The past few weeks had given Kayla more than enough time to see for herself that Ty was truly a changed man. And while they were still taking things slow with their relationship, the fear that had plagued Kayla for so long was finally beginning to disappear.

From her mother's cold expression, Kayla knew nothing she might say would be enough to convince the older woman of Ty's newfound virtues.

Her mom's grip strengthened on her arm. "I think it's time I told you exactly why I feel so strongly about Ty Lawrence. Then I promise never to bring it up again."

Kayla's brow furrowed. It wasn't like her mother to make emotional deals. She glanced at her watch. Ty was meeting her at Chloe's in thirty minutes, giving her little time to get ready. But one look at her mother's pained expression and she knew she owed her the respect to at least listen. She followed her mother into the country-style living room and sat across from her on the pale blue couch.

Her mom tucked an auburn strand of her hair back into the clasp it had fallen from then scooted forward on the cushion. "Your father swept me off my feet the first time I saw him. He was charming, sincere, and everything I'd ever dreamed of. When we got married I had such high hopes for our lives together. He had a good job working in management for a local grocery store, and I planned to stay home and have babies."

Kayla saw the silent quiver of pain reflected in her mother's eyes as she spoke and felt her heart break.

"After we had been married a few years, everything began to change. He lost his job and started drinking. I was blinded by what I wanted to believe until it was too late." Her mom reached out and grasped Kayla's hands. "But it's not too late for you, Kayla. You know Ty is a manipulator and a liar. He's out to win you no matter what it takes, and after he does, then you won't matter to him anymore. You're like a trophy he's set on winning, and once he does, he'll be free to go on to bigger and better prizes."

Kayla flicked at her broken thumbnail as she struggled with how to respond to her mother's pain without negating it. Her mother's harsh view of men had always stemmed from her own experiences. That she knew. But that assessment didn't have to include Ty. At least not the man Ty had become.

"I know you're concerned about me, Mom, and you have every right to be. But you haven't been around Ty lately. He's not the same man."

"People don't change, Kayla. Not really." Her mom reached up to rub the back of her neck and looked intently at her daughter. "I'd love to tell you it's possible for Ty to have changed into some knight in shining armor and the two of you are going to live happily ever after, but that would take a miracle. This is real life where, more often than not, the prince fools around with his secretary or gets himself killed over a six pack of beer."

Her mom was silent for a moment as tears welled in the corners of her eyes. "Just think about what I told you, and please, please, be careful."

"You know I will."

Kayla leaned over and kissed her mom's cheek. Her heart ached for her mother, whose dreams of happiness had been shattered by one man's choices. Even after twenty-three years the pain still refused to leave. But Kayla believed in miracles. And Ty Lawrence wasn't her father. As far as she was concerned, he'd already proven it.

§

"I can't remember the last time I went to the zoo." Ty handed Brandon a bag of popcorn, not even attempting to hide his boyish enthusiasm. "Are you sure you don't want one?"

"I'm sure." Kayla chuckled as she pushed the stroller past the food kiosk and toward the monkeys. Summer was dwindling to an end, but the day was still warm and sunny. "The real question is, are you sure you're going to survive putting up with two preschoolers for the rest of the morning?"

"Are you kidding?" Ty ruffled the top of Jeremy's hair. "They're adorable."

"He sure has latched onto you."

Ty had begged to come along after Kayla had promised Chloe she would watch Brandon and Jeremy for the morning. So far things were working out great. Jeremy had already found a best buddy in Ty and had attached himself to his side. Brandon was content to ride in the stroller Chloe had provided.

Ty scooped Jeremy in his arms and lifted him onto his shoulders as they stopped in front of the chimpanzees. Kayla smiled at the father and son impression. It wasn't hard to picture her and Ty, five years from now, with a couple of children in tow.

Unless her mother's concerns were valid.

"Kayla?"

Ty's voice broke into her thoughts, and she tried to shove the unwanted assumption aside. But her mother hadn't been the only one to plant seeds of doubt in her mind. Jenny and Chloe were still just as upfront with their reservations. It was going to take much more than a free morning of babysitting to convince her best friends Ty no longer had an ulterior motive rolled up in the sleeve of his pinstriped suit.

"Are you all right?" Ty nudged her with his elbow as she pushed the stroller up the slight incline. "You've been awfully quiet."

"I'm fine." She smiled, irritated at herself for letting other people's biased opinions affect her. Ty deserved her trust. They stopped in front of a family of monkeys lying in the sun behind the glass barrier.

"I saw a big front-page write-up on Abbott Financial Services in the headlines. Looks like it's a good thing you got out when you did. Possible indictments, arrests. . ." She saw a shadow cross his face and realized it was probably a topic he'd prefer to avoid. Especially if he knew some of those who might be involved. At least she knew he was innocent. Ty might not have always been on the up-and-up with her in the past, but he wasn't a thief. "I'm sorry. I—"

"No. It's fine. I told you one of the reasons I left was that some unscrupulous things were going on."

"So you think Abbott's guilty?" she asked as they started walking toward the next exhibit. "The article quoted him as defending himself, but the report implied the missing funds were an inside job."

"I want some ice cream." Jeremy's chubby fingers grabbed at Ty's hair.

"Ice cream?" Ty seemed to latch onto the change of subject. "You can't be hungry."

Kayla's eyes widened in amusement, Ty's old employer quickly forgotten. "You've got a handful of popcorn in your hand, and you want ice cream?"

"Yes!" Ty and Jeremy said in unison.

Kayla just shook her head and glanced down at Brandon who lay sound asleep in his stroller beneath the warm sunshine.

"Hurry up!" Kayla laughed at the enthusiastic expression on Ty's face and wondered how she could even think about doubting him. "The rest of the zoo is waiting for us."

Two hours later Kayla spread out a sheet on the picnic table and began to unload the lunch they'd brought. It seemed the ice cream and other goodies picked up along the way had not diminished the appetites of Jeremy and Ty. Even Brandon was awake and ready for his share.

As Kayla passed out peanut butter and jelly sandwiches with apple slices and carrot sticks, she asked Jeremy what his favorite part of the morning had been so far. The four-year-old hesitated only briefly before deciding that petting the goats had been the best part.

"What about me?" Ty shot her a dejected look.

"What was your favorite part?" Kayla asked obligingly.

Ty cocked his head and looked deeply into Kayla's eyes. "Being with you."

"Isn't that kind of sappy?" Kayla managed a chuckle, but her breath caught in her throat.

"What can I say? I'm in love."

Kayla froze for a moment then turned to look out across the green lawn bordered with orange and yellow flowers. Her heart battled with the noise of common sense that seemed to assail her at every turn from well meaning friends and family members. She loved Ty. That had never been an issue. But reestablishing a broken relationship didn't come with a handbook. At the moment she didn't know if she was ready for the next step. She had to come to the point where she trusted him completely no matter what anyone else said. That was the only way their relationship would ever work.

"I'm sorry." Ty tossed the rest of his sandwich into the picnic basket.

She reached out and squeezed his hand. "It's not you."

"You're not thinking of breaking things off, are you?"

She shook her head and ignored the warnings that continued to surface.

"Kayla, if I'm going too fast, I'll slow down." Ty picked a piece of grass at the edge of the blanket and rolled it between his fingers. "You don't trust me yet, do you?"

"I trust you." She wiped a tear that slid down her cheek, wishing she didn't feel so emotional. "But I can't forget how hurt I was when I found out the truth. I don't ever want to go through that again."

Kayla sat silent for a moment, searching for the right words.

"And I talked to my mother this morning." She handed Brandon his sippy cup. "Or shall I say my mother talked to me."

"I can just imagine how that conversation went. It's not a secret she can't stand me."

"She says it's impossible for someone to change as you claim you have. 'That would take a miracle,' were her exact words, I believe."

"It did take a miracle."

She looked up and caught his gaze. "I know, Ty, but religious transformations don't impress my mother."

"What do you believe? Because that's all I care about. I told you from the very beginning that if you told me to walk out of your life and never come back, I would respect your wishes. But that's not what I want to happen."

She blinked back the tears. "I don't want you to walk out of my life."

Ty laced his fingers with hers, the two little ones forgotten for the moment. "As long as we're honest with each other, Kayla, we'll make this relationship work."

❦

"How were the boys today?" Chloe plopped herself down on Kayla's couch with a bowl of potato chips, ready for their monthly Friday night girls' time. Pizza and junk food were the standard fare along with heart-to-heart chats that often lasted into the early hours of the morning.

"Your kids were adorable." Kayla tossed Chloe an extra pillow then checked her watch. Jenny was predictably late. "You can imagine how excited they were when they got to feed the giraffe."

"I understand that finally beat out feeding the goat on the excitement scale." Chloe picked up the rolled newspaper Kayla had left on the lounge chair earlier and popped off the rubber band. "Is this today's paper?"

"Yes. I haven't even had a chance to look at it."

Kayla ducked back into the kitchen to grab the rest of the snacks she'd whipped together this afternoon. Seven-layer dip with corn chips for Chloe. Chocolate chip cookies for Jenny. When Kayla returned, Chloe was busy scouring the entertainment section.

"Nick's sister is writing a sort of 'Dear Abby' column for the *Farrington Chronicle* now." Chloe flipped back to the front page. "By the way. What company did Ty work for in Boston?"

"Abbott Financial Services."

"There's an article in here about them."

"They've been in the paper a lot lately. The government is investigating the company." Kayla set the food on the coffee table. "What does that article say?"

"Police brought a man here in Farrington in for questioning last night regarding an estimated $175 million believed to be missing."

"Someone here in Farrington?"

"They're trying to prove the books have been altered for the past few years. Ty worked with finances?"

Kayla shot a piece of popcorn at Chloe, hitting her target. She didn't like the obvious conclusion. "Don't start with this again. I know for a fact that Ty wasn't at the police department last night."

"Had a hot date?"

Kayla's stomach knotted. "Actually, no. He canceled. Some emergency came up at work, and he had to stay late."

Chloe didn't have to say anything for Kayla to know what her friend was thinking. Kayla stared out the window overlooking the apartment's manicured lawns. She still believed he may have lied to her in the past, but even the old Ty wouldn't have done anything illegal like embezzle a fortune.

Chloe folded up the paper and set it down. "Don't worry. I may not completely trust Ty, but even I can't see him involved in a fraud case."

"Of course he wouldn't be." Kayla pushed aside any doubts that were rising to the surface. The whole thought of Ty being a thief was...ridiculous. "If Ty said he was at work, then that's where he was."

As long as we're honest with each other.

Kayla shook her head. "The article doesn't matter. I have chosen to trust Ty. If he needs to tell me something, then he will."

The doorbell rang, and Kayla jumped up from the couch to get the pizza she'd ordered.

As long as we're honest with each other. As long as we're honest.

Chapter 7

Three weeks later Kayla hurried up the stairs to her apartment, wondering how Ty could have forgotten his wallet in her apartment. She'd cleaned up the living room last night and didn't remember seeing it anywhere. Normally he was the organized one in contrast to her typically chaotic routine. Something she knew annoyed Ty to no end. She could pull off a five-course dinner for twelve in her sleep, but forget trying to keep a balanced checkbook or her tax information up to date. She was every accountant's nightmare. And the reason she'd had to hire one herself.

She fumbled to find her keys in her purse.

Ty moved in beside her, casting a shadow over her purse. "Can I help?"

Kayla laughed and scooted him aside with her hip. "Your wallet's not going anywhere, and trust me, you don't want to stick your hand in here."

Ty leaned against the door frame, waiting until she finally was able to swing open the door.

"Happy Birthday!"

The handle of the door hit the wall with a thud. Kayla jumped. A dozen of her friends stood beneath a long banner in her living room, announcing in bold letters that today she turned thirty.

Ty entered the room behind her, ducking to avoid a tangle of balloons and streamers that skimmed the ceiling. "Are you surprised?"

"Surprised? I had no idea!" Kayla smiled at Chloe, Jenny, and some of her other friends from church. "And Ty's wallet?"

"All a ruse." Chloe stepped forward to give her friend a hug. "We just wanted to remind you that your twentysomething years are over. It's a new decade for you, sister."

"She's right." Jenny stepped up and wrapped an arm around Kayla's shoulder. "And you know what happens when you hit thirty."

Kayla placed her hands on her hips and quirked an eyebrow at her friend. "Since you're already there, I am sure you'll have lots of advice."

"Very funny." Jenny laughed then waved her hands at the guests.

Kayla greeted everyone as she made her way to her dining room table. "Mom. The cake is beautiful." Kayla hugged her mother who stood beside the table, thankful they'd chosen simple pink roses rather than a black, over-the-hill theme. "And you actually kept this from me."

Her mom's grin widened. "Trust me—it wasn't easy."

"It never has been, has it? I still remember two or three surprise parties you tried to throw me as a child. Somehow I always found out."

Ty scooted up beside Kayla and laughed. "I knew there had to be a devious streak running through you."

The smile on her mother's lips vanished as she excused herself to pour a glass of punch on the other side of the table.

Ty nudged Kayla with his elbow. "I wasn't trying to offend her."

"Don't worry about it."

Kayla frowned, wishing she could take her own advice. Why couldn't the two people she loved most in the world get along?

Chloe cut the cake while Jenny served the punch and passed it out to the guests. Once everyone was served, Chloe motioned toward the others in the room. "Since everyone has cake now, why don't you all sit down? Kayla, we chipped in and got you a little something."

Jenny handed her the gift.

"You guys are too sweet." Kayla set her cake plate down and ripped open the foil wrapping paper to reveal a brand-new food processor.

"You needed a new one," Chloe said, collecting the used paper. "It seemed like the perfect gift."

"This is great. All except the fact that I'm thirty now. I was hoping to forget that tiny detail."

Ty slid in between Kayla and Jenny on the couch, and she caught her mom's disapproving frown across the room. Somehow Kayla was going to have to find a way for a truce.

"To Kayla." Ty held up his cup of punch. "To the best girl a guy could ever find."

"Then let's just hope she finds the right guy." Her mother's cold words seemed to hover in the room before she stood and stalked toward the kitchen.

No one spoke. The tension in the air squeezed at Kayla's chest. She glanced at Ty, wishing she could erase the hurt in his eyes—and the disappointment in her mother's.

"I'm sorry. I'll. . ." Kayla stood, not knowing what to do. Talking to her mother would do little to change the situation. "Please, everyone. There's plenty of cake. Eat up."

Kayla made a hasty exit into the kitchen to find her mom. The chocolate cake she'd just finished soured in her stomach. Somehow she would have to find a way to bring out the white flag and form a truce between Ty and her mom— before Ty decided Boston wasn't so bad after all.

Her mother leaned against the counter with her hands gripping her temples. She'd aged the past few years, and while she still had the energy of someone a decade or so younger, life had left its mark in the creases of her face.

"You had no right to say that, Mom." Kayla folded her arms across her chest and bit back the sharp words she wanted to spout out. "No matter what you think about Ty, he doesn't deserve to be humiliated in front of all my friends."

"Really?" Her mother shook her head. "Well, someone in this family needs to hold on to a little bit of common sense, because you don't have any left."

"Because I love Ty?" Kayla squelched the urge to scream. "You don't get it, do you?"

"Get what?"

"The fact that I'm old enough to make my own decisions on who I let into my life."

Her mom fell back against the counter and continued to press her fingertips against her forehead.

A wave of concern took precedence over her frustration. "Are you having another one of your headaches, Mom?"

"Yes, but it's nothing."

Kayla started digging through one of the upper cabinets for a bottle of pain-killers before handing her mom two of the pills. "I need you to accept him as part of my life."

The older woman turned to face her daughter. "Maybe when you have your own children someday you'll understand what I'm going through. Kayla, I watched that man lie to you and hurt you, and I don't want it to happen again."

Kayla winced at her mother's pointed words. "It's not going to. If you would take the time to get to know Ty, you would see he's not the same person he was a year ago."

"He's a charmer, Kayla. He knows how to get what he wants. How is that any different from a year ago?"

Kayla bit her lip. It was useless trying to get her mother to understand. "You're just going to have to trust me."

"I trust you. That's not the problem. The problem is that I don't trust him. What about the government's investigation into the company he used to work for? Have you stopped to consider he could be part of it? I don't want you to go through the pain you went through all over again."

"Ty's not involved." Kayla braced her arms against the counter and shook her head. "I don't know what to say, except that I'm a grown woman. If I'm wrong about Ty, which I know I'm not, I'm the one who will have to live with the consequences."

Her mother caught her gaze and frowned. "And that's exactly what I'm afraid of."

🎵

Two hours later Ty poured himself a cup of water from the sink, certain he'd somehow misunderstood Kayla's last comment. "You want me to go to dinner with you and your mother?"

Kayla folded her arms across her chest and frowned. "You sound as if I'm asking you to steal England's crown jewels for me."

He rubbed the back of his neck and tried to put a check on his frustration. A showdown with Mrs. Marceilo was one of the inevitable factors in his relationship with Kayla, but he hadn't expected to end today with having to eat dinner with the woman. That would simply push them into round two. And the possibility of winning the affections of Rosa Marceilo was about as likely as his being called by NASA to oversee their next mission to Mars. Impossible.

Besides, he'd been looking forward to a quiet dinner at the Blue Moon to celebrate Kayla's birthday—with reservations for two. There had to be a way out of this one. "You know your mother hates me, and—"

"She doesn't hate you." Kayla patted his arm and offered him a smile. "She just doesn't. . .like you."

He dumped the rest of his water into the sink, his appetite for tonight's dinner suddenly diminished. "What's the difference?"

"Come on, Ty." She grabbed her purse and car keys off the kitchen's laminated countertop. "The two of you need to get to know each other."

"And you really think this is a good idea?"

"If you see our relationship heading forward, then yes." Her eyes flashed an angry warning. "She's my mother, and you can't blame her for not trusting you. She loves me."

Ty took a step backward and bumped against the counter. *What was this? Accept my mother or you're history?* Now it was his turn to feel the anger swell in his chest. This ultimatum sat about as well as the proposed dinner with her mom. Why did her mom have to be part of the package anyway? His parents were perfectly content to let Ty live his own life and rarely, if ever, butted in on his relationships. While he could understand the woman's hesitations over his past, he was tired of having to prove himself.

"I told her we would pick her up after everyone left." Kayla slung her purse strap onto her shoulder and softened her expression. "Please, Ty. For me?"

It wasn't fair. He'd rather she had asked him to steal the crown jewels. Going to dinner with the woman who'd just cut him down in front of Kayla's friends was asking too much.

He shoved his hands into his pockets, realizing he had little choice in the matter. "I'll go, but know that I'm doing this under protest."

With a nod, Kayla grabbed her purse and followed him out the door before locking it behind her. He took a deep breath as they hurried down the sidewalk and worked to crush his growing frustration. Proving to Kayla he'd changed had been tough enough, albeit necessary. Having to do the same with her mom and friends was enough to make him doubt he'd ever find true acceptance in her life again.

Still, if he was honest with himself, it wasn't Kayla's fault her mother felt the way she did. And besides, what was one lousy dinner in the scope of things? At least Kayla would be happy. Maybe it wasn't asking too much for him to make a concerted effort.

"I have a birthday present for you." He opened the passenger door to let her into the car, determined to shake the dark mood that had come between them.

She hesitated before getting in. "Does that mean you've forgiven me for asking—"

"Insisting."

"Okay. For insisting you have dinner with my mom?"

"Not necessarily." He shot her a grin then hurried around to the driver's seat. "Just remember—they say good things come in small packages."

Reaching into the glove compartment, he pulled out a red envelope and handed it to her.

Kayla ripped into the envelope and took out a pair of tickets. "We're going to the symphony?"

"In Boston."

Her face broke into a smile. "Do you know how long it's been since I've gone to a concert? This is wonderful!"

"I thought you might like a nice evening to dress up. Dinner's included."

"Thank you." Kayla turned to him, her face hovering inches from his.

Ty swallowed hard as he breathed in the sweetness of her perfume. As hard as it had been, he'd respected her wishes to take things slow, but starting over had proven far more difficult than he'd imagined. His heart had never let go. Unable to stop himself, he cupped her chin in his hand and reached over to kiss her. His heart pounded as he responded to her nearness, but the promise to let her set the pace convicted him.

He pulled back. "I'm sorry—"

"No. I'm sorry."

His heart sank at her declaration. He tried to read her expression, but all he could see were the tears welling in her eyes. "For kissing me?"

"No. I shouldn't have put you in such an awkward position tonight." She ran her thumb down his cheek and smiled. "Maybe I'm the one who doesn't deserve you."

"No. That's definitely my role." He breathed out a sigh of relief, reminded of all the reasons he'd decided that winning her back was worth it. He needed Kayla in his life, and if that meant including her mother, then so be it. "Then I'm not sorry for kissing you, but I am sorry for hassling you over dinner with your mom."

"You're forgiven, but that doesn't change the fact that I need you to make an effort with my mother."

"Make an effort?" *Whose side was she on?* "I'm not the one who stood in front of a roomful of people this afternoon and tried to humiliate your mother. If I remember correctly, she's the one who keeps pulling all the punches."

"Ty."

"What? I'm willing to make peace, but she's got to be open to the idea as well."

"You can't make an effort by behaving as if she doesn't exist." Kayla shoved the tickets into her purse then snapped it shut. "I'll call her and tell her we're on our way."

Ty pulled onto Cranberry Highway, wondering, as he was with Abbott Financial, if a bomb weren't about to explode.

❧

The phone rang a half dozen times then switched to the answering machine. Strange. Her mother had said she was going straight home. She bit her lip and stared at her cell phone.

"What's wrong?"

Kayla shrugged. "Nothing. I just don't know why she doesn't answer. She told me she was going straight home."

"The ringer could be off, she could be taking a shower—there are tons of reasons why she's not answering her phone."

She dropped her phone into her purse, still irritated at Ty's lack of enthusiasm to meet her mother halfway. She was getting tired of playing referee between two adults. "You're probably right, but she had another bad headache today. I'm worried about her."

Ty drove through the tree-lined streets that led to her mom's house then pulled into the driveway. Her mom's car was parked by the garage door.

"I'll be right back." Kayla unlocked the door and jumped out of the car.

Ty was right behind her. "I'm coming with you."

Kayla hurried up the winding brick path, trying to get rid of the nagging feeling in the pit of her stomach that something was wrong. Shivering from the cool, fall breeze, she rang the bell several times before scrambling for her key in her purse so she could open the door.

"Mom?" She stepped into the three-bedroom home.

Mail was strewn across the floor of the normally tidy entryway. A sweater lay in a pile on the floor beside it instead of on the coatrack.

"Mom?" She walked through the kitchen, then rushed down the hall.

Kayla froze in the doorway of the master bedroom. Her mother lay face down beside the bed.

Chapter 8

Kayla felt her lungs constrict. Her mother's hands lay beside the green comforter that had slid onto the floor. Blood trickled from her forehead, staining the beige carpet. Ty gripped Kayla's elbow, but she couldn't move. She'd let her mom leave the party with an ultimatum that she accept Ty into her life, or else. Or else what? She had no right to speak to her mother that way... and now she lay unconscious on the floor. If she died...

Ty knelt beside her mom. "She's breathing, Kayla."

She tried to swallow the knot of fear—and guilt—that rose in her throat. "She told me she was dizzy, and all I did was give her some pain medicine. I should have noticed something was wrong."

"There's no way you could have known, sweetie. I'm calling 911." Ty pulled his cell phone from his back pocket and flipped it open. "It's going to be okay."

Kayla fell to her knees beside her mother. *It's going to be okay. It's going to be okay. . . .* Ty was right. An ambulance would come to take her mom to the hospital. They'd run some tests, and in the end everything would be all right. Fifty-three was too young to die.

"Mom?" She pushed away the blood-stained strands of hair that stuck to her cheek. The left side of her face drooped, and drool ran down the edges of her mouth. How long had her mom been lying here?

Ty's voice and the rest of the bedroom faded into the background.

There was no response. No acknowledgment of Kayla's presence. Only the slight rise and fall of her chest beneath her flowered blouse.

Kayla tried to steady her own ragged breathing. "It's going to be all right, Mom. I'm here."

"Kayla?" Ty crouched beside her to wipe away her tears with his thumbs. She'd been crying and didn't even know it. "I'm going to wait outside for the ambulance. Are you going to be all right if I leave you for a few minutes?"

Kayla nodded then gripped his shoulder. "I'm scared, Ty."

"Your mom's too stubborn to let something like this get the best of her." He tilted up her chin with his fingertips and caught her gaze. "With the Lord's help we'll get through this, Kayla. I promise."

❦

Twenty minutes later Ty pulled his car out of the driveway behind the ambulance and followed it down the highway toward town. Rows of trees had already begun to turn from summer's shades of green into their yearly fall array of scarlet, orange, and yellow. In a few short weeks, piles of fat pumpkins would lie for sale in front of the farms, and the cranberry bogs would be flooded in order to harvest the crimson fruit. But instead of enjoying the scenic drive, he saw the landscape blur before him.

He reached over and took Kayla's hand, pulling it to his chest. "I'm sorry, Kayla. I know how close you are to your mother."

Kayla stared off into the distance. "I never thought of her getting sick. Not yet anyway. She's my mother, invincible and timeless."

"Don't give up yet." He squeezed her hand, wishing he could do more than simply offer words of encouragement. "She's strong. With your help—with our help and the Lord's—she'll pull through this."

"I should have seen something was wrong."

Ty thumped the palm of his hand against the steering wheel, understanding far too well the intense feelings of regret. "You have to let it go, Kayla. The last thing your mother needs right now is for you to beat yourself up because you missed something that wasn't there. She's going to have her own battle to win, and you'll have to be there for her 100 percent."

"I know. It's just weird all that goes through your mind at a time like this." She glanced at him as he crossed an intersection behind the ambulance. "Nothing's ever going to be the same again, is it?"

"Probably not."

Life was good at bringing unanticipated changes. Something he'd seen far too often in his own life. Sometimes it threw a curve ball—like Kayla calling off their engagement. Only God could have taken that situation and brought good out of it a year later. There had been plenty of other unexpected twists, like finding out his mentor and boss was a man with no scruples and even fewer morals.

"Kayla, I'm sorry about something else. I should have given your mother a chance. I wasn't the one to forgive, and I haven't been much of an example."

"I know, more than anyone else, how difficult she can be. I just wanted things to work out between the two of you, and now. . ." She looked down and fiddled with her purse strap. "Ty, she doesn't believe in God. She told me once she'd seen too much pain and heartache in her life—in this world—to justify the existence of a God. And if He did exist, she didn't want anything to do with Him."

The feeling was uncomfortably familiar. How many times had he told God he'd never believe because a good God wouldn't leave a child to starve in Somalia or let things like 9/11 happen? He'd finally realized he'd been blaming God for man's choices. Not that it made things any easier.

"I guess your mother and I have more in common than I realized. For too long I tried to make God into what I wanted. Problem is, I found out He doesn't work that way. People want a God who will fulfill their desires and leave them feeling like they're in charge. Instead, Jesus calls us to take up our cross and follow Him."

"That's pretty profound, isn't it?"

They were both quiet for a moment as he followed the ambulance toward the hospital. God wasn't a deity to be put into a box and brought out like a genie in a lamp. He'd learned that lesson all too well. Following Jesus called for a full-time commitment. No one said that taking up a cross was going to be easy. It was something he was still trying to get right.

Kayla looked over at him. "What if it's too late? I'm not ready to lose her."

Ty turned the corner into the hospital parking lot and for the first time in his life prayed for Rosa Marceilo.

Ty stood in the doorway of the third-floor hospital room and watched Kayla sleep. The padded chair looked anything but comfortable. Just like the lump that had lodged in his throat and wouldn't go away. The MRI had confirmed a stroke, and while it was possible she would fully recover, Rosa Marceilo's life and that of her daughter had more than likely changed forever.

Kayla opened her eyes then slowly sat up to stretch her back. "I hadn't planned to fall asleep."

"I went for a walk." He pulled the other chair up beside her. "I knew you were tired and didn't want to wake you. How is she?"

"She woke up a little while ago, confused but thankfully calm when I told her what had happened. I'm hoping she'll sleep through the rest of the night." Kayla stifled a yawn. "What time is it?"

"Ten thirty." He held up the boxed dinner. "Are you hungry? I brought you a sandwich. All they had left at the deli was tuna fish."

Kayla looked at the box of hospital food and wrinkled her nose. "I'm sorry. You're sweet, but I don't think I can handle fish right now."

"We could try the cafeteria if they're open." Ty dumped the box on the chair beside him when she didn't respond. "How are you doing?"

"I'm still in a daze. I just can't believe all this is happening. I'll have to let my apartment go and move back home."

"Don't make any rush decisions tonight, Kayla."

"What other alternative do you see? There's the business, employees to deal with, and Mom's house—"

"Kayla. You don't have to go through this alone. Let me in. Let me help."

"With my mother?"

He leaned toward her and rested his elbows on his thighs. "You let me know what you need, and I'll do it."

Kayla smiled for the first time all night. "You're welcome to plan out the menus for next week, and I'll need another cook—"

"Funny."

"Why don't we go check out the cafeteria?" Kayla stared at her mom. "She's sleeping, and I could really use some coffee."

"And a shoulder to lean on?"

"Yeah. Especially that."

❦

Kayla chose a table in the back corner of the cafeteria, away from the group of nurses who chatted over cups of coffee. She stirred her own drink and watched the sugar slowly dissolve. The doctor's prognosis was still inconclusive. Possible surgery. . .inevitable extended physical therapy. . . This wasn't a simple take-two-aspirin-and-call-me-in-the-morning situation.

Ty slid into the chair across from her and slapped his hands against the table. "I convinced the chef to whip up a burger for you before he left for the night."

"You didn't." Kayla's stomach growled, reminding her that lunch had been hours ago and the piece of birthday cake hadn't been enough to take the edge off her appetite.

"Extra pickles, hold the mayo. Just the way you like it."

"Thank you."

"You're welcome." He leaned back, balancing his chair on two legs. "When my grandfather was sick, I had to learn that if I didn't take care of myself, I couldn't help him. Let me take you home after you're finished eating."

"Mom needs me here."

"Yes, she needs you, but Kayla, you have to realize she has a long road ahead of her. This isn't going to be over in a few days or even a few weeks. If you burn out from lack of sleep or not eating right, you won't be able to help her."

Kayla fiddled with the sugar wrapper in front of her, trying to calm her nerves. She'd never imagined how one moment in time could change her life so dramatically.

"Considering that tomorrow I'm going to have to turn in my notice for my apartment, talk to Jenny about working full-time, find out what kind of long-term care insurance my mom had—"

"I thought we just decided you can't do any of those things tonight."

"I know, but I have to do something. She's just lying up there, helpless." The reality of the situation hit her afresh, and tears began to flow down her cheeks. "I'm scared, Ty. I don't want to lose her this way."

"She has a good chance for a full recovery. The doctor said so."

"I am going to move into her house," Kayla said decisively. "She's going to need me once she comes home."

"I have to admit that makes sense. What can I do?"

"I need to find a mover."

"Consider it done." Ty held out his arm and flexed his muscles.

"Very funny." Kayla shot him a wry grin. "The house needs to have a few things done to get it ready for winter. Mom usually loves working outside, but that won't be possible for a while now."

He reached out and tucked a strand of her hair behind her ear. "It's going to be all right."

"Maybe. You never expect something like this to happen." She grasped his hand and pressed it against her cheek, wondering how she ever could have doubted him. "And there's one other thing. I'm sorry about all the things I said in the car. I can't blame you for my mom's unhealthy attitude toward men."

"Forget it."

"Kayla? Ty?"

Kayla turned to see the minister from their church, Randall Jenkins, walk into the cafeteria.

"I forgot to tell you I called the prayer chain at church," Ty told Kayla as the gray-haired man walked toward their table.

"I'm sorry I took so long to get here. I was in a meeting and just got your message." The older man pulled up a chair. "How is she?"

"She had a stroke and is paralyzed on her left side. It'll take a long time, but the doctor said a full recovery is possible."

The minister laid his hand on Kayla's shoulder. "I'm so sorry. What can I do?"

Kayla shrugged. "I don't know right now. She won't be home for a while. I'm only down here now because she's sleeping."

"I want you to know there are a lot of people at church who are willing to help. Once she's home, we can help provide meals and even someone to stay with her when needed."

Kayla felt the flow of tears begin again, overwhelmed by the show of love as the older man began to pray for complete healing for her mother as well as strength for her in the coming weeks.

Kayla looked up when he was finished. "Thank you."

He shoved his thick glasses up the bridge of his nose. "We're here for you. Call me if there's anything else that needs to be done."

"I appreciate it, too, Pastor Jenkins." Ty reached out to shake the minister's hand.

"Take my advice, Kayla. Go home and get some sleep."

Kayla yawned. "I will. Besides the fact that I'm out-numbered, I'm too tired to argue."

The waitress slid the plate of hamburger and french fries on the table in front of Kayla. Ty handed her the salt and pepper. "Then as soon as you're done eating, let's get you home."

Chapter 9

Kayla stifled a yawn and tried to concentrate on the fresh basil she was chopping. Between trying to keep the catering business going, packing up her apartment, and visiting her mother every day for the past two weeks at the hospital, she was exhausted. She yawned again then set down the sharp knife, forcing her eyes to focus. If she wasn't careful, she'd do something foolish and be the next one taken to the emergency room. And that was something she couldn't afford.

The back door squeaked open, and Jenny tottered through the entryway with two heavy sacks of fresh produce in her arms.

"You're early." Kayla smiled, wishing it was as easy to change her mood as it was to plaster on a happy face.

"Traffic was light. And besides, got to be prompt for the boss." Jenny flashed her a grin. "She can be an ogre at times."

"Very funny." Kayla couldn't help but chuckle at her friend's jovial expression. Jenny had been a lifesaver the past two weeks, not only in filling in where needed but also helping to keep Kayla's spirits up.

"How's your mom?" Jenny set the sacks on the counter then slid off her fleece jacket. With October halfway over, the lingering Indian summer that had kept temperatures pleasant was quickly fading into winter's cooler weather.

"She's making slow progress, but at least it's progress. I'm hoping she'll be home by the end of the week."

"That's good news, but I know all of this is hard on you." Jenny squeezed Kayla's shoulder before hanging her coat on the rack behind the door. "I keep telling you to take some time off. You have enough qualified staff to fill in the holes, and I can run a tight ship. You don't have to do everything."

Kayla reached for the half dozen eggs she'd boiled earlier and began chopping them. An afternoon off was tempting, but one look at this week's schedule was enough to remind her they needed every person working full-time. "You know I appreciate the offer, but I'm the one Mom's counting on to ensure everything goes smoothly."

"An afternoon off won't bring about the demise of the company." Jenny started unpacking the produce, and while her motherly tone spoke volumes, Kayla didn't miss the gleam in her eyes.

Kayla turned to Jenny and set her hands squarely on her hips. "What is it? You've got that I'm-dying-to-tell-you-something expression on your face."

"Who me?" Jenny laughed then held up her left hand. "Greg finally asked me to marry him last night."

"And you were going to tell me when?" Kayla squealed and grabbed her friend's hand, staring at the pear-shaped diamond. "It's stunning."

"I know. I never knew he had such good taste."

"He chose you, didn't he?" She gave her friend a hug. "When's the big day?"

"Sometime in the spring." Jenny went back to unloading the sacks. "What about you and Ty? You don't talk about him very much anymore. Isn't it about time for the two of you to follow us down the road toward marital bliss?"

Kayla frowned and dumped the basil and eggs in with the fresh crabmeat, wondering when Jenny had begun rooting for the man who once broke her heart. More times than she could remember she'd wanted to bare her heart to Jenny and Chloe, but something had always stopped her. Her mother's outburst at her birthday party had cinched her resolve to keep the details of their relationship to herself. This was just something she would have to handle on her own. Still, no matter what the rest of the world thought, Ty didn't need to prove himself to her. He'd already done that.

Kayla reached for a handful of scallions and started chopping again. "Knowing the way everyone feels about him, it's been easier just to keep our relationship private."

Jenny folded up the sacks and stuck them in a drawer. "You know we never meant for you to feel that way. The rest of us are just. . .cautious."

"Even after all this time? Surely even you can see he's changed, Jenny."

"Honestly, I'm starting to like the guy, but it doesn't matter what I think. You trust him, don't you? That's what counts."

The phone rang, and Kayla picked up the cordless receiver, thankful for the reprieve from Jenny's question. Of course she trusted Ty. It was everyone else who refused to give him a second chance. "Marceilo Catering."

There was silence on the line then those two haunting words again.

"He's guilty."

Kayla slammed down the phone.

"Wrong number?"

"Something like that."

A chill ran down Kayla's spine. She wasn't ready to connect the dots yet, but something wasn't right. Following the articles in the newspaper had continued to reveal that Abbott Financial Services was in serious trouble with the government, though no arrests had been made. A hundred and seventy-five million dollars couldn't have vanished without help. She'd known a year ago that Richard

Abbott was grooming Ty for a position on the company's management team. He'd been next in line for chief financial officer and would have been the youngest ever to be appointed. Had Ty left the company in hopes of avoiding a bomb dropping, or had he truly been unaware of what was going on?

"Kayla."

She jerked her head up and caught Jenny's gaze. "Sorry."

"What's wrong?"

"Nothing. I'm just tired this morning." She'd tried hard to ignore any red flags, certain they were only her imagination working overtime. She had no idea who had been behind the phone calls she'd been receiving the past few days. And she hadn't told anyone. Not even Ty.

He's guilty.

The menacing words echoed though her mind, but she was still convinced even the old Ty wouldn't have stooped to defrauding the company. She'd never believe that. This was Ty. The man who loved her. Who visited her mom in the hospital. Arranged a group of guys from church to move her out of her apartment. Bought her tickets to the symphony. . . .

The blade of Kayla's knife stopped midstroke. "What's today?"

Jenny looked up from the schedule she was going over. "Thursday."

"No." Kayla waved her hands in front of her. "I mean, what is the date?"

"October twelfth."

"Oh no."

"What's the matter?"

Kayla set down the spoon she was using to blend the crab mixture together and reached for her purse. Digging through the side pocket, she pulled out the red envelope. "This is what's the matter."

"What is it?"

"The tickets to the symphony. Ty gave them to me for my birthday."

"When is the concert?"

"Tonight. And I forgot."

"Uh oh."

"Uh oh is right."

"Tonight's the Bunners' anniversary party." Jenny left the clipboard on the desk and crossed the tiled floor. "I can handle it, Kayla. I might be a mathematician in disguise, but I can do this."

"Are you sure?"

"Haven't I been trying to get you to take some time off for days? This is perfect."

"Maybe you're right. Last night he insisted on taking me out to eat, and I almost fell asleep over dinner." Kayla leaned against the counter and mentally went over her schedule for the day. "I'll have time to go to the hospital this afternoon when the luncheon is over. That will still leave time for me to get ready for the symphony."

With renewed energy she sprinkled bread crumbs over the crab mixture. Tonight wasn't a kink in her schedule; it was time with Ty. Something they both needed. Feelings of fatigue washed over her, but she ignored the impact. She could handle it.

If only she could ignore those two words.

༖

Ty knocked on Kayla's door at half past six. He'd heard the fatigue in her voice when he called her and had tried to convince her to stay in tonight. They could always go another night, but she had been insistent that she wanted to go. Not that a night out wouldn't be good for her, but she needed sleep more.

When she didn't answer, Ty knocked on the door again.

"Kayla?"

Digging into his pocket, Ty pulled out the key Kayla had given him in case of an emergency. This might not be technically classified as an emergency, but she should be home and wasn't answering. He was worried about her.

"Kayla," he said again, stepping into the apartment. Boxes lined the living room wall, ready for the people from church who were coming on Saturday to move her belongings to her mother's home.

"Kayla, it's Ty."

There was no answer. Ty glanced at his watch. Where could she be? She knew he was planning to pick her up for dinner.

Walking toward the couch, a wave of relief swept over him. Kayla lay curled up with a thick afghan covering her; she was sound asleep. Her cheeks were tinged with a hint of pink, and he resisted the urge to brush back a curl that had fallen across her forehead. Part of him still didn't believe he deserved her, but God had been gracious enough to grant him a second chance to win her heart.

All that stood between them now was Richard Abbott and her mother's approval. Ty's visits to the hospital had already begun to bring out a softer side of Mrs. Marceilo, and Kayla never had to know the police had questioned him regarding the missing money. Or that they were still looking into his involvement with the missing funds. He'd find a way to avoid any backlash.

"Tell her."

Ty frowned at the insistent voice in the back of his mind.

"Tell her."

The words came again, but he ignored them. He couldn't tell her. If he wanted her to trust him, telling her would only serve to drive a wedge between them. And that was something he couldn't afford. Ty tiptoed into the kitchen where he'd seen a pad of paper and pens and scratched out a note to let her know he'd come by. He'd been right when he'd tried to encourage her to skip tonight and go to bed early. She was exhausted. There would always be another night at the symphony.

Setting the note on the coffee table, Ty turned to leave.

"Ty?"

He stopped in the entryway. "Hey. You weren't supposed to wake up."

"What time is it?" Kayla sat up and rubbed her eyes.

"Six thirty."

She rubbed her hand on her forehead. "I'm sorry. I must have fallen asleep."

Ty bent down to kiss her. "And that's exactly what you're going to do. I'm leaving, and I want you to get ready for bed."

"I can't, Ty. I've been looking forward to tonight." She struggled to get up, but he gently pushed her back onto the pillow.

"Kayla. You haven't even had time to think about tonight. All you need right now is to get some sleep. We'll do it again. I promise."

"But Jenny's covering for me at work and—"

"It's okay."

Kayla ran her fingers through her hair. "I'm sorry."

"For what?"

"For disappointing you."

"For disappointing me? You could never disappoint me."

Kayla's face broke into a smile. "I wish that was true. I've fallen asleep on you two nights in a row."

"I hope that isn't an indication of how boring I am."

"Don't worry. I can't imagine life with you ever being dull."

Ty leaned against the couch's armrest. "Just promise me that as soon as I leave you'll go to bed. These last couple of weeks have been hard on you, and you need to get your rest. Promise?"

"I promise."

"Then kiss me good night, and I'll leave."

"Tell her."

Ty ignored his conscience or God or whatever it was and instead reached over and kissed her again, wishing he didn't have to go. "I'll call you in the morning."

He walked out of the apartment, locking the door behind him. Surely God didn't expect him to tell Kayla everything that was going on. He'd risk losing what he'd worked to fix between them. No. That was a chance he simply wasn't willing to take.

Kayla aimed the can of polish at her mother's dining room hutch and sprayed the lemony scented liquid onto the wood. Except for a few pieces of furniture still left to dust, she'd managed to do a thorough cleaning of her mother's entire house in one afternoon. Three weeks of trying to schedule her life around hospital visits and catering jobs had left her too exhausted to worry about the layer of grime accumulating in her mother's normally spotless house. Having her mother at home now added a new dimension to the situation, but at least she wouldn't have to make the daily trek to the hospital.

The loud crack of splintering wood sounded from outside. Kayla turned to the large picture window overlooking the front lawn. Last time she'd looked, Ty had been raking the leaves in her mom's yard. What was he doing now?

An unmistakable thud followed. Kayla dropped the spray can on the hutch and ran to the front door.

Outside, Ty lay on his back beside a thick tree limb. Kayla's throat constricted. This couldn't be happening. Her mother lay inside barely able to function, and now Ty.

I can't handle any more, Lord.

She ran across the yellow grass, the scene a blur from tears that threatened to escape. By the time she reached him, he was trying to sit up.

She stumbled over the limb. "You're okay?"

"I'm fine."

"What were you doing?" Kayla knelt beside him, wanting to slug him for scaring her. "You might have broken something."

"Trust me. The only thing hurt right now is my pride." Ty stood to brush off a layer of dirt from the back of his jeans.

"You're sure you're not hurt?"

Ty walked around, as if to prove everything was in working order. "I'll have a few sore muscles, but certainly not anything to worry about."

"What were you doing up in the tree?" Kayla stood up to face him as a surge of anger coursed through her. He had no right to take chances and worry her this way.

"I was trimming a couple of those branches. Didn't want them to fall on the house. The second branch didn't fall, but I did." Ty rubbed his left elbow with his hand then stopped. "Why are you crying?"

She jutted out her chin. "I'm not crying."

"Then what is this?" He brushed away a tear from her cheek. "I'm okay, Kayla. Really."

She pressed her fists against her hips and fought the urge to lash out at him. "I'm not crying. I'm mad."

"Mad?" He pulled her toward him, but she pushed him away.

"Yes! Mad because you took a stupid risk and climbed my mother's tree. Mad because you fell out and scared me half to death. . .and mad because. . . because I can't lose you, too."

Silence hovered between them for a moment. Ty pulled her to him and hugged her. She could feel her heart pounding against his chest and hated the way she kept falling apart without any warning.

"You could have broken your neck or something." She looked up at him. "I can't handle anything else."

"Come here." Ty sat on the grass and pulled her down beside him. "You've been through a lot these past few weeks. Personally, I think you've done remarkably well."

She shook her head. "Remarkable because I'm having panic attacks every other day? This isn't me, Ty."

"Stop trying to be superwoman and let people help you." Ty grasped her hands and leaned forward. "And it's okay to cry."

Kayla frowned. Maybe he was right, but she was tired of crying and feeling as if she carried the weight of the world on her shoulders. She was tired of being tired. The doctors estimated a six-month recovery for her mother. If she couldn't make it three weeks without falling apart, how would she ever get through the coming months?

"I don't think I can do this, Ty. The home health nurses are great, but what about when that's over?"

"One day at a time is all you have to worry about." He tilted her chin up with his thumb.

"Didn't Jenny say she'd organize some women to help you clean?"

"Yes, but—"

"No buts. You should have asked for help. I'm here. Jenny and Chloe are willing to do anything for you. The church has offered to help. How does that verse about sharing one another's burdens go?"

Kayla cocked her head and shot him a smile. He was right. As always. The one person who could give her the push she needed to get going in the right direction again.

"What is it?" Ty asked.

"You should see yourself." She pulled a leaf from his hair.

"What?" He shook his head, and another leaf tumbled to the ground.

"You're a mess."

"And you're changing the subject."

Kayla jumped up and headed for a pile of leaves Ty had raked earlier in the day. She'd been cooped up inside long enough. What she needed right now was an old-fashioned leaf fight.

"Don't you touch that pile." He reached for her arm, but she was quicker than he was. "I'm not cleaning up this yard again."

"Oh, really?"

Kayla scooped up an armful of the crisp leaves, and as soon as Ty was close enough she threw them at him.

"Two can play this game, you know." Ty gathered up a pile.

The leaves hit Kayla and fluttered to the ground as she scooped up another load and aimed for her target. Before she could let go, Ty ran toward her and tackled her, pinning her back to the ground.

"Give up?" Ty teased.

"Never." She blew a leaf off her face.

"Say uncle."

"Never!"

Kayla began to laugh as Ty reached for her sides and started tickling her. Squirming unexpectedly, Kayla slid out from under him and ran back to the tree.

"Are you giving up already?" Kayla poked her head out from behind the tree to watch him where he stood.

"No." His expression turned serious. "It's just good to see you laugh."

Kayla leaned against the rough bark. "Has it been that long?"

"Yes, it has." He walked toward her.

"You make me happy. That's why I couldn't stand it if something happened to you."

He gathered her into his arms and kissed her. "I always want to make you happy."

She felt a hot blush cross her cheeks. "We're in the middle of my mother's front yard."

"I'll stop." He kissed her one last time on the tip of her nose. "You're just hard to resist."

Kayla stepped back, looking at his tall, lean frame, and gave a prayer of thanks to God for bringing him back into her life. "I need to check on my mother then finish cleaning the house."

"And I need to finish up here as well." Ty's cell phone beeped, and he grabbed it off the porch railing.

Kayla brushed off the front of her pants. "Who is it?"

Ty frowned and shoved the phone into his pocket. "It's nothing important. Just work."

"That was more than a my-boss-wants-me-to-work-overtime look."

"Everything's fine. Really." Ty grabbed the rake and eyed the scattered leaves. "And it looks as if I have just a few things to get done before dark."

৺

Ty waited until Kayla was back inside the house before pulling out his cell phone again. He'd almost broken down and told her the truth about the investigation, but the last thing she needed was another problem dumped on her.

He punched in Penny's number, thumping his foot against the ground until she answered. "Penny, it's Ty. What's going on?"

Silence filtered across the line for a moment until Penny spoke. "I thought you might want to know they found a stack of papers with your signature on them. And let's just say these weren't authorization forms to buy envelopes from a discount store."

"What are you talking about?" Ty combed his fingers through his hair and stared at the ground. "You know I'm clean, and I've given the government everything I have against Abbott—"

"I'm not sure that matters anymore. The government's fraud team isn't going away, Ty, and they're not stopping with Abbott."

Ty snapped his phone shut, wondering when the noose was going to tighten further and if there was anything he could do to stop it.

Chapter 10

"What about this one?" Jenny stood in front of a three-way mirror dressed in a satin wedding gown with embroidered flowers on the bodice. Tiny beads sewn into the skirt glistened in the soft light of the boutique.

Kayla reached down to spread out the ivory train then let it tumble to the ground in gentle waves behind Jenny. The Bee Gees played "How Deep Is Your Love" in the background, adding to the romantic ambience of the shop. Plymouth's Wedding Boutique had everything, including veils, hats, jewelry, and shoes, and was the perfect first stop for any bride-to-be.

Kayla folded her arms across her chest and eyed the gown. "It's beautiful, but so was the last one. And the one before that. . .and the one before that."

"That's the problem." Jenny laughed. "Just when I think I find something I like, another one catches my eye."

Kayla chuckled at her friend's indecision. Choosing a wedding dress was proving to be more complicated than solving a complex mathematical equation. And they'd yet to look at flowers, music, and menus. At this rate six months wasn't going to be nearly enough time to plan the couple's wedding. Kayla had already decided they were going to have to take another afternoon off at some point and go into Boston where the selection catered more to Jenny's nontraditional tastes.

Kayla, on the other hand, loved the elegant feel of the shop. Dresses with long trains, white gloves, and pearl-studded veils. . . She took a step back and stared at her friend's silhouette in the mirror. A year ago she'd been the one standing on the low stool, modeling dress after dress for her own wedding. She'd chosen a matte satin gown with a sweetheart neckline and an A-line skirt that had formed a chapel train in the back. Returning it to the shop without ever wearing it had been enough to leave her in tears. But even that hadn't been as painful as finding out Ty wasn't the man she'd thought he was—or had wanted him to be. That revelation had ripped her heart in two.

She took in a deep breath and pushed away the memory. Things were different this time around. The thoughts gnawing at the back of her mind were nothing more than symptoms of her own insecurities.

"Kayla?"

Kayla glanced up at her friend. "Sorry. What did you say?"

"What about this one?" Jenny held up a lacy gown with dozens of white pearls sewn into the bodice.

Kayla pressed her lips together and tried to stay focused on Jenny. Today was her day, and she wasn't about to put a damper on it because of her own complicated love life. "I like it, though not as much as the one you're wearing."

"It's too simple, isn't it?"

"I didn't say that." Kayla eyed the dress. "It's only that the last one was too fancy, and the one before that didn't have enough lace."

"It's a bride's prerogative to change her mind." Jenny straightened the tiara atop her head and turned to the saleswoman whose fixed smile implied she was used to fluttery brides who had no idea what they wanted. "Where's the one with the pale champagne organza fabric? I'd like to try it on again."

Kayla browsed through the racks while the saleswoman went to look for the dress. "I loved the shimmering champagne-colored dress, but the diamond tiara has to go. Way too gaudy in my opinion."

Jenny studied her reflection in the mirror then wrinkled her nose. "You're right."

Still waiting for the saleswoman to return, Kayla perused a nearby aisle before another dress caught her eye. "Look at this one."

Kayla ran her fingers across the satin material. The fitted bodice featured a U-shaped neckline and pearl accents. Roses and a trail of silver leaves ran down the skirt. If she was the one looking for a wedding dress, this one was close to perfect.

Except, of course, she wasn't looking.

"You should try it on."

Kayla's brow puckered at her friend. "I'm not engaged."

"You practically are."

"This is your day." Kayla studied the detail in the embroidered stitching across the bodice. It was completely different from the one she'd bought a year ago—but then she and Ty were completely different people today.

Jenny nudged Kayla with her elbow. "Try it on."

"Would you like to try that one as well?" The saleswoman appeared behind them.

"No, but my friend would."

Before Kayla had a chance to argue, the two women steered her into the dressing room. Moments later she stood in front of the mirror, the bodice and slimming waistline fitting to perfection. Small pearls graced the sleeves as well as the bottom edges of the dress.

"It's breathtaking, isn't it?" Kayla could hardly believe her own reflection.

Her cheeks were tinged pink, and she looked like a princess who'd just stepped out of the pages of a fairy-tale book. It took little imagination for her to picture Ty as her knight in shining armor coming to rescue her.

"Now you just have to get Ty to pop the question," Jenny said.

Reality smacked the air out of Kayla's lungs. She wanted him to ask her, but life had turned into a complicated muddle of confusion between caring for her mom and running her mom's business. Keeping up a relationship in the twenty-first century had nothing to do with castles and handsome knights. It had everything to do with honesty and trust.

"Our relationship isn't as simple as yours and Greg's."

"No relationship is simple." Jenny handed Kayla a gauzy veil with rhinestones and drop pearls surrounding the headpiece, then helped her slip it on.

It was a perfect fit for the dress. "If he does ask, will you be my bridesmaid?"

"You know I will." Jenny reached around the layers of satin to give Kayla a hug. "He makes you happy. I can't deny that."

He's guilty.

No! Kayla stared at her reflection in the mirror and tried to ignore the words that had continued to repeat over and over in her mind. "You're right. Ty does make me happy. Very happy."

If that were true, though, why did it sound as if she were trying to convince herself?

☙

Ty rang the doorbell to Kayla's mother's house then took a step back on the wide porch. Six months ago he never would have considered coming to Rosa Marceilo to talk about her daughter. She would have kicked him out in an instant. Today he stood at her front door, ready to wave the white flag if necessary. No matter what her stance, he was determined to do things right this time. And despite the obstacles that still seemed to stand in their way, he wasn't prepared to put off their wedding any longer.

A home nurse opened the door then escorted him into the living room where Mrs. Marceilo sat in a recliner.

"Ty?" While her speech had improved tremendously with therapy, her left arm and leg still hung limp. "Kayla's not here right now. She—she's out with Jenny."

"I know." He shoved his hands into his back pockets. "I came to see you, actually. Do you have a minute?"

A crooked smile crossed her face. "I'm not going anywhere, and I. . .I can't get up to kick you out, if that's what you're worried about."

The plump nurse stood in the doorway to the kitchen. "May I get the two of you some tea?"

Mrs. Marceilo nodded. "That would be nice, Hillary. Thank you."

Ty sat across from Kayla's mom on the faded blue couch, and it struck him how much Kayla had given up to move in with her mom. The country decor of the living room was a far cry from Kayla's more traditional tastes. She loved her dark mahogany furniture bought from local auctions, brightly colored wall murals, and shelves filled with books and photos. Most of the pieces she'd collected now sat in storage.

He fiddled with the edges of the embroidered pillow beside him. "How are you feeling?"

"My speech is improving, but I forget what I want to say. . . half the time. Physical therapy's a. . .nightmare, but they've tried to. . .convince me it's the only way I'll walk again." She grasped her limp arm then let it fall onto her lap.

"Kayla told me they expect a full recovery."

"P–possibly. I suppose that depends on. . .on how hard I work." Mrs. Marceilo repositioned the afghan on her legs. "You. . .don't have to bore us both with a bunch of small t–talk, Ty. I've never hid the fact I. . .disliked you, and I'm b–betting you've felt the same way."

Ty stared at the framed quilt hanging on the wall behind Mrs. Marceilo's head and sent up a prayer for guidance. Apparently his regular visits to the hospital had done little to ease the strain of their relationship. Not that he'd expected to be received like the prodigal son, but something had to be done to ease the tension between them, for Kayla's sake, if nothing else.

The woman brushed a wisp of auburn hair from her forehead. Despite Kayla's heavy workload, he knew she managed to fix her mother's hair every morning, help her dress, and put on her makeup. It was a gift that had helped to build back the woman's confidence.

She pushed up her glasses and eyed him closely. "Even I have to admit. . . something's changed about you."

Her statement caught him off guard.

"Excuse me?" Ty leaned forward. He'd expected her to continue shooting barbs at him, not handing out hope for a truce.

"The Ty I knew wouldn't have made. . .daily visits to see some old woman unless it. . .unless it somehow fit into his agenda to get. . .what he wanted." Her expression softened slightly. "As hard as it is for me to admit. . .you've been there for my daughter."

Hillary brought in a tray with two cups of tea and a plate of cookies. She held the smaller drink in front of Mrs. Marceilo. "Can you handle this? It's hot."

"I'll be fine, thank you." Mrs. Marceilo took the cup with her good hand and drew it to her lips.

Ty waited until the nurse had left the room before continuing. "I know I've made mistakes in the past, but I love your daughter, Mrs. Marceilo."

"And for whatever reason. . .she says you make her happy." Mrs. Marceilo set down the tea and reached for a chocolate chip cookie from the end table beside her. "These are my weakness."

Ty smiled and took one for himself. "Your daughter makes me happy, too. That's why I'm here."

"I had a feeling this. . .this visit didn't have anything to do with me."

He cleared his throat, wondering if the momentary truce would last once he stated his real reason for coming. "I want to ask Kayla to marry me, and I would like your permission."

A frown appeared on her face, deepened by the droop on her left side. "I don't recall you taking the time to ask my—my permission the last time you asked her."

Ty tried to ignore her disapproving gaze, wondering if she enjoyed making him squirm. Christ might have forgiven all his past mistakes, but that didn't always take away the sting of guilt. Or the burden others placed on him. "There are a lot of things I regret in my past. I want to do it right this time."

Mrs. Marceilo took another long sip of tea before saying anything. "Three months ago I—I would have thrown you out of the house at this point."

He noted the slight gleam in her eye. There was no doubt about it. She was enjoying herself.

Ty relaxed a bit. Two could play the game as well as one. "And today?"

"Somehow you've managed to convince me. . .you care about my daughter. And not only. . .her, I might add, but her decrepit mother as well."

"I beg to differ with that description."

"Always the diplomat, aren't you?" Mrs. Marceilo laughed, but a warning flashed in her eyes. "Don't ever walk out on her, Ty Lawrence, because if you do, I—I'll come after you. I won't have my daughter set up like a. . .like a trophy on some mantel. . .then forgotten. Do you understand me?"

"Yes, ma'am." While he intended to keep his promise, he also took her warning seriously.

"You'd better." Her hand began to shake, and she set the cup down. "I have to admit. . .I don't understand the changes."

"Or believe them?"

"Not completely."

Ty rubbed his jaw and prayed for an answer. "Christ, and the sacrifice He made, changed everything for me."

"That is what Kayla keeps trying to tell me." Mrs. Marceilo shook her head. "I used to believe. . .God cared about me. Then my husband left. . .me alone with a seven-year-old daughter and a trail of grief."

"I spent a lot of time blaming God for man's mistakes. Or more often than not, for my mistakes. He does care, Mrs. Marceilo. And so do I."

Tears pooled in her eyes, but she remained silent.

Ty leaned forward to rest his elbows on his thighs. "I'm not one to make promises lightly, Mrs. Marceilo, but I do have one—no, two—that I want you to hear. I promise to take care of your daughter and always put her first. And I also promise to take care of you."

Mrs. Marceilo blinked away the tears. "I never planned to like you. . .let alone allow you to marry my daughter."

And for the first time in a long time, Mrs. Marceilo smiled at him.

❦

Two hours later Ty sat across from Kayla at the small table in the back of the restaurant, wishing he'd chosen a more creative way to propose than over dinner. The soft music and candlelight were nice, but nice couldn't compete with the first time he asked her to marry him. Sailing around Nantucket Island with caviar and a hired musician wasn't easy to compete with.

Ty squeezed the lemon into his water then took a sip. "I visited your mother today."

"I really appreciate the effort you've made with her." Her smile confirmed the fact that swallowing his pride and talking to her mother had been worth it.

"A box of chocolate truffles now and then goes a long way."

"I'll settle for prawns and shrimp tonight. The menu looks divine."

A ponytailed waitress approached their table. "Are you ready to order?"

Kayla told the waitress what she wanted then scooted her chair back from the table. "I'm going to run to the restroom and wash my hands before they bring out the appetizers if you don't mind."

"Of course." Ty felt for the small velvet box in his sport coat pocket as she walked away and thanked God for second chances.

❦

Kayla pushed her way through the crowded bar, wondering why they couldn't place the restrooms in a more convenient location for those in the restaurant. The lobby was filled with people waiting to be seated. Four years of waitressing in college made her sympathetic toward the employees who'd go home after closing with sore feet and aching backs. Not that she didn't still get her fair share of aches and pains after being on her feet all night for a catered event, but it still had to be easier.

Past the bar was a narrow hallway. A woman wearing a black dress and high heels stopped in front of Kayla, blocking her way.

Kayla tried to move past. "Excuse me."

The woman shoved a lock of thick, dark hair from her shoulder but didn't move out of the way. "I hope you enjoy the prawns."

Kayla shook her head. "I'm sorry."

"The chef was guilty of overcooking mine, but you're a bit of a chef your-self, aren't you? You understand the challenges of preparing that perfect meal. Especially for such a large crowd."

Kayla reached up to rub her temple. Her head was beginning to pound from the loud music coming from the bar. "Do I know you?"

"No. But I know a lot about you, and I have a message for your boyfriend."

"You must have the wrong person."

"I don't think so. Tell Ty to watch his back."

The woman brushed past Kayla, knocking her into the wall. By the time she regained her balance, the woman was lost in the lobby crowd. Apprehension swelled through Kayla's chest. It was time for her to stop pretending everything was all right in her relationship with Ty. That he hadn't been involved in some-thing at Abbott Financial Services.

Fear rose in her throat as she hurried into the bathroom and locked the door behind her. Stepping up to the sink, she stared at her reflection. Her eyes had dark shadows beneath them from lack of sleep. Her cheeks were flushed, but she wasn't sure if it was from the warmth of the restaurant or the encounter in the hallway.

She pressed her hands against her chest. Her heart was racing so hard it pounded in her ears. She glanced at her left hand and rubbed the empty space on her finger. She'd hoped Ty was going to ask her to marry him tonight. Her mother had been vague about his visit, but what other reason would he have had to come out to the house to see her mom?

Someone tried the handle then knocked on the door. Kayla jumped. If it was that woman again. . .

"Is someone in there?"

"I'm coming." Kayla splashed water on her face and quickly dabbed it with a paper towel.

The room blurred before her as Kayla walked back to the table. She slipped back into her chair then pushed the plate of appetizers the waitress had brought while she was gone toward the middle of the table.

Ty reached out to take her hand, but she pulled away. "What's wrong? You look as if you've been crying."

"I need to get out of here." She grabbed her purse from the chair and slung it across her shoulder. "You and I need to talk."

Chapter 11

Ty slammed the car door then shoved the keys into the ignition in order to start the heater. He still had no idea what he and Kayla were doing sitting in the parking lot of the restaurant—without having eaten dinner—the night he'd planned to ask her to marry him. Somewhere, between ordering shrimp and washing up in the restroom, she'd shoved their entire relationship to the edge of a cliff and left it dangling without any explanation.

He'd planned for tonight to end with her saying yes to his proposal. Instead, he looked at her rigid figure beside him. Jaw clenched, lips pressed together, hands clamped tightly. . . The only other time he remembered her being this irate was the night she called off their engagement. Acid churned in his stomach as he gripped the steering wheel. That wasn't going to happen again. He wouldn't let it.

He popped the peppermint he'd grabbed on the way out of the restaurant into his mouth then fiddled with the plastic wrapper. "What's going on, Kayla?"

She folded her arms across her chest, still staring straight ahead. "Why didn't you tell me the government is investigating you in connection with Abbott Financial Services?"

Her words struck like a sledgehammer against his chest, and he fought to catch his breath. "I—I didn't tell you because I didn't think it mattered. I'm innocent."

The moment the words were out, he realized he'd said the wrong thing. Negating the situation also negated the importance of her in his life and his need for her. But that wasn't true. All he'd ever wanted to do was protect her, to protect their relationship.

He cleared his throat and hunted for an explanation that would make sense. "I—"

"You didn't think it mattered?" Her voice rose a notch. "Of course it matters. How can we have a relationship based on trust when you won't talk to me about things that affect your life?"

"Kayla, I'm sorry. I didn't want to drag you into it."

"No." She turned to him, her eyes flashing with anger beneath the white light of a streetlamp. "You didn't think I'd let you back into my life with a possible indictment hanging over you."

Her words pinned him against the wall and condemned him in one fatal swoop. But there was more involved. Hadn't he wanted to protect her? "It's complicated, Kayla."

"I don't care how complicated things are. You should've told me."

He drew in a ragged breath. Trying to protect her was nothing more than an excuse. He'd ignored the Spirit's nudging to tell her the truth, and now he was paying for his own foolishness. "You're right. I was afraid I'd lose you. I didn't want you to think I'd been involved in anything illegal, to give you any reason not to trust me."

"Well, guess what? That's exactly what you did. And it's about to get even worse." The rosy flush in her cheeks was gone, replaced by a white pallor. "I've been getting phone calls."

Ty shook his head. "What do you mean?"

"Someone's been calling me, presumably to convince me you're guilty, and then tonight—"

"Whoa, slow down, Kayla. You never told me any of this."

"The same way you didn't tell me? Just remember I wasn't the one trying to hide something from you. I was hoping the phone calls were nothing but pranks or the wrong number. Tonight all the dots finally connected." She grasped the door handle as if wanting to escape. "I thought our relationship had changed this time, Ty. You told me honesty and trust were the keys to making this relationship work. . .but you lied to me."

"Wait a minute." He wanted to reach out to grasp her hand, but he stopped himself. "I never lied to you."

Her brow furrowed into a narrow line. "You never lied? The police interviewed you, didn't they?"

"They interviewed all the employees who worked for Abbott during the past five years. It's procedure."

"And the night you told me you were working late?"

He closed his eyes and tried to remember the details of that day. There had been a family emergency with one of the employees, and his boss had asked him to oversee the end of the month accounting. In the middle of updating the computer, the police had called. He'd spent an hour being grilled on everything from his job description to Abbott's lunch habits. It hadn't been an experience he'd like to repeat. But he hadn't lied to her. He just hadn't told her.

"I was working late that night. The police called me in about seven. I might not have told you about the interview, but I never lied to you."

"Tell me, Ty. Does the president of Farrington Cranberry Company know the last employee he hired to oversee his financial status might be indicted for fraud?"

"That's not fair, Kayla—"

"Isn't it?" Every ounce of trust he'd gained back from her during the past couple of months vanished into the cold night air. "I don't know, but when I hire a person I like to make sure there's no chance they might spend the next thirty years in prison."

His stomach knotted at the statement. Losing his current job had been an issue he'd chosen to keep shelved in the back of his mind. No doubt the only reason he hadn't had to hit the unemployment lines was because his new boss was an old friend from college who knew that while his personal life might have been marred with a few imperfections, his professional ethics were spotless.

Right now, though, his concern had to focus on Kayla. "Tell me what happened tonight."

She blew out a hard breath. "A woman stopped me at the restaurant and wanted me to give you a message. She said you needed to watch your back."

"Who was she?"

"How should I know? Some woman in a black dress, who wasn't there to be my new best friend—I can tell you that much."

"I don't understand." Ty pounded his hands against the steering wheel. *Abbott.*

The noose was tightening, and this was a message. A message that they were watching and could get to him—and Kayla. Ty felt his forehead bead with sweat despite the cold weather. It had been foolish to believe all of this would go away without Kayla's finding out. Foolish to think he could hand over convicting files without Abbott's turning against him. Foolish not to have listened to the Spirit's urging to tell her the truth from the beginning.

A trickle of fear seeped through him, growing each moment as he tried to digest the implications. How low would Abbott stoop to ensure he wasn't implicated? The police had questioned Ty regarding the papers with his signature, and he thought he'd convinced them they'd been forged. The pieces were starting to come together. Was it all simply a warning to be quiet or part of a setup Abbott was putting together with the help of his lawyers? Ty had believed that cooperating with the police was all he needed to do, but now with Kayla involved. . .

He turned up the heater a notch as the outside temperature continued to drop. "Tell me more about the phone calls."

"Someone apparently thinks you're guilty, and for whatever reason they want me to know."

He hated the edge of bitterness her voice held. God had given them both a second chance, and for him to have blown it was almost more than he could handle. "I should have told you, and now. . ."

"And now what?"

"I need you to believe I was never a part of anything illegal." He looked up at her, but she avoided his gaze. "I turned in documents to the police that I hoped would lead to implicating Abbott. But Abbott's going to do everything he can to make sure he's not the one who takes the fall."

Ty thought back on the past few weeks. The car that had followed him. Misplaced items at work and at home. He'd tried to chalk it up to coincidence, but now he knew that wasn't true. Abbott was looking for something. Warning him they could get to Kayla. And they would do anything to save their own skins. Leaving the company might have been the right decision, but it had put him at the top of Abbott's list.

She folded her arms across her chest. "I want you to take me home, Ty."

He looked up at her, wondering what to do now. What could he say to make things right? "Don't do this, Kayla. We can work this out."

The hard lines that had marked her face earlier had softened into a look of sadness. What hurt him most of all was that he'd let her down. Why hadn't he trusted their relationship enough to tell her?

"I'm sorry, Ty, but it's too late this time."

☙

Ten minutes later Ty watched Kayla slip into her mother's house without a look back. He'd told her once that their relationship would make it as long as they were honest with each other. Pulling out of the driveway, he pushed on the accelerator and sped down the road, wondering how he could have neglected the very thing he'd assured her was most important.

He slammed his fists against the steering wheel. Trust was something one earned, a fact he knew all too well. Yet in the process of proving himself to her, he'd managed to destroy everything he'd worked so hard to gain. And possibly lost Kayla in the process.

Something ran across the road, and he jammed his foot against the brake to miss it. The car skidded sideways, striking the edge of the sidewalk with a jolt. The seat belt jerked against his chest as the car came to a stop.

For a full thirty seconds Ty didn't move. The quiet roar of the engine competed with the accusations filling his head.

"Lean on Me."

He barely heard the words through the muddle. The wind whipped across the windshield. A car honked in the distance. Even the pounding of his heart seemed to echo in his ears.

"Lean on Me."

He stared at the dashboard. This time the words filtered through the noise of the chaotic world around him. He'd worked so hard in the past year to make things right: with God, with Kayla. And he thought he'd succeeded until tonight. The words *Lean on Me* echoed through the recesses of his mind. Maybe that was the problem. Everything had been about his getting things right. Had he forgotten to put God in the equation?

Pastor Jenkins had preached Sunday on how salvation was a gift of God's grace. Never something a man could earn on his own merits. The thought was sobering. He'd spent his whole life working to get ahead, and his efforts had gained him huge financial success and status. But success came with a cost, and the price tag had been too high. He'd lost Kayla in the process. Yet even after realizing he needed a Savior, he'd continued to go at things his own way.

Choosing to follow Christ wasn't the end. For too many years he'd only listened to his own voice. He was going to have to make it a habit to stop and listen to the Spirit's prompting. Learning to be quiet and hear God's voice might have kept him from losing Kayla.

Ty held up his hands in defeat. *I need Your help, Lord. Help me to listen for Your voice.*

He pulled back onto the road again, fighting the strong urge to drive back to Kayla's. There were too many things left unsaid between them; too many things needing to be resolved.

"Lean on Me."

Slipping into the turn lane, he swung a right toward his apartment. He still had no clue what the future held, but for the first time in weeks he knew he didn't have to go through it alone.

ॐ

Kayla thanked Hillary for staying late then walked the older woman to the door. Locking it behind her, she slumped against the wall. The last couple of hours had played out like a bad movie. She'd been certain Ty's visit to her mother would end with a proposal tonight; then everything changed in an instant.

Turning off the lights, she walked down the hall to check on her mother who'd gone to bed early and was snoring softly in her room. Kayla stood in the doorway of the bedroom and smiled at the look of peace on her mother's face. Her left eye still drooped, and the road ahead wasn't going to be easy, but her mother would make it.

Kayla sat down on her bed, wishing a good night's sleep would erase the weeks of fatigue that were piling up. Picking up her Bible from the bedside table, she flipped open the pages. Between running the business and taking care of her mom, she couldn't remember the last time she'd had a quiet time with God. Or how long she'd been trying to handle everything on her own. Somehow she'd let her spirit become a dried-up well in the middle of the desert.

I just can't do this anymore, Lord.

She opened to the first chapter of second Corinthians, a recent passage in one of Pastor Jenkins's sermons, and started reading. The apostle Paul had always been a superhero in her eyes. The list of things he endured for the sake of the gospel read like a *New York Times* bestselling thriller.

Pulling her legs up under her, she stopped at verse 6. Paul wrote how suffering produced patient endurance. How could suffering produce patience? Kayla rubbed her temples with the tips of her fingers. She'd never been shipwrecked or left in prison or even gone without a meal. Her struggles were real, but in the scope of what many had to endure, she wasn't sure they even counted as trials. On top of that, patient endurance read more like an oxymoron than a word of encouragement.

She reread verses 3 and 4. " 'Praise be to the God and Father of our Lord Jesus Christ, the Father of compassion and the God of all comfort, who comforts us in all our troubles.' "

All our troubles. Her mom's stroke. Ty's betrayal. The load of running the business while caring for her mother.

She continued reading the chapter, stopping again at verse 9. " 'This happened that we might not rely on ourselves but on God.' "

The truth seared through to her heart like a hot iron. That was what was missing in her life. How long had she spent her time relying on her own efforts to take care of everything? She claimed to follow Christ but was all too quick to grab the steering wheel and head off in her own direction. Controlling the business. Controlling her mother's recovery. Controlling Ty.

Tears she'd held back for weeks poured down her cheeks like healing rain, and the love of her heavenly Father enveloped her. The future was still uncertain, but one thing wasn't anymore. This time she was going to put her trust in the One who created her.

ॐ

Ty parked his car in his spot then locked the doors before heading up the sidewalk toward his apartment.

"Ty Lawrence?"

Ty stopped short of the small patio and turned around. "Yes?"

"My name's Samuel Lance. I'm a law enforcement officer for the State of Massachusetts." The man flashed a badge beneath the bright streetlamp as he took a step toward him. "You're under arrest for accounting fraud and other illegal activities in connection with our recent investigation into Abbott Financial Services."

Chapter 12

Kayla combed out a section of her mom's hair, then clamped it into the curling iron, wishing she could spend the rest of the morning in bed. She'd finally fallen asleep around one, but her dreams had been filled with Ty. Already she missed him, torn between her heart's longings and the common sense that constantly reminded her she needed to stay away from him. Even putting her trust back into God's hands had become a minute-by-minute effort.

"Are you almost done?"

Kayla's focus switched back to the task at hand. "One section left."

Her mom worked to fasten the top button of her blouse that had come undone. "You know you don't have to do my hair every morning, Kayla."

"I know I don't have to, but I want to." For once she was thankful for the distraction. Between her mom and the business, staying busy would make the pain of letting Ty go easier. Or at least she hoped it would.

Her mother's hand shook as she fought with the shirt.

Kayla reached down to help. "Let me do that—"

"No!"

Kayla drew back her hand and bit her lip as her mom continued to struggle. Her fingers fumbled with the buttonhole. It was all Kayla could do not to finish the chore herself. Finding the balance between helping her mother and letting her struggle to relearn simple tasks had proved to be difficult. The stroke had added depression to the list of symptoms her mom had been forced to accept. All of which added up to a new dimension of tension between them.

Her mother jerked the button off and threw it onto the floor. For a few seconds neither of them moved.

"I'm sorry." Her mom let her good arm drop into her lap defeated.

"It's okay." Kayla moved the curling iron to the last section, deciding to leave the button on the floor for now.

"No, it's not." Her mom's leg shook. "Since when do I have to rely on—on my daughter and nurses to button my shirt?"

Tears pooled in her mother's eyes. Kayla set the curling iron down and wrapped her arms around her. Frustrations over her relationship with Ty seemed minimal compared to the life-changing challenges her mom faced.

Kayla bit back her own tears of empathy. "I remember when I was in third grade and I wanted curls like Abigail Mentor's. You must have spent an hour fixing my hair every morning before school."

"And your curls were much prettier than Abigail's. . .weren't they?" Her mother's smile emphasized the droop on the left side of her face, but at least she seemed to have forgotten the button for now. "I wanted to see you last night. How was your dinner with Ty?"

With Ty on the top ten list of topics to avoid, Kayla hadn't expected the subject to come up and wasn't sure how to approach it. Another argument was the last thing she wanted. "I understand he came to visit you yesterday."

"He did. . .and we had a nice time. What happened at dinner?"

Kayla quirked an eyebrow at her friendly tone. "There's nothing to tell."

Her mom strained to look up at her. "Don't tell me the two of you. . .got in a fight?"

Kayla shook her head, confused. Even after her mom had agreed to keep her opinions of Ty to herself, nothing had really changed. The stroke had just postponed the inevitable explosion she was convinced was coming. Genuine interest in their lives wasn't what she'd expected.

Kayla began to comb the short curls into place. "Why the change of heart, Mom? You're acting as if you like him. But he's the bad guy, remember. The one who's stealing your daughter away, bound to break her heart."

"Not according to everything. . .I've ever heard from you." Her mom pointed to a gold-foil box on the bedside table. "You'd be amazed how far a box of chocolates goes when you've been living on hospital food."

"He said something about that." She still didn't get it. Since when did peace break out? "He was going to ask me to marry him, wasn't he?"

Her mom reached up to push a curl into place on the side of her head. "I'd say that's between you and Ty."

"Mom. I need to know."

"He came to ask my permission to marry you."

"And you agreed?"

Her mom nodded slowly. "Lying in a hospital bed for almost three weeks makes. . .you look at things differently. He's good to you. And as much as I haven't wanted to admit it, he's been. . .good to me as well."

Kayla sprayed some hairspray to set her mom's hair in place, making a mental note to schedule an appointment with the hairdresser for a perm. Her mom did have a point. Making sure the outside of her mother's house was ready for winter was only one of the things he'd done to help ease Kayla's load. He'd fixed the garbage disposal, insulated the windows, changed the smoke detector batteries, and the list went on and on.

Her mom slid on her glasses. "He also mentioned how easy it is to blame God for our mistakes. I can't say. . .I've ever really thought about it that way."

Kayla squeezed her eyes shut for a moment and sent up a prayer for wisdom. If she was going to rely on God for His wisdom and help in her life, now was as good a time as any to start. If her mother was opening her heart to God, what she needed to tell her about Ty was going to make things worse. How many people had been turned off from God and consequently church because of the behavior of the very people sitting inside?

"There are some things you need to know about Ty, Mom."

Kayla sat down on the edge of the bed beside her mom and told her everything. From Ty's involvement in the government's investigation into Abbott Financial Services, to the strange phone calls, to the woman at the restaurant. The emotional weight she'd carried home the night before had shifted from anger to sadness. Maybe reality would hit her at some point. Right now she still felt numb.

"I'm so sorry you've had to go through this." Her mom reached out and grasped Kayla's fingers. "And I know this is going to sound. . .crazy coming from me, but I think you need to consider the fact that Ty's innocent."

Her brow pinched together. Those were the last words she'd expected to hear from her mom. "Whether or not he's innocent isn't really the point. He kept the truth from me. That's not a relationship to base a healthy marriage on. And it goes back to the same problems we dealt with a year ago. It's a matter of trust."

"What if he was simply trying to protect you?"

Kayla shook her head. She couldn't believe what she was hearing. Unplugging the curling iron, she marched across the room and opened the heavy mauve drapes. Outside, dark storm clouds reflected her mood. Why was her mother defending Ty? A box of chocolates wasn't nearly enough incentive to blind a person to the truth of the situation.

Her mom struggled to add blush to her cheeks. "I'm serious, Kayla. Even after everything you've told me. . . something's not right."

"It seems pretty straightforward to me." She folded her arms across her chest, resisting the urge to take the makeup brush away from her mom to finish the job herself. "The bottom line is, whether or not he was involved, the fact remains that he didn't trust me enough to tell me what was going on. How could he hide the fact that he's one of the government's suspects? It doesn't get much bigger than that."

"I've kept things from you throughout the years to protect you."

"I'm not a child anymore, Mom. I don't need to be protected."

The doorbell rang, and Kayla fled from the room, grateful for the interruption. Since when did her mother defend Ty and his underhanded actions? If anything, her mom should be on her side; but instead it was as if she'd fallen into Alice in Wonderland's rabbit hole and ended up in the twilight zone.

The doorbell chimed again. Kayla glanced at her watch as she hurried through the living room. Eight in the morning was too early to expect company, and Hillary wasn't coming for another hour.

Kayla paused at the door. If it was Ty, she didn't want to see him. She might have realized she couldn't do things without her heavenly Father's help, but that didn't mean she was ready to deal with the emotional tsunami Ty was certain to evoke.

Leaning forward, Kayla glanced through the peephole, then let out a sigh of relief. Chloe stood on the porch dressed in a red jacket with a matching knit hat and gloves.

Kayla unlocked the door and flung it open. "Hey, this is a nice surprise."

Chloe stepped out of the cold and into the warm entryway before giving Kayla a hug. "Honey, I need to talk to you about something."

"And how are you this morning? You always were one to get straight to the point." Kayla caught Chloe's frown, and a shot of adrenaline flashed through her. "What's wrong, Chloe? Is it Nick or Jenny? Or the boys?"

Chloe stood in the entryway and pulled off her gloves. "No, sweetie. I hate to be the bearer of bad news, but it's about Ty."

"What's wrong, Chloe?"

"He called Nick last night a little after nine."

Kayla's head began to spin. Ty had left her place around seven, and she assumed he'd gone home. If he'd been in an accident, or even worse—what if Abbott had done something to him? "What happened? Is he hurt?"

"No, honey. Ty's been arrested."

Kayla felt her knees give out as Chloe helped her to the couch. Surely she hadn't heard her friend correctly. The company might be under investigation, but that didn't mean Ty had been a part of the corruption.

He's guilty.

She dismissed the condemning words that had haunted her the past few weeks. Ty couldn't be guilty. Sure, she'd been furious with him for not telling her the truth. For not trusting her to be able to handle what was happening in his life. But she'd never believe he could have been involved in something criminal.

She rubbed the back of her neck and stared at a spot on the carpet. When was the last time she'd had the carpets cleaned? She'd need to call and have someone come out—

"Kayla. Are you all right?"

"No." She shook her head and tried to erase the distractions as she looked up. "This can't be happening, Chloe. I don't understand."

Chloe sat across from her and took her hands. "Ty's worried about you. He insisted I come to your house and tell you in person. He didn't want you to find out on the phone or, worse, on the news."

Kayla glanced at the television that sat in the corner of the living room. Abbott Financial Services was no mom-and-pop business. They'd made the Fortune 500 list the past three years in a row. Ty's face would be plastered across TV screens and newspapers from Boston to San Francisco. The very thing he'd hoped to avoid.

"What's he been charged with?"

"Securities fraud and inflating stock prices. He was picked up last night by the Securities and Exchange Commission that's working with local law enforcement."

"What about Richard Abbott?"

"He could always be next. But, according to the prosecuting attorney, the evidence doesn't point to him."

"I don't believe it." Kayla pinched the bridge of her nose with her forefingers, refusing to cry. "This is serious, isn't it?"

"Very."

"And what if he's guilty?" Kayla's voice caught in her throat.

Chloe squeezed her hands. "I know none of us has been very supportive of your relationship with Ty, but that doesn't mean I think he could be guilty of defrauding a company of millions of dollars. All you can do right now is take things one day at a time and pray. Nick's a good lawyer and will do everything he can to get him off."

Put your trust in Him, Kayla. That's all you can do.

Kayla tried to steady her breathing, repeating the words over and over in her mind. "Is Nick there with him?"

"He's working to get him out on bail, but that's going to be tough. He promised to call me as soon as he finds out anything."

Kayla walked to the window. She thought her world had fallen apart last night when Ty admitted he was under investigation, but she'd never believe he was guilty of accounting fraud. Surely her instincts weren't that far off a second time.

"I have to do something." She stared out across the yellow lawn trying to work her mind around both Ty's arrest and what she needed to do about it. "I'll call Jenny and ask her to cover for me today."

Chloe got up and stood beside her. "What are you talking about?"

"Penny was Ty's secretary in Boston, and she worked for him for years. She has to know something."

"I'm sure the police have already questioned her, Kayla."

209

"I know, but they might have missed something, and I have to know the truth about him this time." Everything suddenly became clear. Maybe it was crazy, but there was no way she could stay here and wait for something to happen. Penny would have access to inside information that might prove Ty's innocence. "I'm going to Boston."

☙

Kayla shifted her umbrella to block the downpour as she ran toward the Abbott Financial building. Shivering beneath her long black coat, she wondered for the umpteenth time if her impulsive decision had been a mistake. She hadn't even taken the time to try to call Ty after Chloe's bombshell announcement. If the authorities would even let her talk to him.

She shivered again, but this time it wasn't from the cold. She needed answers before she could face him. Going to his old place of work had seemed to be the first logical step. Or at least it had seemed logical at the moment Chloe told her Ty had been arrested and Nick had just been brought in as his criminal lawyer. She was no Sherlock Holmes, but she was on the verge of another broken heart and had to do something. Besides, no matter how jumbled her personal feelings were at the moment toward Ty, she wasn't going to walk away this time without finding out the entire truth.

The four-story building rose before Kayla. Standing on the edge of the sidewalk beneath the outside awning, she stared up at Abbott Financial Services before taking a deep breath and heading inside. Her mother's insistence on Ty's innocence had surprised her—and convicted her. What if he was innocent and had only meant to protect her?

She crossed the lobby's polished tile floor, knowing that for now she owed him the benefit of the doubt. His methods of trying to protect her could be discussed at another time.

Five minutes later the elevator stopped on the third floor, and the doors opened to reveal the large reception area. It had been over a year and a half since Kayla had walked into the plush Boston office. Nothing had changed, from the overstuffed gray couch and chairs to the rich purple and silver accents.

"May I help you?" A receptionist looked up from a computer screen and waited for her response.

Kayla's stomach lurched.

You can do this.

She cleared her throat and caught the young woman's gaze. "I have an appointment with Penny Waterford."

The receptionist glanced at the calendar in front of her then raised her penciled brows. "You have an appointment with Miss Waterford? She's an executive assistant who doesn't normally talk to clients."

"I spoke to her this morning, and we're having lunch."

"O–kay." The woman picked up the phone, mumbled a few words, and hung up. "She'll be out in just a minute. Take a seat over there."

Kayla had just sat down when Penny walked into the room. The woman had cut her blond hair into an attractive bob, but other than that the petite assistant looked the same as when Ty had first introduced them at a company Christmas party two years ago.

"Kayla, it's good to see you again." Penny held out her manicured hand in greeting. "I was surprised to hear from you and even more surprised when you said you wanted to meet me here in person."

"I appreciate your taking the time to see me. Is there somewhere we could talk in private?" She wasn't in the mood for small talk and formalities.

"There's a bistro down the street." Penny slid a black coat on over her stylish purple skirt and blouse. "It's close enough to walk to and stays pretty quiet during lunch."

"That's fine."

Fifteen minutes later they were seated at a corner table with bottles of sparkling water. Aromas of garlic and onions coming from the kitchen did little to whet Kayla's appetite, and she wasn't sure if she'd be able to eat the chicken salad she'd just ordered.

"I was so upset when I heard about Ty's arrest this morning." Penny took a sip of her drink, seemingly relaxed despite the heavy atmosphere that must pervade the office after yesterday's arrests. "He was always a good boss. He worked hard and treated me well."

Kayla poured her flavored water into a glass full of ice. "Who do you work for now?"

"The big CEO himself. Richard Abbott."

"Wow! That must have been a nice promotion."

Penny set down her drink and nodded. "His secretary went on maternity leave then quit, and let me tell you, the extra income that comes with working for the CEO of the company can't be beat. Unless you count the recent government investigation."

"I'll get straight to the point, Penny. You knew Ty better than anyone I can think of here in Boston. Have you been in contact with him since he left?"

"Sure. He's called me several times over the past few months. We all knew the government was asking questions, and he seemed interested to know what exactly was going on. I always assumed it would disappear. I never thought anyone I knew, especially Ty, could actually be guilty."

Kayla leaned forward in her chair. "You don't think he did it, do you?"

"I—I don't know, Kayla." Penny's friendly smile faded. "I hate to burst your bubble, but as much as I liked Ty, I think the authorities have the right man this time."

The dozen or so tables around them blurred from view as the walls closed in around her. The instrumental music in the background churned in her head like fingernails on a chalkboard. Voices slurred together into a muddled roar.

Kayla tried not to panic. "What are you saying, Penny?"

"They think he tried to clear most of the damaging stuff from his computer, but they were still able to find enough evidence to obtain an arrest warrant. Apparently he also handed over some documents to the police implicating Richard Abbott, but from what I heard, most of those documents were well-thought-out forgeries."

"What?" Kayla shook her head. Ty might be brilliant when it came to numbers, but forgeries? It didn't make sense.

"I'm sorry." Penny took another sip of her water. "I know you didn't come here to hear me confirm what the police are saying, and I wish I didn't have to, but as Abbott's own protégé, Ty was next in line for the job of chief financial officer. He had access to files and data that few other people in the entire company had."

Kayla knew she was grasping at straws, but she wasn't ready to stop yet. "Do they think he was the only one involved?"

"The authorities are looking at two other top managers. I knew them both. It's been a tremendous blow to the company, though we're all hoping we can put the scandal behind us as soon as possible in order to move forward."

"I guess I thought this all had to have been a big mistake. I mean, Ty and I have had our differences, but he's not a criminal." Kayla's temples began to pound. Something wasn't right, but she had no idea what. "Had you ever noticed anything out of the ordinary when you worked with him?"

Penny fiddled with the paper napkin between her fingers. "I debated whether or not I should pass this on to you, and I'm still not sure—"

"I have to know the truth."

"I had noticed some discrepancies for the past year or so and decided to start keeping copies of files." Penny pulled a flash drive from her purse and set it on the table. "I handed this over to the police three days ago, keeping copies for myself. I never told Ty what I was doing. I guess because I didn't believe he might be guilty. But all that's changed now, Kayla. I'm afraid the police have the right man. As far as I'm concerned, Ty's guilty."

Chapter 13

Kayla clicked on the small fringed lamp in her mother's living room then fell back against the couch cushions. The hour-and-a-half drive home from Boston to Farrington hadn't been enough time to erase the shock of Penny's convicting words. Instead, it had resurrected all the old feelings of mistrust Kayla had managed to store away in the back of her mind these past few months, and brought with it a finality she hated. Ty was guilty, and there was nothing she could do to change that.

She rubbed the back of her shoulder with her fingertips to loosen the heavy knots in her muscles. Having Ty back in her life had been like the answer to an unspoken prayer. She'd never loved anyone the way she loved him. Even talking with him last night hadn't completely taken that away. But now everything had changed.

She'd tried to find a hole in Penny's story, anything that would prove Ty's innocence. But Ty's former secretary had no reason to lie to her. Penny's heart wasn't involved, allowing her to see the truth for what it was. Something Kayla had been unable—or perhaps unwilling—to do. Failing to see the truth at this point would do nothing but bring her even more heartache in the future. Just like telling him good-bye might not be something she got over quickly, but it was what she had to do.

She picked up the cordless phone off the end table and dialed his home number, realizing her mother had been right all along. People didn't change. Not really anyway. Ty was no different from the man he'd been the day she broke off their engagement. Whether or not he was guilty was no longer in the equation. He'd purposely kept too many things from her. And she couldn't pretend any longer that it was all right.

The phone rang a half dozen times then switched to the answering machine. She took a deep breath to steady her nerves. "Ty, this is Kayla."

She squeezed her eyes shut, wishing all this would go away. But the words *He's guilty* wouldn't let her forget.

Her hands shook as she held the phone against her ear. "Listen. I know you're in good hands with Nick, and I'm sorry for all that's happened, but I can't do this any longer. Please don't call me or try to contact me. I'm sorry. . . ."

Kayla hung up the phone, not knowing what else to say. Maybe because there simply wasn't anything left to say. She'd taken a chance and given away her heart, quite certain now that she'd never get it back.

The next morning Kayla piped the last layer of crimson frosting on the three-tiered wedding cake, then stood back for a final inspection. The Walker-James wedding had quickly become the wedding of the year in the small town of Farrington. Two families in the cranberry business who'd lived in the area for generations were finally tying the knot, and the fact that Marceilo Catering had been chosen to do the wedding was an extra bonus for the small company.

Kayla had decided to finish the cake at the church, which was now in the final stages of preparation for the seven o'clock ceremony. Jenny was on her way in the van with the majority of the food they would be serving from the newly refurbished kitchen; it was in the building's east wing where the full dinner reception would be held. Round tables with lacy white covers had been set up, along with yards of white and ruby red tulle, elaborate rose petal centerpieces, candles, and twinkling white lights.

She should be pleased with her staff's efforts, but instead the wedding only served to remind her of everything she'd lost. She'd seen clips on the news last night of how Ty had been released on bail until the upcoming trial. Chloe had told her that, despite his continued stance that he was innocent, he'd also lost his job with Farrington Cranberry Company.

She set the empty frosting bowl in the sink and turned on the hot water. A part of her felt guilty for not being there for him. He'd stayed beside her every step of the way of her mother's recovery, from visiting her in the hospital to helping out at the house. Wasn't that enough to prove the man had changed?

The door banged open against the inside wall as Jenny entered the kitchen with her hands full of boxes of appetizers. "Kayla, we have a problem."

Thoughts of Ty vanished for the moment. There was a job to do, and it was up to her to run things in a professional manner. "What's wrong?"

Jenny set the containers on the counter and frowned. "One of our suppliers called ten minutes ago. He can't get the strawberries he's been promising me all week. Off season or not, the bride wants chocolate-covered strawberries."

"Then we'll give her something even better."

"What?"

Kayla rested her hands on her hips. "Is it too late to make those chocolate mousse dessert puffs we served last week? They were a huge hit and not too hard to make for an up-and-coming caterer like you."

Jenny grinned as she glanced at her watch. "I can have them ready by four, which should give us plenty of time."

"Good. I'll help you unload the van then finish setting up here while you take care of the mousse. What about the other staff?"

"They'll be back here in a couple of hours with the rest of the food. Everything's on schedule."

"Great." Kayla headed for the van.

"Wait a minute, Kayla." Jenny started to follow then stopped. "Are you okay about all of this? I mean a wedding probably isn't on your top ten list of jobs you'd like to take right now with all that's happened in the past twenty-four hours."

Kayla shrugged, wishing her friend hadn't brought up the subject. "I can't exactly turn away business because I can't win at romance."

"I saw him on the news last night."

"So did half the state of Massachusetts." Kayla hurried out the back door and shivered at a gust of wind. Tonight's predicted snowfall would either add a romantic touch to the wedding or cause havoc in getting the guests here. She was fervently praying for the former.

Jenny hurried outside behind her. "I think he's innocent."

Kayla braced her hands against the van door before popping it open. Why couldn't everyone just drop it? The last thing she needed right now was a distraction. And thinking about Ty was a distraction. He was out of her life, and nothing anyone said or did was going to change that. "How could you have spent the past few months believing I was making another mistake, and now, when I finally see the truth, decide the man is innocent? Don't do this to me, Jenny. I can't handle it."

"I expected you to believe him."

Kayla felt her blood pressure rise as she grabbed a large container of cut-up fruit. "What I think doesn't change the reality of what happened."

"What if he was set up?"

Kayla froze. "What are you talking about?"

"I was over at Chloe's last night. Nick's looking into this angle. There have been too many strange things happening. The phone calls you received, the woman at the restaurant, Ty being followed and his house gone through—"

"What? He never told me about that." Kayla swallowed her irritation. She piled another container on top and hurried back into the church.

"Just hear me out, Kayla." Jenny grabbed the groom's cake and followed on her heels. "Nick's theory is that someone, namely Richard Abbott, is trying to scare Ty. He might not fight back if he knew they were watching him and could get to you."

Kayla spun around and planted her fists on her hips. "So what do you think I should do? Call him and tell him everything's okay?"

Jenny seemed to ignore the hint of sarcasm in her voice as she set the cake down on the counter. "I think you need to pray about it, but Ty was at Nick and Chloe's house last night as well, and in all honesty I think he's more upset about losing you than the upcoming trial. And you have to admit, no matter how professional you try to be, you're just as miserable. I don't know what'll happen, but my gut tells me there's more going on here than we can see from the surface. Ty might have been a workaholic in the past, and while it might have affected your relationship, it's not a federal crime to be a jerk. Richard Abbott, on the other hand, apparently has a few skeletons in his closet that they're looking into. If the theory's true, I know even you wouldn't want Ty to take the fall for some rich man and his lawyers. And you certainly won't want him to go through this alone."

Kayla felt her lungs constrict, and she fought to breathe. What if he was innocent and she wasn't there for him?

Jenny moved in front of Kayla. "What does your heart say? Not your head or the facts. What does your heart say?"

"I don't know."

Kayla set the food down on the counter and clenched her fists at her sides. It wasn't fair. How had things gotten so complicated? She needed some time to think. . .and pray. She caught Jenny's gaze. "I know we've still got a lot to do, but you're right. I need some time to pray. Thirty minutes. An hour tops."

Jenny smiled and nodded. "You got it."

❦

Kayla walked down the center aisle of the auditorium toward the prayer room, stopping on the thick carpet to finger a red satin bow that hung on the end of one of the pews. Those setting up for the wedding must have gone to lunch, because the sanctuary was quiet now. A quiet that would be replaced this evening with the joyful presence of family and friends of the couple who were pledging to spend the rest of their lives together.

She made her way toward the prayer room, feeling a sense of despondency grow with every step. Sunlight filtered through the stained-glass window above the front baptistery, casting a golden glow over the large brass archway decorated with white organza and roses. Candles graced the front pews, adding to the romantic feel of the room.

Had it been only a few short weeks ago when she had tried on a satin gown in the shop with Jenny and dreamed of her own wedding day in this very church? She thought she'd been given a second chance for love with the man who'd captured her heart. All she had left now were the shredded remnants of her heart. . . and lost dreams of what they could have had together.

What do I do now, Lord?

There were no answers this time, only the steady pounding of her heart. Her heart.

Words spoken to her by her mom and friends flooded through her mind. *What does your heart say, Kayla, not your head? . . . What if he's only trying to protect you? . . . He's stood by you during your mother's illness. . . . Ty's innocent. . . .*

Ty's innocent.

But was he? Kayla pressed her fingertips against her temple. Was God using her friends and family to show her the truth?

Kayla slipped into the prayer room and sat down on the empty wooden bench. "I don't know what to do, Lord. I don't know if I can go through the rejection again if I'm wrong."

She fought to clear her mind, searching for the words as she spoke aloud. "What if he is guilty? That means he's lied to me, and even if he is innocent, he never told me the truth about what was happening. Trust will always be an issue between us."

Kayla drew a tissue from the box beside her and blew her nose, wondering if Nick's theory had any merit. Even if Ty was innocent, the case wasn't going to disappear tomorrow. Abbott must be desperate to end things. Stock prices for the company had already dropped significantly as shareholders awaited further news from the government's investigation. And in the meantime Abbott would have the financial backing to do whatever it might take to frame Ty.

She held her head in her hands. Sixteen months ago Ty's true character had come out—even when she didn't want to see it. But things were different this time. Hadn't Ty proved he wasn't the same man? That he'd truly decided to follow Christ?

Convicted, she picked up her cell phone to call Ty.

"Kayla?"

She turned to the door, but all she could see was a dark silhouette of a man. The figure lunged toward her and grabbed her arms. The cell phone flew out of her hand and slammed against the wall. She tried to scream, but instead a blistering pain shot through her head, then darkness.

Chapter 14

Ty sat on the edge of the twin bed and stared at the colorful wall decal of Winnie the Pooh. Nick and Chloe had been gracious enough to give him a quiet spot in Brandon's room where he could spend some time thinking and praying. The thought of sitting home alone had become anything but appealing.

He clasped his fingers around the edges of the mattress, still wondering when he'd wake up from this nightmare. Four months ago he'd walked out of the executive office suites of Abbott Financial Services, certain he'd be able to find a way to help convict the company's crooked CEO. Somewhere along the line the tides had shifted, and now he was the one with the Securities and Exchange Commission, along with a half dozen other entities, breathing down his neck

This wasn't the way things were supposed to play out.

I don't understand, God. I gave my life to You, and now I'm looking at the possibility of spending the next twenty years in prison for something I didn't do.

None of it made sense. Not that he'd ever believed becoming a Christian guaranteed a happily-ever-after life, but what happened to "Ask and you will receive" or "Come to me, all who are heavy burdened"? Between his relationship with Kayla, her mother's stroke, and the fallout from Abbott Financial, he'd worn out his knees spending time in prayer. And for the first time he was beginning to wonder to what avail.

Ty picked up a throw pillow from the bed and flung it against the pale blue wall. Admittedly part of this whole mess was his fault. How much had he lost because of his decision to keep things from Kayla? In an attempt to shelter her from the truth, he'd pushed her away, losing any trust that had been gained between them.

He glanced around the small room that looked like a scene straight out of Pooh Bear's Hundred-Acre Wood and felt the heavy ache of loneliness. Losing his career and facing jail time were difficult enough to comprehend. Losing Kayla was even worse. He'd imagined them with children five years down the road: a boy and a girl, or maybe two of each. He really didn't care as long as they could be a family. That was all he'd ever wanted.

I don't understand, Lord.

He gazed at the Bible lying on the edge of the bed but didn't pick it up. He'd spent half the morning searching for a word of encouragement to hold on to. Some promise that offered relief in the light of losing everything. But nothing had spoken to him. Instead, resentment began to take root. Leaning on Christ was a day-by-day challenge he was still working to get right. And with the way things were spiraling out of control, it was getting harder by the minute.

A knock on the door jerked Ty from his brooding. "Come in."

Nick entered the room carrying a tray of food. "Chloe thought you might be hungry."

Ty glanced at the covered dish and glass of milk and felt his stomach churn. "Not really, though I do appreciate the offer."

Nick handed him the tray despite his disinclination. "Take my advice and eat what you can. Facing what seems to be an uphill battle might take away your appetite, but you can't afford to get sick."

Ty offered him a wry grin. "Did Chloe tell you to say that as well?"

Nick laughed. "Apparently you know my wife."

"Enough to know I'll never be able to repay her. . .or you." Ty set the tray in his lap and felt a twinge of appetite return as he took off the cover and the savory aroma filled his senses. Meat loaf and mashed potatoes would go a long way to keep up his stamina. "Both of you have gone far beyond the role of lawyer and hostess."

"Don't worry about it." Nick leaned against the door frame. "I would have done the same for someone else. Well, I might not share my wife's meat loaf with just anyone, but hey. . .what are friends for?"

Ty took a bite and smiled. "I can see why you're not keen on sharing your wife's cooking."

"And we've got some cherry cobbler as well if you'd like to join us in the living room."

"I just might do that." Ty took a second bite then held up his fork. "Can I ask you a spiritual question first?"

"You bet." Nick slid into the rocking chair, pushing the footstool aside with his heel.

"I'm sure Chloe told you Christianity is a new thing for me." Ty stabbed at a green bean then frowned. "I guess the bottom line is that I'm grappling here as to how to justify God's presence in my life when I'm in the midst of losing everything I have."

Nick blew out a long breath. "I'd say that's a question man's tried to work out for centuries. Where's God in the midst of pain?"

Ty nodded, certain there wasn't going to be a simple answer to his problem. "I feel as if God has abandoned me and expects me to figure things out on my own."

Nick leaned forward to rest his elbows on his knees. "I don't think I've ever told anyone this, but before Brandon was born, Chloe had a miscarriage. It was one of the worst experiences of my life. Realizing I'd never be able to hold the child we'd waited and prayed for was hard. Watching Chloe suffer was even worse. She went through a time of severe depression, and I was helpless to do anything about it. I asked myself some of the very same questions you have to be asking yourself right now."

"So what did you do?"

"I was forced to answer one challenging question. Did I believe God was in control of everything, including His plans for my family? The truth was, if God wasn't in control of everything, I had no reason to continue to follow Him. In the end it boiled down to a simple matter of faith."

"We live by faith and not by sight." Ty poked at the mashed potatoes with his fork, finding the words hard to come to terms with. "That's a tough concept to grasp. Especially for someone used to dealing with concrete numbers and facts."

"Or like a lawyer forced to deal only in evidence?" Nick leaned back in the chair and shook his head. "We want something we can hold on to, but God's ways are never man's. I made myself look back at other times in my life when God's presence was unmistakable. He didn't leave me then, and every day I choose to believe He won't leave me now, either. Listen—I know you're not looking for a sermon here, but Hebrews says we're to hold unswervingly to the hope we profess, for He who promised is faithful. Nothing you experience here on earth can begin to compare with the reward of heaven Christ has in store for us."

Ty set the tray on the bed beside him and tried to digest everything Nick said. "I can't say my faith has been holding steady these past few days."

"The Bible also says we are blessed when we persevere under trial, because we will receive the crown of life God has promised to those who love Him. It's worth it, Ty."

"Deep down I know it's worth it." Ty looked up and caught Nick's gaze. "But what if the court convicts me? I'll have lost my job, my reputation, and Kayla. . . ."

He squeezed his eyes shut at the reminder. Losing Kayla would always be what hurt the most.

"I don't know, Ty. All I can do is promise to do everything in my power to ensure the truth becomes known." Nick rocked back in the chair. "Have you thought about calling Kayla? She has to be frantic."

"The message she left on my answering machine made it quite clear as to what role she wants me to play in her life." As much as he didn't want to admit it, things were over between the two of them, and he respected her enough to step out of her life if that's what she wanted.

Nick cocked his head. "What's the old saying? It's a woman's prerogative to change her mind? I wouldn't give up on her yet."

"More wisdom from Chloe?"

Nick's boisterous chuckle filled the room. "If it were up to her, she'd plunk the two of you down in a locked room together and keep you in there until you work it out. She hates seeing her friend hurt. And besides that, I'd say she's developed a bit of a soft spot for you for some reason."

Ty let out a deep sigh, wishing he could say the same for Kayla after all that had transpired in the past twenty-four hours. "It's nice to know a couple of people are in my corner."

"We'll get you through this." Nick stood and clasped Ty's shoulder. "Keep your eyes fixed on Him. He'll never leave you."

"I'll keep reminding myself."

"And for the record." Nick stopped in the doorway. "I think Chloe's right about Kayla. Sometimes you have to take a chance. It's not as if you're going to lose anything."

"You've got a point there." Ty grabbed his cell phone out of his back pocket and stared at the number pad. "Maybe it is time I took that chance."

ॐ

By the fourth phone call, Ty felt the lump of concern in his chest begin to swell. Where was Kayla? He'd called her cell phone, but no one had answered. Next he tried her mom's house, her office phone, and even Jenny.

He stalked down the narrow hallway and into the living room where Nick was working through some files at his desk. "Something's happened to Kayla."

Chloe jumped up from the floor where she'd been reading a book to her boys and moved beside her husband. "What are you talking about?"

"I don't know for sure." Ty rubbed the back of his neck wondering when the nightmare of the past twenty-four hours would disappear. "I can't get ahold of her, and no one has seen her."

Nick took off his reading glasses and swiveled the chair away from the desk. "She's probably running errands for tonight's event. She mentioned it yesterday." He looked to his wife. "What was it?"

"They're catering the Walker-James wedding."

Ty leaned against the half wall that separated the living room from the entryway. If something had happened to her because of his involvement with Abbott, he'd never forgive himself. What if subtle warnings had just escalated into a calculated attempt to silence Ty?

Beads of sweat collected on his forehead. "What if Abbott got to her?"

Nick shook his head. "There's no reason for Abbott to call attention to himself at this point. If he's guilty he's got you where he wants you. His best move is to stay out of things, and he's smart enough to know that."

Ty wasn't convinced. "I spoke with Jenny a minute ago. She's at the church, and she hasn't seen Kayla for the past four hours. You know Kayla. She'd never leave a job without telling someone where she's going. Even Jenny's getting frantic."

"Where was the last place Jenny saw her?"

Ty worked to steady his breathing. "Jenny said they spoke after lunch at the church, and Kayla told Jenny she needed an hour or so by herself to pray. Jenny went back to finish up some of the food for tonight, but when she returned with the rest of the staff, Kayla wasn't around and she hadn't finished any of the wedding stuff. All she could figure was that she went to the church's prayer room and fell asleep. We all know how tired she's been lately. She went to check on her but saw no sign of her. That was twenty minutes ago."

Chloe dug into the pocket of her jeans then tossed her husband the car keys. "I'll stay with the boys and make some phone calls. You two go find Kayla."

Ten minutes later Ty and Nick pulled into the church parking lot. With the wedding scheduled to start within the next two hours, the parking lot was already filling up with some of the wedding party.

Jenny was inside pacing the kitchen floor, her cell phone pressed against her ear. She held up her finger and motioned for them to wait. A moment later she snapped the phone shut. "She's never done this before. I've called everyone I can think of; no one's seen her, and she isn't in the building."

"What about her car?"

"It's gone as well. None of this makes sense. We all know she was under a lot of pressure lately, but she'd never walk out on a job. Never."

Ty still hadn't shelved his theory that Abbott was involved. "Show me where you think she was last."

Jenny stumbled from the kitchen then scurried down the center aisle of the church auditorium. In the dim light of the room, a half dozen people bustled around, making final touches in preparation for the ceremony. The door to the prayer room was half open. Jenny pushed it the rest of the way then slipped in before them.

"As I told Ty, I can't be certain this is where she went, but she headed this way, and it's a place she likes to come when she needs a few moments of peace."

Ty glanced around the room. Approximately six by six, the room was painted in subtle hues of blue, with no furnishings other than a wooden bench and three other chairs. A large painting of the cross hung on the back wall. On either side, light filtered through stained-glass windowpanes. The only other thing in the room was a potted plant in the corner. No place to hide anything. No clues that even placed her in the room.

He glanced behind the ceramic pot just in case. "Wait a minute."

"What is it?" Jenny stepped up beside him.

Ty bent down and picked up a cell phone that had fallen behind the plant. He didn't have to take a second look to know it was Kayla's. "She's been here."

The phone had a long crack along the side. Something had happened in this room. Ty's own cell phone rang, and he reached into his pocket to answer it.

"Ty, this is Penny. Abbott's got Kayla."

Chapter 15

Ty parked his car at the marina then checked the time on the dashboard. He had three minutes to spare. Penny's instructions had been explicit. Twenty minutes to get there. Find his friend's boat, the *Angelina*. And come alone. Any signs of police involvement meant he'd never see Kayla alive again. He felt for the tiny tape recorder in his front pocket that Nick had handed him at the church and wondered if he'd made the right decision to bring it. Abbott wasn't a fool, and Ty wasn't willing to risk Kayla's life. Even if it meant Abbott won in the end.

He moved to the end of the floating walkway, replaying Penny's message over and over in his head. The thought that Penny might be involved sent a shudder of fear through him. He was still uncertain if his former secretary was simply being used as a pawn in Richard Abbott's game or if she'd been on his side all along.

Either way Kayla's life was in danger.

He stared out across the blue waters of the harbor, took in the details of the scene, and remembered all the summer days he'd spent out on the ocean with his parents. Somewhere, among the dozens of boats, was Kayla. It took him two and a half minutes to locate the *Angelina*. The sleek vessel was tied up at the end of one of the floating walkways, not in its usual slip. Convenient if Abbott was planning a quick getaway. But how did he find the key?

Abbott sat near the helm wearing a sweater and khaki pants. If it were possible, the man looked worse than the day Ty had walked out of the office on him. Pallid skin, thick jowls, thinning hair, all signs of stress. . .and guilt as far Ty he was concerned. Penny stood beside him, her hand possessively on his arm.

Where was the loyal secretary he'd worked with for three years? He'd considered her a friend. "You've been in on this all along, Penny?"

Penny avoided Ty's gaze. "What can I say? Abbott pays well."

"Glad you could make it, Ty. Your friend's boat is a beauty." Abbott pulled off his sunglasses. "I'm considering making an offer on one myself. Of course, I'm prepared to put out quite a bit more on a bigger one. Oh, and if you're wondering how I got the key, well, let's just say I have my ways." He laughed.

Ty drew in a deep breath. *Where are You, God?*

He stepped onto the familiar boat, wishing the marina weren't so quiet. The weather was too cold for most people to consider going out today despite a clear sky and calm sea. Somehow Abbott had even managed to use the weather to his advantage.

Abbott tapped a gun at his side. "Don't get too close, please, Ty. I wouldn't want anything to happen to you."

"Where's Kayla?" He refused to play the old man's games.

"Twenty-eight feet, pedestal steering, three-blade propeller—"

"I said, where's Kayla?"

"You always were so focused on the task at hand, weren't you, Ty? You need to relax. That's what I've done. Look at me. I've shed the tie and suit jacket and replaced it with something a bit more casual. Why? Because I realized life's too short to follow the rules."

"You know I couldn't care less about your plans to spend more of the company's money, Abbott. I want—"

"I know. You want Kayla." He finished the last sip from a wine glass as he maneuvered the boat away from the dock and toward the open waters. "Search him first, Penny."

Ty stood rigid as Penny patted him down. She drew the tape recorder from his jacket pocket and threw it onto the deck.

"I'm disappointed, Ty." Abbott twisted the stem of his wine glass between his fingers and shook his head as Penny stepped away from Ty. "Weren't my instructions explicit enough? Twenty minutes. Come alone. No police. Did you actually think a tape recorder fit into the equation? I'm tempted to end this whole thing right now without your ever seeing Kayla."

Ty pressed his lips together, certain that any signs of begging on his part would only end up provoking the man.

Abbott waved his hand in Penny's direction. "Bring her out, Penny. Though I will warn you, Ty. Don't try anything else foolish. Trust me. You'll regret it."

Thirty seconds later Kayla stumbled onto the deck in front of Penny. Ty moved to help her, but Abbott reached out and stopped him with the barrel of his gun.

The boat rocked beneath him. Ty forced himself to stay where he was, his focus now on Kayla. "Are you all right?"

Kayla nodded then took a seat where Penny told her. When had life spun so completely out of control that he'd been the cause of Kayla's kidnapping? He could see the fear in her eyes, mixed with hope that he'd do something to save them both. His head began to pound. Nothing made sense. Kayla sitting with her arms tied behind her; Penny taking orders from Richard Abbott.

Abbott, on the other hand, seemed to feel no remorse over the situation. "Penny's the perfect secretary, you know, especially when it comes to gathering information from the enemy."

Ty decided to ignore the implications. All he knew was that he'd trusted Penny, and she'd betrayed him.

Just as he'd betrayed Kayla.

Ty tried unsuccessfully to swallow the lump in his throat. A little of his own medicine perhaps? He hated the fact that he'd hurt her. Hated more that he was the cause of her being hurt again. If only he'd been able to protect her. . . . "So what happens now?"

Abbott slid his sunglasses back on as the shoreline grew smaller. "I suppose you have the right to know. I'm just sorry I don't have the time to let the law take care of things. It would have been nice to see you rot in jail the next twenty years. That's what you'd planned for me, isn't it?"

Ty shook his head. "I have the right to know what?"

"Face it, Ty. With all the bad publicity the company is looking at right now because of your case, shareholders are nervous. I can't let the company go bankrupt. I have to think of its future."

"You should have been thinking about the future of the company when you stole from its assets." Ty took a step toward Kayla. "Besides, you can't seriously think you'll get away with this."

"Trust Me."

Ty felt a tiny seed of confidence grow. This wasn't over yet. What had Nick said? It all boiled down to a simple matter of faith. Either God was in control of everything, or faith in Him was empty. He was going to choose to walk by faith.

He took another step forward.

"Stay where you are." Abbott held up his gun and shook his head. "Here's how I see it. I've already managed to create enough evidence to keep the DA, the SEC, and whatever other organization you can think of busy with evidence to convict you. They'll find some of the money—enough to satisfy them—in an offshore account connected to you. So, yes. I know I'll get away with it. The whole world now knows that Ty Lawrence is nothing more than another power-hungry executive who tried to make a fortune the wrong way. You'll never be able to stand up to the big boys."

"Think what you like, but you know you can't get away with this."

"Oh, really?" Abbott cut the engine, walked across the deck and shoved Kayla's chin up with the butt of his handgun. "Because here's the way it's going to play out, and, frankly, you don't have any way to stop me."

He pulled a folded piece of paper from his pocket with a gloved hand. "This is a signed confession and suicide note, written by none other than Ty Lawrence. No one will question when a man recently arrested and facing the reality of spending the next few decades in jail kills himself on his friend's boat after murdering his ex-fiancée. Penny was always so good at passing along information, like the fact that your friend's boat, the *Angelina*, is docked here for the winter."

"Why this boat?"

"It's the perfect place for a murder-suicide, isn't it? And saves me a cleaning bill for the mess you'll leave behind. With that and the physical evidence, the police will have no problems proving the theory correct." Abbott leaned against the railing, looking confident. "Once I am cleared of being involved in any wrongdoing, I'll be free to leave the country. Health reasons, you know. The doctor says I'm working too hard. I'll resign from my position as CEO; then I can spend my millions where no one can touch me."

A cold wave of horror swept over Ty, but he wasn't willing to end things yet. "The police won't stop looking for all the money, and eventually you'll slip. One day they'll tie it to you."

Abbott moved back toward the helm. "Maybe, but $175 million is worth the risk, don't you think? Though if you hadn't started turning in data to the police, I'd planned to wait around until I had at least a quarter of a billion."

Ty glanced at Kayla. He couldn't stand seeing her sit there with her hands tied behind her back and a bruise marking her cheek. All he had left to fight with were his words. "I don't think any amount of money is worth the risk. And there's something else I find interesting. You taught me everything I know about negotiating. Surely you don't think I'll simply agree to go along with your little plan."

"Penny, tie him up. I don't want you to finish your grim deed, Ty, until we're out to sea." Abbott glanced at his watch. "Don't worry, though. It will all be over in thirty minutes. We've got another boat coming to pick us up, but of course you won't need a ride at that point, will you?"

Ty felt a shudder whiz like a bullet up his spine. The man was insane.

Penny grabbed a length of rope and had Ty sit in a chair beside Kayla. "You know you can still get out of this, Penny."

Penny looked at him. "Last time I heard, the law doesn't take too kindly to premeditated murder. I'd say that puts me in pretty deep."

Abbott laughed as Penny wrapped the rope around Ty's wrists. "You could have had all of this, Ty. Never understood that storing-up-treasures-in-heaven garbage. Seems to me this is reality, and enjoying it right now makes a lot more sense."

"Except heaven's real, too, Abbott. Just like hell."

Ignoring Ty's response, Abbott called to Penny to throw him another drink from the cooler. She grabbed one and tossed it toward Abbott, but her aim was too long. Distracted, Abbott turned to catch the bottle. Ty scrambled to untie the rope before Penny could tighten the knot. There was no time to think. He lunged for Abbott. Caught off guard, the portly man didn't have a chance. Ty slammed into his right side. Abbott's attempted shot clipped the bow of the boat.

Ty kicked the gun out of the man's hand and shoved him to the ground face down. Within seconds two federal agents appeared on deck from the cabin below. One of them jerked Abbott to his feet then slapped a pair of handcuffs onto his wrists. The man was still trying to catch his breath as the other agent radioed for backup then read him his rights.

Ty hurried to release Kayla. "Are you all right?" He drew her into his arms, needing to convince himself she was alive and this was over.

"I think so." She slid her wrists out of the first knot. "What is going on?"

"I have no idea, but with Abbott in handcuffs something must be going right finally."

As soon as the rope came off, Kayla reached up and wrapped her arms around Ty's neck. "I've never been so glad to see you in my entire life."

He looked down at her and tilted up her chin with his thumb. "Does that mean you forgive me?"

Her smile worked to melt the anger that bubbled inside him toward Abbott. All that mattered anymore was that she was okay.

She nodded her head. "I let fear blind me from the truth. Deep down I knew you were innocent. I just hate that it took a crazy man to show me the truth."

He pulled her close, relishing in the softness of her hair, the sweetness of her perfume, and the touch of her skin. "It wasn't your fault, Kayla. I should have told you the entire truth a long time ago."

"Yes, you should have."

He ran his finger down her cheek. "I promise I won't keep things from you ever again. In wanting to protect you and our relationship, I almost lost you. It's a matter of trust, something I want our marriage to be based on."

"Is that a proposal?"

"I'm sorry to interrupt, Ty." Penny walked toward them, the bottom of her Windbreaker flapping in the wind. "You did well. I'm sorry you both had to go through what you did, but we got him. The entire conversation was being recorded. Richard Abbott isn't going to see the outside of a prison for a very long time."

He shook his head, his arm tightening around Kayla's waist. "That's wonderful, but I don't understand, Penny. You're working for the government?"

"Retired Petty Officer Penelope Waterford at your service, sir." She saluted as one of the uniformed agents approached. "And I'm sorry about the phone calls and the encounter at the restaurant."

Kayla's eyes widened. "That was you?"

"Pretty good disguise, wasn't it?" She shook her head as one of the agents dragged Abbott off the boat. "Abbott thought he needed to send warnings that showed he could get to you whenever he wanted to. In order to ensure he continued to trust me, I had to go along with it."

"Penny was honorably discharged from the navy a few years ago." The stocky blond man shook Ty's and Kayla's hands, introducing himself as Agent Stevenson with the Securities and Exchange Commission. "We recruited her to help take down Abbott from the inside. Unfortunately, he's good, and we always seemed to be a step behind him. When Abbott told Penny what he planned to do, she came up with this plan and hid us down below. She vouched for your innocence the whole time. I'm glad to see she was right."

Ty felt himself relax as the boat sped back to the marina. The reality of spending the next twenty years in jail began to fade. "What about the charges against me?"

The man repositioned the bill of his baseball cap. "I'll need you both to give a complete statement, but I don't think it will take much to convince the DA and the government that you're innocent, Mr. Lawrence. And Abbott won't be going anywhere for a long time."

The second officer docked the boat then shut off the motor. "I need to ask the two of you to move off the boat. We'll let you know when our men are finished, but for now it's a crime scene."

❧

Kayla ignored the throb in her head as Ty helped her off the boat and focused instead on how everything in her life had just changed—again—in the past ten minutes. A test of faith? Perseverance in the midst of adversity? Whatever it had been, she felt as if she'd failed the exam.

"I'm sorry, Ty."

He wrapped his arm around her shoulder. "For what?"

She looked up at him, afraid he'd disappear and she'd wake up in the boat again. "For not believing you."

"I'm the one who should be asking for your forgiveness. I should have told you the government had questioned me. I just never imagined things getting this out of control."

She laced her fingers in his as they slowly walked down the floating walkway toward the other end of the marina. "I'm still reeling from everything. I thought you were guilty, and then Penny was involved."

He leaned down and kissed the top of her head. "I'm sorry about all of this."

"As long as we're all okay." She breathed in the salty sea air that mingled with his aftershave lotion.

"So." Ty stepped off the walkway and turned her toward him. "Where were we when Penny, my former-secretary-turned-criminal-accomplice-turned-hero so rudely interrupted us?"

The gentle waves lapped against the shore. A seagull cried out overhead. But all she saw at the moment was Ty. "If I remember correctly, I think you were proposing."

"Was I?"

"Yes, you were. And I was about to say yes." She shot him a wide smile.

"Well, if you were about to say yes, then I'd better hurry up and pop the question."

Kayla looked up at him. Her toes tingled with anticipation, and her heart felt as if it were about to fly out of her chest.

"Kayla Rose Marceilo, the worst thing that's happened to me in the past forty-eight hours was the thought of losing you. It seemed worse than the pending trial or even facing the reality I might go to jail. I need you to be a part of my life, because I love you." He brushed back a strand of hair the wind had blown across her cheek. "You help me be a better man, Kayla, and I want to spend the rest of my life with you."

Kayla felt her chest swell with emotion as she gazed into his eyes. "Ty, there's nothing else I'd rather do than spend the rest of my life with you."

Ty pulled her into his arms and gently kissed her on the lips. "I take it that's a yes?"

"Oh yes, Ty." She giggled as he kissed her again. "Definitely a yes."

Chapter 16

Kayla stood in front of the full-length mirror and fingered one of the small pearls that graced the sleeves. The satin skirt, with its trail of roses and silver leaves, served as a reminder that God really had worked things together for good. In the past three months, Ty had been exonerated by the government, and her mother, while still not back to work, was able to walk again.

Kayla felt a ripple of peace flow through her. Nightmares from the day Richard Abbott had grabbed her from the prayer room had completely vanished. No longer was her heart overcome with fear of the future. Instead, she saw only possibilities and the rich future she and Ty could have together.

Jenny walked into the sunlit dressing room carrying the veil.

"It's breathtaking, isn't it?" Kayla gathered the skirt and spun around to face her friend. Today she really did feel like a princess about to marry her prince. No more doubts or uncertainties. Only a calm assurance she was following God's will.

"So how does it feel to know that in less than an hour you'll be Mrs. Ty Lawrence?" Jenny asked.

Kayla's smile reached the corners of her eyes. "Like I'm flying on top of the world."

"I'm glad to hear that." Jenny handed Kayla the same gauzy veil with rhinestones and drop pearls she'd first admired at the boutique then helped her slip it on. "Though I'm still not sure how you were able to schedule your wedding before mine."

Kayla laughed. "Because I've always wanted a Valentine's Day wedding, and I'm not waiting another twelve months."

Jenny nudged Kayla with her elbow. "I should have agreed with your offer to have a double wedding."

Kayla smiled then glanced at the clock on the wall. The forty-five minutes left until the ceremony seemed like forever. Lifting up the front of her dress so she wouldn't trip, she headed for the small balcony outside the room.

Jenny hurried behind her with Kayla's satin slippers. "Where are you going?"

"I just want to take a peek and make sure everything is ready." Giddy excitement wouldn't allow her to stay cooped up in the small room any longer.

"Chloe is down there right now, double-checking everything, and besides, Ty is going to see you if you stand there."

Ignoring her friend's counsel, Kayla leaned against the railing and glanced over the balcony onto the wooden church pews where Jenny and Chloe had transformed the simple sanctuary with roses, white organza, and candles. Soon the lights would dim, and the string quartet would start playing. It was everything she'd ever imagined her wedding day to be.

"Kayla?"

She ducked behind the railing at the sound of Ty's voice. "Ty? You're not supposed to see me yet."

"What?"

Jenny leaned over the balcony. "She said you're not supposed to see her yet. It's bad luck for the groom to see the bride before the ceremony."

"Tell her I don't believe in bad luck."

Kayla crouched behind the wooden balcony rail, working to keep her balance without ripping her dress. "I don't either, but it's. . .tradition."

"What?"

Jenny pulled her cell phone from her pocket, punched in a number, then waited for it to ring.

Kayla glanced up at Jenny. "Who are you calling?"

A cell phone rang from below the balcony. "Ty, here's Kayla."

Kayla stared at the phone Jenny shoved in her hand. "Okay, isn't this a bit silly?"

Ty laughed on the other end of the line. "I agree. Tell your friend she's nuts."

Kayla pressed the phone to her ear. "I could give her the phone, and you could tell her—"

"No!" Ty laughed. "I might not have you exactly where I want you, but at least I can hear your voice."

"Forty-five minutes and I'm yours."

"There's still the ceremony, the reception—"

"And a week in the Bahamas." Kayla moved back from the edge of the balcony and sat down in a chair, letting the yards of fabric swirl around her.

"Now you're talking." The line was quiet for a moment. "Kayla?"

"Yes?"

"I love you."

"I love you, too."

Kayla clicked the phone shut and sent a prayer of thanks to God that everything was right in the world.

Lisa Harris

Award-winning author, Lisa Harris, has been writing both fiction and nonfiction since 2000, and has more than fifteen novels and novellas in print. She currently lives with her family in Mozambique, Africa where they work as missionaries. Visit her Web site at lisaharriswrites.com and her blog at myblogintheheartofafrica.com.

SEASONS OF LOVE

Elizabeth Goddard

Dedication

Dedicated to my loving husband, Dan; my four beautiful children, Rachel, Christopher, Jonathan, and Andrew; and my ever-supportive parents. Special thanks to Chief Arthur Parker of the Carver, Massachusetts, police department; Flax Pond Farms; Centennial Cranberry Farms; and Brian Kendig for helping me to understand encryption software.

Prologue

I've got a proposition for you. Call me," a familiar voice crackled from the answering machine.

Grandpa? Riley O'Hare set her sack of groceries on the counter as she replayed the message.

The clock on the sage-colored wall displayed six thirty. Grandpa was on the East Coast. No way would he still be up at nine thirty. She'd have to wait until morning before she could call him. She hated waiting and stared at the ceiling while the annoying computerized voice detailed the time and stated that she had another message.

"Riley, it's Eric. You there? I tried to reach you on your cell today. I'd love to have dinner with you tonight, but I've got that meeting with Tom Carling at Solution Sciences, remember? Actually, you could join me. It never hurts to have a beautiful woman on your arm. Italiano's at six thirty."

"Too late," she said and huffed at his comment. It irritated her that he acted as though they were supposed to have dinner tonight. When would he get it? He didn't seem to understand that things were over between them. Riley shuddered.

Eric Rutherford only saw her as eye candy to impress his colleagues. Everything revolved around his work as a business consultant—though she couldn't blame him for that. Her career as a regional account executive for Morris & Associates consumed her, as well. Most people didn't have time to live their own lives anymore.

Anxious to be rid of thoughts of Eric, she hit the DELETE button hard and long. The answering machine responded that all messages had been erased.

"What? Argh." Riley examined the caller ID list to see whose calls she'd missed since she'd just accidentally trashed all the messages. John's work number appeared last. She called her brother back, getting no answer; then she tried his cell. Still no answer, so she left a message.

After she finished putting away the groceries she'd grabbed on the way home from work, she popped precooked chicken strips onto a paper plate and into the microwave, then pulled the tab off a diet soda. It fizzed over the top and onto her beige blouse. "Ack!" She whirled around and held it over the sink. When the soda's overzealous carbonation died down, she wiped the can with a paper towel and set it on the counter while she cleaned.

Frustration overwhelmed her. She didn't have the energy to cook a decent meal. Life had been hectic since graduating from college with a business degree. Three years of her life had flown by since then. Was this what it was all about?

Riley sat at the kitchen counter and ate her chicken strips, her thoughts never far from her grandfather's call. She retrieved the client folders stashed in the side pockets of her soft leather briefcase. If she wasn't traveling on business, she brought work home every night. After she plopped down on the sofa to read through the files, she pulled her lip ointment from her pocket to moisten her forever-dry lips, then pressed the POWER button on the remote control to watch a twenty-four-hour news station.

She looked at her Swiss watch. Seven o'clock. *Okay, I give.* Riley slid her cell phone from its holder and started to dial then realized she hadn't called Grandpa in a while and couldn't remember his number. Worse, she hadn't bothered to store it in her new camera phone that her brother, John, had sent. She found Grandpa's number in the address book on her laptop, cringing at the thought of waking him. It would be ten o'clock his time.

After the fifth ring, she changed her mind, but before she could end the call, he answered. "Hello?"

Startled by the sound of his voice, Riley hesitated.

"Hello? Who's there?" Her grandfather's agitated tone caused embarrassment to wash over her. She'd woken him. "Riley, is that you?"

She smiled as warmth flooded her. "Grandpa, I'm sorry to wake you."

༄

Unable to sleep, Riley stared at the ceiling in her bedroom. She exhaled and rolled to her side—again. The glowing green numbers of the alarm clock read three thirty. Her grandfather's proposition had thrust her thoughts into chaos. She wondered how she could possibly consider it. She loved him and had heard the desperation in his voice. No one else had any interest in carrying on the family business. Riley's mother had died a year ago, and her aunt lived in Chicago with her family. A few distant cousins lived in the area. They always managed to help with the harvest, but they had high-paying jobs in the city.

Who would take the farm if not her?

Her grandpa had said that he knew she loved the place as he did, and she had her business degree. True, she'd spent much of her childhood at Sanderford Cranberry Farms and managed to be there for harvest as often as possible, taking a week of vacation. But what he asked was a lot—he wanted her to give up her life in California and move to Massachusetts to run things.

Still, she couldn't let go of the idea. If she accepted, she would also have an opportunity to be near her brother, John, and his family, who lived in Plymouth—a short drive from the farm. She'd only learned of his existence two years before, when John had found his biological mother—Riley's mom. Her mother had told her that she'd given up a child for adoption before she was married to Riley's father. Riley's grandmother had not wanted the embarrassment of an illegitimate child. Her church friends would have been aghast.

Riley had always wanted a brother, so she was thrilled when John and his family came into her life. She was so proud of him. A sharp programmer, he had been courted by the National Security Agency to work as a cryptographer. He was fun, too, always leaving her clues to solve some puzzle he'd concocted.

A deep love for John and his family had taken root in her heart—especially for his son, Chad, now two years old. Though it surprised her, she had been overjoyed when John asked her to become Chad's guardian should anything happen to him and Sarah. John's adoptive parents had died years ago, and Riley sensed that Sarah didn't much like her own family.

She glanced at the faint glimmer of the golden letters on her Bible. She needed to pray about this decision and give herself time to consider the possibility. But she felt so far away from the Lord. Weeks had passed since she'd read His Word. With her demanding job, she hadn't made time to meditate on scripture. If she prayed for an answer, would she even hear God over the continual distractions?

Peace eluded her.

Someone pounded on the door to her apartment. Riley froze. Why would anyone disturb her at this time of night? Her heart raced. She sent up a prayer for protection, hoping that God would hear. The banging continued, forcing her out of bed. She slipped on her robe, crept to the door, and looked out the peephole.

Eric!

Shocked that he stood on the other side of the door, she backed away.

She wanted to throw open the door to give him a piece of her mind for disturbing her in the middle of the night, but she thought better of it. He swaggered back and forth then leaned against the door, mumbling her name as he pounded.

He's sloshed!

"How dare he." She stilled, realizing her mistake. She didn't want him to know she was awake and standing by the door. In fact, for all he knew, she wasn't even home but out of town on business, which was usually the case. A friend could have taken her to the airport.

Panic shuddered through her. She'd tried to end her relationship with him and had finally resorted to ignoring his persistent phone calls. At first, she'd gotten caught up in his career aspirations. But it quickly became clear that Eric was never content. He always wanted more. He wanted more from her, as well, but was unwilling to make a commitment, and she cringed at her own blindness.

Her stomach churned as Eric slammed his fist again. She leaned her head against the door, uncertain whether to answer him in order to tell him to leave. She backed farther away from the door. The man wasn't even a Christian. "Oh, Lord. How could I have let things go so far? Forgive me."

A neighbor's voice echoed through the corridor. She looked through the tiny hole to see who it was. "What's going on here? Can't you see she's not home?" Charles from across the hall stood in his doorway wearing shorts.

"Thank you," she said softly, even though he couldn't hear her.

"Mind your own business, buddy!" Eric slurred; then he disappeared from sight. Riley hoped he had a ride home in his condition.

She opened her door a crack then whispered, "Charles, is he gone?"

Charles had disappeared, as well, but then he burst through his door wearing jeans and a T-shirt. "I'm going to make sure that friend of yours doesn't drive home drunk." He ran through the corridor and down the steps.

Riley closed her door, locked the dead bolt, and stumbled to the sofa. She crumpled, her body trembling as she cried. Eric's behavior was getting out of hand. She wiped her eyes and stared at the pair of gold-framed pictures on the wall, illuminated by the soft glow of a small accent lamp. The one on the right depicted a large palm tree waving in what appeared to be the Holy Land; it read BE STILL AND KNOW THAT I AM GOD. The one on the left portrayed a man looking up into the night sky; it read SEEK THE LORD WHILE HE MAY BE FOUND.

They were cheap, decorative gifts from a friend when she first moved into her apartment. As she stared at the artwork, she realized she'd never even stopped her busy schedule to consider what they said or meant.

Until now.

Despite Eric's intrusion, the question of whether to accept her grandfather's proposal remained at the forefront of her thoughts. She bowed her head and swallowed the knot in her throat. "Thank You, Lord. I think I have the answer before I even asked."

She went back to bed and allowed exhaustion to overtake her.

☙

Riley awoke to the trill of the phone on the nightstand. A glance at the clock told her she'd overslept.

She lifted the receiver. "Hello?"

"Riley?" Her father's drained voice jolted her wide awake.

She sat up in bed. "I'm here. What is it?"

"Your grandfather had me call you. He couldn't stand to give you the news himself. I'm sorry. It's your brother, John. . . . He's dead."

Chapter 1

Carver, Massachusetts

M ornin', sleepyhead."

"It's not like we have to milk cows or anything, is it?" Riley rubbed her sleepy eyes and groggily dragged herself through Grandpa's sixties-style kitchen. After two weeks, she was still trying to unpack and settle in and hadn't yet grown accustomed to her grandfather's early hours.

Ding. Her grandfather pressed a button, and the microwave door popped open. The microwave didn't seem to fit in this retro kitchen. He yanked out his coffee cup then proceeded to spoon instant coffee into the steaming water.

"Wouldn't you prefer a cup of freshly ground French vanilla cream?" Riley pushed the START button on the automatic coffeemaker. She should have set it for automatic brew last night but forgot.

"I haven't got any use for that fancy, newfangled coffee." Her silver-haired grandfather grinned at her, producing a wide display of crow's-feet around his still-bright blue eyes. Thick gray brows arched as he puckered his lips to sip the steaming mixture.

Riley turned her back on him and stifled a laugh. She checked the water level on her own coffee. She never waited until it was finished brewing and poured her nondairy creamer into a large I LOVE CALIFORNIA mug, then followed it up with the half cup's worth of coffee brewed so far. She sipped it and turned to lean against the white counter. Her gaze skimmed the kitchen before resting on Grandpa.

No wonder his farm was in poor condition. Grandpa hadn't upgraded anything in over forty years. Well, except for the fact that he'd bought a microwave. He'd kept the farm small, while others had expanded and diversified; some had even grown to handle all of the processing of their produce, whether cranberries or some other crop.

Her grandfather began shuffling pots and pans around in the cabinet, finally producing a large flat skillet. "Bacon and eggs?"

A twinge of nausea rolled in her stomach at the thought of bacon sizzling this early. She covered a yawn and glanced at the clock on the oven as she sat down at the table. Five thirty. "Thanks, but no. I'll just have my granola breakfast bar."

Though Riley's reddish blond hair wasn't quite long enough to stay permanently within the butterfly clip, she attempted to pin it off her neck. She groaned inside because she should be making breakfast for her grandfather, not the other way around. But she wasn't much for cooking, nor was she big on breakfast. She had a feeling a lot of things were about to change.

A blond-haired, two-year-old boy toddled into the kitchen, rubbing his squinting eyes. *They already have.*

"Morning, Aunt Wiley." The sweet syrup of his voice poured over Riley's heart, stirring her love for him and a fierce grief over his loss.

"When am I going home?" He climbed up into her lap, and she lovingly placed her arms around his soft, cuddly body in a tight hug.

Riley's heart felt as if it would break in two at his question. How would she ever explain to him that his parents were never coming back? With sorrow-filled eyes, she looked up at her grandfather, who'd stopped placing slabs of bacon on the skillet. His mouth was turned down, revealing an entirely different set of wrinkles than when he smiled. He returned her stare and nodded his support.

The boy rested his head against her chest, and she caressed it with her chin while struggling for the right words. "I don't know, Chad. Don't you like your room here?" She winced at her completely inadequate answer.

Bacon crackled on the stove. "Sonny boy, would you like breakfast?" Grandpa tried to sound cheery for Chad's and Riley's sakes, but she didn't miss the grief in his tone.

The child lifted his head and shook it. "Ceweal. Don't you have my ceweal?"

Riley ruffled his blond hair. "Of course we have your cereal. You had it yesterday and the day before, remember?"

Her chest tightened with pain when she considered all that had happened in the last few weeks. After attending John and Sarah's funeral, she'd flown back to California and packed her things and moved to Massachusetts to run the cranberry farm and care for Chad.

Riley placed him in a high chair and began gathering a bowl, spoon, milk, and his honey-toasted oat wheels from the pantry. It all seemed surreal as she performed the tasks without thinking. She watched Chad spoon his cereal into his mouth, finding it hard to believe that she was his legal guardian.

When she had agreed to take care of Chad should something happen to John and Sarah, it hadn't entered her mind that their worst fears would come true. They'd been killed in a car accident. Sometimes people experienced a sense of foreboding. Had John felt an impending tragedy? Is that why he'd been so anxious to make arrangements for Chad?

She stood and shook away the grievous thoughts. Despite all that had happened, she was glad she could be here for Chad. And though the farm was in a sad state of affairs, she would do what she could to help her grandfather. That is, if he would listen to her. They'd already had a few heated discussions because he didn't want to move into the twenty-first century. She shook her head. A positive result, though, was that she would be far away from Eric. And maybe, just maybe, she could find a little time to herself. Time with God.

Grandpa crunched his bacon and shoveled scrambled eggs into his mouth. She hadn't noticed when he sat down. "Tell you what," he said between bites. "You go get ready for the day. I'll cut this little boy's hair."

Riley gasped. "You wouldn't dare." She leaned her nose against the top of his blond curls. "I love his hair. Don't you dare touch it."

"He looks like a girl. Needs to look like a man if he's going to live on my farm." Grandpa stiffened as though he realized he might have said too much.

Chad looked at her grandfather over the edge of his cereal bowl, his face contorted. He wasn't yet comfortable with his new home and didn't understand. Riley wondered if he ever would.

She eyed the phone book on the counter. If anything, she needed to get advice about how to explain to a child that his parents were never coming back. "I think it's a good idea, after all. Maybe you could just trim it a little. Nothing dramatic, okay?" She raised her eyebrows in question at her grandfather, making sure to keep the twinkle in her eyes.

Grandpa winked. "After our morning walk, then."

Riley's insides warmed. Her grandfather had gladly included Chad on his daily walks.

In her room she spent time reading her Bible and talking to God in prayer. After she'd showered and dressed, she grabbed the phone book. She wanted to get started early today, taking inventory of her grandfather's situation by beginning in the office of Sanderford Cranberry Farms. She thumbed through the yellow pages. The ancient phone mounted on the wall shrilled, the sound sending her back to her time on the farm years ago. She let it ring, thinking to let the machine answer it because she needed to get to work.

After the tenth ring, she realized that Grandpa wasn't answering—and neither was his answering machine, because he didn't own one. She laughed and shook her head at the caller's persistence then picked up the receiver. "Hello?"

"Yes, is this the Sanderford residence?" a familiar, smooth male voice asked.

"Um, yes, it is. May I ask who's calling, please?"

"Ms. O'Hare, is that you? This is Zane Baldwyn."

John's business partner.

"We met. . .at the—"

"I remember." She hadn't meant to cut him off.

She recalled his trimmed black hair and cobalt blue eyes. Grief and confusion had been written all over his face. He'd been John's friend for years. The reminder sent an ache through her heart and the acknowledgment that she'd have to make time to talk to him. But not today.

His stiff white shirt and navy designer suit had reminded her of Eric, and she'd felt an instant aversion toward him. She gritted her teeth. It was a premature judgment, but at the moment, she wanted to rid her mind of corporate images. "I'm sorry, I was just heading out the door. I've got a busy day ahead of me. Is there something I can do for you?" Moving from California and adjusting to her new status as a mother had put enormous pressure on her, giving her the sense that if she didn't get on top of things, she'd soon be bogged down by it all.

"Look. I apologize that I approached you at such an inopportune time as a funeral."

She shook her head as she recalled that he'd been tactless, inviting her to lunch as if he were hitting on her—at a funeral of all places. "I forgive you. Anything else?"

"Yes, actually. I really need to speak with you." He hesitated then added, "It's about John, of course. I don't want you to get the wrong idea."

Too late.

"Bernard's at noon?"

This guy was Eric all over again. She had no idea where Bernard's was anyway. "I'm sorry. I really don't have the time today. I've got a child to care for and a business to get familiar with. I've never been a mother before. . . ." Riley covered her mouth, appalled at her babbling. "Can you tell me whatever you need to say over the phone?"

"No. Please, Ms. O'Hare. . .Riley. May I call you Riley?"

Chad came screaming into the kitchen, his hair shaved close to his scalp. Her grandfather followed. Riley gasped. "What happened to his hair?"

"Excuse me?" the voice from the receiver asked.

"I'm sorry, Mr. Baldwyn, I have to go." Riley hung up the phone.

Chapter 2

Zane Baldwyn slammed the cordless phone into its cradle. "Women!"

Chelsea peeked into his office. "Everything all right, Mr. Baldwyn?"

He'd told the young receptionist months ago to stop chewing gum. The habit was unprofessional. But he could tell by the way she spoke that she'd stored it away in her cheek, probably thinking he wouldn't notice.

"Yes, fine. Thank you." Her question reminded him that he needed to close his door if he wanted privacy. John had left his office door open the night he'd died in the car accident, enabling Zane to overhear a message he left for his sister, Riley. Though he didn't know what good the information would do him if he could never talk to her.

"I don't know. Sounds like you're having girl trouble to me." Chelsea began chewing her gum again, apparently having forgotten Zane's request.

He sent her his practiced none-of-your-business look—the one he'd used countless times in the past on meddling employees in previous companies—because he was afraid his words would come out too harsh to the inexperienced recent high school graduate. She stopped in midchew to look down at the files she clung to; then she tapped them with her long, red fingernails.

"I'd better get busy on these." She disappeared from the doorway.

He'd often heard her talking about her dates. Maybe she could help, after all. "Wait, Chelsea." Zane sprang from his chair to follow her.

She rushed back through as he exited, and they collided, scattering the files over the deep maroon carpet. He could tell by the blush on her face that she might have a crush on him.

Great. He had planned to ask her about how to meet with a woman who wasn't interested in him. But now he wasn't so sure that was a good idea.

"Here, let me help you with those." Zane dropped to the floor to scoop up files with Chelsea.

The girl giggled. "Oh, thanks. I'm really sorry. I heard you call my name, and I was just coming back when—"

Zane held up his hand to stop her. "Chelsea, it's okay. Really. Completely my fault."

She batted her eyelashes and began smacking her gum. Zane paid close attention so that he would not accidentally touch her hand in the process of picking up the files. On second thought, maybe it would be a good idea to stifle any ideas that Chelsea might have about him.

"The reason I called you is that I changed my mind. I do, in fact, need to discuss something not of a business nature," he said.

Chelsea slowed her chewing. An expectant smile lifted her flushed cheeks.

Oh no. This wasn't going as he planned. "There's a woman."

Her brown eyes peered into his. They were both on their knees, picking up files. Her face was entirely too close. Did he imagine a slight pucker on her lips?

Beads of sweat popped out on his forehead. "Another. . . uh. . .woman."

Her lips formed into a slight frown, almost pouting, and she returned to the task of retrieving papers and files.

"The truth is. . .well. . .I'm not very good with women. There's someone I'm trying to meet for lunch, and she turned me down. What can I do?"

Chelsea finished picking up the files, and Zane stood along with her. He handed the manila folders over. "Mr. Baldwyn, I'm not sure why any woman wouldn't want to go out with you."

Zane's neck grew warm, and he tugged at his collar. "Well, thank you, Chelsea. I don't know what to say."

He strolled with her into the reception area of Cyphorensic Technologies. The luxury office suite had been his decision. In his opinion, the impressive mahogany-paneled walls depicted success.

With his business savvy and John Connor's programming skills, he'd been convinced there was nothing to stop them. Now Zane believed he'd made a horrific mistake in inviting John to leave his stable, well-paying job to partner with him. He'd pounded himself with guilt day and night, wondering if John would still be alive today if he had stayed at his corporate job.

Even if John had not died in the accident, Zane knew that John's marriage had suffered from the long hours he spent developing software for the company. Pain shot through his stomach, and he placed his hand over his midsection. He needed an antacid.

"Mr. Baldwyn?" Chelsea broke through his thoughts. She'd shuffled behind her desk now and gazed up at him with sad puppy eyes. "I'm sorry about Mr. Connor. I know that has to be what's been bothering you."

"Thanks. I apologize if I've not been myself."

Zane stared down at the blond-streaked brunette. She wore too much makeup to his way of thinking. He felt sorry for her. With all that had happened, he had no idea if he would be able to keep her employed. They had no business to speak of yet. But Zane had been wooing his prospects.

"That's all right. I understand. Now, about this woman you're interested in.

You really like her, don't you?" She grinned at him like a Cheshire cat.

An image of John's sister, Riley, played across his mind. Zane had never met her in person before the funeral, but John had recently displayed her picture in his office, even proudly placing it on his desk, which was usually off-limits to anything but his computers.

He chuckled. After Zane's two attempts at talking to Riley, he decided her personality was sorely lacking in warmth. "I'm not sure that I like her. I don't even know her." He leaned against the desk. "Tell me. What do you suggest I do?"

"Well, if she won't go to lunch with you, find a reason that you have to talk to her or be with her. It's hard to know exactly because I don't know the specifics."

Zane stared at Chelsea. Of course he had an important reason to speak to Riley. That's why he had invited her to lunch. Then it dawned on him. "Chelsea, you're a genius."

He was thinking in terms of business prospects. He didn't need to do lunch with her. He only needed to go to the cranberry farm to speak with her.

"Oh, Mr. Baldwyn, you're just saying that. But you know what I'll do? I'll pray for you." She smiled up at him; then the phone rang, and she answered. "Cyphorensic Technologies. May I help you?"

Zane took that as his cue to leave and headed back to his office. *Pray for me?* He stifled his laugh until he'd closed his office door. "Crazy girl." Did God actually answer prayers? Did He care about everyday life?

Zane pulled open the top drawer of his desk to grab his car keys then reconsidered. He paced across the Persian rug centered in the room. If he appeared at Sanderford Cranberry Farms, he'd need to have a very good reason. He couldn't just tell her that he'd overheard something he shouldn't have.

Maybe he did need Chelsea to pray, after all. Her proclamation brought a smile to his lips. He hadn't considered praying in years, since he was a child even. His mother had been consistent in her efforts to make sure he attended Sunday school and church. But that was where it all ended. He'd made himself into what he was today, no thanks to God.

He hurried out of his office and into John's, flipping on the light as he strode through the door. John's desk sat near the far wall, a computer credenza behind it. Pain gripped his stomach again, a manifestation of his grief at having lost his business partner and friend. He eased into John's chair as if it were sacred. There had to be something in John's office—a memento that he could deliver to Riley, giving him the excuse he needed to speak with her. Then he would know whether or not to broach the subject of the phone call.

Zane tried to rub the tension from his neck and face. It was no use. What difference did his knowledge of the call make anyway? Without a programmer to write the software, Cyphorensic Technologies could not continue forward.

He'd been a vice president for a software company for years. But it had been a constant battle to do things his way. So he'd gone to work for another company as the CEO. Only this time the board of directors blocked his decisions. Zane started Cyphorensic so that no one could tell him how to run it. He'd funded the entire thing himself, planning for the months it could take before the company began to stand on its own.

Zane wasn't a programmer. But he couldn't let the company fall apart. As much as he hated to think of replacing John, he needed to hire a programmer as soon as possible. The new employee would not be a partner this time. Zane hoped he would find someone who could pick up where John had left off.

Zane spun around in the Aeron chair—the only chair for hard-core programmers, John had insisted. He stared at John's special desk system, all designed for maximum efficiency, free of clutter and knickknacks. His laptop briefcase remained where Zane had seen him place it. The man was relentless, planning to stay late the night he died. But Zane had insisted otherwise because John needed to focus on his wife, his marriage.

Two more monitors sat on a table nearby, everything networked seamlessly. But John had preferred his laptop. Zane opened the black canvas case to pull out the lightweight computer. Though he'd not spent the countless hours that John had invested in writing thousands of lines of code, Zane knew enough to understand the documentation John placed within his program, explaining each segment. He unzipped the middle section of the case.

His heart skipped. No laptop. He stuck his hand down into the dark case, just to be certain he wasn't missing something. Nothing. He laid the briefcase on top of the credenza and leaned back into the chair, his hand over his mouth. He spun around again to face the desk.

A wireless mouse rested on a brown leather computer sleeve. Zane had mistaken it for a mouse pad at first. He sighed his relief and opened the sleeve. No laptop. He placed his elbows on the desk and rested his head in his hands as he tried to recall the events as they happened.

John had closed the laptop, pulled the cords and wrapped them up, then stuck it all in the laptop briefcase. Zane had stood on the other side of the desk and watched him, reminding him that he shouldn't take his work home with him. He didn't want his friend to do anything to further jeopardize his marriage for the sake of Cyphorensic. Zane had escorted him out to the parking lot and watched him drive away to pick up his wife for a romantic dinner.

Zane's heart pounded, and his breathing grew rapid. He jumped up and tore over to the other computers. Except for the monitors, the hardware was gone.

He slid his cell from his pocket and phoned Sarah's mother, who'd been named the estate executor, to question her about any computers in John's house.

John had promised Sarah he'd keep his work away from home. And true to John's word, he'd done just that. All computers remained here, at Cyphorensic.

Not good.

He gasped in disbelief.

John's words to his sister echoed in Zane's mind. . . . *"Riley, are you there? . . . Listen, I sent you something. Watch for it. It's important."*

As John hung up the phone, and before Zane entered his office, John had said, "It might be a matter of life and death."

As the words of that night reverberated in his head, Zane's pulse hammered. What had John gotten himself into? Whatever it was, it appeared to involve Cyphorensic Technologies' software, hence the stolen hardware. He yanked the phone to his ear and started to dial the police.

Wait.

He replaced the receiver. The last thing he needed at this juncture of the start-up company was to tie up Cyphorensic in some sort of technoscandal. John had some prior illegal cyber dealings, but he'd come clean. Zane trusted him. But what if something had changed?

His gut told him that whatever John had sent to Riley was related—maybe he'd even sent the software itself in an effort to keep it safe. Zane had to find out if Riley had received whatever John sent her.

Forget finding a memento to take to Riley. He rushed through the plate glass door of his fledgling company, ignoring Chelsea's questioning calls, and hurried to his luxury car, sliding into the tan leather driver's seat. As he turned the key in the ignition, he clenched his jaw in resolve. The suspicion that had bothered him since John's accident wrapped around his mind, growing stronger. Something was amiss in the circumstances surrounding his partner's death.

Zane clenched the steering wheel. He had to find out what his partner had deemed a matter of life and death and had sent to his sister. He floored the gas pedal and headed to Sanderford Cranberry Farms somewhere on Cranberry Highway.

Chapter 3

R iley held Chad in her left arm and one of the inspirational pictures she'd brought from California in the right. It would serve as a daily reminder of her new life of peace. She almost laughed out loud. So far, things had been anything but peaceful.

She followed Grandpa through the door of the small, one-room cottage that served as the main office of Sanderford Cranberry Farms. He set a laundry basket full of Chad's toys and a blue-jean quilt on the floor. Riley released her squirming nephew and placed the picture on top of a stack of boxes.

Grandpa flipped on the fluorescent lights while Riley opened the window shades. Give her sunshine over artificial lighting any day of the week. She smiled. After all the time she'd spent working in the skyscrapers of corporate America, that should become her new motto.

Though large maple and oak trees shaded the old structure, as she looked though the window, she had a clear view of the acres of cranberry beds, including the new ones that Grandpa worked to prepare.

The familiar light gray monolithic computer sat like a fossil on the corner of an old aluminum desk.

"When was the last time you turned this thing on, Grandpa?" Riley shoveled around the stacks of papers and musty cardboard boxes, stubbing her toe against one of the taupe filing cabinets. She pressed the POWER button on the vintage CPU. The slumbering machine hummed and churned, beginning to boot up.

Grandpa released a deep sigh. "I'm trying, Riley. It was part of my plan to grow the farm—get modernized. But I've struggled with using the thing. Millie from the church was coming for a while to get it running. She tried to enter information into the accounting software she took the liberty of buying for me, but she said it was too slow. And your brother's wife, Sarah, looked at it for me. She said she'd come back to help me, and she did spend one morning that next week. She said I needed a newer computer, though."

"Well, no kidding. This is a 486 processor."

"It's all Greek to me. And that Millie, I thought she always had her eye on me, even when your grandmother was alive. She offered to help, and, well. . .I was desperate. Makes me feel sick."

"I'm sure that Millie honestly wanted to help you, Grandpa. You shouldn't feel guilty for accepting it." Memories of her grandmother and the time Riley had spent with her making cranberry recipes played across her mind.

"Well, I do. Your grandmother suffered the last few years of her life when the cancer got her." Grandpa lowered himself into a chair on the other side of the desk and stared at his hands. "I can't tell you how much it breaks my heart to lose John and his pretty wife like that, when we'd only just found him. And with your mother gone, too. . . I had hoped that the farm would continue on in the family like it has all these generations." He lifted his gaze to Riley. "But I look around and everyone has gone off to bigger and better things. Your aunt's in Chicago with her family. There's no one left. I thought if I expanded and turned it into something big, like Farrington Cranberries, I wouldn't need to pass it on to family, except I'm too old and too tired to do it."

He sat up and stared at Riley, a big smile forced on his face. "But now you're here."

Riley kept her mouth closed. She wanted to tell him it wasn't possible, but what did she know? "Haven't they moved into all processing, including distribution?"

"Yes. It's crazy thinking, isn't it? The least I could do, though, is increase the business by adding more beds and maybe diversify into something else. I should have done that years ago in order to keep up. I was just set in my ways. I'm not telling you this to disrespect the memory of your grandmother in any way, but her illness. . . Well, it depleted the savings."

"We don't have to talk about this right now if it's too painful." Riley's heart ached for the loss of her grandmother. She hated seeing her grandfather like this. As she watched the monitor come to life, she felt pleased that her grandfather had made the attempt, but she couldn't stand to see him disappointed.

"No," he said, "I need to bring you up to speed. I planned to create more bogs and purchased a dozer to do the job. After I figured how much I would have to pay someone else to do it, well, I realized I could do it myself and bought a 1982 model."

"That's great!" *Over twenty years old?*

"You haven't heard the rest. It has mechanical problems. Worthless. I took out a loan on it, and now with the two bad growing seasons in a row, I'm struggling to pay for the thing." Grandpa frowned. "I should have told you all of this before you committed to come here. I'm sorry."

Riley rushed around the desk to place her hand on her grandfather's shoulder. "No, you did the right thing. Me being here is the right thing." She watched Chad playing on the floor, and her insides rolled with anguish. "We're going to grow this farm. I'm going to help you make it happen. For you. For Chad."

Though the loss of her brother remained at the forefront of her mind, joy surged inside at the thought of building something worthwhile. Chad had lost his parents. He was part of her family now. She wanted to be the best mother she could be, and she would build this business for him. And for her brother.

"Aunt Wiley!" Chad maneuvered his way over to her and raised his arms. She picked him up. He pointed behind her, and she spun around to see a large poster of the Sanderford Farms brand—a huge cranberry stood out in the middle of it. "Cwanbewy?"

"That's right, sweetie. It's a cranberry. We're on a cranberry farm." Chad jumped down and toddled over to touch the picture hanging on the wall, but he couldn't reach it.

Riley turned to smile at her grandfather but continued to speak to Chad. "When I was a little girl, my grandfather used to tell me all about the cranberries. Do you know where the word *cranberry* comes from? Some of the first people to settle our country—the Germans, for one—called it a crane berry at first because when the vines are blooming, they look like a crane. That's a type of bird."

"Cwane?" The child gave his best effort to pronounce the word. Riley thought Chad spoke well for his age.

"That's right. Eventually, the word changed to *cranberry*."

Grandpa winked at her. "He's a bright boy. And I knew you were the one. You always loved the farm so much." He stood and reached for Chad. "I'd better get this little guy out of your hair while you take a look at all the paperwork. I've got chores to do, and he can go with me."

"Thanks. I won't be long. Just want to get organized."

Chad screamed in Grandpa's arms and reached with all his strength back toward Riley. "Oh, all right, you." She took Chad back into her arms and shrugged at her grandfather. "It's no problem. That's why I brought his toys."

Riley didn't want to put Chad into day care. He'd lost his parents, and she wanted him to spend as much time as possible at the farm and with her and Grandpa.

Her grandfather left the office, and Riley put Chad on his quilt to play with his brightly colored toys. She moved behind the desk and surveyed the mess. By the look of things, her grandfather wasn't big on paperwork, but that was no surprise. He'd always loved the outdoors.

The first thing on her agenda was to contact the dozer salesman about his faulty equipment. She shuffled papers and came across the late payment notice, among many others, and finally discovered the seller's name. It took only ten minutes on the phone with the new-and-used dozer dealer, Chuck Sorenson, to learn that he would not change his as-is warranty policy. Still, she could detect no intent in the man to sell broken tractors. It was simply the way of things. He'd given her the phone number of a mechanic.

Chad wandered over as she picked up the phone to dial the mechanic. She offered the boy a piece of chocolate, hoping to distract him, but he wanted both the chocolate and for her to pick him up. She obliged, holding him in her right arm and the phone to her ear in the left. The first opportunity she had to go to town, she would have to purchase a cordless phone. It was impossible to get things done while attached to the desk.

A gravelly voice answered. She pictured the man on the other end covered in grease.

"Yes, I need a mechanic for a 1982 dozer." As Riley waited for the mechanic's reply, she noticed Chad's mouth encircled in brown. She couldn't see his fingers as they gripped her shoulders out of her line of sight, but she imagined them to be chocolate dipped.

"Give me your information. I've got five ahead of you," the mechanic said.

Chad began to whine. Riley shushed him and kissed him on the forehead.

She gave her name and told the man the equipment was at Sanderford Farms on Cranberry Highway. He told her he'd already looked at that dozer and that Robert Sanderford had not been able to pay. Riley's pulse pounded in her ears, along with Chad's whining. Why hadn't Grandpa told her?

She would do her best to negotiate. A knock drew her attention. A business-man appeared in the window of the door.

Riley panicked. What else had Grandpa left out? Was the man a banker or with the IRS? As he reached for the knob, Riley turned her back to him, wrapping the cord around her and Chad. The boy protested. Dread swelled in her chest, and her palms grew sweaty. She shuffled Chad in her arm.

"Listen, Mr.—" The door slammed behind Riley. When the mechanic did not offer his name, she continued. "Mister, I'm desperate here. What if I agree to pay after this year's harvest?"

"Ma'am, I need to be paid for the work. I don't operate like you cranberry farmers. I can't wait until after the harvest when you get paid. I've got a family to feed."

Riley huffed, her mind scrambling for a solution. She whirled around to face the desk again and, too late, remembered she'd turned her back to her untimely visitor.

Oh. Great. Zane Baldwyn. She smiled and motioned for him to take a seat. "I understand. I'll come up with something. You said you'd looked at it already, though. Can you give me your estimate?"

"Give me a minute. I've gotta find it." The sound of a diesel engine revved through the receiver.

Riley acknowledged Zane with a nod. Rather than sitting, he chose to roam around the office, moving and touching things. She stiffened at his boldness and wished the man didn't remind her so much of Eric. He had always been so overbearing, controlling. He had to have his way. Hadn't she told Zane that she wouldn't have time for him today? Yet there he stood, forcing her to see him. She'd come three thousand miles to get away from her ex-boyfriend. But it seemed that he was in the room with her.

Zane turned to look at her as if he knew she'd been staring. She tried to avert her gaze, but his cobalt eyes wouldn't let her. He gave her a genuine smile, though she had the feeling that sorrow over the recent death of her brother dampened it. His clenched jaw relaxed as he looked at her then at Chad. He removed his suit coat and slowly approached as he reached out his hands to the candy-coated boy.

Riley widened her eyes in surprise. She was even more astonished when Chad relinquished his hold on her and scrambled into Zane's arms. He strolled around the office, uncaring that Chad was a detriment to his starched white shirt. Amazing. He cooed and soothed the child. Riley wanted to slap her forehead. Of course Chad would know Zane.

The mechanic returned to the phone and told her his price. She gasped and said thank you then hung up the phone. When she returned her attention to Zane, Chad was asleep in his arms.

Unexpectedly, warmth flooded her heart.

Chapter 4

With Chad nestled in his arms, Zane watched Riley. Her face had been pale as she hung up the phone but had transformed into an expression Zane couldn't read as she glanced at Chad. Had he offended her by taking the boy? She opened her mouth to say something but hesitated, shuffling papers on the desk instead.

"Mr. Baldwyn. What a surprise." She finished repositioning various-shaped white and yellow papers, then stacked them in a neat pile.

"I see that I've interrupted something important. My apologies." He motioned toward the quilt on the floor to indicate his desire to lay Chad on it. "May I?"

His question seemed to jolt Riley from her somber mood, and she skirted the desk. "Yes, of course. Here, let me take him." Her hands touched Zane's chest as she attempted to wrestle the boy from him. "I'm sorry I didn't think to put him down myself."

Zane edged away from her. "No, I've got him. I can do this."

Riley placed her hands on her hips, appearing a little incensed. But then she relaxed and gave Zane a lopsided grin. "Thank you." She looked at the floor as if the words were difficult to say. "I appreciate you watching him like that."

"Not a problem." Zane bent down with Chad and gently placed him on the quilt. Once certain that Chad would remain asleep, he stood and faced Riley again.

He'd been angry and frustrated when he realized the computer hardware—all of John's work and the future of Cyphorensic Technologies—had been stolen. He rushed out of his office to get here without finding an excuse to talk to her. As she looked at him, he realized he didn't have a clue how to broach the subject.

Of course he didn't need an excuse. He could simply come out and tell her he'd overheard John's message. Confront her. But she might not be willing to confide in him, a complete stranger to her. For all he knew, she could be part of the problem. He scratched his head and avoided her gaze while he considered what to say.

A picture rested on top of a box, and he picked it up, examining it while he gathered his wits. It read SEEK THE LORD WHILE HE MAY BE FOUND. The notion unsettled him. Zane put the picture back in its place. He should have calmed down before coming here. He must find out what Riley knew, if anything, and if she'd found the item—a password, a program or file, or what, he didn't know—that John had sent to her.

As he opened his mouth to voice his question, he noticed something about Riley that had escaped his attention before. He couldn't be sure, but the Riley in front of him was somehow different than the Riley in the picture in John's office. Interesting.

Strawberry blond hair struggled to escape her apparent attempt to pin it away from her face. The Riley in John's office had straight blond hair. He didn't believe it was a simple matter of hair coloring; even the face was slightly different. He would have to examine the photo to be certain.

"Um, the reason I stopped by is. . . Let me start over." *Man, you're bungling this.* He was an executive, an entrepreneur. Why was he stumbling over his words?

"Yes? I'm waiting. I've got a lot to do. . . ." Moisture appeared in her eyes. Her day didn't appear to be going too well. She turned away from him to squeeze between boxes and filing cabinets in order to get behind the old-fashioned desk, though not the sort of antique that would be worth anything.

It was then he noticed the chocolate smeared over the shoulders of her white T-shirt. He grabbed a tissue out of the box on her desk and handed it to her. Too late, he realized his blunder. He hadn't meant to embarrass her.

"Thank you." She took the tissue from him and wiped her eyes. "I'm sorry. It's been a hard day. I didn't realize it was so obvious."

Zane knew his sudden appearance in her office didn't help matters. He probably only reminded her of John. He took another tissue from the box and moved around the desk, wanting to laugh at the horrified expression on her face. "Turn around."

"What—what are you doing?" Her jade eyes peered up at him. He couldn't be certain, but he thought he saw fear and anger raging behind them.

"I'm not going to hurt you. I simply want to wipe the chocolate off your shirt. It's a really nasty habit, you know."

Realization dawned on her face, and she laughed and showed him her back.

"Chocolate, that is. I take it you're an addict, have a problem." He wiped at the brown splotches then decided the tissue wasn't the answer. "Have you got any water?"

She turned back to face him. "Really, this isn't necessary. I'll have to spray it with stain remover. You talk like you know about chocolate; don't you know it stains?"

"I do; that's why it's imperative that we remove it immediately." Zane spotted the wipes on top of the filing cabinet and pointed. "Those—they'll do." Before he could move, Riley dashed around the desk as if uncomfortable in close proximity to him. Her presence had an odd effect on him. She had single-handedly subdued his anger.

Riley lifted the container. "Empty. But I've got diaper wipes. They'll work."

While she rummaged through the diaper bag, he allowed his gaze to roam over various statements and late notices. It wasn't enough that her brother had died. She also had to deal with this mess.

Riley yanked a wipe out of the box and held it up, her eyes full of mischief. "If I were you, I would worry about the chocolate on my own shirt."

A smile erupted on his face, and he felt it all the way into his heart—a surprising but pleasant sensation. "This old thing? I'll just toss it."

Laughter gushed from her, the sound a symphony to his ears. The telephone rang, discharging the magic of the moment. Zane put his hand on the handset, considering answering it.

"No. I'll get it." Riley furrowed her brows, a warning in her eyes as she rushed to the desk. She stuffed the wipe into his hand before she yanked the annoying device to her ear. "Sanderford Farms."

Reprimanded, he made his way to the chair on the other side of the desk, feeling like a nuisance while he listened to her conversation. He could tell his presence made her uncomfortable.

Cranberry farming. An idea began to formulate in Zane's mind. He closed his eyes and smiled, tuning out Riley's phone conversation. He enjoyed it when things seemed to fall into place like so many carefully placed dominoes. And things were falling into place.

Sitting in the Sanderford Cranberry Farms office relaxed him. He'd overreacted. He decided that he would inform the police of the hardware theft, after all. His strong suspicion that John's death was more than a coincidence was just that—a strong suspicion—probably not enough to convince the police of foul play. He doubted the police's search for missing hardware would materialize into a cyber scandal.

Zane stepped outside to make the call to the police. If there was a connection between the computer theft and John's death, Zane needed to find out on his own. He could do that and still protect his unsullied start-up. He returned to the office to find that Riley remained glued to the phone.

Zane didn't feel comfortable with Cyphorensic Technologies going forward until he discovered what had happened to his friend and his wife, and to the software. In the meantime, he needed information that Riley might have. She appeared to be consumed with making a failing business work and did not act at all like someone who held a big secret in the palm of her hand.

Zane was an entrepreneur. He couldn't help but be interested in all the possibilities that could come out of cranberry farming, including a new challenge.

Riley hung up the phone, slamming it a bit harder than necessary. She rubbed her temples.

Zane's chest swelled with admiration for the strong young woman. Add "new mom" to her task list. He hoped he wasn't making a mistake in offering his help, but somehow her vulnerability had penetrated his better judgment. That much he recognized.

She was John's sister. Chad, John's son. Zane owed it to his friend and partner to help his sister make this work. If he discovered what he needed to know in the process, so much the better. He noticed her staring at him and became aware he'd been caught up in his thoughts. He stood.

She folded her arms across her chest and raised her eyebrows. "You know, you never did tell me why you dropped by. I know it wasn't for pleasantries, since you've already stated at the funeral and on the phone that you needed to speak to me. It was important. Remember?"

"I have a proposition for you." John heard Chad begin to squirm on his quilt. He'd have to do quick work, convince her to agree before she had time to reconsider.

Her incredulous expression urged him on. "John talked a lot about the cranberry farm—intrigued me. I'm an entrepreneur; I'd love to help in any way that I can." He stuck his hands in his pockets to hide the fact that he was nervous, an altogether new emotion for him.

"Look, I'm not sure what you have in mind, but this business is family owned and operated. It's not like you can get it ready so that you can take it IPO or whatever it is you do. I know your type." Riley applied ointment to her lips and rubbed them together then tucked the small container back into her pocket.

She would be as much of a challenge as the business itself. Even better. "No, no. You misunderstand me."

"What about your company? How would you have the time?"

Zane peered out a window that was in need of a good scrub and watched a man head to the office. He had to hurry. "I can't do much with the company right now. I lost my key programmer. My only programmer." He turned to face Riley. "But you know that. Cyphorensic is on hold for the moment." Or at least until he decided how to proceed with it. Sensing her rebuff, he continued. "Think of Chad, if not yourself. Let me do this for Chad, for John's memory. I can help you. It's apparent you need assistance."

The door swung open, and Zane flinched. Had he won her over?

The man stepped into the room then removed his straw hat and nodded at Zane. He looked at Riley. "Ma'am. I've already spoken to Mr. Sanderford, and he told me to come speak to you since you're running things now. Sure wish you would've shown up sooner. Thing is. . .I've had to take another job." He lowered his head. "I'm sorry about that. I've got two teenage boys starting to drive. That comes with a big insurance bill." The man grinned as if he hoped to ease the tension.

Zane wanted to smile at the timing, but he couldn't. He hesitated before looking at Riley, because he knew the turmoil on her face would affect him.

Chapter 5

Oh great! The day could not get any worse. Riley steeled herself against an onslaught of tears growing behind her eyes. She would not allow herself to break down. "I'm really sorry to hear that—Mr. Finickes, is it?"

She'd only met the man a few days before, but her mind was in overdrive, trying to grasp her new responsibilities plus all the changes that had happened in her life in such a short time.

"Can you give us two more weeks?" She held her breath.

The farm helper looked at his hat. "Ma'am, I'm sorry. My new employer needed someone starting this week. If I want the job, I've got to start now." He looked up at her, regret in his expression.

"I understand. Tell you what. I know we probably owe you something. Why don't you come by tomorrow, or later in the week when you get the chance, and I'll have a check ready for you." Riley could sense Zane watching her, and it unnerved her.

He'd made a valid offer to help with the farm, but she felt pressured and did not appreciate his interference. She could do this job herself, though Mr. Finickes didn't have the greatest timing in the world.

"Thank you, ma'am. Later on this week, then." He placed his hat back on his head, stood tall, and smiled at her before exiting with an added bounce to his step.

Riley opened desk drawers and shuffled through pencils, paper clips, business cards, and an array of disorganized junk, looking for a bottle of painkillers. A sticky blue substance covered her fingers, and she looked for the source. A leaking ink pen. She wiped at the goop with a tissue but only succeeded in smearing the ink, which left a stain.

The pounding in her head began to increase in intensity, and if she didn't stop it soon, she could be facing a full-blown migraine. The bills and late notices drew her gaze as though they screamed at her, demanding her attention. Unsuccessful in her search, she sighed as she closed the drawer and returned her attention to Zane.

"You know, I appreciate your offer. I really do. But I can handle this on my own. It's a great opportunity for me." If she could make it work, that was. She could think of nothing worse than failing and adding to Grandpa's disappointment.

Chad stirred on his blanket and sat up, his pudgy cheeks red. He squinted then rubbed his eyes. "Mommy?"

Pain shot through Riley's tender heart at his words, and she shared a look with Zane. His gaze spoke volumes to her that he cared deeply for the child. She rushed to Chad and picked him up. "No, sweetie, Mommy's not here. It's Aunt Riley."

The inadequate words caused her to frown. For Chad's sake, she wished she could become his mother; then he wouldn't have to grapple with a situation he couldn't understand. She'd not had the opportunity to call a counselor for advice yet, though she would probably speak to the pastor at her grandfather's church as he had suggested.

"Here, honey, let me get you some juice." The yellow top of a sippy cup protruded from the elastic side pocket of his diaper bag. She pulled at it, but the bag wouldn't relinquish its hold.

"Allow me." Zane pulled the apple juice out and handed it over to Chad, who smiled at him. It was obvious the boy returned Zane's affection.

She understood why Chad loved him so much. He was kind and considerate. "I should probably get back to work, Mr. Baldwyn, and I'm sure you've got something you must do, as well. Again, I appreciate your offer, but I can handle this." Riley hoped she sounded convincing; the pressure in her head was mounting, and she didn't have an inkling how to get on top of things now that Chad was awake.

Zane jammed his hands into his pockets and paced. "May I ask you a question?"

Though his manners were endearing, the man couldn't take no for an answer. She gritted her teeth to contain her frustration. After her experience with Eric and now Zane, Riley began to wonder if all men were bullheaded.

"Go ahead."

"Don't think me rude, but how do you plan to run this business and take care of Chad?" He pinned her with a blue-eyed stare.

She bristled and opened her mouth to speak, but he held up his palm to stop her. "Let me at least help you get organized, get things running smoothly. It's what I do. I can see that you've come into an impossible situation."

Zane pulled his other hand out of his pocket and moved close to Riley. "I feel like I need to do something for John, for his son and sister. Don't deny me this." He leaned in and kissed Chad on the cheek.

The tender kiss startled her. She stiffened at his nearness. His cologne fogged her thinking, and she backed up to clear her mind.

"What do you know about cranberry farming? You're a computer geek, for crying out loud." Riley pressed her dry lips together, hoping she hadn't offended him. "When would you have time to do this, and how would you work? Are you even willing to get your hands dirty?"

Zane grinned at her onslaught of questions. Not the effect she'd been shooting for. He unbuttoned his left shirtsleeve and began to meticulously fold it over until it reached his elbow. Then he started on the other, again taking time to be precise with each crease.

"First of all, I'm not a computer geek. Your brother was, remember?" His smile faded at his mention of John. He placed his hands on his hips. "I'm ready to get my hands dirty. I'll work part-time in the morning for a few weeks, months, however long it takes. I'll take care of Cyphorensic and other business in the afternoon."

He came across as ridiculous, standing there with his sleeves rolled neatly to his elbows, yet his starched white shirt looking as though it had been painted by an artist working in chocolate. Riley covered her mouth to hide her smile.

He raised his arms in question. "What? You don't believe me?"

"So you're really going to just throw that shirt away?"

Zane's eyes widened; she'd caught him off guard. He looked down at his shirt as if seeing Chad's artwork for the first time and laughed.

His laughter sent an unexpected thrill through her heart. She'd been wrong. Zane was not like Eric. Her ex-boyfriend would never have the desire or need to help anyone—unless he had an ulterior motive. Still, she'd been a poor judge of character in the past and couldn't be certain of Zane's intentions. She cradled Chad in her arms, desiring to focus on the child and, for the moment, put aside her concerns about Zane's true reasons for wanting to help.

"All right."

His cheerful expression turned serious, his smile fading. "You won't regret this, Riley. May I call you Riley? I'm not sure we ever established that."

His eruption of words made her dizzy. "Yes, yes, you can call me Riley."

❦

As Zane pulled into the parking lot of the two-story business complex that housed Cyphorensic Technologies, he tried to relax. He'd made the decision to help Riley on the cranberry farm in order to search for what John had sent her, or at least to earn her trust so that she would tell him. But while he was in the farm office, he couldn't think of anything he wanted to do more than help her. He owed that much to John. But he had to admit it wasn't the best business decision he'd ever made. Against his better judgment, he'd offered to spend time organizing things and getting the farm ready for expansion. All he'd really needed to do was be forthright and ask her about John's message.

He slammed the car door and pressed the security alarm button on his key fob as he headed toward the building. Something about Riley, her desperate need, or possibly the combination of Riley holding Chad and her desperate need, had touched his heart. Awakened it. Made him feel alive. It astounded him that with everything he'd done with his life, he'd never felt this way before. And he wanted to feel this way more.

Zane stared at the gold-etched name of his lifeless company; then he pushed through the plate glass doors of Cyphorensic Technologies to see Chelsea stashing personal items into a cardboard box. He stopped in the middle of the small lobby. "What are you doing?"

She curved her lips without flashing her usual bright smile. "Mr. Baldwyn, sir, you don't need me. There's nothing going on here. Hardly anyone ever calls. And except for when Mr. Connor was still alive, well, no one stops by anymore. I wanted to be a receptionist so I could see people. I love people. I've filed everything there is to file. Twice."

She smacked her gum in sheer freedom. "Besides, I got a new job. I'll be working for a veterinarian. I love animals. Oh, and I almost forgot. The police are here. I didn't know that Mr. Connor's computers were stolen, but I showed them his office."

Zane hesitated, absorbing her news as he stared at her. He hadn't noticed any cruiser in the parking lot. "They're here?"

"They only just showed. They're looking around Mr. Connor's office, taking pictures and prints, I think." She cleared her throat. "The investigating officer said he needed to ask you questions. He's so cute."

Zane sighed. "Well, I'm here now." He headed back to John's office.

"Mr. Baldwyn. Glad you could make it." One of the two uniformed officers greeted him with a smile. "I'm Sergeant Draper."

"Sorry I'm late. I phoned in not that long ago. Figured it would be awhile before anyone showed."

The officer's smile flattened, but he maintained his friendly, relaxed stance. He proceeded to question Zane regarding the theft. Zane answered with the facts, leaving any of his qualms out of the equation. No need to introduce his theories at this point.

"Your alarm system's been disabled. I suggest you invest in something that can't be disabled through the simple cutting of wires."

The information startled him. Had setting the alarm become such a rote operation that he'd failed to notice the system hadn't armed? "Thanks. So what happens next?"

"There's been a rash of electronic thefts in the area lately. TVs, stereos, and computers. Unless you have something else to add. . ."

Zane shook his head. What was he going to say? His partner had died in a car crash a month ago but had sent something he thought might be a matter of life and death to his sister? He'd had a nefarious history of hacking? "I need to take some files home. That's okay, isn't it? I'm a workaholic."

"I think we have all we need." Sergeant Draper nodded his dismissal of Zane and headed out of John's office along with his partner.

A rash of electronic thefts. Zane tugged at his collar. Was he being paranoid to think that the stolen hardware had anything to do with John? Still, there was his strange comment about life and death. . . .

Zane stood in the hallway and watched them stroll through the reception area. Chelsea's smile brightened. Sergeant Draper lingered longer than necessary before leaving. Once the officers were gone, Zane approached Chelsea. She resumed stacking various pictures of family members and friends into the box next to something pink and fluffy that Zane didn't recognize. He knew she was right, of course. There was no reason for her to remain at Cyphorensic. She was a vivacious, attractive young woman and needed interaction.

"I mean, if things were busy, I wouldn't leave you. You could count on me. But except for Mr. Connor's client, well, you don't need me."

Zane froze. "What did you say?"

Chelsea stopped chewing and gave him a look that said she thought he was old and losing it, apparently forgetting her earlier infatuation with him. Zane knew she hadn't intended to appear that way, but it cut him nevertheless.

"I said you could count on me if things were busy. . .if you needed me." She went back to smacking, even attempting a bubble. "But you don't."

"You said something about Mr. Connor's client." Zane didn't want to sound as though he wasn't aware of any clients. Probably Chelsea had misunderstood.

"There was that one man who came to meet with Mr. Connor. Twice, I think. I told him that you were out of town, but he insisted on meeting Mr. Connor."

Fire seared Zane's stomach, and he groaned.

"Are you all right?" Chelsea reached out to touch his shoulder.

"Yes, fine, thanks. I just need to get my antacid. The twenty-four-hour stuff isn't any match for my ulcers. I need the name of Mr. Connor's client so I can contact him and let him know what happened, that John died in an accident."

Chelsea's face went pale. "I—I don't know his name. He didn't give it. I'm so sorry. I'm a lame receptionist, aren't I?" She plopped into her seat and looked at him for validation. Zane feared she would cry.

"It's all right, Chelsea. No need to be upset." *The only person who ever came through the doors and you failed to get his name?* "What can you tell me about this man? Who did he work for?"

She looked up at him, stricken. "If I knew that, don't you think I would have gotten his name?"

Zane could only frown at her. He couldn't conjure a smile, even for Chelsea.

"Quite right. Well, I guess this is good-bye, then. I wish you well." Frustrated, he moved to head to his office.

"Mr. Baldwyn?"

He stopped and turned to face her again. "Yes?"

"I can tell you the man sort of scared me. He had black hair and wore an expensive-looking black suit, kinda like you do, only you usually wear blue or dark gray."

"Scared you?"

She nodded.

"Why did he scare you?" Chelsea was inexperienced. She was being melodramatic.

Eyes closed, she paused as if in deep thought. "I have a photographic memory. Did I ever tell you that? I can see him in my mind right now. Well, for one thing, he wasn't warm and friendly. Usually people are friendly to me. Oh, oh. And I remember Mr. Connor wasn't pleased to see him, at least at the office."

Heat rushed up Zane's neck. "Did Mr. Connor actually say that?"

Chelsea's cheeks reddened enough to be seen through her heavy makeup. "Um. . .yes. I'm sorry. I overheard him."

"Thanks for the information. If you think of anything else, I'll be in my office or Mr. Connor's."

He left the reception desk and hurried down the hall to John's office. He rummaged through the desk drawers, searching for anything that would tell him who John's visitor had been. For all he knew, it could have been a friend. The way that Chelsea presented it, the man had been a client. Still, he wasn't Zane's client, and John hadn't mentioned him.

Nothing was safe here—that is, if the thieves had left anything. Zane retrieved empty boxes from a spare room they'd used as storage and began packing anything that appeared important from John's office. They'd taken the computer hardware and all of the storage media. Zane stashed manila folders, hoping they would contain hard copy of pertinent information, into the boxes.

He went through the same drill in his own office and stuck the boxes in the dark corridor. He hadn't realized it was so late and flicked on more lights as he went back to John's office to make sure he hadn't missed anything.

Then he saw it.

The picture of John's sister, Riley, sat on the desk in a small bronze frame. He examined the photo closely. He was right. She looked very different in this photo, and his gut told him that it wasn't her. Yet John had said it was his sister. Zane placed it on top of the files in a box and headed out the door to load his car.

With all the boxes secured in the trunk and on the seats of his car, he hurried back to switch off the lights and lock the doors. When Zane returned to open his car door, movement in his peripheral vision caught his attention. He looked at the corner of the building to see a shadow skate into the darkness.

Zane jumped into his car and sped out of the parking lot. If he wasn't convinced before that John's death had been no accident, he was now. Since the thieves were still lurking around the office, then perhaps they had not retrieved what they were searching for. That put Riley and Chad in danger, as well. He took comfort in the fact that she'd allowed him to work with her. At least he would be on hand if protection was required.

After bringing the boxes up to his condominium and stacking them in his home office, Zane swiped the photo of Riley out of the box and found a lone soda in the sparse refrigerator. It would be a long, grueling night, but he needed to get started searching through the documents if he was to make any sense of it all.

He reclined on his navy blue leather sofa and gazed at Riley's photo while he sipped, the carbonation burning his throat as it went down. No, the woman in this picture was not Riley. Warm images of the feisty woman he'd spent the morning with floated through his tired mind.

Chapter 6

A bright blue sky promised a glorious day and, Riley hoped, a better one than yesterday. She covered a yawn as she carried Chad, who was still sipping on his cup of milk and wearing footed pajamas, to the Sanderford Farms office. The structure rested across the circular drive from Grandpa's farmhouse.

Zane's sleek, black luxury car was parked in front. Her heart skipped a beat. The unexpected reaction to seeing he'd arrived early aroused mixed emotions, and she couldn't decide if she should smile or frown.

She'd wanted to spend time with Zane going over Grandpa's plans for expanding the farm and had counted on Grandpa taking Chad for the morning. But he'd mentioned working on the pumps for the irrigation system and left early. He must have unlocked the office door for Zane. Since she'd agreed to allow him to assist in the business, she would have to remember to give Zane his own key. She pressed her lips to Chad's forehead and tousled his already mussed-up hair then opened the office door.

Zane stood behind the desk, holding a spray bottle and cloth, dressed in a cream-colored sweater and blue jeans instead of a designer suit like he'd worn the two times she'd seen him. He looked up from orderly papers and files and sent her a brilliant, heart-stopping smile.

"Good morning, Riley." His blue eyes glistened with warmth as he moved around the desk in one fluid motion.

Riley shut the door behind her and clung to the knob as if it would give her strength to fight the strange weakness in her legs. "You've been busy."

"How's my boy this morning?" Zane reached out his arms, and Chad allowed Zane to take him. He rested his head on Zane's chest.

Zane scrutinized the child's hands. "What, no chocolate today?"

"Shh." Riley glared at Zane. "You know he understands you, right?"

Chad lifted his head to Riley. "Candy?"

"No, sweetie. Aunt Riley won't make that mistake again. At least not in the office while I'm working."

Chad scrambled down and toddled to his toys left on the quilt from yesterday.

Zane stuck his hands in his pockets. "You know, even the best moms hire babysitters sometimes, that sort of thing. It wouldn't hurt to get help with him. In fact, he might enjoy going to a day care."

His words sounded like an affront to her. She crossed her arms and glowered. "Only yesterday you questioned how I could run the business and give Chad the time he needed. Were you just using that to get your way? I thought you were here to help." Her pulse pounded in her ears.

"Calm down, Riley. I did say that, and I meant it. I wasn't using your predicament with Chad." He shifted closer to her and placed a tanned hand on her arm. "I was merely thinking of you. You looked tired and drained. And Chad would enjoy time with other children. You can still be his primary caregiver."

She turned away from him and took a calming breath to rein in her irritation. The man acted as if he knew more about parenthood than she did. Her incompetence frustrated and embarrassed her. The inspirational picture she'd brought in yesterday remained where she'd placed it, and she held it up to the wall, trying to decide the best place to hang it. "How—how do you know so much about kids?"

"I don't want to give you the wrong impression. I know hardly anything about children. Really." He hesitated as if carefully considering his next words. "I only repeated words that John said to his wife. He told me they'd had marital troubles since Chad's arrival. It seems obvious to me that it would be difficult— things wouldn't be the same. I babysat for them a few times to help. That's why Chad and I are buddies."

Riley whirled to face him again. "No way."

He laughed. "Yes way." A distant look appeared in his eyes, and he frowned. "But then John began working too much, hardly ever went home. He said he needed the extra time because he was in the most intense part of the project." Zane shook his head then focused on Riley. "So how about you? You appear to be experienced with children. I'm impressed by the way you handle Chad."

Riley wanted to hear more about John's work, but she sensed that Zane's intention had been to revert to the original subject. "Babysitting was my business in high school. I was even certified."

"Certified?"

"Yeah, at the local hospital they taught classes that included CPR and offered babysitting certification."

"Well, you know what you're doing. I apologize if I overstepped."

She dismissed his words with a wave of her hand and returned her attention to the picture. "No. It's all right. I think you mean well. Babysitting is one thing. Parenting is totally different, which I'm finding out. It's just that I'm not ready to let anyone else have him right now."

Zane sighed behind her.

"He just lost his mom and dad." Riley's words came out shaky, and she wiped at the sudden tears, grateful she wasn't facing Zane. "Sorry. I miss John."

Zane tried to turn her and pull her into his arms, comfort her, she knew. Riley would have none of it. "No, I'm fine."

Zane handed her a tissue. She breathed deeply, took it, and gave a short laugh. She looked back at the picture.

"This says to be still and know that I am God." She sniffled as emotion continued to batter her insides. "I don't even know if John knew God. Never asked. Can you believe that? I never asked. What kind of Christian doesn't ask her brother if—"

She peered at Zane's speechless expression. "I'm sorry. I didn't mean to have an emotional breakdown on you."

He narrowed his gaze as if in deep contemplation while he stared at the picture. For the first time, it occurred to Riley that Zane might not be a Christian. She hadn't considered it either way until that moment.

He caught her looking at him, and his reverie fell away. "Look, why don't you give me a tour of the farm. You can tell me what you and your grandfather want to do here. I mean, give me the entire picture. I want to know your greatest dreams for this place. That would go a long way in helping me to know what direction to take. Organizing paperwork is one thing. But I love to make things happen."

Once again Zane had changed the subject, but his talk of dreams pleased her. "That sounds like a great idea. I need some fresh air. I'll get Chad's stroller. Do you mind watching him while I run to the house?"

"You know I don't."

When Riley returned with the three-wheeled jogging stroller, she set it on the lawn outside the office. She unlatched the tab to unfold it and yanked on the handle. It snapped into place. She bounded up the steps and opened the door to peek in.

"Chad, I brought you a change of clothes; then we can go for our walk."

Zane sat behind the desk, holding Chad, who pointed at a slim, charcoal-colored laptop computer. He whispered into the child's ear before he looked to Riley and smiled.

"I don't blame you for bringing your laptop. Who could work on that old computer?" She motioned toward the antique slumbering on the side table.

"You're only correct on one count. I can't work on that old computer. On the other, you're wrong. This isn't my laptop. It belongs to Sanderford Cranberry Farms."

Riley's mouth dropped open. She gathered her wits and said, "What are you talking about, Zane? I don't even know that we can afford a new computer right now. We've got other problems. Like a dozer that needs repairing." Though the new laptop thrilled her and she chided herself for sounding ungrateful, Zane had overstepped.

Pleasant voices resounded from the device speakers, causing Chad to giggle. Zane slid him off his lap and onto the chair as he stood. "Relax. They don't cost all that much. I stopped at a twenty-four-hour shopping mart this morning. If it bothers you that much, just consider this the beginning of much-needed cash flow—a loan to help get things moving."

She thrust her hands onto her hips. "I have my own laptop. You should have said something. You could have used mine." Riley scratched her head. "I was thinking of using it—just hadn't gotten that far yet."

"You think I don't have one I could use? I run a computer software company, remember? If you want to itemize this for your business, it has to be used for business." Zane frowned, his disappointment evident. "You know, I really thought you'd be pleased."

Why couldn't she be happy that he'd taken the initiative? She should have expected that from him, an entrepreneur. Instead, she'd ruined the moment. It astonished her that his hurt expression bothered her as much as it did.

She relaxed and slid her forefinger along the top of the sleek machine. "I'm sorry for making such a fuss. You're right. We do need this. Thank you for thinking of it."

The man amazed her. He'd only spent one morning in her office, and that was to convince her to let him help. He hadn't wasted any time getting to work.

"You worry too much. I know you want this place to be a success for your grandfather. And it will be. Things aren't as terrible as they seem. Show me the farm. I'll work on a tentative business plan. In fact, we won't even wait for the plan to get started on things. Like, say, the dozer." Zane raised his eyebrows and tilted his head toward the window.

"You didn't!" Riley rushed to the window to peer out. A tow truck was in the process of hoisting it onto a trailer. Her grandfather stood talking to one of the men. "I take it Grandpa knows and approves."

"Let's see. His words exactly were, 'My granddaughter's as smart as a whip.'"

She jerked her face from the window to stare at Zane, looking for a trace of sarcasm. The warmth in his eyes coaxed her suspicions away.

"He's right. Riley O'Hare has everything under control because she hired a consultant to get things moving," he said then winked.

Her spirit surged with hope. She grinned at him. "I have to admit. . .you're good."

❧

Zane strolled next to Riley as she pushed a napping Chad in a big-wheeled jogging stroller along a dirt path toward the cranberry beds. Her hair appeared lighter in the sunshine. It bounced at her shoulders with each step she took. The breeze swept a few errant strands across her face.

She flashed a smile his way. "I have to be honest with you. With myself. I'm starting to realize that I don't know anything about the business of cranberry farming. I think Grandpa has expectations because I have a business degree. But that doesn't mean anything."

The undeveloped road swerved to the right, and they followed its course. A lush green meadow surrounded by ancient oaks extended for several acres to Zane's left.

"I'm sure you know more than you think," he said.

"I practically grew up here. Lived here most of the time in the summer. Of course, during harvest season, everyone pitched in. But I only saw things from a child's point of view. I came out a few times as an adult. I realize there is much more to running a farm now that I'm living here."

Riley sounded winded, so Zane grabbed the handles. "Here, let me."

She relinquished control and stepped to his side without disturbing their cadence. "I should be in better shape than this. But I haven't exercised in a few months. It's amazing how quickly you can get out of shape."

Zane stared straight ahead, focusing on the road. He'd noticed Riley's slender, appealing figure. He chided himself for allowing his thoughts about her to veer from anything other than business—something he struggled with, the more time he spent with her.

"I can tell you the basics. My great-grandfather purchased the eighty acres that is now Sanderford Farms. There's only about ten acres producing cranberries, a pond, thirty or forty acres of woodland. I'm not sure on all of the numbers, but Grandpa knows, and he can tell us. Plus there's a reservoir for use with the bogs. It's quite a process. Actually, now that I think about it, Grandpa should be showing both of us all of this. I haven't exactly had the time to refresh myself with the details."

The young woman had already faced quite a challenge, yet she appeared to stand ready to tackle another. Zane felt a rush of admiration for Riley and drew a deep breath.

"Oh, so now you're getting winded. Let me take it, then. We're almost there anyway. Look, you can see the dikes," she said.

They strolled to stand on heaped-up dirt surrounding the cranberry beds. Sprinklers doused the plants with water.

"All that green covered with pink and white flowers you see is the cranberry runners. Surprising how thick they grow, isn't it?" Riley shook her head, her expression bright, beautiful.

Zane scrambled down the dike and stepped over the irrigation pipe to take a closer look. He stared in awe at the millions of shiny red-green leaves, swelling up the runners. "Truly amazing. I've spent most of my time in office buildings, working in front of a computer. I regret that I haven't taken more time to enjoy nature." The fresh air and the vegetation had a calming, therapeutic effect on him. Yet it was Riley's youthful excitement that fascinated him.

"Grandpa started dozing new beds in April. He said it had taken too long because he had to make sure they were level and he wasn't experienced in using a laser level." Riley laughed. "But he's trying."

She continued strolling. "Then he'd spread six inches of clay over them for the first layer. But that's when the dozer broke down. We've still got to put down six to eight inches of organic material like loam or peat, then sand. That'll take weeks, so depending on how long it will take that mechanic you hired to repair our dozer, I think we may miss planting new fields for this season. Even so, any new vines would take at least five years to give us fruit."

Her words stunned him. He hadn't considered that it would take so long; he'd hired a mechanic without doing much research. The news that he'd miscalculated goaded him. "Then why were you trying to hire a mechanic yesterday?"

"What? I'm not saying it's the way things will go. I just don't know. But we can always try. We don't want to lose an entire planting season."

Impatience threatened to rob Zane of enjoying the farm tour and Riley's presence. He felt for his cell in his pocket as he considered the possibility of getting a new dozer.

Chad squirmed, waking up. Riley handed Chad his drink then stood to face Zane. He'd learned his lesson and felt certain that she would not approve of the purchase. With his limited knowledge, it would be an impulsive action at best.

"I think Grandpa wishes he could diversify into every aspect of cranberry processing. But that is beyond the realm of possibility to me."

A chill of exhilaration raced through Zane. It amazed him how the idea of expanding this farm excited him. Riley's jade eyes peered at him as though questioning his thoughts. A slight grin spread over her lightly freckled cheeks. She wore minimal makeup, enough to accentuate her eyes and lips. He thought her face was flushed from the exercise, but the red on her cheeks deepened.

She looked away from him. "I'm not sure what you do and don't know about cranberries. So just ignore me if I tell you something that you already know. But these are not actually real bogs in the true sense. The cranberries have to be dry while they grow in the peat and sand. It's only during the harvest that the bogs are flooded and the cranberries float to the top. That's why they're called bog rubies."

"I didn't realize that. See, you know more than you think."

"Well, I've helped with harvest over the years as often as I could, even after we moved to California. I've been researching on the Internet late at night, too, to help fill in the blanks." She grinned.

Chad threw his cup on the road, and Riley huffed. While she leaned over to pick it up, Zane released the child from the captivity of his stroller. Chad delighted in running in circles.

Zane studied Riley then said, "I know that harvest season is in October, right?"

"Yes, the bogs are flooded. That's when all of the equipment is put into use and the extra workers are needed."

"Well then, we've got some time. It's only the end of June." Zane cringed at his words. He hadn't planned to work here through October. He needed to resolve if and why John was murdered—and find his missing software—before then. If only he knew what he was looking for.

He watched Riley hold hands with Chad as they danced around in a circle, trusting and innocent. He could potentially resolve the mystery if he told her of his suspicion of John's murder and asked her to tell him what John had sent. He'd made a mistake. He should have presented her with his suspicions yesterday instead of this plan to help her. But it wasn't a scheme; he was genuinely pleased to think of making the cranberry farm an operation that she and her grandfather could be proud of.

If he solved the puzzle surrounding John's death today, he would still want to do that.

But he couldn't stand to think of the outcome of relating his suspicions. The woman juggled too many things already. She didn't need or deserve to have fear heaped onto her already-full plate. An unpleasant thought occurred to him, causing his heart to palpitate. How would Riley react when she learned of his deception? He pushed the anxiety away, out of his mind. No, he would try to discover the truth on his own, protect her for the time being.

John would have sent something ordinary, and only a person aware that the item was a clue to a puzzle would think to engage in solving it. He didn't think Riley had known her brother long enough to be aware of that side of him, but he wasn't sure.

"What are you thinking about?" Her pleasant voice brought him back. "You can't fool me. I see those wheels turning."

She stopped playing with Chad and drew him into her arms then came to stand before Zane. "Something's bothering you. What is it?"

Surprised, he said, "You know me that well already? I need to be more careful."

He turned to face the road back to the house and office. "We should get back."

"But I haven't shown you the equipment or pump."

"I've seen all I need to see for now." He knew his words came out cold, and her confused expression cut him to the core. Though he was connected to Riley and cared about her because she was John's sister, he was beginning to have feelings of a different nature for her. And it scared him. He'd already lost everyone he'd ever cared about.

Chapter 7

After lunch, Riley went back to explore the farm. She'd lost track of time, and as a result, they would have to eat a late dinner. While she stored the stroller in the mudroom, Chad wandered through the entryway to the kitchen. She trailed behind him then marched to the sink to wash her hands and splash water over her face.

"Juice, juice. . ." Chad pointed to the plastic apple juice container she'd left on the counter earlier. Only it was empty.

"I'm sorry, it's all gone. How about water?" She filled his cup with the filtered bottled water she'd purchased. Every time she watched Grandpa drink from the tap, she squirmed. She wasn't accustomed to drinking the hard water on the farm.

The child took a sip then threw the cup on the floor, shaking his head. "No. I want juice."

Riley huffed and lifted Chad, hoping to distract him. "How about milk?" She set him in the high chair and buckled him in. "Better yet, how about chocolate milk?" At the moment, she didn't want to risk his discontent with her new suggestion and would try anything to please him.

Tired and frustrated, she allowed her mind to think about her life in California. After a long day, she had time to kick off her shoes and recuperate, even though she had brought work home. Things were different with a child.

She opened the freezer to rummage through its offerings. Grandpa stomped his boots outside before entering the mudroom. He appeared in the kitchen wearing socks, his clothes covered with grease and dirt.

Riley gasped. "Grandpa. You look a mess."

"The irrigation pump's broken. It's beyond repair, so I'm going to need a new one."

She closed her eyes at his statement. Everything was breaking at once. She stifled her desire to ask him if he'd replaced or upgraded anything in all these years. She was here to help, not hurt.

"I've got to get cleaned up. Say, you wouldn't mind popping in a frozen dinner for me, would you?" he asked.

Riley stared at the diminishing contents of the freezer. "You know, I need to do some shopping. I'm sorry that we've been eating everything. I need to share the responsibilities; I just haven't had time."

Though she'd decided to live in her grandfather's house and divide the expenses, she hoped to have a place of her own at some point.

"Grandpa, what do you like to eat?" She glanced at the tray standing by his favorite recliner in the living area. "You can't exist on TV dinners all the time."

"If you want to cook something for you and Chad, I might share a bite with you." He grinned. "Whatever you decide will be fine with me."

After washing his hands with grime-removing soap, he grabbed a glass from the cabinet and filled it with water from the faucet. She would have to encourage him to clean up in the bathroom. Maybe she could talk him into drinking purified water, too.

He emptied the glass then sighed. "You know, your grandmother did all the cooking. I never learned. Since it has been just me here, it hasn't been worth the effort." He headed through the living room and up the stairs to his bedroom.

Great, just great. Not only was she going to raise a child and run a farm; she'd have to learn to cook. She understood her grandfather's sentiment, because she hadn't made the effort to cook for herself much, either, but she'd soon have to pick up the skill. She looked over at Chad, who busied himself with the empty plastic juice bottle he'd somehow managed to reach from the counter.

"I'm sorry, I forgot all about your chocolate milk." Riley retrieved the jug from the fridge and noticed this would be Chad's last cup until she went to the store. Unless, of course, he was willing to accept water. Maybe she could stretch it into two cups if she only poured him half. She stirred in some chocolate syrup, something she kept on hand for stressful moments. After handing the cup to Chad, she poured a spoonful of the delightful syrup and stuck it in her mouth.

She closed her eyes and enjoyed the sweet taste, willing the stress away. "Mmm."

Zane's words about getting help with Chad came back to her as she watched the two-year-old sip with delight. He looked at her, his eyes wide with pleasure.

"Good, isn't it?" she asked.

He nodded.

Her heart ached at the thought that Zane could be right. If only she had a little help with the child, she could get on top of things around the farm. Who was she kidding? She needed to work on more than the business. The boy needed decent, healthy food. Fruits and vegetables. Her shoulders sagged as she leaned against the counter. So far she'd been a complete failure as his guardian.

She hadn't prepared ahead of time for dinner and would have to scramble to pull it together. Then she needed to run to the store. She ran her hand through her hair, thinking she'd give almost anything to take a nice, relaxing shower right now.

Grandpa would go to bed early—because he woke up much too early in her opinion—so she would have to take Chad with her to shop. She reminded herself that he was all she had left of her brother, and she would do whatever it took to make things work. Besides, she couldn't afford child care yet.

Gravel crunched outside. Riley leaned over the sink and looked out the kitchen window. Zane's car pulled to a stop. Her heart jumped with pleasure. She chided herself for her unwarranted reaction. She knew little about him and would have to exercise more self-control over her emotions. Still, it surprised her that he'd returned, and she wondered if he'd forgotten something.

She rushed to the door and opened it. His eyes brightened when he saw her. "Pizza, anyone?" He held up three large boxes.

Relief flooded Riley. "You're a lifesaver. But then, I suppose you already knew that. Come in." She held the door open for him as he entered the kitchen through the mudroom.

He placed the boxes on the counter. The pepperoni pizza steamed when he lifted the lid. "I didn't know what kind you liked or how much to get. But almost everyone loves pepperoni."

"Pizza, pizza!" Chad bounced in his high chair.

"And I already knew that the little guy likes pepperoni. That's what we had when he stayed with me."

Riley couldn't believe her good fortune. "You know, I appreciate this. I can't tell you what great timing this is."

He flashed his smile before grabbing a slice and holding it out to her. "Aren't you hungry?"

"Yes, thanks. Let me grab a few plates first." She retrieved dishes from the cabinet. "Grandpa will be excited. All he ever gets are those frozen dinners. He's cleaning up and should be down in a while."

Riley took a bite. Cheese strung from her mouth to the pizza, unwilling to let go. She saw Zane watching her. Embarrassed, she grabbed a napkin and wiped her mouth.

She sat down at the table, and Zane joined her. They made trivial conversation, chatting about the weather and the next day's agenda. Riley finished her second piece and was about to consider a third when she noticed that tomato sauce covered Chad's face and clothes.

She frowned. "Solving one problem only creates another. He'll have to go straight to a bath after this."

"Maybe not," Zane said. "I usually just wipe him up with a wet washcloth, and then he's good to go. I mean, I would hate to think that I only created more work for you." Teasing glimmered in his eyes.

"No, no. That's not what I meant. But I do have to ask, why did you come back? Why the pizzas?"

"Well, I felt bad for the way I rushed out on you today. I had things I needed to take care of. I thought we could talk more about the business—get to know each other better in a more relaxed atmosphere. You know, without the pressure of a workday." Zane set his pizza crust on the plate and gave her a serious look. "That's all right, isn't it?"

"Yes, it's fine. I can't thank you enough. I was just about to stick something in the oven. That is, if I could find anything."

His relaxed tone soothed her nerves. It pleased her that he seemed to care about the farm and was taking it seriously. Though she understood the reason he gave—that he felt he owed it to John—she found it hard to accept that sort of concern, kindness. But Riley wanted to believe him. She couldn't help but like Zane.

"You're going to spoil me if you keep this up. First the mechanic, then the laptop, and now pizza! What next?"

The spark in his eyes sent a thrill through her. To avoid his gaze, she wet a cloth at the kitchen sink then began wiping Chad off in his high chair, though she mused that hosing him down might be a better choice.

"Riley?" Her stomach swirled at the way he said her name. She closed her eyes. She needed to rein in her emotions now if she was going to make it through this evening.

He continued even though she hadn't answered him, "If it would make you feel more comfortable, you and Chad could freshen up while I clean up the dishes. Besides, your grandfather hasn't eaten. I can visit with him while I wait."

The man thought of everything. Though Riley loved his considerate nature, her grandmother's words flitted through her mind. *If it seems too good to be true, it probably is.* She thrust the negative thought away and turned to face Zane.

Grandpa whistled as he strolled through the living room and into the kitchen. "I smell pizza." His eyes widened, and he smiled with pleasure as he stuck out his hand to Zane. "Well, what do you know? Did you bring those pizzas? You might give my Riley some competition if you're not careful."

Riley smiled at her grandfather's teasing reference to her cooking, or lack thereof, and offered him a plate of the Italian food. "Grandpa, I need to get cleaned up and so does Chad. You don't mind visiting with Zane while I do that, do you?"

"Not at all. He's a fine young man."

Riley pulled an unwilling Chad out of his chair. "Come on, sweetie, don't you want to take a bath?" She headed up the stairs, trying to decide how to keep her eye on him while she cleaned up.

Zane's unexpected appearance was a pleasant surprise. But she reminded herself that she wasn't exactly the best judge of character. She'd spent over a year with a self-centered control freak, all the while thinking he was her dream come true. Riley groaned. Zane's interest was a business one, connected to her brother, and she shouldn't allow her thoughts to venture anywhere else.

She entered the bathroom with Chad, turned on the water to ready his bath, and grinned. *At least until I get to know him better.*

♥

Riley descended the stairs into the living room. After his bath, she'd given Chad to the men to watch while she washed up. Grandpa lounged in his recliner watching a game show, his eyelids drooping. He'd probably retire to his room soon. Zane sat on the sofa, a sleeping Chad leaning against his arm. He smiled as she approached but appeared tense. She wasn't sure if he was afraid of waking Chad or if she'd taken too long to get ready.

"I'm sorry. I didn't mean to make you wait." Riley paused in the center of the room, looking at the occupied recliner and sofa. The only place left to sit was next to Zane. "You really don't have to stay."

Zane furrowed his brows and stared at her as if trying to read her meaning. "I don't want to keep you from doing anything."

"No, it's all right. We can talk about the farm. Right, Grandpa?" she asked.

In response, her grandfather rose from his exhausted stupor. He turned to grasp Zane's hand and shake it. "It was nice chatting with you, son. I've got an early morning, and it's my bedtime."

They bade Grandpa good night. Riley hoped they wouldn't wake the sleeping boy. She sat in the warm chair her grandfather had vacated but noticed it wasn't positioned in a way conducive to conversation. "Why don't we go to the kitchen table? I can make us coffee."

"What about him?" Zane tilted his head toward Chad.

"I'll put him to bed." Riley carefully peeled Chad away from Zane, tiptoed up the stairs, and placed him in his bed.

By the time she returned to the kitchen, the aroma of fresh-brewed coffee wafted through the air. "You can't help yourself, can you?"

Zane looked up from pouring the brew into a mug. "What? Should I just wait for you to do everything?"

She warmed at his thoughtfulness. Still, for some reason, it frustrated her. "No, but you could at least let me do something. I read that when they designed instant cake mix they decided to leave in a few steps, like adding eggs and water, so that the homemaker would feel useful."

He laughed. "Okay, so I'll let you make the coffee next time."

Next time?

He handed her the I LOVE CALIFORNIA cup, steaming with black liquid. "I assume this is yours." He grinned. "Sorry, I don't know what you take, so you'll at least have to do that yourself."

"Give me that." She reached for the nondairy creamer and dumped a spoonful in.

He shook his head. "I can't do this." He smirked before continuing. "I can't let you go on with the wrong impression about me—again. Your grandfather made the coffee while you were cleaning up earlier. Said he liked the instant but that you were 'dead set on your fancy brew,' to put it in his exact words. All I had to do was walk in here and push the button to start it."

"Well, now, that makes me feel better." She sipped the hot drink while questions about the man standing in her kitchen reeled in her mind. "So why don't you tell me about yourself. In only two days, you've turned yourself into a necessity at Sanderford Cranberry Farms, but I don't know a thing about you except that you were John's business partner."

Zane took a long drink of his coffee. Riley wondered how he could swallow it when it was piping hot. "Me? There's nothing too interesting about me. But maybe you'd like to talk about your brother. I know that you two only learned of each other a couple of years ago. And with you living across the country, you probably didn't get much time with him or his family." He moved to the kitchen table. "You would like to talk about him, wouldn't you?"

The pain she felt over her brother's death had become far too familiar. And she hated it. She swallowed the lump that formed in her throat and joined Zane at the table. "Yes. You're right. I would. So tell me, how did you two meet?"

"John and I have known each other since grade school. I wouldn't say we were friends, though, until high school, when I was going through some...things. We became close. He was like a brother to me. We attended different colleges. Public for him, private for me. But we stayed in touch. I knew him to be brilliant, and when I decided to start Cyphorensic, I discussed everything with John. He left a good job with great company benefits to join me."

As he spoke, Riley watched his handsome face contort. Lines she hadn't seen before appeared out of nowhere, making him look older than before.

He paused and scrutinized the knots in the pine table. "I can't tell you how sorry I am for your loss. That's why I want you to believe me when I say that I really want to make your farm a success."

His need for her approval took her by surprise. A myriad of emotions swelled inside, creating nervous flutters in her stomach, and she searched for a way to dispel them. "Would you like more coffee?"

She retrieved the carafe from the counter and set it on the table between her and Zane, like a protective barrier—though she wasn't quite certain what she needed protection from.

"No, thanks." He toyed with his empty cup, waiting for her response.

"Zane, I believe you. I know this has been quite a blow to you, too, not only in terms of losing a friend, but to your business, as well." Riley cleared her throat, trying to recover from the shakiness she heard there. "Have you hired John's replacement?" It was painful to speak of her brother. She was grateful for the coffee and took a big swig.

Zane rose from the chair and jammed a hand into his jeans pocket. He paced across the linoleum floor while he rubbed his chin. Riley had noticed that he often took time to consider things before he spoke. She liked that about him.

"I haven't been able to go forward, for reasons I can't explain right now." He stared at her as he sat down, leaning over the table to look intently into her eyes. "When was the last time you actually spoke to John? I mean, did you have a chance to talk to him before he died?"

Riley sighed. "Thankfully, yes. We only spoke every few weeks or so. If he didn't call me, I'd call him. Sometimes I'd talk to Sarah or Chad."

Zane frowned, and his expression took on that deep, contemplative look she'd become accustomed to, though it was usually interspersed with smiles. She reminded herself that the discussion of John was painful for him, as well.

"What about the night he died? Did you talk to him then?" Zane's gaze was penetrating, his expression serious.

"No. He'd called that night. But I didn't talk to him."

"Then how do you know he called? He left you a message?" Zane leaned forward. "What did he say?"

"I don't know if he left a message because I mistakenly deleted them. I know he called because I saw his number on my caller ID. I tried to return his call. Got no answer, so I left a message."

Zane's shoulders sagged. "What time was it when you checked messages—do you remember?"

Something in his tone sent prickles over her. He sounded like a cheesy detective questioning a suspect on a prime-time police drama. She rubbed her arms to take away the unexpected chill.

Unnerved by the conversation, Riley stood up. "Can you tell me why you want to know?"

He stiffened. "I'm sorry. I didn't mean to upset you."

"I know. It's just me. I'm tired, and talking about John, well, it's just too painful right now, I suppose. Look, could we do this another time? I mean, I want to talk more. I'd love to hear stories of my brother, since you knew him far longer than me." She smiled at him, hoping to ease the tension.

His expression relaxed, and he smiled gently. "Riley, truly. . .I didn't mean to overstep. But you're right. It's getting late, and I have an early day tomorrow. I need to get on top of all that paperwork." He flashed her another smile.

After Zane left, Riley locked the doors. She climbed the stairs and peeked in on Chad. Still sleeping. She wanted nothing more than to plop down on her bed, but she noticed a pile of envelopes on the pillow. Grandpa had placed her mail there instead of putting it in the office. Probably afraid her junk mail would get lost. She laughed and rummaged through the stash, some of which was forwarded from her California address, then tossed the mail into a cardboard box to be dealt with later. She still needed to unpack.

As she readied herself for bed, she couldn't stop thinking about Zane Baldwyn. She didn't doubt that his intentions to assist her with growing the farm were sincere. But his questions had sent a suspicious chill up her spine. She chided herself for revisiting the ridiculous notion. She'd probably misunderstood his intent and had overreacted. It wasn't as if she hadn't been emotional of late. Still, the niggling thought that he was after something wouldn't leave until she drifted off to sleep.

Riley woke with a start and sat up, her heart racing. Sweat beaded on her brow. The images came rushing back. She'd dreamed she was married to Eric. He was the absolute worst husband, thoughtless, inconsiderate. He traveled constantly and never had time for her, just like her father. Riley lay her head back against the pillow and let out a soft cry. In the dream, Eric's face had morphed into Zane's.

Chapter 8

Stupid! Stupid!

Zane slammed the door to his condo behind him. His car keys jingled when he tossed them onto the coffee table. The place smelled stale, neglected.

If it had been physically possible to kick himself, he would have. Instead, he settled for berating. He'd handled it all wrong, bungling his attempt to question Riley without raising her defenses or alerting her to his predicament. If he could solve this mess without involving her, it would be for the best. The last thing he wanted to do to John's grieving sister was create fear. Nor did he think it would do any good for her to discover her brother had been murdered. Zane could prove none of it. Yet.

It was a delicate balance—convincing her of his sincere attempt to help Sanderford Cranberry Farms while using the opportunity to sleuth. If he had learned anything about Riley O'Hare, it was that she had a few trust issues.

Slipshod, Baldwyn, truly slipshod.

The bottom line was that he didn't know how to question her and should have waited for a more suitable opportunity. He'd pushed things. So far, he'd gone about winning her confidence all wrong. He'd suspected that she didn't trust him from the beginning, so he'd labored to win her favor.

He thought he'd gained ground as he watched her warm smile, enjoyed their banter. But it was she who'd disarmed him and won his esteem. He laughed at the irony and headed for the shower.

Despite his best efforts, he'd only succeeded in ruffling Riley's feathers with his assistance, rather than pleasing her, right down to making coffee. Her first reaction to almost everything he did for her was to take it as a personal affront to her abilities. He was trying too hard.

He showered and dressed then fell into a plush chair in the corner of his home office. Cardboard boxes from Cyphorensic were stacked and organized along the far wall, beckoning him. He ran his fingers through his still-wet hair and wondered why he'd dressed instead of getting into bed. Might as well get to work. He skimmed through papers in one of the boxes. Then another. When he looked up at the atomic clock, it read 1:00 a.m.

If he had done too much damage with his questions, Riley might not allow him back into the office, into her life. He couldn't risk it. He grabbed his keys and rushed out the door to head back to the Sanderford Cranberry Farms office. He should retrieve as much information as he could from the dinosaur computer and finish organizing the endless piles of papers. It would be pleasant to walk into a thoroughly scrubbed and orderly office tomorrow, as well.

Until Zane figured out what was going on, he would not let any questionable activities rest. While talking with Robert Sanderford tonight, he'd learned that Sarah had used the office computer. If she'd used it for even thirty seconds, she might have hidden information that would help Zane—if that had been John's plan. There was no way for him to know for sure whether Sarah had been involved unless he copied and examined the files on the computer.

In the meantime, he could possibly get an overview of Sanderford Cranberry Farms by looking at the files, depending, of course, on whether anyone had bothered to update things.

After the drive from Plymouth to Carver, Zane turned onto Cranberry Highway. Before long, he pulled into the entrance to Sanderford Cranberry Farms and turned off his headlights as he headed toward the office. He didn't want to disturb anyone. As the tires of his car crunched against the gravel driveway, they seemed to shout his presence, and he winced, hoping no one heard.

Rather than slamming his car door, he pressed it shut until he heard the required click. He crept up the steps to the office and searched through his key ring for the one Riley had given him earlier in the day.

One of the keys engaged the lock, and Zane exhaled. The thick smog polluting his mind suddenly cleared. He hadn't known what he was looking for until that moment.

The key!

He shut the door behind him and leaned against it, allowing the exhilarated pounding of his heart to calm. Why hadn't he thought of it before? The criminals who'd stolen the Cyphorensic computers needed the key to the encryption code, or the software would be of no use to them. Still, it didn't make sense. John was developing software to create a new encryption standard, but it wasn't finished. Why steal it? Though he didn't understand everything, Zane had at least figured out what John had hidden away somewhere, and his strong suspicion was that John had mailed the key to Riley. Only she would not recognize it for what it was.

In the dark, he stumbled to the desk and flipped on the banker's lamp, hoping the low lighting would be sufficient for him to see while he copied files. While he waited for the old computer to boot up, he spotted one of the scripture pictures that Riley had hung on the wall. The dim light on the desk wasn't bright enough for him to make out the words, so he strolled over.

285

He read it in a hushed tone. " 'Seek the Lord while he may be found; call on him while he is near.' Isaiah 55:6."

A sense of peace settled upon him, unnerving him. He backed away from the image. First Chelsea had said she would pray for him. Now his path had crossed with Riley, another Christian. She believed that it was her obligation to evangelize everyone, or at least she'd been upset with herself for not asking John if he had known Christ. It surprised Zane that she hadn't asked him yet, and he wondered what he would tell her if she did.

Sure, he was a Christian.

He believed in God and His Son. He'd learned all of that as a child. But he wasn't so sure that God cared much about the everyday details of his life. God hadn't exactly been there for him when things had fallen apart in high school. But John had. And Zane had picked up the pieces and made a success of his life.

He shook his head. Some success. His partner and wife were dead, and more than Zane's company was now at risk. The idea that God was trying to reach him for some reason wouldn't let go. Did God do that? Zane wasn't sure, but there was no way that he would believe God had gotten rid of John just to get Zane's attention. No. If he'd learned anything in Sunday school, it was that the human race lived in a fallen world. God wouldn't do something bad to achieve something good. Zane nodded to himself. Instead, He would act like any good manager and take something that had gone horribly wrong and create something good from it.

That was all Zane was trying to do here—solve a mystery to bring order back. Still, he wondered why God hadn't involved Himself in Zane's family crisis when he was in high school.

His ulcer flared, and he went back to the desk to find the bottle of antacid he'd stuck in the top drawer. He popped two of the pills and swallowed them dry; then he stuck a disk into the computer's drive and began the laborious task of copying files.

This would take awhile.

In the meantime, he opened drawers and pulled out all the items, organizing them while he waited. For all he knew, Riley had received the item John had sent and simply stuck it in a drawer, not realizing its importance. Nothing he did could be counted as a waste of time.

He smiled to himself. Though Riley could blame most of the disorganization on her grandfather, Zane had seen her in action and was convinced she'd learned all she knew from Robert. John was her half brother, but they were complete opposites. John was a well-oiled programming machine with a brilliant mind that seemed to border on insanity at times. He could not exist if anything was out of place. Riley seemed to thrive amid disorganization.

As he thought of Riley, warmth spread through his chest. In only a matter of a few days, he'd begun to care about her as more than John's sister. It sickened him to think of her reaction once she learned of the initial reasons for his pro posal to help the cranberry farm. She would be angry and disillusioned. She'd lose faith in him. He was a fool to allow himself any attachment to her.

Zane shrugged off the nagging thoughts and focused on the task at hand. He filed every loose paper in its own category in manila folders, trashed others, and organized the boxes based on the dated information to be dealt with later. He swept the floor and shined the windows as well as possible in the darkened room. All the while, he continued to insert disks into the computer and copy the files. He was amazed at the amount of information on the machine, since it didn't sound as though Robert Sanderford had spent much time on it. Though he could have searched the computer itself without copying the files, he didn't want to take a chance that he would need access to the information again and for some reason that access would be denied. Riley might decide she didn't want his help anymore.

By three in the morning, he'd finished copying the last of the files and uncluttered the office of most of the excess papers. He would head home and attempt to get a few hours of sleep. Tomorrow morning he would return to the farm, then spend his evenings searching for John's key.

He thought of Chad, Riley, and Grandpa and prayed to God for the first time in years. He had to find the key to decipher John's code.

Before someone else did.

Chapter 9

After a difficult night of tossing and turning, Riley woke early and joined Grandpa for breakfast. She noted he was running behind this morning. She spoon-fed oatmeal to Chad to be sure that he ate something, because half of the mixture had already ended up on the floor. Grandpa slurped his instant coffee while he read the morning paper. She cleaned up the breakfast dishes and continued to peek out the window, eager for Zane to arrive.

"What's eating you this morning, Riley?" Grandpa tilted his head enough to peer at the paper through his bifocals.

She pulled up a chair and sat down at the table. Chad sipped the last of the milk. "Am I that obvious?"

"You've had four cups of coffee already and are brewing more. You've looked out the kitchen window between every spoonful of oatmeal and every dish you put away."

"I thought you were reading the paper," she teased. It probably didn't take much effort for him to see that she was about to burst. "I didn't sleep well last night. I'm just anxious to get things moving for you. That's all."

Anxious to throttle Zane is more like it!

She had awakened in the night after a bad dream and slipped out of bed to head to the kitchen for warm milk but remembered she had to save the last of the milk for Chad. When she'd looked out her bedroom window, she'd seen a light on in the office and Zane's parked car. By the time she'd slipped on her robe and hurried down the stairs, he'd gone. She couldn't imagine what he would be after in the middle of the night. Had he left something? Nothing could be that important.

More than anything, she wanted to believe the best about him. She liked him. But his questions to her about John had seemed more like fishing than curiosity. She'd been tired and emotional about the discussion of her brother and had dismissed the nagging in the back of her mind that Zane wasn't being up front with her—that he was hiding something.

She wished she didn't jump to the worst conclusions about people, but her time with Eric had left her unable to trust. He'd told her he cared for her, and at first, it seemed that he did. But over time, Riley came to realize that only work mattered to him. Eric had used her, allowing her to take the blame for a disgruntled client when, in fact, the blame was all his.

Seeing Zane in the office at three in the morning had aroused her questions about his motives once again. For some reason, she felt betrayed. Used again. Nausea rolled through her stomach at her disappointment. She would confront him as soon as he arrived. Grandpa's chair scraped across the floor as he scooted from the table. The sound jolted Riley back into the present.

"Well, I'm off. Zane and I had a good talk last night. I need to check all our equipment to see what else needs to be repaired or replaced."

Riley's heart jumped. "Grandpa, I need to speak with Zane first when he gets here. Alone. Would you mind watching Chad for me for a few minutes while I do that? Then I'll take him to the grocery store with me. I can't put that off any longer. We'll have something home cooked for dinner tonight, I promise." She hoped it wasn't an empty promise.

"Sure, I can play with Chad while you take care of your business. I think I hear Zane's car now."

Riley placed a hand over her stomach as if it could quiet the turmoil inside. "Let me wipe Chad off first." She wetted a paper towel and cleaned his face, hands, and high chair. She needed to calm down before she went into the office. If anything, she'd need her mind to be clear before confronting Zane and his smooth talk.

The door stuck as she tried to plow through, bruising her arm and shoulder. She hurried across the circular drive between the house and the small office, then thrust the door open to confront Zane.

He stood behind the desk, opening the new laptop. When he saw Riley, he smiled and held out his arms as if showing off the fruit of his labor. "For you."

As she scanned the small room, she was speechless. The entire office appeared clean, swept, and polished. Even the outdoors appeared brighter through the sparkling windows. Though the cardboard boxes remained, they'd been repositioned in an out-of-the-way part of the room. Each corner of each box appeared perfectly aligned. The desktop held no scattered, waiting-to-be-filed papers.

Her mouth dropped open.

"It's—it's truly amazing." Riley placed both of her hands on her head, scrunching her hair between her fingers. Relief swept though her in the form of sheer pleasure. "So this is why you were here in the middle of the night?" She frowned, remembering she'd been quick to judge him.

"I couldn't sleep. And, well. . .please don't take this wrong, but I couldn't stand the thought of facing this disorganized office another day. Now we're good to go. I wanted to research for the business plan today, but something else has come up." He looked down at the keyboard and began typing while he stood.

She strolled to the desk, disappointed. "You're leaving? You just got here." Embarrassment flooded her at her words. She'd sounded too needy. "I understand, though. You probably have plenty of other things to do." She hoped she was wrong.

"I'm not leaving—just have to take care of a few other things first."

An image of Chad and Grandpa flashed across her mind. "I almost forgot, I left Chad with Grandpa for a few minutes. He said he had things to do, so I don't want to leave him too long. I've got to go."

Zane stared intently at the computer screen without responding. Riley wasn't sure if he was listening as she said, "I want to be involved in everything to do with the farm, but I really need to go grocery shopping. So I hope there's nothing you need me for this morning."

She crept backward, figuring his mind was focused on something other than her.

Without looking up from the computer screen, he said, "Wait up. I'll go with you."

Flabbergasted, Riley hesitated before responding. "You're going grocery shopping with me? What on earth for?"

He closed the laptop and rounded the desk. "Actually, I need to get some sort of work clothes. I thought we could do that, too."

His words continued to stun her. "Farm work clothes?"

"That's right. Remember I said I was willing to get my hands dirty? Well, I can't do that in these clothes." He motioned to his green polo shirt and pale slacks. "Isn't there a farm supply store where I can purchase the appropriate clothing?"

"Like a pair of overalls and a plaid shirt?" Riley smiled at him and nodded. He continued to surprise her, thrill her. "Sure, come on. We'll go to Carver Farm and Pet Supply. Grandpa has always gotten his work clothes there. I used to love to go there with him as a child. It's a great place to chat with the locals, too."

☙

Riley and Zane pulled into Sanderford Cranberry Farms after several hours of running errands. She unbuckled Chad from his car seat and detached it from Zane's vehicle while he opened the trunk and removed plastic grocery bags. The items he'd purchased today would allow him to work in the field without concern. She smirked at the thought, thinking she would believe it when she saw it. Zane was the ultimate professional, and he looked the part. Yet she couldn't believe how rugged and handsome he appeared after he'd changed into his work boots and jeans.

By the time she'd ushered Chad to the doorstep, Zane was back outside for more of the groceries. He stared into the distance toward the cranberry fields as he strolled to the car. She laughed at his eagerness to work with his hands. When everything had been unloaded, Zane hurried back to the office and Riley worked to tidy the kitchen.

Just as she finished putting away the groceries, Zane rushed in and grabbed her arm. "Come on. I want to show you something."

The excitement on his face made her curious, but Chad's eyes were drooping. She gave him a regretful frown and said, "I'm sorry, but it's going to have to wait. The little guy needs a nap."

"No, you can bring him, too. Put him in the stroller." The man was as giddy as a child.

Riley strapped a sleepy Chad into the jogger, and they headed toward the cranberry beds. When they cleared the two large maples that hid their view of the crop, Riley saw her grandfather's dozer pull to a halt in one of the new beds. She gasped and covered her mouth.

"They brought it this morning while we were shopping. See, that's your grandfather working the thing. I told him not to mention we expected it today so that it would be a surprise."

In her excitement, Riley started running with the jogger. Zane kept up with her though he wore new work boots. Gravel crunched behind them, and they skirted the road to allow a truck pulling a trailer heaped with loam to pass.

"Zane, I don't know what to say to you. How?"

His grin spread from ear to ear. "I made phone calls on my cell on the drive to and from the farm. It's amazing how much work you can get done that way. I scheduled for the loam to be delivered—after the dozer, of course."

"No, I mean—and don't take this wrong—but what about the money?"

Zane stopped Riley and turned her to face him. He stuck his hands into his pockets and stared at something in the distance. "Because I'm no longer paying your brother a salary, I'm funneling it into the farm instead. I'll work it out on paper. I know this is what he would have wanted."

Riley swallowed the lump emerging in her throat, uncertain about Zane's decision to put his money into the farm.

His expression became serious, his eyes penetrating as he looked at her. "Don't worry about me, Riley. I have income from other investments, and I'd set aside money for my enterprise with John. Cranberry farming is a minor detour. You can consider me a venture capitalist, if you want—I'm investing in Sanderford Cranberry Farms."

She nodded her acceptance. When they made it to the newly dozed bed, Grandpa climbed out of the huge machinery, smiling bigger than she'd seen him since she moved here.

※

For the next several weeks, Zane labored with Riley and her grandfather on the cranberry farm, preparing the new beds while caring for the established crop. They finished by adding a layer of peat and topping it with six inches of sand.

Cranberry vine cuttings were spread then plowed into the soil with a harrow. The newly planted beds were then irrigated. By the end of July, all that remained to do until the harvest was to weed, mow the dikes, and watch for pests.

It was laborious, but Zane had never been happier in his entire life. Working with his hands had a therapeutic effect on his body, ridding him of stress. Though he'd planned to create a business plan for the farm, he and Riley decided that, given the fact the growing season was upon them, it was more effective and morale boosting for everyone, especially her grandfather, to see progress through planting new beds. There would be plenty of time once that was done to work on expanding even more, maybe diversifying into other crops. Robert Sanderford had plenty of acreage for that.

Zane worked the farm during the day, spending any extra time with Riley and Chad, then devoted his evenings to going over the computer programs and files, looking for a clue that would point him to the decryption key—the only thing that could decode John's encryption algorithm. Though the police had apprehended the electronics thieves, Zane's computers were not in the hoard of stolen property, and the case remained open. Since they had exhausted all leads, the investigation had stalled. And still, the mystery surrounding John's death remained.

⍝

As the end of September neared and the time to harvest the cranberries grew closer, Zane walked across the dike, watching the sprinklers jet water over the growing plants, and he couldn't help but think about his budding relationship with Riley. He connected with her in a way he couldn't explain. Her inner strength drew him. Her sense of humor helped him to laugh at himself.

Since he'd arrived to help at the farm, he'd watched new growth appear on the vines, elongating the stems covered in leaves. Eventually, pink and white flowers had given way to tiny green pinheads. Now as he scanned the beds overflowing with the ripened berries, he hoped that his blossoming relationship with Riley would also bear fruit.

But he'd kept something hidden from her. The heaviness pressed down on him, drowning him in a bog of guilt. He shook his head. If he wanted to build a lasting relationship, he'd have to construct it on a strong foundation. He needed to tell her the truth.

A gusty breeze bathed him with water droplets from a nearby sprinkler, and he took a deep, calming breath. Somehow the fresh air and sunshine made all his problems seem smaller, less pressing. His mind was clearer, more astute now than it had ever been. What did he really know anyway? John and his wife had died in a car accident. Someone had stolen his computers. Could the two incidents be unrelated? He could have only thought he saw someone lurking at the office and overreacted. He had nothing to go on and knew that if it weren't for the peace he felt working on the farm, he would have gone crazy with the effort of wondering if John's past had ensnared him once again, leading to his death. Zane could know nothing for certain until he found the key.

More than anything he wanted to move past his mistakes, his paranoia. He needed to tell Riley the truth. She'd placed more pictures with Bible verses on the walls of the office. Her faith was a strong and important part of her life, so he'd read the verses and thought about them. The latest one was his favorite. The scripture said there was a time for everything. He allowed the verse to linger in his mind. . . . *A time to plant and a time to harvest.* A few of the words resounded in his thoughts. . . . *A time to love and a time to hate.* He hoped for the former rather than the latter when he told her the truth.

"Zane!" Riley waved her arms from the road and sauntered toward him. As he watched her slim body maneuver over the dikes with grace, he wondered if working on the farm had been the therapy, or if working with Riley was the real reason for his contentment.

He strolled toward her to meet her halfway. It was time to tell Riley the truth.

Chapter 10

Riley studied Zane as he headed toward her across the dike. It amazed her to see the transformation that had taken place in him over the last several weeks. He'd replaced his business suits with jeans and work shirts, but the change had penetrated deeper than just the clothes on his back.

As he approached with a gleaming smile that appeared to go to the depths of his soul, he tried to avoid one of the far-reaching sprinklers by running. He ended up thrusting his arms in a defensive posture as he passed the onslaught, getting sprayed anyway. His laughter resounded in her ears, making her heart skip. She licked her dry lips and reached for the ointment in her pocket.

Zane came to stand before her, stuck his hands in his pockets, and grinned down at her. "What's up?"

"Why don't you join us for dinner tonight? You always rush off. But how about some of my home cooking instead?" She stared at the ground, suddenly embarrassed. "I've been practicing and learning new recipes."

He laughed at her comment but didn't respond.

"You don't have to be afraid. Grandpa says I've improved. But I can see in his eyes that he misses my grandmother's cooking. He can't fool me there."

The light breeze whipped a strand of hair across her eyes. Zane reached over and pulled it out of her face then tucked it behind her ear. She gazed into his intense blue eyes and tried to hide from him how his simple touch had affected her.

"I'd love to join you, but. . ."

Though her grin remained in place, her disappointment sent a pang of regret through her. She licked her lips. "But?"

"I have a better idea. Let me rephrase that. Not better than eating your home-cooked food, I'm sure." He took her hand in his, causing her heart to race. "I have something important I need to talk to you about. I'd like to take you out to dinner. Alone. Maybe Grandpa could watch Chad for a while?" He raised his eyebrows.

Riley wondered when she would stop being surprised by anything Zane did. "Well, I still have to cook for my guys, but I suppose I could wait to eat with you." She paused while she considered her next question then asked, "Can you tell me what this is about? Have you finished the business plan? Or is it something else?"

"I'm researching before I put the document together, but that isn't what this is about." He furrowed his dark brows, his expression serious. "This is something else. You'll have to wait."

Riley wanted to question him further. She wondered if he had decided to stop working on the farm and simply put the business plan together at home. After all, he'd devoted much more time and effort to this place than she ever expected of him.

"Well then, I'll see you this evening. Is six all right? That will give me time to feed Chad and Grandpa then clean up the kitchen." She grimaced when she considered how tired she would be by then, but she looked forward to going to dinner with Zane.

"Six it is. I want to mow the far side of the dike; then I'll go get showered and changed." He grinned and turned his back to her as he strolled toward the mower.

She shook her head. She never would have thought he would do this sort of work. And like it. Though he hadn't said it in so many words, she could see by the calm expression on his face and his relaxed posture that the farm had been good for him.

As she meandered next to the cranberry beds, hope swelled inside her that Grandpa's farm would eventually bring in more money. With Zane's help, they'd been able to make use of the planting season instead of putting it off for another year. Depending on what he came up with in his business plan, the next few years could mean big growth for Sanderford Cranberry Farms—if that was what her grandfather truly wanted.

Since John had considered Zane a worthy business partner, Riley measured the possibility of Zane staying connected to the farm in some way. Though he'd never indicated he would work with them from now on—he'd make a great consultant—she wanted him allied with them in a more permanent fashion. Still, Sanderford Cranberry Farms had been family owned and operated for ninety years, and she wasn't sure how Grandpa would feel about a partnership with Zane.

It saddened her to think that part of her grandfather's dream was not only to expand the farm, but to make it a family legacy for generations to come. With the rest of the family deserting the farm and going to take jobs in the city, no one was left to run it. Except Riley. She'd always treasured her time with her grandparents when she was growing up and loved the excitement of the harvest and the festival. But Riley and her mother had been whisked away by Riley's father to the other side of the country, all for the sake of his job.

Though her father remained consumed with his business in California, they'd spoken over the phone several times since her move, and he promised to come to the farm for Christmas.

The holidays. The familiar pain over John's death surrounded her heart as she yanked the back door open and went into the kitchen. She decided to bake a one-dish recipe for easy cleanup rather than the five-course meal she'd planned to impress Zane with, giving herself more time to prepare for the date.

She pulled out a baking dish. He hadn't said it was a date, only that he needed to speak with her, that it was important.

Elsie entered the kitchen. "Hi, Riley. Chad's asleep. Can I help with anything?"

Riley shook her head and placed some ground meat in the microwave to defrost it. "No, thanks anyway. If Chad's asleep, you can go home." The tall brunette teenager had been an answer to prayer. She was Millie's granddaughter and lived only a couple of farms down on Cranberry Highway. Riley suspected that Millie's original intent of offering Elsie as a babysitter was to give Millie an additional reason to speak to Riley's grandfather.

"Okay, I'll see you tomorrow after school, then." The fifteen-year-old grabbed her satchel and headed out the door to walk home.

After mixing together a casserole, Riley popped it into the oven and set the timer for an hour then headed upstairs to get ready while Chad slept. If things went as planned, she'd have time to spend reading her Bible. After checking in on Chad, still sleeping in his toddler bed, she took a shower.

She reminded herself that Zane had not said it was a date. But it was difficult to keep from getting excited about the prospect of spending time alone with him, discussing anything at all over dinner. She wondered why he couldn't tell her in the office. In fact, they'd been alone when she'd come to the cranberry beds to invite him to dinner.

She knew she shouldn't harbor hope that his invitation had been a date disguised as something else. Though her relationship with Eric was in the past, thoughts of him still haunted her at times—maybe because he'd tried so hard to keep his hold on her, refusing to accept their breakup. Sometimes she feared she would open the door and see Eric standing there. A crazy thought, she knew. At first, Zane's workaholic attitude had reminded her of Eric. But as Zane had mentioned a few times, she'd had the wrong impression about him.

And he was right. Zane was nothing like Eric. Zane appeared to care about people, considering how every action taken and every word spoken would affect them. Eric, on the other hand, was greedy and self-serving.

Now that she considered it, when she had learned about her half brother in Massachusetts, Eric hadn't expressed any interest in the situation until she'd told him how John was hoping to develop new hack-proof encryption software. She regretted that slip of her tongue, but in her excitement, she hadn't thought to keep secrets from her boyfriend. For all she knew, he'd shared the news with some of his high-level business contacts and the vultures had circled, wanting in on the cyber action.

But John never said a word.

Riley wrapped a towel around her wet hair and peeked in on Chad. He slept curled up in a ball in the corner of his bed. She hurried to the chair in her room and grabbed her Bible off the side table. Taking a deep, calming breath, she reminded herself that she'd come to the farm to find peace and have time with God, not to rush through everything or become stressed while she prepared for dinner with Zane.

She tried to clear her mind of distractions and focus her thoughts on the Lord, but she couldn't quit thinking about Zane. There was something she needed to discuss with him, too, and she might as well do it tonight. She'd been remiss in allowing herself to care about him. Zane had said he believed in God. But did believing in God make someone a Christian? Or was it trusting in God? She remained unconvinced about his commitment to the Lord, not because he'd declined on several occasions to attend church with her, but because he avoided any discussion about God. But then, Riley hadn't always been ready to discuss her relationship with God, either—something she should have freely shared. She frowned then prayed for God to make her stronger.

She turned to Matthew 10, where she'd left off reading. "I am sending you out like sheep among wolves. Therefore be as shrewd as snakes and as innocent as doves." The words pierced her heart with conviction. She thought again of Zane's comments to her. *"I don't want to give you the wrong impression."*

Riley considered everything she knew about Zane. Frankly, it wasn't much. As a person, he was kind and considerate, hardworking. Still, a niggling doubt in the back of her mind continued to bother her.

He'd put an unbelievable amount of time and effort into Sanderford Cranberry Farms, for John's sake, he said. She believed him. But she knew he'd neglected his own company, because every time she questioned him, he told her he'd put Cyphorensic aside for a while. But why? Clearly, there was much about him she didn't know. She had trouble buying the fact that an entrepreneur such as Zane would put anything, especially the company he'd started, on hold. She pushed the unwelcome thoughts away, because she appreciated and wanted Zane's help. Still, she had to guard her heart somehow. She didn't relish the thought of being hurt again.

A child's cry reached her from across the hall, and she rushed into Chad's room. She pulled him out of his bed and discovered his body was on fire with fever.

℘

As Zane readied himself for dinner with Riley, he tried to get his mind off the possible outcome. He wasn't sure how she would respond when he told her what he'd kept from her all this time. But because he finally believed the crisis had long gone and that he'd been wrong about everything, he hoped her reaction to the news would be a mild one. With that behind him, perhaps he could tell her he was interested in pursuing a relationship. He blew out his breath, anxiety burning in his gut. He'd never been good with women.

He needed to focus on going forward with Cyphorensic again. Because nothing had surfaced regarding his stolen computers, John's brainchild of new encryption software was gone. Zane had been unable to locate a copy of the software, which frustrated him. He couldn't imagine that John hadn't kept a copy somewhere. Zane had no choice but to return to his original vision for Cyphorensic as a computer forensics software provider.

Of course, there was still the possibility that the criminals who stole John's software would attempt to use it, but they'd have to break John's code first, which was unlikely. Though it had never been far from Zane's mind, he needed to begin the search for John's replacement. In truth, no one could replace John—either in terms of his brilliance or in terms of his friendship to Zane. But it was long past time to put the past behind him and return to his normal life.

When he finished showering, his cell phone vibrated on the dresser and he picked it up. Riley's number flashed across the display, and he clenched his jaw. He dialed into voice mail to retrieve the message, hoping their plans hadn't changed.

Riley's worried voice resounded through the small device, explaining that Chad suffered with a fever and she didn't feel comfortable leaving him. Zane returned her call, and Robert answered. He said that Riley had been in contact with a nurse and had given Chad a fever reducer. Zane snapped the cell shut, feeling both disappointed and concerned over Chad at the same time.

He ordered in Chinese, and after he finished eating, he reclined on the sofa and fell asleep.

Buzz. Buzz. Buzz.

The vibration stirred Zane from a deep slumber, and he fumbled for the phone in his pocket. He glanced at the clock as he flipped open the device, which displayed Riley's number. One thirty in the morning.

Apprehension coursed through his body. "Hello?"

"Zane! I've been trying to call you. Why haven't you answered? You won't believe what's happened."

The distress in Riley's voice urged him to the door. He grabbed his keys and left the condo. "Calm down, Riley. Is it Chad? Is he all right? Call the doctor." He climbed into his vehicle and spun out of the parking lot.

"No, Chad is fine. I gave him a fever reducer. It worked. It's the office—someone has ransacked our office."

Chapter 11

Chad fell back to sleep while Riley clutched him, waiting for Zane to arrive. She felt guilty that she still held on to the child, but she wanted to know that he was safe and secure after what had happened. The police had already come and gone, which reassured her. She tiptoed up the stairs and laid him back on his bed.

After taking care of Chad, she returned to the kitchen and poured herself another cup of coffee, realizing that she wouldn't get any sleep tonight. Grandpa leaned against the counter with his cup, lost in thought. Though she'd tried to contact Zane before the authorities, he hadn't responded to her initial attempts to reach him. Now as she considered her actions, she wondered why he was the first person she'd thought to call.

She tried him again after the police had left. It had seemed surreal when the two cruisers raced up the cranberry farm drive. She'd answered a series of questions and was told to expect an officer from the Bureau of Crime Investigation to take photos and recover prints the next day.

Headlights flashed through the kitchen window. Riley and Grandpa headed out the door to greet Zane. He stepped out of his car, and without thinking about her actions, Riley flew into his arms. He held her tight as if it were the most natural thing to do. The warmth and security she felt within his muscled frame comforted her. When she became aware that she was clinging to Zane, she distanced herself.

"I'm...um...sorry about that. It's just that this whole mess..." She gestured toward the office and averted her gaze from his questioning eyes.

"No, no. It's all right."

Zane nodded to Grandpa. "Sorry you've had to go through this, Robert."

"It's not your fault, son." He placed his hand on Zane's shoulder and squeezed. "I'm just glad you finally got here to help calm Riley down."

Wide-eyed, Riley gazed at her grandfather. "What's that supposed to mean?"

"Come on. Let's go inside." Zane gave her a sympathetic smile and grabbed Riley's arm.

"You kids have fun. I'm heading back to bed." Disgruntled, Grandpa turned his back to them and walked to the house. "I'll listen for Chad. No need to worry."

"Can you tell me what happened?" He started toward the office.

She ran ahead and stood in front of the door. "No, we shouldn't go in here. Let's talk in the kitchen."

"We won't go in. But I want to see for myself."

"All right." Riley opened the door for him.

Brows furrowed, Zane stood in the doorway, his gaze roaming over the destruction. With a deep frown, he nodded at Riley. "I've seen enough. Now tell me what happened."

She descended the porch steps and walked with him to the house.

"I got up to check on Chad because of his fever. I saw lights on in the office again, and at first I thought it was you. So I dressed and came outside in time to see the vandals drive away."

He held the door for her as she entered.

"Did you see what kind of car they drove, their license plate?"

"It was too dark to read the license plate, but I saw a sedan. Not sure of the make. It looked like an expensive model, though. I've already told all of this to the police." Riley shuddered when she considered how close she'd come to walking in on them.

Zane pulled her to him, embracing her. "Are you cold?" He rubbed her arms to generate heat. But instead she felt the warmth rushing to her cheeks.

"No, I'm really not cold. Just shaken. Oh, Zane, the longer I stared at the papers strewn over the floor and the overturned boxes, the angrier I became. It's so. . .frustrating."

She pushed away from his attempt to console her. "I don't understand why anyone would do this. It makes no sense. And all the hard work you've done is for nothing. It's not like we have a problem with vandals out here. What do you think, Zane? Why would someone do this?"

His expression grim, he said, "I can't tell you how relieved I am that you didn't walk in on them. There's no telling what they might have done. In fact, don't come out here at night alone for any reason." He nailed her with a convicting stare. "What if something would have happened to you? What about Chad?"

"But I thought it was you." Her voice cracked with emotion.

He placed his hands on Riley's shoulders. "I'm sorry about that. About everything." He hung his head. The stress and tension she'd watched dissipate from him over the last several weeks were back in full force.

A sense of foreboding pressed against her thoughts. Zane's strange questions came to mind. *"Did you have a chance to talk to him before he died?"* All her doubts about his reasons for working on the farm whirled in her head, creating a tumultuous whirlpool of suspicion. But she'd put them to rest already and tried to dismiss them again.

"Grandpa said that no one has ever done this before. I'm thankful they were only interested in destroying the office and didn't venture to the house. I get the sense they were looking for something, but I can't imagine what. Can you?"

A shadow flashed across Zane's features. Riley's pulse raced. Her mind played tricks on her, persuading her to suspect that the vandalism was related to Zane and not to Sanderford Cranberry Farms.

I don't want to give you the wrong impression. His earlier words danced in her mind, mocking her.

She turned her back to him and began rinsing out her coffee mug at the kitchen sink. "Do you think it was vandals, Zane, or do you think they were looking for something?" *And what?* She wanted to voice her last question but dreaded the answer; she could hardly breathe while she waited for his reply.

It never came.

Riley lifted her face and stared at the ceiling, taking a deep breath. She turned to face Zane, and what she saw in his eyes shredded all that was left of her hope.

❦

The look in Riley's eyes squeezed Zane's chest like a vise. He'd never meant for this to happen, for things to go this far. His mind reeled from the shock that Sanderford Farms had been targeted. Why had they waited until now? Zane rubbed his stubbled jaw.

He hastened to Riley, put his hands on her shoulders, and peered into her eyes. They shimmered with a mixture of hurt, anger, and distrust. "Remember when I asked you to believe me, to trust me, when I said that I was helping with the farm because I owe it to John—for your sake and Chad's?"

She nodded slowly.

A sharp pain shot through his chest at what he was about to tell her. "Riley, I think you need to sit down."

She snapped out of her stunned expression and pulled away. "No, tell me everything. Now." Her voice sounded distant, unfeeling.

He grabbed her, forcing her to face him. "I meant every word. In fact, it didn't take long for my desire to help you with the farm to become something I wanted to do for you, regardless of John."

Riley stumbled to the chair and slumped into it. "Tell me why you came to work here. The truth."

Zane ran both hands through his hair and blew out a breath. *Where do I begin?* "The night that John died, I heard him leave you a message." He cleared his throat. "The corridors in our office suite echo, and well. . .John hadn't closed

301

his door. I mistakenly overheard him."

Riley quirked her left brow. "And?"

"I heard John say he'd sent something to you. Then as he hung up, he said it might be a matter of life and death. He sent something he considered to be very important to you, Riley."

Riley covered her face with her hands then let them drop to her lap. "What else?"

"It wasn't until after the funeral when I decided to look at John's laptop that I discovered it missing along with all of his hardware and storage devices. I just. . .couldn't bring myself to go into his office. Had to give myself time."

She pushed herself from the chair and moved to face him. "So what are you saying, exactly? I still don't understand why you came to work here." Her voice was riddled with emotion. "Unless you're looking for whatever the vandals were looking for here, too. That's it, isn't it?"

Her brows knitted in confusion, and her pain was evident in her frown.

With all of his being, Zane wanted to make her understand. "I never intended to use you. I only wanted to protect you. You have your hands full, and I wasn't sure about any of this anyway." Still, he kept the burden of John's possible murder to himself.

"Did they find it?" she asked.

He shrugged. "I don't know. Do you remember getting anything from John in the mail?"

"If you could tell me what we're talking about, that might help."

Riley's voice sounded steady, and she appeared more composed, more accepting of the circumstances. Despite the situation he'd placed her in, she remained resilient.

"My vision for Cyphorensic was to enter the growing computer forensics field." He glanced at Riley and noted a question in her eyes. "Computer forensics is used by investigators to determine if illegal activities have transpired on a computer system. I brought John on board, but because he'd already begun work on creating a new standard in encryption code—meaning hack-proof code—that's the direction we took. I can count on one hand the programs out there that are considered undecipherable. The government uses them."

His explanation complete, he shrugged. "That's where we're at. The only conclusion I can make is that whoever stole the computers must have wanted John's software. But they can't open it because John's work can't be hacked. Obviously, they're looking for the key to crack the code."

Riley shook her head. "Why would they think they could find it here? A password, for crying out loud."

"Not just any password. John would have created a complicated algorithm."

What would Zane have done had he needed access to the software?

"Great, just great." Riley rubbed her arms.

"Hold on." Zane paced as he thought. Riley waited, seeming to understand his need for concentration. Then it dawned on him. "That's it."

"What's it?"

He gripped his chin. "They must have hired another hacker to break the code but were unsuccessful. It's the only explanation. Apparently, their tactic hasn't worked, and now they're searching again. They must think I've hidden it somewhere."

"Still, why don't they just confront you? Ask for it?"

"Hear me out. I've wondered why they haven't confronted me, too." Zane hesitated. He didn't want to reveal to Riley that he believed John had been murdered or had been involved in something illegal. "Maybe they hope they can find John's key by following me. If they were to confront me too soon, they might risk losing the key for good, now that John is gone."

Riley shook her head, her expression grave. "Zane, eventually, if they don't find this. . .password. . ."

"That's why we have to find it first."

"But I still don't know what we're looking for."

"What we're looking for is both simple and complicated. John enjoyed creating puzzles to solve, hidden treasures. John has hidden the key. He has left us the clue of where to find it. I'm sure of it."

"So what is the clue? The sooner we get this solved, the better." She thrust her hands on her hips, determined.

"Well, there's another problem. I don't even know what the clue is." He dispelled her wide-eyed expression with a wry grin. It relieved him to see her appear to have overcome the situation. Her strength amazed him.

More than anything, he wanted to pull her into his arms, but he steeled himself and instead raised his arms out to her as if making an offering. "I'm so, so sorry, Riley. I never meant for any of this to happen. I thought I would figure it out, that I could manage it on my own. I didn't want to give you something else to worry about."

She pressed her lips together and turned away then began wiping the kitchen counter. She stopped. Her actions indicated that she still held animosity toward him. He watched her reach into her jeans pocket and pull out a small tube, probably her lip ointment. A familiar, nervous act he'd seen her perform numerous times. When he considered all he'd come to know about her, down to her constant need to moisturize her lips, a sense of longing coursed through him.

"You'll have to bear with me, Zane. This has been information overload for me. Right now, I just don't know what to think. I do know we've got to find that clue. You should have told me this from the beginning."

Riley twisted her hair back and pinned it with a clip she'd pulled from a drawer. He watched her reflection in the glass of a picture hanging on the wall.

And then he knew where John had hidden the clue.

Chapter 12

Zane unlocked the entrance to his condo, the events of the night reeling through his mind. He closed the door behind him, locked it, then shut his eyes and leaned back against the sturdy steel casing. The cold penetrated his clothing while he repeatedly knocked the back of his head against the door, furious with himself for allowing the situation to escalate.

He'd finally become convinced that he'd made a mistake—that the stolen computers were a simple matter of theft with no ties to John. But he could afford no such errors again. Come morning, he would hire his own private investigator.

He flipped the switch on the wall, but the sofa lamp did not yield its light. Fear gripped his gut.

He stood motionless and listened, hoping he hadn't stumbled into trouble.

After his eyes adjusted to the moon's rays filtering through the blinds, he recognized the same chaos he'd witnessed at the Sanderford Farms office. Only the culprits had done much more damage to Zane's residence. His leather sofa had been upended, along with the lamp and side table. The chairs had fared no better.

He hoped the culprits wouldn't decide to return. Zane could not understand what good could come of scattering papers and overturning furniture in order to search for their treasure. If anything, he believed it would only make the hunt more difficult.

John had counted on his need for order to alert Zane to his clue. He clenched his jaw, gritting his teeth. The item had been before John the whole time, sitting on the desk in the open, when it should have been hanging on the wall out of his workspace. He was relentless to keep his desk tidy and free of anything that would distract him from his work, considering even a picture clutter. No one would have noticed an object out of place in John's logically arranged office. No one except Zane. Yet he had missed it.

It had been John's life insurance; of that, Zane felt confident. Somehow, John's plan had ended in disaster.

Zane had failed miserably, as well. He'd noticed the oddity, but because he hadn't realized he would need the information, he'd deleted the file from his mind. So it didn't register as anything but peculiar. He supposed the shock of the theft had skewed his ability to focus.

He picked his way through the living room over to the kitchen to flip on the fluorescents then crept down the empty corridor, remaining alert to any intruders, and into the office. He flicked the switch. Again nothing. The lamp in the office had also been overturned. Zane made a mental note to replace all of his lighting with overheads.

A bright ray of moonlight gleamed through the window, illuminating the one item he'd been searching for. He stepped softly, careful to avoid damaging any of the files or knickknacks that lay scattered over the dark carpet. The image of Riley's look-alike stared up at him in the shimmering light like a shining specter in the dark room. Zane reached down to retrieve it. The picture appeared undamaged, but someone had stepped on it, cracking the glass and overlooking its significance.

He pulled the photo out and tossed the frame back into the disaster area. The glass clinked as it hit the floor, but another slight jingle caught his attention. *Of course!* The clue was inside the frame. Zane recovered it and discovered a gold chain taped to the backing.

Bingo!

He dangled the chain in the moonlight. Still, he had no idea what it meant, only that it should lead him somewhere. Exhaustion overwhelmed him. He wanted to sit down but didn't have the energy to return the furniture to its proper position. There wasn't any point in calling the police, because he knew he wouldn't be giving them the evidence they would need to tie it all together—John's clue. He couldn't afford to lose the clue when he'd only just found it. Would they believe him anyway? Before heading to bed, he made sure to check all the closets and possible hiding places. He clutched the chain and the photo as he strolled to his bedroom, hoping he still had a bed to lie in.

It remained in its rightful place. Relieved and surprised at the same time, Zane plopped down on the soft mattress. He stared at the chain. Finding the clue was only the first piece of John's convoluted puzzle. He grimaced at the thought.

☙

Unwelcome sunlight flickered through the window as rustling leaves seemed to clatter outside, igniting Zane's headache. Groggily, he rolled out of bed and scowled at the disaster area that had been his home. The clock on the wall read eight thirty—he'd overslept. He headed for the bathroom and gaped at his coarse appearance. Shadows circled his eyes, and he needed a shave.

First, he would brew coffee to clear his mind. Last night he'd been too worn out to consider the events with clarity. But Riley had never left his thoughts. She'd lived in his dreams. He'd hurt her by not being honest when he'd only tried to protect her, keep her from having another burden to add to her struggle. Now she had the trouble despite his efforts, and to make matters worse, he was afraid that she might erect a barrier between them. He had no idea if it could ever be torn down. He believed he'd made headway in earning her trust, but for what reason if it all came to this?

He splashed water over his face and dried it. Grabbing the chain and photo, he strolled to the kitchen, ignoring the untidy heap along the way. He laid the items on the counter and, after starting the coffee, decided to shower while it brewed. The photo drew his attention, and he stared at it. The woman held a cell phone to her ear and wore the same gold chain around her neck, but with a small locket affixed to it.

Riley must have the locket. That was what John had sent to her. Zane phoned her while he waited for the shower to steam.

No answer.

Thirty minutes later, Zane had dressed and was on his way down Cranberry Highway toward Sanderford Farms. He tried calling Riley but received no answer at the house. The day they'd gone shopping, she had purchased an answering machine, complaining about people who were hard to reach. He tried the farm office and left a message. It was reasonable to think that they were on the farm, especially with the imminent harvest.

Zane peeled through the entrance and down the gravel road. A luxury sedan that he didn't recognize was parked in the circular drive. He recalled Riley's words that the vandals had driven an expensive-looking sedan.

He tried to steady his breathing, but the events of the past evening would not allow him to do so. As soon as he stopped his vehicle, he exploded from it and dashed up the office steps to whip the door open. Empty.

He ran to the house, fueled by fear and adrenaline. Without knocking, he burst through the back door and, seeing the kitchen vacant, yelled Riley's name.

A dark-suited man stepped into the living area doorway, his eyes narrowed as he scrutinized Zane.

Oh no! Riley!

Rage pounded through his heart. In two steps, he stood before the stranger, fist drawn.

Riley appeared in the doorway. Her eyes widened, and she gasped. "Zane, no!" She stepped between him and the man.

Seeing her unharmed, he slumped against the wall, relieved. "Riley, you're all right."

He looked at the stranger standing next to her. The man wore a smirk on his face. Zane wanted to punch him anyway.

She placed her hand on his arm, its calming effect working. "Yes, I'm fine. Now what about you? You look like you've seen a creature from the latest horror flick."

"I thought. . . I thought. . ." He pushed away from the wall and paced, running his hands through his hair. "I'm sorry. I suppose after everything that has happened I thought the worst when I saw the unfamiliar car outside, and then I came in here to see him standing there. . . ."

She smiled in sympathy, yet she appeared tense and uncomfortable. Zane assumed she hadn't forgiven him for his duplicity.

Realization dawned in her eyes. "Oh, Zane, this is Eric Rutherford. Eric, Zane Baldwyn."

Zane nodded his acknowledgment, as did Eric, but neither shook hands.

Riley moved into the kitchen and sat down at the table. "I'd prefer we talk in here; Chad's napping. Eric and I were. . .friends. . .when I lived in California. His arrival is an unexpected surprise." Eric pulled out the chair next to Riley and sat, placing his hand on hers. He laughed as his gaze slithered to Zane and back to Riley. "Come now, Riley. You know we were more than friends. Be honest with Zane." He kissed her hand.

Riley pulled her hand away, her face ashen.

Pangs of jealousy sliced through Zane's exposed heart. "I called but couldn't reach you."

"You did? That's funny. I didn't hear it ring, and I don't see the little red light flashing." She pushed away from the table and strode to the machine on the counter.

"There was no answer," Zane said, never taking his eyes from Eric. He didn't like the man.

Riley pushed buttons on the device. "Strange. It seems to be working."

Eric stood, as well, and buttoned his black suit coat. Zane cringed, wishing he'd dressed professionally today. Feeling humiliated already after his wrong assumptions, it would go a long way toward giving him a sense of authority.

"You were putting Chad down for a nap. I unplugged the phone, thinking you wouldn't want the boy disturbed." Eric came to stand behind Riley and placed his hands on her shoulders.

She turned to face him, looking like a cornered animal. "Zane, why were you trying to reach me?"

"It can wait." Zane didn't know how much he could say in front of Eric. "I've got things to do. It was nice to meet you, Eric."

Zane turned and left the house, wishing there was something he could do to extract Riley from Eric's possessiveness. But he had no right to act out of jealousy. No right to interfere.

❦

Grandpa appeared in the doorway. "Who's your friend, Riley?"

Thankful for Grandpa's arrival, she escaped Eric's assertive overtures and grabbed her grandfather's arm. "Grandpa, this is Eric Rutherford. He's a friend from California."

The older man thrust out his hand in his usual warm manner. "Glad to meet you, son. So you knew my Riley in California?" While keeping his attention on Eric, he ambled to the sink to fill a glass with water.

"Yes, we were close. I'm surprised she didn't mention me. So sorry to hear about her brother. Since I had business in Boston, I took the opportunity to stop for a visit. In fact, I'm taking a few extra days after my business is complete."

Riley closed her eyes. Nausea gripped her already-tumultuous insides, and her spirits sank. *No, no, no.*

Eric was the last person on the planet she wanted to see right now, if ever. She needed to speak to Zane, unload her torrential emotions.

Go home, Eric.

Given that Zane had tried to contact her and leave a message, she considered that he'd possibly discovered something to help them solve this ridiculous puzzle. She glared at Eric for his interference and would have growled at him if her trusting grandfather were not in the room.

Grandpa spoke to Eric about the plans for the farm and Riley's part in it, bragging on her. Riley felt the heat warm her cheeks, but her embarrassment stemmed from the fact that it had been Zane who'd gotten things rolling, not her. Her heart skipped at the thought of seeing him preparing to slug Eric. He'd tried to save her from someone he thought was a danger to her. She wished she hadn't stopped him.

Zane had appeared crestfallen when Eric took her hand. It hurt her to see him like that. She'd have to explain Eric's presence once she had a chance to speak to him.

Both Grandpa and Eric stared at her, waiting for a response. "I'm sorry. Were you talking to me?"

"I just told Eric that he's welcome to stay here on the farm when his business is finished. We've got plenty of room, and that way he won't have to drive back and forth to see you."

The room tilted, and Riley leaned against the counter. She remained stunned for a moment while she contemplated a response. Grandpa had already made the offer; he didn't understand Riley's animosity, and she didn't want to seem rude to either of them. At least she would have time to come up with an excuse before Eric's minivacation.

"That's very kind of you, Grandpa. Thanks for coming by, Eric." Hearing Chad's cry, she jumped at the chance to leave. "I've got to check on Chad."

It was a struggle to contain her irritation with Eric, but it was best not to offend him, especially in front of her grandfather. He wouldn't understand her rudeness and would be disappointed in her.

When she reached Chad's room, she wiped away his tears and pulled him to her. After changing his diaper, she took him to her room to play on the floor while she tried to pray. She looked out her window toward the Sanderford Farms office.

Zane's vehicle was gone.

Chapter 13

Azesty autumn breeze wafted over Riley as she strolled near the cranberry beds. After the police had dusted for prints and completed their investigation, she'd spent the rest of the morning cleaning up the office. Alone. Eric had gone back to Boston to work, and Zane had never returned. Elsie had stopped by the farm after a short school day and offered to stay with Chad—an answer to Riley's prayer for help today. More than anything, she needed to calm her frazzled nerves. Last night's break-in and Eric's arrival this morning had almost brought her to her knees, as well it should. She needed to spend time in prayer. But she couldn't.

She bristled in irritation that she'd been kept from speaking with Zane. He had something to tell her. She knew because he'd all but said it when he mentioned that he'd tried to call her. She could see in his eyes that he wanted to talk to her alone. But he'd left the farm. She cringed when she thought of his hurt expression when Eric had acted as though she belonged to him.

Last night she'd learned that Zane had not been truthful about working at the farm. At first, the knowledge of his deception had hurt. The pain had gone deeper and felt more personal than it should have, surprising her. But she'd had time to consider his reasons and understand them. For now, she intended to focus on searching with Zane for whatever John had hidden.

Still, she wondered what else he kept from her. She believed in Zane, but a certain part of her remained unwilling to trust him completely.

The brilliant crimson fruit helped to calm her spirit, and as she stared down at the beds, she decided the ripened crop did, indeed, deserve the name *bog rubies*. The bright yellows, golds, and reds of the autumn trees accentuated them. During the next few days, Riley, Grandpa, family, and friends would be busy with the laborious task of harvesting the berries. First, they would flood the beds with water from the reservoir using the new pump.

Riley had hired help three weeks ago to assist Grandpa with inspecting the cleaning machine and conveyor and to make sure spare parts were on hand. Once the process began, the crop would not wait while repairs were made. She'd prepared meals to feed the workers ahead of time and frozen them.

It occurred to her that her grandfather had purposefully failed to mention the impending harvest when he'd invited Eric to stay. He probably expected

Eric to join in the work like the others. She laughed out loud at the ridiculous thought of her all-business ex-boyfriend knee deep in water, booming the berries. She hoped the labor involved would be enough to send him away.

Weariness filled her at the thought of the endless hours of work that would consume her over the next two or three days. At least less time would be needed since Grandpa's antique walk-behind harvester had been replaced with a new riding one, though they would use the old one as well. She was thrilled that she could be part of her grandfather's life and the farm once again. She never dreamed her world would change so dramatically in such a short period of time.

Moisture brimmed in her eyes. She believed that leaving behind the corporate stress and Eric and moving to this peaceful farm was the answer she was looking for. But as she walked along the dikes, she realized she didn't even know the question. All she knew was that she longed for an inner peace, yet even as a Christian, she felt as though peace eluded her.

As she drew in a deep breath, the earthy smell relaxed her. She could at least try to pray. *Father, please bless my grandfather's cranberry crop and help him build the legacy he's desired for so many years. Please help me to be a good mother to little Chad. And help Zane to know You in a deeper way. Please keep us in the palms of Your hands and protect us.*

Riley swiped her wet eyes then opened them.

A blurred figured in a business suit approached. She sighed with relief when she recognized Zane rather than Eric.

His professional appearance surprised her. She'd grown accustomed to the farm work clothes and admitted she liked him better in them. "What's with the suit? Did you have a meeting this afternoon?"

He cocked his head. The warmth in his eyes had disappeared. "As a matter of fact, I've contacted a security company to install an alarm at both your office and home. But you have to remember to arm it or else it won't work."

Though the vandalism was not something to laugh about, his tone brought a chuckle from her. "You say that as if you know from experience."

His expression looked serious, scolding her lightheartedness. "Last night I returned to my condo to find it in worse shape than your office."

She inhaled sharply. "Oh no! . . . Zane. . .I'm so sorry to hear that."

"I've hired a private investigator."

His news stunned her. "You did? Do you think that will make any difference?"

Zane reached into his suit pocket and pulled out a gold necklace.

Riley scrunched her face. "What's that for?"

"I have a photo that John claimed was you, but it's not. The woman is wearing a gold chain like this, only it also has a locket on it. Do you know where the locket is?"

Riley racked her memory then shook her head. "Sorry, Zane. I've never seen that before. Why are you so sure that I would have it?"

Zane stared off in the distance, frowning. Riley was certain her exasperation mirrored his. "John said he'd sent you something. This is part of the clue. It has to be the locket. You have to have it if we are going to resolve this."

His cold stare sent a chill over her. What had happened to the warm and friendly Zane with the magnetic smile? She couldn't hide her disappointment.

She touched his arm. "If it will make you feel better, I'll look through my stuff. I still have boxes to unpack. Can you believe it? I just—I don't remember getting anything from him. But I could have been distracted with attending his funeral and the move here."

His sympathetic smile encouraged her that the Zane she'd come to know was somewhere inside. She wondered if Eric's appearance had anything to do with Zane's sudden change toward her. Or maybe his friendliness had been part of his ruse to gain access to the farm in his search. Now that she was aware of his scheme, he no longer needed to pretend.

He stared at the ground and kicked at an errant weed with his polished black shoe. He reminded Riley of a little boy who'd been caught stealing candy. "There's something else."

Here it comes. She shook her head and turned her back to him, not knowing if she could handle anything else.

"What is it?" Her voice came out breathy, weary.

"Remember when I told you that after your brother left you a message that night he said to himself it could be a matter of life or death? I've believed from the beginning that John's death was no accident."

The meaning of his words gripped her mind and took root. Stunned, she whirled to face him. "Wha–?" The strength in her legs gave out, and she plummeted.

Zane caught her and pulled her to him, maintaining a tight hold as she sobbed against his expensive designer suit.

All the anxiety and worries she'd kept inside in an effort to remain strong rushed out. Questions and accusations reeled in her mind, tormenting her soul. John murdered? Sarah, too? Or had she just been in the wrong place? It was too much to grasp. Her heart ached for her brother's family, for Chad.

Lord, why has this happened?

Zane's voice continued to comfort and soothe in the background of her anguish. When her tears were spent, remorse filled her that she'd exposed her emotions to Zane, and she pushed away from him. She avoided looking at the damage she'd done to his suit.

She pulled a tissue out of her pocket that she kept on hand for Chad and wiped her eyes and nose. "Who, Zane? Who killed my brother? Do the police believe this?"

He gripped her shoulders. "Calm down. One question at a time. I haven't exactly shared my theory with the police."

"What? Why not?"

"Because John left his clues for us to decipher. Not the police. Besides, all I have is suspicions, nothing concrete."

"So what? Isn't that their job to figure out?"

Releasing his hold, he sighed heavily. "But all I have is something John said and his clues—or at least one of them. Let's go with what John's given us first."

He stepped closer and peered into her eyes. "I didn't want to tell you this because I wanted to spare you, but I feel I've lost enough of your trust already."

❦

Zane's heart ached as he looked at Riley's contorted, pain-filled expression. Anger surged through him that he'd decided to reveal his belief that her brother was murdered. Had his reasons for telling her been all wrong? He'd wanted to regain her trust. Instead, his decision had caused her more pain.

"I should go. I've hurt you enough for one week." He started back to the office, where he'd parked in the drive.

"Wait."

Zane closed his eyes. He didn't know why she'd said the word, but it pleased him. He turned to look at her.

"Could you walk with me a bit? Unless, that is, you have to work." A tight smile tugged at her cheeks.

At the moment, Zane couldn't think of anything he'd rather do than be with her. Nor could he recall any other pressing business for the day. He offered his arm. "Shall we?"

She wiped her eyes again then hooked her arm through his. Though they strolled without speaking, a quiet comfort settled over Zane, and he hoped she felt it, as well. He thought of things to say, conversation starters, but didn't want to disturb the mood. Riley needed time to assimilate what he'd told her.

Their walk took them to the acreage beyond the cranberries amid an abundance of colorful oaks and maples.

When Riley stopped, she faced Zane and grinned. "Sorry about your suit. Do you think you can get that out?"

He glanced down at his soiled shoulder. "This old thing?" The words reminded him of the chocolate incident, and when he saw the sparkle in her eyes, he knew she'd remembered, as well. They both laughed.

"That's a good sound to hear from you. I'm worried about you." He tipped her chin with his thumb to scrutinize her tearstained face. "You know if there was any other way, I wouldn't have told you."

The diminutive smile on her face faded. "You have to tell me everything. I'm a big girl. You shouldn't have kept anything from me. He may have been your partner, but he was my brother." Her lip quivered, but she breathed in and controlled her emotions.

Though Riley's earlier outburst was understandable considering the news he'd given, he admired her attempts to remain strong. But he worried that she allowed herself no outlet.

She closed her eyes as if considering her next words. "If whoever killed my brother is searching for this, aren't we in the same danger?"

"Honestly, I think they realize their mistake in losing John. He was the brilliance they needed to complete their project. I don't think they will make that mistake again."

"Some family and friends helping with the harvest will be arriving tonight."

"You'll be safe surrounded by people."

"What I mean is that I won't have much time to find that locket. That's the key to all of this, isn't it?"

Her concerned expression ripped through the barrier of his control, and he placed his hand gently at the back of her head, pulling her toward him as he wove his fingers through her hair.

She didn't resist.

Her soft lips beckoned him, and he leaned down to meet them, pressing his own against their warmth. Powerful emotions erupted in his soul from the simple touch of his lips against hers.

He released her and backed away, swallowing to fight the sudden dryness in his mouth. "I shouldn't have done that. Forgive me. You're in an awful state of mind. I didn't mean to take advantage of you."

He thrust his hands into his pockets. "We should get back."

Riley appeared dazed at his actions, shoving his guilt deeper. What more could he do to hurt her?

Chapter 14

Wearing waders the next day, Zane stood knee deep in the bog and wiped the sweat from his forehead with a gloved hand. After several hours of pumping water from the reservoir into each of the beds, he was spent. But daylight remained, and Robert Sanderford had finished his turn driving the eggbeater, a machine that spun reels to churn the water. Zane needed to try his hand at it.

In one of the other beds, Gerome Mays, a distant cousin, used the old walk-behind harvester. Though it took longer, it still accomplished the task. Zane climbed onto the tractor, not much larger than a riding lawn mower, and began the process of stirring up the water. Liberated berries already bunched together, floating in the bog like pieces of a jigsaw puzzle. The machine chugged along at two miles an hour. Zane watched in amazement as the ripe berries, filled with small pockets of air, floated to the top after they separated from the vines.

Once he felt comfortable with the machinery, he allowed his thoughts to drift, mesmerized by the noisy engine and the reel agitating the bog. Despite the burden of knowledge he shared with Riley regarding the events surrounding John's death, they both needed the break that concentrating on the harvest brought. Working with his hands was good therapy.

Riley paced along the dike as if she were on the sidelines watching a football game and waved at him, cheering him on. Her face was bright with excitement, and he was pleased that she'd been able to take her mind off their predicament. Seeing her observe him caused a sense of pride to swell in his chest. Being able to witness the fruits of their labor and take part in the harvest filled his heart with more joy than any business endeavor he'd achieved in the past.

As he turned the machine in the bog, he considered that the true meaning of life had evaded him. What good was it to be a successful businessman if you had no one to share life with? He frowned, his thoughts agitated like the water beneath him. Though he'd paid for Cyphorensic Technologies' office lease a year in advance because he was offered a deal for doing so, without software and a programmer of John's caliber, there was no company. Could he find an adequate replacement for John?

He noticed Riley again. This time she held Chad in her arms, and he waved at Zane. He smiled at his little guy.

His little guy?

Zane's heart warmed at the thought. He admitted he'd grown to love Chad as if he were his own. His gaze wandered back to Riley. Without a thriving business, he believed he couldn't offer them a future. More than anything, he wanted to give her security, stability.

When he glanced back to the dike, Riley and Chad had disappeared. Just as well, because he didn't need the distraction. He'd never intended to work at Sanderford Farms for this long. But he had expected to complete his search before now. Once the harvest was over and he finally presented the business plan to Riley, there was no reason for him to stay on.

He turned the machine again and saw Riley standing on the opposite bank, Eric at her side. Zane allowed a low growl to escape, knowing it wouldn't be heard over the eggbeater's racket. He didn't trust Eric and didn't understand why the man insisted on pursuing Riley when it was clear she had no interest. At least Zane hoped it was clear. Maybe he was only fooling himself. Eric could be the sort of man Riley needed. She had to think of what was best for Chad. Eric had a job. Zane had a defunct company. Still, he didn't like Eric.

Riley smiled at Eric, and they walked off together. Zane cared deeply for Riley, and he wondered why it took Eric's appearance to make him realize how much. He scowled as he watched Eric put his arm around her and pull her close to him as they strolled away. He couldn't believe the man had the audacity to show up at the harvest and not be prepared to get his hands dirty.

The churning complete for this bog, Zane stopped, engaged a lever to lift the reel out of the water, then turned off the engine. He dismounted, stepping into the floating rubies. Gerome's wife, Leiann, stood on the dry dike and offered Zane a large Styrofoam cup.

Eager to drink, he nodded his thanks then gulped the cool, tart lemonade. When he finished, he smiled. "Thanks. I guess I was too thirsty to speak."

She gestured to the house, a twinkle in her hazel eyes. "The women have pulled out the snack trays if you'd like to take a break."

Zane glanced at the bog where Gerome still labored. "What about your husband? Maybe I should go take his place while he eats."

"No, no. I gave him a bite before he started." She looked down at her feet then back at Zane. "I've got on my waders, so I can take him a drink."

Zane headed toward the house, wondering if he would have any time alone with Riley. He hadn't heard if she'd discovered anything, though he was certain she would tell him. But with a home full of cranberry harvest workers, some of whom would remain at the house for the next several days until the task was complete, he doubted she'd had ample opportunity to look.

As he approached the gathering, he saw Riley exit the back door with a covered dish. She set it on a long table covered with food. Friends and family members congregated around the tables; some entered the house itself. Zane washed his hands in the portable washbasin then found the large jug of lemonade and refilled his cup. He maneuvered his way through the friendly faces whose names he was only beginning to learn and approached Riley at the far end of the table. She was uncovering the plastic wrap from a dish of cheese-filled celery.

Zane stood next to her and faced the small gathering that he'd decided yesterday was too large for the required work. But he supposed it was tradition and a reason to bring people together.

One of Robert's church friends picked a piece of celery off the serving dish. Zane smiled at him before finishing off his lemonade. The man ambled down the table, selecting food and placing it on his plate.

Zane caught Riley's attention. "How are you?"

"I'm fine, thanks. But I think we're past the small talk, don't you?"

Her comment startled him. Something was definitely agitating her. He studied her before tilting his cup to toss the remaining ice into his mouth. He crunched on it. "All right, then. Have you found anything?"

"Are you serious? I did as much as I could before this harvest business escalated. It's really bad timing if you ask me. You should have told me everything weeks ago."

Again, Riley's feisty words startled Zane, and he stopped smiling at the people mingling and eating and faced her. She wore a peculiar expression on her face that he couldn't read.

He gripped her elbow and ushered her away from her serving position to the side of the house. "What's going on? Is everything all right? I mean, besides finding the locket. I already know that part of the equation."

"Sorry, I'm tired. And we still have several days to go. I'm not used to this continual labor. . .and entertaining. But don't get me wrong—it's fun in its own way. Besides, this is the life I've chosen, and I'm sure I will grow to love it." She stared at him, and he caught the flicker of a question cross her features. "Next year, that is."

"Yeah, next year." Zane hesitated, considering his words. "You'll be okay, you know? Things are progressing very well on the farm. You have a feel for how to run things now. And you can always call me if you need me." He cringed, wishing he hadn't said it. It sounded too. . .final.

A swaggering peacock dressed in a dark blue polo shirt and tan slacks approached from a distance. *Eric.* Zane scowled.

"What's wrong?" Riley spun to look and released a slight groan.

He suspected her agitation had more to do with her ex-boyfriend than with the requirements of the harvest. He'd been surprised when she explained her previous relationship to Eric. Zane couldn't imagine her falling for someone like him.

"Hi there, Zane." Eric nodded and sidled up to Riley.

Zane stifled the smirk that threatened to erupt when he saw Riley's subtle shudder. "Hi there, yourself."

"How does it feel to work on a cranberry farm?" Eric smiled and cocked his head as if interested in Zane's reply.

"It's hard work, but I've enjoyed it." Remembering his earlier annoyance with Eric's unwillingness to help, he added, "You might try it yourself."

He instantly regretted the words. Riley stood slightly behind Eric and glared at Zane. The last thing he wanted was to have Eric get involved with the farm. Evidently, Riley felt the same way.

❦

At home that night, Zane scrubbed off the grime and dressed. He'd received a phone call from Tom Ackley, the private investigator he'd hired. He was pleased that Tom had done such quick work, though he wouldn't give Zane the specifics over the phone. After arming his upgraded security system, Zane headed to a nearby grocery store parking lot.

He sat down in Tom's midsize car and nodded at the man in the driver's seat. "Tom."

"Thanks for meeting me." He wore an expensive suit similar to the design that Zane preferred.

An executive friend working for one of Zane's previous employers had given him Tom's name. "No problem. I hired you, remember?"

Tom chuckled at Zane's comment.

"What have you discovered?" Zane's palms grew moist with the anticipation of possible answers to this dilemma.

Tom pulled a manila folder from the space between his seat and the console. He retrieved the photo of the woman whom John claimed was his sister.

"Did you find out who she is? What's her name and connection to all of this?"

Tom frowned. "You're not going to like it."

Pain erupted in Zane's stomach, and he pressed his hand on his midsection then leaned against the headrest.

The private investigator handed him another picture. It was smooth and glossy, cut from a magazine. "The February edition of *Tech-It* magazine."

"What? Are you saying that the photo on John's desk is not a real person?"

"It is a real person. . .a model. I'm saying this photo is an image taken from that magazine. Maybe your partner thought she looked like his sister, and since he didn't have a picture, he used this."

Zane couldn't hide the disappointment in his voice. "Thanks for the work, Tom. Do you have anything else?"

"Not yet."

"All right, then."

The two men nodded, and Zane exited Tom's vehicle to climb into his own and head home. He'd needed to check whether the woman's identity was also part of the clue. John had created a photo-quality image from a picture in a magazine for use in his insane puzzle. Why? Though Zane still ached for his friend, he hoped that wherever John was right now, he could look on and get some sort of satisfaction out of knowing that Zane and Riley were striving to solve the puzzle. Zane remembered the regret Riley expressed because she hadn't discussed God with John. The thought left him unsettled.

He was beginning to see that he couldn't manage his life on his own. But he'd kept himself closed off from God for so long that he didn't know where to begin.

ॐ

Riley gripped the floating rubber tube called a boom as she helped the others corral the crimson sheet of bog rubies close to the conveyor belt that would propel them onto a platform. Booming the berries had always fascinated her as a child, but she'd never been allowed to help with this part of the harvest. Urging the berries forward in the water took more strength than she would have thought. Though Grandpa had protested at her involvement because there were plenty of other workers to help, she held her ground, wanting to experience everything.

She caught sight of Chad standing next to Millie and Elsie, and she waved at him. She hoped he would grow up enjoying the experience of the cranberry farm as she had. Once the berries were tightly packed, floating near the equipment, Zane, Grandpa, and others moved inside the circle to begin scraping the carpet of crimson fruit onto the belt, where they were cleaned. When the platform had reached its capacity, the contents were dumped into the freight car of an 18-wheeler that was then sent to one of the independent cranberry handlers.

Grandpa did not belong to the large co-op with which 70 percent of the Massachusetts cranberry growers were contracted. The cost to join was high, and he wouldn't get paid until the cranberries were actually sold by the handler. She intended to speak with Zane for his business advice on whether to remain independent or belong to the co-op. The advantage of joining would be a three-year, fixed-rate contract.

Riley labored alongside the others for two more days. Though she enjoyed every minute of it, the entire process was all-consuming. They'd already said good-bye to several of their helpers as the bogs began to empty and the guests began to vacate the house.

Too exhausted to remove her waders, she meandered away from the activity toward the grove of trees where Zane had kissed her. She could still feel the warmth that had flooded her being at his tenderness, even though it had been a few days ago. If only the kiss had occurred under different circumstances than after learning that he believed her brother was murdered. But his response to his actions had left her confused about his feelings and intentions.

The gloomy thought that she hadn't asked about her brother's relationship with the Lord continued to surface, bothering her. Yet it also reminded her that she needed to broach the subject with Zane, as well. Time after time, she'd worked up the courage to speak with Zane, but he'd continued to change the subject or allow other interruptions. She had to know before she allowed her feelings to go any deeper for him. Already the man had made inroads into her heart without her realizing how far.

All she had longed for was a simple life. Instead, her life had become more complicated since the day Zane arrived at Sanderford Cranberry Farms.

Chapter 15

Nonsense, we can go together." Grandpa paced in the kitchen, dressed in his best jeans for the harvest festival.

"You're all ready to go, though. It's going to take me awhile. Call your church friends back, Grandpa."

For the last few years, the largest cranberry grower in the region hosted a festival for all to celebrate the harvest. She wanted to be excited, but she was too exhausted. If it weren't for the fact that she'd agreed to meet Zane there, she would skip it altogether.

Riley handed Chad his juice cup then rubbed her aching head. The harvest had zapped all her energy. Though the crop had been trucked off the farm two days before, she still hadn't recovered.

Grandpa came to Riley and placed his hand on her shoulder. "All right, then. I'll go without you. But only because I can see you need a little time to yourself." He grinned and gave her a loving pat.

"You'd better hurry before they leave without you," she said.

"How about I take little Chad with us. Millie will be there. She loves to see him."

"What about her granddaughter, Elsie?" Relief washed over Riley. She longed to soak in a hot bath to ease her aching muscles. She couldn't help but smile about the fact that her grandfather had grown to like Millie, after all. He'd made healthy progress, finally getting on with his life after the death of her grandmother. She grinned when she considered that much of that growth had occurred since she'd arrived.

"I'm sure she'll be there, too. Don't worry about us; we'll have a good time."

"Let me grab his things, and don't forget to take the car seat," she said.

After seeing Chad and Grandpa off, Riley locked the door and bounded upstairs to start her bathwater. She'd spent yesterday rummaging through her things, including the ten moving boxes that had remained in the garage, still packed. Though her heart ached for her brother—and even more now that Zane had told her he believed John was murdered—she began to feel angry with John about the mystery he expected her and Zane to solve. She couldn't understand why he hadn't spelled things out so they could understand.

Riley soaked in the tub until the water turned cold. The bath eased her tension, and she felt relaxed. She even sent up a silent prayer for the discovery of the elusive clue. In the mood to look special, she searched through the closet, looking at her nicer clothes that she hadn't worn in months, since caring for a child left a spot on every shirt she owned.

She held a tan outfit against her body and stared at the mirror, frowning. The pantsuit needed something extra, maybe jewelry. She hoped to look special for Zane.

For Zane?

Shaking her head, she tugged a dresser drawer open to dig out the jewelry box buried underneath a jumble of undergarments. She tossed them into a cardboard box nestled beside the dresser so that she could get a better look at the contents of the disorganized drawer.

She froze. The cardboard box had rested in that spot for so long that it had become part of the room's decor and had gone unnoticed. She hadn't searched it. Still, it only contained items she'd tossed in recently. She grabbed it and dumped the contents onto the bed. Along with the clothes, several postmarked envelopes—junk mail and solicitations—were scattered amid the heap, and she gathered them together, tossing them as she searched for a letter from John.

One envelope did not have a return address but had been sent to Riley's California address. It had been forwarded to Massachusetts. Then she noticed the Massachusetts postmark. In the midst of all the turmoil, she'd overlooked the letter. The handwriting appeared to be that of a man. Her heart pounded as she searched for a letter opener to slit the top. She hoped this was the item John had sent.

Losing patience, Riley ripped through the paper. She pulled out several folded sheets and discovered a small item in between them.

The locket!

As she examined the shiny, gold-plated square, touching it with her finger, she couldn't believe she had finally found it. Still, what could be so important about a trivial ornament?

She scrutinized the sliding door in the front of the locket. Riley's heart raced. Should she open it or wait for Zane? Upon applying slight pressure with her thumb, the door slid open, and a small square object dropped to the carpet. Riley reached down and carefully picked up what appeared to be the smallest memory card she'd ever seen. It was no bigger than her fingernail.

Fear coursed through her. The information she held in the palm of her hand had meant the difference between life and death to John. Her mood plummeted. Somehow, things had gone awry. She hated that she was in possession of such a dangerous object.

She hurried to dress so she could deliver the news to Zane. The locket would be the perfect accessory to her tan outfit—sure to draw his attention. The ironic notion brought a laugh. Zane had kept the original golden chain he'd shown her. Riley came across one of an appropriate length, though it was silver rather than gold like the locket.

She phoned Zane on his cell. When he didn't answer, she left a message on his voice mail. She tried to keep her voice calm, rather than shaky, but it was no use.

༚

Zane tired of the culinary demonstration and roamed toward the farm stand, avoiding the live band that played on the temporary stage. He scanned the crowd for Riley. He assumed she would have arrived at the festival by now. He checked his watch and noted that dusk was fast approaching. A helicopter offering rides zoomed past, rendering him momentarily oblivious to any other sounds.

A young girl approached him holding glowing neon bracelets and sticks. "Mister, would you like to buy one?"

He patted the young entrepreneur on the top of her head. "No, thanks. Maybe later."

As he sauntered down a walkway rimmed by people pushing their wares, he looked at all sorts of antiques, linens, artwork, and even produce from the local farmers. Completing the harvest had filled him with satisfaction. The celebration festival was for all to enjoy. Without Riley, there wasn't much here to interest Zane. He checked his watch again then spotted her grandfather.

He hurried through the crowd before he lost sight of Robert then touched the back of his arm. Riley's grandfather turned to face Zane, his broad smile growing even bigger.

"Hello, Robert. Enjoying the festival?"

"Grandpa! Grandpa!" Chad came running from a vendor, a stick of pink-and-blue-swirled cotton candy in his hand. Millie wasn't far behind the child. Riley would be near, as well.

A pang jolted Zane's heart at Chad's outburst—he'd begun calling Robert "Grandpa," which was only right. But the child would grow up and not even remember his own father. Still, Zane was grateful that the boy had family to love him.

Robert lifted Chad into his arms, heedless of the sticky mess. Yes, he was loved.

"There's a huge crowd this year. Have you been to a cranberry festival before?" Robert opened his mouth to allow Chad to stuff in the sticky sugar.

"I'm afraid this is my first time." Zane watched Millie retrieve Chad from Robert's arms. Something was going on between those two. He grinned at the thought.

"So, do you know which way Riley headed? I'm surprised I haven't seen her yet."

A nearby carnival ride began booming upbeat music.

"What?" Robert appeared to consider Zane's question. "I'm not sure where Riley is. I haven't seen her. She decided to come later."

Robert's words sank in, filling Zane with disappointment. He frowned and searched the crowd. "How would we find her in all of this, even if she was here?"

"That's a good question. But I wouldn't worry too much. I think she needed time alone. She worked hard. I can't tell you how proud I was to see her standing in the bogs, booming the berries. It was a grand time for all of us." Robert slapped Zane on the back.

Though he knew Riley's grandfather meant to encourage him, Zane became concerned. "I think I'll walk around and look for her."

"All right, son. We'll tell her that you're looking for her if she turns up."

Zane moved closer to the entrance so he could see Riley in case she entered the festivities. In the distance, he spotted Eric strolling the grounds, searching the crowd, no doubt looking for Riley, the same as Zane. He melted back into the shadows. What was Eric doing here? Riley had said he'd returned to California.

Zane didn't feel he could stomach Eric at the moment. He wondered if his enormous dislike for the man could be attributed to the intense jealousy he felt when he saw the two of them together. He wondered if the insane emotion had clouded his judgment of Eric and whether in any other circumstances they might be friends.

He doubted it.

Zane decided to call Riley. When he pulled his cell out of his pocket, he saw that he'd missed a call from her. He surmised that bursts of loud music, helicopter rides, or the throng had distracted him when she'd called. His concern mounting, he hoped it wasn't important and that she only meant to tell him she was on the way or already there.

He dialed into voice mail then saw Riley moving between people. She appeared flushed and anxious. He stepped from the building's edge where he'd hidden from Eric, only to witness the man edge toward Riley. When Eric reached his prey ahead of Zane, Riley visibly stiffened. At least Zane had no reason to be jealous.

He realized what nagged him about Eric. Riley's distaste for him had become apparent to all. Zane could not believe a man with Eric's intelligence would not heed the signals Riley sent him. Yet here he was, three thousand miles from his home, pursuing a disinterested female.

As Zane watched Eric head to the Ferris wheel with Riley in tow, he wondered what the man was after.

Chapter 16

Eric tightened his grip on Riley's elbow as he ushered her toward the Ferris wheel. She glared at him. "You're hurting me. What's the matter with you?"

His expression turned ominous, sending panic through her. "We need to talk."

Her ex-boyfriend's grip remained unyielding as they stood in line. To Riley's dismay, Eric had timed his carnival ride excursion at the right moment, and after a quick word with the ride operator, they were quickly escorted into a cozy car all to themselves.

She buckled in and leaned back against the red vinyl cushion, wondering what had just happened. Her intentions had been to find Zane and tell him she had discovered the locket that held the key to their mystery. Within the few minutes of her arrival at the festival, the horde of people had grown, and she'd shuffled along with them in her search for Zane. Oh, how she wished she'd found Zane before Eric had appeared out of nowhere.

He was scaring her.

She twisted a small topaz ring on her finger, avoiding Eric's stare, then mustered her courage and raised her head to face him. "I thought you'd gone back to California, that the work that brought you to Boston was finished. Surely you can't still be taking time off. What are you doing here?"

"No, Riley, I'm not vacationing. As a matter of fact, I didn't accomplish the work I flew here to do. Yet."

Riley shifted in her seat under his menacing gaze. The carnival worker finished loading excited passengers on the wheel, and it began to rotate. A breeze lifted Riley's hair from her face, cooling her.

A pleasant tune signaled a caller on her cell. Her heart skipped, hoping it was Zane. His number appeared in the small window. She pressed the RECEIVE button. "This is Riley."

"Are you all right?" Zane's voice barreled through the phone, wrapping her in assurance.

She looked at Eric, who watched her like a bird of prey, readying to strike. She measured her words carefully. "I'm. . . fine, thanks. Where are you?"

"I'm down below. If you look out, you can see me." Riley leaned to the side but saw no one she recognized in the crowd. "I'm sorry, there are too many people. But it's good to know you're there." She looked at Eric again. For some reason, she feared he might grab the phone from her. She tightened her grip then banished the ridiculous thought.

"I saw you come in, but then Eric rushed you onto the Ferris wheel before I could get to you."

His words warmed her. If only he had made it in time. "The ride will be over soon enough."

"Hang in there." He laughed. "Sorry, I didn't mean to make a joke out of it. I called because you looked. . .uncomfortable."

"That's putting it mildly, but you're right—this, too, shall pass. I'll see you on the ground. Oh, wait!" Riley could not tell Zane of her discovery with Eric listening. "I left you a voice mail. Did you get it?"

A barrage of noise invaded her phone, and she couldn't hear Zane's voice. She'd lost the connection, so she pressed the END button.

Feeling confident after Zane's encouragement, she glared at Eric. "You still haven't answered my question. What are you doing here? I know you have no interest in this festival. And you should know by now that I have no interest in you."

A condescending grin spread over his mouth. "I assure you, the feeling is quite mutual."

Stunned by his comment and his strange behavior, she didn't know how to respond and instead watched the beautiful scenery as the wheel made its way around. While she gathered her thoughts, she stared at the lights glistening in the distance with the falling darkness. The raucous sound of the carnival seemed to grow louder, even at the top of the ride. The aroma of hamburgers and hot dogs drifted up on the breeze.

"I'm sorry, you'll have to explain to me again, then, why you insisted that I ride the wheel with you if you don't enjoy my company," she said.

She'd never seen this side of Eric before, even after all the time she'd spent with him. As memories raced through her mind, she remembered occasions here and there when he'd revealed a different part of himself.

He stared into the distance as if contemplating his response to her. His dark hair rustled in the wind. She examined his handsome profile and considered the fact that the behavior he exhibited tonight had been within him the entire time she'd known him. But her feelings had erased any negative thoughts she may have had at the time because she'd cared about him.

Sitting before her was the real Eric. And she still cared about him as a person who needed God, but no longer as a man she'd once considered spending the rest of her life with, though he'd never asked.

As if in response to her thoughts of marriage, an image of Zane made her heart skip. She shook the presumptuous thought from her mind.

"Where is it?" Eric continued to stare out the side of the car and did not turn when he addressed her.

Immediately her thoughts went to the locket, and she placed her hand over it where it hung around her neck. Panic exploded from within and rushed through her body, sending moisture to her palms and trembling to her limbs. She fought to hide the emotion in her expression and thanked the Lord that Eric had chosen not to look at her.

How does he know?

"What?" she managed to say through an emotion-filled throat.

He picked that moment to face her, but his expression appeared relaxed. "Where is it? You know what I'm talking about." The mocking she'd heard in his earlier tone was gone, but his gaze pierced her, showing that he meant business.

She could not believe her ears. He had nothing to do with any of this. "Eric, I really don't have a clue what you're talking about. Did I take something of yours when I left California? Just tell me. You can have it back!"

"Your brother, John, sent it to you. I want it."

Her mouth went dry as she stared at him. If only he'd asked her yesterday, she could have told him the truth when she said she didn't know where it was. Now if she said that, he would know she was lying. Eric knew her too well.

"I—I don't know what you're talking about." It couldn't hurt to try the tactic once more.

He leaned forward. "Come now, Riley. I know you're lying."

Grief rushed through her soul as realization flooded her mind. She'd been only too thrilled to tell Eric about John's talents and his encryption project. Nausea roiled in her stomach, and she gripped her middle, bending over. Riley had been foolish to think she could share information, even if it was with her boyfriend—someone she thought she could trust.

As a business consultant, Eric had high-level connections, and his knowledge had leaked to the wrong party. She groaned as she continued to clutch her stomach, sick that she had brought this upon her brother. She no longer cared if she exposed her emotions.

The man already knew everything.

Eric unbuckled and moved next to her. He leaned closer and spoke softly into her ear. "If you give it to me, no one else will get hurt."

Images of Chad, Grandpa, and Zane tore through her mind. She cried out to God. What should she do? Would giving the memory card to Eric release them from danger? Or would it put them at further risk? They could tell the police about Eric and his connection with John's murder.

John's smiling face appeared in her mind. How she missed her brother. Fury surged through her that Eric had taken him from her.

She turned to face him, the heat of her rage exploding. "You! You murdered my brother!" She slapped him full across the face.

He covered his cheek with his hand as he winced. "It wasn't me, Riley. I didn't do it. All I did was share information about your brother's skills with an interested client. Believe me, had I known who I was dealing with, well, I would have stayed far away. I'm sorry about that. But it's too late now. They're breathing down my neck to retrieve the information your brother sent you."

His hand dropped to his side, revealing his reddened face. Eric appeared to revert to the man she'd been attracted to months ago. He huffed and rubbed his hands together. "Please understand." He paused as he swept her hair away from her face. "I'm just trying to keep anyone else from getting hurt. Namely, you." He lifted her hand and kissed it.

She knew he intended to turn his charm on her since his fear tactics had not worked, but his touch repulsed her.

She had to get off this ride.

҈

Zane's patience ran thin. With the crowd growing for the evening festivities, he couldn't pace as a way of relieving his tension. He'd never realized how many turns a Ferris wheel could take. Maybe it was standard at all carnivals and he hadn't paid attention. He made his way through the line of grumbling people while excusing himself. He explained to any who challenged him that he needed to speak to the carnival employee.

The man stood jesting with another worker and appeared to ignore the Ferris wheel.

"Excuse me, sir," Zane interrupted.

The man shoved his baseball cap up on his head to reveal questioning dark brown eyes. He tilted his head in reply to Zane.

Zane noticed the man's name on his flannel shirt. "Carl, I'm wondering about how long your ride has been running. Please don't misunderstand. I'm not challenging your abilities as a ride operator; I'm just curious. Is this normal?"

Carl's friend slapped his back and left him. Carl returned his attention to Zane and rubbed his gray-stubbled chin. "A guy wanted extra time with his girlfriend." He revealed an impish grin and lifted the corner of a green bill out of his shirt pocket, enough for Zane to see he'd been paid one hundred dollars. "He made it worth my while."

Zane gritted his teeth. "I'll pay you double to stop it."

Carl grinned and rubbed his chin again, as if considering the proposal. Zane surmised that the man didn't intend to make things easy. "All right. I never said

329

how long I would keep it running." He cleared his throat and motioned for Zane to follow him away from the crowd. "You can slip it in my hand. The two hundred dollars, that is."

Zane pulled his wallet from his slacks and unfolded it. Comprehension dawned like the beginning of a bad day. He'd planned to get money at an ATM at the festival, but he'd been consumed with finding Riley.

"I have to get cash."

The man shrugged and started to march back to the waiting line.

As the wheel turned, Zane heard Riley's voice when her car whirled past. She was in distress.

Zane grabbed Carl's arm. "No, wait!"

Carl turned a threatening glare on him, causing Zane to release him. "I'll give you four hundred if you'll stop it while I go get the cash."

"I'm not stopping it until you give me the money."

Incensed, Zane raised his voice. "Look, you're going to have to stop the wheel sooner or later. Look at all those people in line."

Carl shrugged. "It's a carnival; they're used to waiting."

Zane growled at the insensitive ride operator, feeling as though he'd caused the man to run the thing longer than he had planned. He should have waited. He walked away from Carl and rushed over to the operating equipment. In his desperation, he sent up a prayer that he would know how to stop the Ferris wheel before Carl stopped him.

Chapter 17

The ride wrenched to a stop, sending the cars swinging violently, the huge wheel grinding in protest on its axis. Riley plunged forward, but her safety belt held her, securing her to the seat. The force thrust Eric across the small platform because he'd failed to strap himself back in.

He gripped his head and groaned.

She heard a ruckus below and peered over the edge of the car as far as she could to see what was happening. Two men struggled near the Ferris wheel's operating stand. A familiar tall figure reached for the controls, while the carnival worker wrapped his arms around him, trying to stop him.

"Zane." She drew in a sharp breath.

Other men rushed to them and pulled the two apart. She heard Zane's prominent, authoritative voice taking control of the situation. He pointed at the ride operator and spoke in an accusing tone.

Eric righted himself on the seat. Blood trickled from a gash in his temple. "Your new boyfriend can't save you, Riley. In fact, you're the one who needs to save him. Give me what I want."

Riley looked at Eric, surprised at what she heard in his voice. "You're afraid, aren't you?"

The wheel started again then paused to allow passengers off each of the cars. The process of disembarking the riders continued.

"Yes. I'm afraid. And you should be scared, too." He spat the words. "Are you happy now?"

Riley closed her eyes, overwhelmed as a sense of peace wrapped around her. She knew that someone had to be praying for her at that moment. She opened her eyes to stare at Eric and realized that she felt sorry for the man.

"Well, I'm not scared. God is going to protect me."

Eric leaned back against the seat and laughed. "When we get off this thing, you're going with me, and I'm going to make you hand over what John gave you."

"Zane will be waiting for me." As soon as the words left her mouth, it was their turn to exit the car.

A man apologized to them for the inconvenience. Riley looked for Zane, expecting him to be waiting for her, but she didn't see him. "Where's the man who was here?"

"Which one, lady?"

"The one—"

Eric thanked the worker and hastened Riley away, his grip tight. Screams of fear and excitement bombarded them as noisy rides thrust their occupants about. Deafening music boomed from all sides. Riley could see how it would be easy for Eric to abduct her in the midst of the throng. No one would even hear her scream.

"Okay, Eric. I give."

He turned to face her and paused to look around at the multitude of festival attendees. "That's better."

"Promise me that no one else will get hurt if I give it to you." She held her breath as she fingered the locket.

"I promise. Do we need to go somewhere, or do you have it with you?"

Riley glared at him, gripping the clue that John had given her and yanking it from her neck.

A disbelieving grin spread across Eric's face, and he released his grip on her. "Oh man, you've got to be kidding me. You were wearing it this whole time?" He glanced behind her and stiffened.

Riley pressed the locket into his hand then darted away from him, rushing through the onslaught of bodies. She dared not look behind her. She ran full force into a man's chest. He gripped her arms and pushed her away to reveal his face.

"Riley?" Zane wrapped his arms around her and held her close.

All the tension of the last hour came flooding out in a torrent. There was nothing she hated more than tears. But she couldn't help the emotional release.

People jostled against them as they stood in the center of the fray.

Riley leaned her head back to see Zane's face. He released her. She looked at his tailored blue shirt.

"You're going to have to toss another one, I'm afraid," she said, sniffling again. She dug through her small purse for a tissue without success.

Zane ushered her over to a bench, grabbing a napkin from a concession stand on the way. "Here, try this."

She took it and wiped her eyes then her nose. "Where were you? I got off the Ferris wheel, and you were gone."

"I'm sorry about that. They took me to the security office where I explained about my response to the ride operator's misconduct. Someone paid him to leave the ride going longer than usual. That kept me from being there to wait for you. I should have left matters well enough alone. The ride would have stopped on its own—eventually."

She blew her nose again. "No, it's okay. You tried."

"Riley, tell me what happened up there. What did Eric want?"

She breathed deeply through her nose. It still made a sniffling sound. "Oh, Zane. You're not going to believe this."

Concern and warmth brimmed in his eyes. "It's all right now. You're okay. I'm not ever going to let that man near you again."

Zane's chivalrous words touched her, and she patted his hand. "Calm down."

He returned her smile but with a question in his eyes.

"I think we've seen the last of Eric," she said.

A child climbed up onto the bench next to Riley and tried to hand her half of his hot dog slathered with mustard and ketchup. His mother squeezed next to him, crowding Riley and Zane.

Zane stood and urged Riley to follow. "Let's find a place where we can talk."

He held her hand as if he was never going to let her go. Yet his touch felt nothing like Eric's unwanted, painful grip.

"What about Chad? Grandpa? I forgot all about them. Have you seen them?"

"Yes, more than an hour ago. They were enjoying themselves. Millie and Robert were taking good care of Chad. I don't think you need to worry about him. He's in good hands."

Riley followed Zane on shaky legs. Her entire body felt like Jell-O, trembling from her encounter with Eric. They found a small coffee kiosk. Riley stayed with Zane while he purchased drinks.

He flashed his card at her. "At least someone here takes these."

They settled nearby at an out-of-the-way picnic table.

"Okay, take a long swig of that. Give it time to clear your mind. Are you hungry? I'm sorry I didn't think of food."

"I couldn't eat right now. My stomach's too upset."

Zane sipped coffee and stared at her over the rim of his cup. She could see that he wasn't going to push her to tell him about Eric. She'd been bursting to tell him her news, and with all that had happened, she wasn't sure where to begin.

In the beginning. . .

The gentle voice nudged her heart, delighting her, and she laughed.

Zane cocked a brow. "Something funny?"

"Nothing, really. I was just wondering where to begin."

"In the beginning."

She nodded. "That's what I hear."

Riley told Zane about Eric's involvement and the part she'd played in her brother's demise.

He reached across the table to hold her hand. "You couldn't have known. Don't blame yourself. John's occupation wasn't a secret."

She relished his comforting words and touch. There was no doubt that she would have to ask God to help her forgive herself. The urge to talk about her relationship with God spilled over, but she bit her lip. She knew Zane wouldn't want to hear it now. But when?

Lord, please help me to speak to him when the time is right.

Nor would he want to hear the worst part of her story. She hesitated while she considered how to break the news to him.

❧

Zane's insides ached as he watched Riley. He was grateful that the scoundrel hadn't hurt her. He played with her fingers, hoping to help her relax. At the same time, he fought his own frustration. It would go a long way to relieve his anger if he could get his own hands on the man responsible for John's death. Yet according to what Riley said, Eric hadn't known anyone would be hurt.

Riley's words that they would not see Eric again echoed through Zane's mind.

Too bad.

Zane froze as the thought grabbed him.

"Riley, why won't we see Eric again?"

"Excuse me?" She drove her fingers through her tousled hair, weaving it out of her face.

"You said we wouldn't see Eric again."

She frowned and took a sip of her coffee.

"Riley. What did you give him?" Zane stood up from the picnic table. "Did you find the locket?"

"Yes, I rushed to the carnival to tell you—then Eric grabbed me." She frowned. "I'm so sorry, Zane. I had no choice."

Zane sunk back to the bench. He was grateful for Riley's safety. That was more important than anything, especially a ridiculous clue. But without the locket, they could go no further in solving John's puzzle.

Riley's eyes widened, and she covered her mouth while she reached into her pocket. "You're right, the coffee helped clear my thoughts. I was so focused on the locket, and Eric upset me. I forgot."

A mischievous smile spread across Riley's face. "I said that I gave him the locket. But I didn't give him this."

She held out her palm. A tiny square rested in the center of her hand.

A memory card.

Chapter 18

Riley held Zane's hand as she followed him through the festival crowd then to the parking lot. He headed in the opposite direction of her parked car.

"My car is that way," she said.

He continued in the same direction and increased his pace; he noticed Riley lagging behind and pulled her along.

"But what about my car? I could just follow you."

"No way. I'm not letting you out of my sight." Zane opened the door to his car for Riley. "I want you to see this through with me. We can get your car later."

He stroked her cheek with his thumb and pressed his lips into a tight smile.

Riley nodded her agreement and climbed in. She called her grandfather to check on Chad, and she explained about Eric. Millie and several others had stopped over to visit after leaving the festival, relieving her of concerns. She reminded her grandfather to arm the security alarm.

Sooner or later, Eric would discover that she hadn't given him all that he'd asked for. She silently prayed for him, concerned for his life in all this chaos, as well.

She reached under the seat to adjust the legroom and found Zane's computer. He slid into the driver's seat and shut the door.

"Are we going to look at the memory card now?" she asked.

"Afraid I'll have to get an adapter—a card reader. So we're going to an electronics store."

Zane started the car, and they exited the parking lot to head toward Plymouth on Interstate 44.

"So what's stored on this thing? What is so important that it cost John his life?"

"I thought I knew. But I'm not so sure anymore. I've been hoping that John stored an extra copy of the new encryption software so that I would still be able to go forward with the business." He paused as he merged to head north. "But now I don't think I want software that someone is willing to kill for."

"What else could it be?" Riley gripped her seat as Zane passed the slower traffic.

"We'll find out as soon as we see what's on that card. Could be the software itself or other files that John wanted us to see. But there's something else. I haven't told you everything. John had a run-in with the law a few years ago. He illegally hacked into—well, you don't need to know the details."

Riley's curiosity was piqued. "So what are you saying, Zane? That my brother was a hacker and this whole thing has to do with something illegal?"

Zane looked out the driver's window. She wished he'd keep his eyes on the road.

He returned his attention to driving. "It's possible—in fact, it's probable—that Eric's friend wanted John to hack into someone's system. But his moonlighting activities have taken Cyphorensic down with it. It's either that, or they simply wanted what John had been developing for Cyphorensic—a new hack-proof algorithm. Then they could offer it to the highest bidder. But obviously, they're still searching for something. I thought they were looking for the key, because they have his software—they stole the computers, remember?" He chuckled. "But they couldn't get into John's stuff."

"What do you think they're after if not the key?"

"Well, let me just say that we may have the same problem. If the key isn't on the minidisk, then we can't open it."

Riley sighed and stared out the window. She shook her head and frowned, saddened by thoughts of everything that had gone wrong in the last several months.

Still, she had Chad, and her grandfather appeared to be happy. The same peace that surrounded her while she was in Eric's company on the Ferris wheel burned inside her. She turned to look at Zane, who concentrated on driving.

"Something happened to me while I was with Eric." She looked out the window again.

"I'm sorry I didn't stop him from taking you on that ride. You're okay, aren't you? He didn't physically hurt you, did he?" Zane placed his right hand over hers and steered with his left one.

"No, nothing like that. In fact, it has nothing to do with Eric."

"I'm listening." He shot her a wry grin.

Riley hesitated, considering how to explain it. "I hated my life in California. I was so preoccupied with my job that I barely had time for myself. And no time for my relationship with God." She held her breath, waiting to sense any tension in Zane as she broached the subject.

When he said nothing, she continued. "I wanted to break up with Eric. In fact, I did, but he wouldn't accept it. I thought coming all the way across the country and giving up my career would change things. I believed living with Grandpa and working the farm would bring back the wonderful feelings I had when I was a child."

"Riley, we're all looking for anything to fill the void, to make us happy." Zane exited the freeway, drove down the frontage road, and turned right, into a large shopping center.

"When I finally moved here, I prayed and read my Bible. It was almost as though I was trying to force things to happen."

He frowned as he pulled into a parking spot.

"Zane, I found it. I found the peace I've been looking for."

He smiled. "You're coming in, right? I wouldn't want to leave you out here by yourself."

He started to open the door, but Riley grabbed his arm. "Please let me finish."

"All right." Zane shifted in his seat, turning his full attention to Riley.

Riley's heart warmed to think that he was willing to listen, though he had to be anxious to review the information on the disk. But she felt a heavenly urge to tell him everything.

"I found that peace when I was on the Ferris wheel with Eric. I finally understood God's peace could come in the midst of striving. It's not a matter of what's going on around me—if I'm busy or if I'm not. It's a matter of what's going on inside of me and if I'm able to receive His peace in all circumstances."

He narrowed his eyes as if contemplating her words. "And what about now? Do you feel it?"

She nodded and grinned. "I do."

He gripped the steering wheel and stared out the windshield. "Well, at least one of us has found the answer. Shall we go?"

She swallowed the sudden knot in her throat and got out of the vehicle. His response was not what she'd expected. Still, she knew she'd done the right thing by telling him of her experience. God would have to do the rest.

They rushed into the large discount electronics and appliance store. Zane headed straight for the ministorage devices and searched the aisle.

A store clerk wearing a red polo shirt joined them. "Can I help you find something?"

Zane glanced at the man's name tag and held the memory card up between his fingers. "Yes, Darryl, I need an adapter to run this on my laptop."

❧

Zane got into the car and tossed the small sack containing the adapter in the backseat. He'd hated the disillusioned expression on Riley's face when he hadn't responded as she expected. He was happy that Riley had found contentment. And. . .it gave him hope.

He started the car. "You ready?"

She nodded, appearing preoccupied.

"Do you think your grandfather would mind if we did this at the farm?"

Her eyes widened; then she smiled. "You know he wouldn't. Thanks. I mean, for thinking of me. I'd like to check on Chad."

"Thought so. We need to be there, too, in case Eric shows up again." Zane put pressure on the accelerator to bring them to the speed limit. In less than half an hour, he could have the information in his hands that could solve John's puzzle.

They rode in comfortable silence, though Riley's words about finding God's peace would not be quieted in his mind. He glanced over at her several times as she stared out the passenger window.

"All right." He winced, wondering if he was making a mistake. But Riley had come to mean more to him than anything. He didn't want to let her down. He could at least try—for her.

"All right, what?"

"All right. If it's time to talk about God, I'm ready."

A beautiful, breathtaking smile filled her face, and the previous stress appeared to melt away, revealing an inner glow. No, this idea had not been a mistake.

"I grew up in church. My mother made sure to take me every Sunday, so I thought I knew God, or at least that I knew who He was." His throat tightened as the memories he'd pushed down for years began to surface.

"It's really strange, but the last person I spoke to about this was your brother, years ago when we were in high school."

A look of awe crossed her face. She moved her lips as if in silent prayer. "I'm glad you're telling me this."

Zane took the exit to head back to Carver and Sanderford Cranberry Farms. "My brother drowned when he was a senior. I looked up to him, idolized him. He was only two years older than me and on the swim team. Can you believe it?"

Though the words came out with difficulty, Zane found that an enormous weight began to lift as he shared with Riley. "We all took it hard, of course, but none took it harder than my father. He had big plans for my brother, and when he looked at me, his entire attitude changed. I thought he wished I had died instead."

Riley placed her hand on his arm. "Oh, Zane, you must be mistaken. I'm sure he loved you very much."

"I know you mean well, but you didn't know my father. He ended up leaving us—me and my mother. Don't misunderstand; my father was wealthy, and we were well taken care of, but he divorced my mother and moved to Europe. I never saw him again. All I have left of him is the money he willed to me when he died four years ago."

"And your mother? Where is she now?"

"A cemetery near Plymouth."

Silence filled the vehicle, but this time tension accompanied it. Zane knew the tension emanated from him alone.

"If you're wondering what this has to do with God, I'll tell you. I couldn't understand why my brother died and my father left. Why should I count on God after He let me down? So rather than relying on Him, I've relied on myself, working hard to make it where I am today." The words sounded crass even to his own ears.

Riley gasped. "But, Zane, you can count on Him."

"That's what your brother told me." He turned into the entrance of the farm and continued toward the house.

"What did you say?"

Zane glanced at Riley, and the look of wonderment on her face took him by surprise.

"Your brother told me that I can count on God and His Son. John was there for me during that difficult time in my life and has been my closest friend since. That is, until he died."

"Zane, I know what you must think. That whether John was killed in an accident or murdered, how can you count on God? But we don't see the larger picture around us. He was there for me on the Ferris wheel with Eric. I know it."

☙

John was a Christian!

Zane's words thrilled Riley, and she wanted to weep for joy, but she'd cried enough for one day.

As Zane pulled around the circular drive to park near the house, Millie and her granddaughter stepped through the door. Riley got out of the car.

Millie came over to hug her, a large handbag hooked in her elbow. "Riley, dear, I just put Chad down. Your grandfather was a bit nervous. Afraid he wouldn't be able to get the poor child to sleep, so Elsie and I stayed to keep him company."

"Oh, thank you. I'm sorry I'm so late. Did Chad do all right, then?"

Millie waved her hand to throw off any doubt. "He was a complete angel. Exhausted, but an angel. We were just leaving, but come inside, and I'll show you what I've done. I prayed for you this evening, dear. Don't know why, but just felt I needed to do it. Is everything all right?"

Warmth filled Riley at Millie's words. "Everything is fine. Thank you for your prayers. I felt them."

Riley noticed Zane removing his briefcase and his purchase from the car as she followed Millie into the house.

Once in the kitchen, the older woman pointed out a large plate of chocolate chip cookies. "I made grilled cheese sandwiches, too, thinking you might be hungry when you got in. They're wrapped in foil on the counter, probably still warm."

Riley looked around the sparkling kitchen. Millie had left no evidence of her culinary endeavors but the food to be enjoyed. "Thank you, but you really didn't have to do all of this."

"Nonsense. We've got to get home, so I'll leave you in your grandfather's good hands." Millie's face brightened when she mentioned Grandpa.

Zane entered the kitchen just then, and he and Millie exchanged farewells. Grandpa escorted Millie to her car then returned to the kitchen. "Thought you'd never get here, but now that you are, I'm exhausted. You wouldn't think me rude if I went to bed, would you?"

"Grandpa, this is your house. Don't be ridiculous." Riley pecked him on the cheek.

"Night, all." He disappeared up the stairs.

Zane slung his soft leather briefcase onto the table and began pulling out his laptop. A manila folder slid out onto the floor.

Riley leaned over to retrieve the file. A picture fell out. She picked it up and examined it. A woman who resembled Riley was wearing a locket and holding a cell phone to her ear. "This is the picture you told me about. I've seen this before."

Zane plugged in the computer and booted it. "Probably saw it in a magazine: That's where it came from. For some reason, John created a photo-quality picture from the magazine image to grab my attention in all of this." He frowned.

After attaching the card reader to the USB port, Zane placed the memory card inside and waited for the data to display. He groaned and thrust his head into his hands, grabbing hair with his fingers.

"What is it?"

"We need the key. Why can't I figure this out? It shouldn't be this complicated."

"Maybe I can help. But honestly, I don't understand how it all works. Maybe if you could explain it to me, it would remind me of something important that John said to me. Why don't you tell me exactly what you mean when you say 'key,' for starters?"

"As you know, John was working to build a new standard for encryption. All that means is changing data into a secret code through a mathematical algorithm—one that no one could get into. The problem is that no one *can* get into it." He released a nervous, frustrated laugh. "The only way to read it is to have the key. John's key is a short program, an algorithm like the encryption code itself."

"Then let's go over what we have."

"Nothing. We have nothing." Zane slid away from the table and moved to the counter. He stretched out his arms and pressed his hands against the edge, supporting his body.

Riley persisted. "There has to be something you've overlooked or you're not telling me. We have the disk, and we found the locket—only it was used to give us the disk." Riley closed her eyes and took in a deep breath. "And we have that picture, the first clue."

The picture. A memory flashed across her mind, and she grappled with it, trying to capture the thought. "The picture. There's more to the picture." She took it out of the folder again. "She looks like me, she's wearing a locket. . .and she is talking on a cell phone."

Adrenaline rushed through her. "Zane, I know where I've seen that picture before."

Zane turned to face her. "In a magazine—I told you already."

"No, it's on my camera phone."

His eyes widened. "Give it to me."

Riley pulled the cell from her purse. "He sent me the phone a couple of weeks before he died. I had mentioned I'd like to have a camera phone. I confess I've never learned how to use it to take pictures."

"I need the connections that came with this. Do you still have them?"

Riley retrieved the accessories from her room. "What does it all mean? What's so important about the picture?"

He spoke as he connected the phone to the laptop "If I'm right, the key is in the picture. If John embedded a data stream into this digital picture on your phone, all I have to do is download the picture, and when I open it on the laptop, the code should self-extract. It would then act similar to a virus. In this case, the virus is an algorithm used to open the data."

Riley exhaled, amazed that she'd carried the key with her the entire time.

Chapter 19

Riley leaned over Zane's shoulder to watch as file names appeared on the monitor. It was difficult to comprehend that John had stored the only key on her phone to open whatever valuable secrets were contained on the disk, and she'd unknowingly kept it for him.

This near to Zane, she felt herself breathe in the scent of his cologne. A sudden, unpleasant thought confronted her. Once he finished solving the puzzle, he would be finished with Sanderford Farms because he'd found the key. It had been at the farm, with Riley, the entire time. The fact that she would no longer see him every day, if at all, disturbed her. She believed he would want to spend time with Chad, but it wouldn't be the same.

Riley put her hand over her heart and took a step back from where Zane sat staring at the computer screen. He struggled with his relationship with God. She knew that, yet she'd allowed herself to fall in love with him. She'd been so caught up in the suspense of solving John's mystery that she wasn't sure when it had happened.

"No." The word escaped without her permission. Though she'd thought it was inaudible, Zane glanced back at her.

"No, what? This is exactly what we wanted. This is it. It worked, Riley."

Zane slid away from the computer and stood. "Come here." He pulled her into his arms and held her. "I couldn't have done this without you. You know that, right?"

Though her emotions were in conflict with her judgment, Riley allowed herself to savor his embrace. "That's only because John sent me the key. He could just as easily have put it into your phone."

"True enough. But he wanted the key to be far away from here. And maybe he knew we'd be good for each other." He squeezed her.

A thrill rushed through Riley, and she wondered if Zane felt the same way about her that she did about him. A small comment window appeared in the center of the monitor. Zane had his back to it, so he couldn't see.

Riley freed herself from his embrace. "I think it's finished."

Zane sat in the chair to face the laptop again. He scrolled down the list of file names; then he selected and opened one of them. Riley wasn't certain why he'd singled it out. Copies of e-mails were pasted into a document along with other information.

"What does it all mean?" she asked.

"I'm not exactly sure, but it doesn't look good."

A twinge of panic rippled across her skin.

"It appears to be incriminating information linked to a government official." Zane rubbed his chin. "I don't want to read anything more, nor do I want to hold on to this. It needs to be turned over to the authorities."

"So you think that they used John to hack into the system to retrieve this information?"

"That's exactly what I think. They could have threatened his life or his family. I'm not sure. But he did the work. I believe he gave us the clues to insure his life once he was finished. If something happened to him, then the criminals would be exposed, though they had no way of knowing how. That's where I'm confused, because it didn't work, and because of his death, we now hold volatile information in our hands."

Zane shut down the computer then snapped it closed. Frowning, he stood and looked at Riley. She knew her expression mirrored his.

"John's plan backfired, and he was killed." She wasn't certain she believed that aspect of Zane's theory. Still, the authorities would have to iron out all that had happened and why. "What if, and this is a big 'if,' John's death really was an accident?" Her mind began to wrap around the idea. "What if the bad guys, whoever they are, didn't kill him? He just simply died before they got what they wanted?"

❦

Zane walked down the corridor of Cyphorensic Technologies to make sure the entire premises had been vacated. Though his lease did not expire for another two months, he'd sold the office furniture. There was no reason for him to remain. After all that had transpired over the last several months, Zane could not bring himself to go forward with his company when it had played a role in John's predicament.

His partner and friend had made sure that Zane had the encryption software he'd created. It was on the disk. Though it was only in the alpha phase, Zane was able to sell the code. He put the money into a trust fund for Chad.

Even with all the information that Zane had supplied the investigators, no other conclusion could be reached but that John had been killed in an accident, not murdered, before he had been able to deliver the decryption code to the criminals. Eric's clients. They'd had a need, and he'd supplied the name—John's name. Eric had no knowledge of their dealings with John until they pressured him to help obtain the key. After the police questioned Eric, two men were arrested in connection with attempting to gain unauthorized access into a government computer system.

Zane hoped that Riley found consolation in the fact that John did not seem to have participated in the hacking job by choice. But he was threatened, and in the end, it appeared that he'd had no intention of delivering.

Zane stood in the center of the reception area and turned slowly. His gaze rested on the spot where Chelsea's desk had been. He hoped she loved her new job.

"I'll pray for you." He reflected on her words then whispered, "Thank you, Chelsea."

His heart told him that her prayers had been answered. After the tragedy with his brother and his parents' divorce, he thought that God didn't care about the details of his life. Didn't care about him. So Zane wanted no part of God. His life, to this point, had been built on creating an empire for himself. But it meant nothing.

As he looked at the vacated offices of his venture, the cold, stark truth wrapped around him. He could do anything he wanted, including start a new company, but nothing he did would matter without a relationship with God and His Son.

He reflected on the last few months spent at Sanderford Cranberry Farms. Without a doubt, he knew that God did care about him. He could see it all around him, as well as through the subtle ways God had whispered to his heart.

Zane bowed his head, and in his heart, he humbled himself before the Creator, asking for forgiveness and a new start. Once peace settled over him, assuring him that God had answered, he said good-bye to his company. Zane walked out the door, trusting in God to direct him to his next endeavor.

He turned to lock the plate glass double doors but instead pressed his forehead against one of them. The pain of regret burned in his stomach. He'd never been in the position he was in now—unsure of what he would do next. Learning to trust in God's direction would be a new experience.

Images of Riley and Chad would not let go of him. With a business failure fresh in his mind and on his résumé, he had nothing to offer the woman he loved. He smiled to himself. It was the first time he'd admitted that he loved her.

As Zane pulled the key out of the lock, footfalls interrupted his thoughts, and he turned away from the company doors. Riley approached with Chad in her arms. Zane's heart soared at the sight of her. She released Chad, and the boy ran to Zane, who lifted him with zeal and kissed him on the forehead.

Riley smiled at Zane. He couldn't remember if she'd ever been so beautiful.

"I didn't want you to have to face closing your company doors alone. Sorry we weren't here sooner."

A gust of wind whipped curls across her face. Zane swept the tendrils away from her green eyes, bringing a blush to her cheeks.

"I'm not sure if this is the right time for me to discuss this with you." She blew out a breath. "Grandpa agrees with me. We'd like you to be a partner in Sanderford Cranberry Farms. Permanently. He loves your business plan, your ideas of how to grow the farm to include processing and distribution, and frankly, so do I. It doesn't mean you can't still work in the software industry—"

Zane covered her lips with his fingers then leaned down to kiss her. Chad forced him to end the kiss all too soon. "I thought I knew what would make me happy. But I didn't—that is, until I met you. I can't think of anything I'd rather do than see you at the cranberry farm every day."

In his heart, he thanked God for sending the answer already. He knew the gentle nudge he felt about Riley was God's urging, as well. "But first, I have a question for you, and I'm not sure what your grandfather will think about this."

Riley knitted her brows, and her smile flattened. "What is it?"

"I'm in love with you, Riley."

Moisture brimmed in her eyes, magnifying the love he saw in them. "Oh, Zane." She pressed her lips together and averted her gaze.

Pain ripped through his heart. "I'm sorry if I spoke too soon."

"No, it's just that I don't know where you stand with God."

His spirit soared. "I can settle that for you. I've resolved my issues and allowed Him back into my life." His smile beamed from within.

"Really?" Her face brightened.

"Really."

"I can see it written all over your face. You couldn't have made me happier. I love you, too." She melted into his embrace.

"Are you sure I can't make you happier? Because I haven't asked you the question yet."

Riley pushed away from him to look into his eyes. Her mouth dropped open.

"Riley O'Hare, will you marry me?"

She pressed both hands against her heart, tears streaming. "Yes, Zane Baldwyn, I will marry you!"

"Yes, Zshane Balwin, I merwy you." Chad grinned, revealing a mouth full of perfect white baby teeth.

Epilogue

Riley stood in the foyer of the two-hundred-year-old church, waiting for the oak sanctuary doors to open; then she would glide up the red-carpeted aisle, stepping in cadence to the wedding march. They had planned for a small, quiet wedding.

She'd waited months for this spring day—the season when everything began anew. Both she and Zane needed to put their ordeal behind them and have an opportunity to focus on each other, free from the backdrop of the suspense that had shadowed their relationship. Though she still missed her brother and his wife and regretted the time she'd lost with them, Riley began to accept the loss—especially since she knew that they were with the Lord.

She had settled comfortably into her new role as a mother, and Chad's demeanor reflected his contentment. Though he'd lost both of his parents, all that mattered now was that he was loved and cherished. Zane would make a great father, and in fact, he was already fulfilling that role with Chad. She couldn't wait until they would officially become a family.

Her grandfather had agreed to allow Zane to build a new farmhouse on the property for the Baldwyn family. Riley inhaled deeply and widened her eyes to stem the tide of tears. She didn't want to cry on this day, but she knew she'd end up losing the battle.

"You look beautiful, Riley!" Her father's voice broke through her thoughts. Tall and stately, he paced across the wood flooring in his black tuxedo. He would walk her down the aisle to give her away. It thrilled her to see him again. With him living in California and her in Massachusetts, she wouldn't see him often. He stood teary-eyed, and she hoped he'd shed the tears for the both of them.

"Thank you. You know, in moving here, nothing turned out the way I planned, but at least I met Zane." Riley closed her eyes and inhaled deeply to calm her nerves.

Her sweaty palms made it difficult to grip the crimson-accented bouquet. She twisted the large ruby engagement ring on her finger. She smiled as she remembered when Zane had taken her for a walk among the oaks and maples beyond the cranberry beds. They'd shared a kiss under the trees; then he'd pulled the ring from his pocket. He'd presented her with the gem, explaining that it represented the bog rubies to remind them of how they fell in love.

Amazed, she could do nothing but love him and be grateful to God for bringing him into her life. It seemed that when she had embarked on a search for peace the storms had grown much fiercer. But they lasted only for a time.

Soon the growing season would begin all over again. Her life had changed as quickly as the seasons. As if on cue, the organ chords vibrated through the old structure, pulling her from her reverie, and the doors swung open. Zane stood at the end of the walkway.

Riley's heart pounded, reaching into her throat. She longed to be with him and wanted to hasten through, but the wedding ceremony would not be rushed any more than the cranberries would be hurried to ripen on the vine. As she took her first step down the aisle toward her future husband, she trembled. Her father gently squeezed her arm hooked through his and patted her hand, reassuring her.

She kept her focus on Zane, though she could still see the heads turning to watch her. Some gasped, and others softly remarked what a beautiful bride she made.

Her father spoke in his turn, giving her away. She stepped forward, and Zane took her hand. The pastor began to speak, and in her heart, she believed and agreed to every word. But she hardly heard them as her love spilled over for the handsome man standing next to her.

Once they were announced as man and wife, Zane and Riley shared a gentle kiss that signified the beginning. There was a season for everything, and now Riley would begin a new season of life, one she would spend with the man she loved.

Elizabeth Goddard

Elizabeth is a seventh generation Texan transplanted in southern Oregon near the Rogue River. When she's not writing, she's busy homeschooling her four children and serving with her husband at their local church where he pastors. Beth and her husband, Dan, have been married for twenty years. She enjoys hiking in the redwoods and camping on the Oregon coast with her family. Beth's passion is to fulfill her life-long dream, answering God's call to write.

A Letter to Our Readers

Dear Readers:

In order that we might better contribute to your reading enjoyment, we would appreciate your taking a few minutes to respond to the following questions. When completed, please return to the following: Fiction Editor, Barbour Publishing, Inc., P.O. Box 719, Uhrichsville, OH 44683.

1. Did you enjoy reading *Cranberry Hearts*?
   ❑ Very much—I would like to see more books like this.
   ❑ Moderately—I would have enjoyed it more if _____
   _____

   _____

2. What influenced your decision to purchase this book? (Check those that apply.)
   ❑ Cover   ❑ Back cover copy   ❑ Title   ❑ Price
   ❑ Friends   ❑ Publicity   ❑ Other

3. Which story was your favorite?
   ❑ *Who Am I?*   ❑ *Seasons of Love*
   ❑ *A Matter of Trust*

4. Please check your age range:
   ❑ Under 18   ❑ 18–24   ❑ 25–34
   ❑ 35–45   ❑ 46–55   ❑ Over 55

5. How many hours per week do you read? _____

Name _____

Occupation _____

Address _____

City _____ State _____ Zip _____

E-mail _____

If you enjoyed

Cranberry
HEARTS

then read

PALMETTO
DREAMS

by Terry Fowler